the Glassblower

PETRA DURST-BENNING

Translated by Samuel Willcocks

amazon crossing

Text copyright © 2003 by Petra Durst-Benning
English translation copyright © 2014 by Samuel Willcocks

The Glassblower was first published in 2003 by Ullstein in Berlin as *Die Glasbläserin*. Translated from German by Samuel Willcocks. Published in English by AmazonCrossing in 2014.

Cover design by Marc Cohen

Published by AmazonCrossing

www.apub.com

ISBN-13: 9781477820278
ISBN-10: 1477820272
Library of Congress Control Number: 2014933179

PART ONE

FALL 1890

THE BEGINNING

But glass cups and vessels may become the subjects of exquisite invention; and in buying these we are doing good to humanity.

—John Ruskin

1

Ruth had already gone upstairs twice that morning to try to wake Johanna. Both times her sister had grumbled something that led her to believe—wrongly, as it turned out—that she really was going to get up. *Why do I always fall for it, every single day,* Ruth scolded herself as she climbed the stairs for the third time. The smell of bacon frying gently in the pan followed her as she went. She stopped at the dormer window, stood on tiptoe, and glanced down at the back of the house, where Marie was singing. A spider had spun its web right across the window. Without even noticing the fine patterns spun into the threads, Ruth brushed it away with her hand. Marie was nowhere in sight. Nor was Father. Ruth frowned. By the time either of them smelled anything burning in the kitchen, the bacon and potatoes would be charred to a crisp!

The last time she had come up to try to wake Johanna, she had left the door to the room she shared with her sisters standing open, so she could already see from the landing that Johanna was still not up. Without saying a word, Ruth walked up to the bed, grabbed hold of the linen bedspread, and whisked it off Johanna.

"How can you lie there all covered up in this heat?" she asked, shaking her head as her sister struggled toward wakefulness. Ruth went to the window and opened the shutters wide. Straightaway the bright September sun flooded the room with a dusty light.

Johanna swung her legs over the side of the bed like a rheumatic old woman, groaning piteously but not saying a word.

Ruth glared at her sister one last time and then hurried back downstairs to rescue breakfast. While she stirred the potato slices and bacon bits around the pan, pouring in a little more oil so they wouldn't stick, she thanked heaven that she at least was an early bird.

Even as a child, Johanna had never liked getting up early—she and her sisters had been late to school often enough on her account. And it wasn't just getting out of bed that caused her trouble—she was groggy all morning and no good to anyone before ten o'clock. "It's as though I'd drunk half a bottle of schnapps the night before," Johanna had said once, trying to explain how bleary she felt. Not that she or Ruth had ever drunk half a bottle of schnapps or had any real idea what that would feel like. Knowing that Johanna would be sleepy in the mornings, the three sisters had settled on a housework routine that meant that she didn't have any morning chores, though Ruth sometimes wondered whether this was really the best answer. She sighed. Had their mother still been alive, she probably wouldn't have made such a fuss about it! In many ways, Anna Steinmann had been much more stubborn than her husband. Ruth tried to picture her mother's face for a moment, and felt a pang of sorrow at how hard it was to do so. Ten years was a long time.

The water she had put on to boil for the morning brew began to simmer, shaking Ruth out of her memories, and she promptly took the pot off the flame. She didn't like it when the chicory roots boiled too long in the water—best just to bring them up to a boil from cold, or else the drink was too bitter. Ruth was fussy about this: most of the folks in the village made a brew of dried bits of mangel-wurzel, but she wouldn't let the stuff into her kitchen. She'd rather drink plain water than that swill. Of course, she liked to drink real coffee most of all, but often they couldn't afford enough beans to last the week. Johanna went to Sonneberg every Friday to sell the glass that they had made that week and she always brought back a little bag of coffee beans. Joost Steinmann didn't much care what he put in his cup to drink, as long as it was dark and hot, but he didn't deny his daughters this little luxury. It had become something of a ritual by now; when Johanna came back from Sonneberg, they would treat themselves to coffee and a slice of cake, and a pickled herring that she would buy in town as well.

The rest of the village gossiped about these habits of theirs and said that in Joost Steinmann's house, the women ruled the roost. But it wasn't as though they did whatever they pleased. Certainly within their own four walls the girls were allowed their own way much more than others of their age, but when it came to sheltering them from the wicked ways of the world, Joost could be worse than a mother hen. What if the village choir was rehearsing and they wanted to join in the singing? Out of the question—there might be boys lurking around the streets as they walked back home. And a dance on the night of the solstice? There was no point even asking if they could go. A few years back some of the village girls had gotten together and started a spinning group for the winter, but Joost wouldn't even let his daughters join in this bit of harmless fun. "You'll slip and fall on the ice on your way home and break a leg," he had declared. "Better to stay home and practice your letters." As if books were as enjoyable as a good chat. Ruth swallowed. The gatherings were set to begin again in November, and the other girls would all be sitting at the spinning wheels two evenings a week while she and her sisters sat at home. By the time the spinning circle broke up and the girls walked home through the alleys, laughing, throwing snowballs, and shrieking at the boys chasing them, Ruth, Johanna, and Marie would already be in bed.

It was no wonder that all the boys in the village had gotten the idea that Joost didn't want them paying court to his daughters. The way he looked at any boy who came calling stopped most of them from ever coming a second time.

Ruth went to the table and opened the drawer to fetch out the little mirror she kept there. When she held it out at arm's length, she could see her whole face in it. She was a beauty, and she knew it. She and her sisters had all inherited their mother's fine, even features, and their mother had been an exceptionally beautiful woman.

Ruth heaved a sigh and put the mirror back in the drawer again. What good did it do her to look in the mirror and see a pretty face? Would a man ever kiss her on the lips? Would anyone ever tell her that her eyes shone like amber? That her skin was as clear as a spring morning? If Joost had his way, all three of them would die old maids.

The only man who regularly came to call was their neighbor Peter Maienbaum. Ever since his parents had died a few years ago, one soon after the other, Joost had looked on him as a son, never thinking that he too might turn into a skirt chaser. But judging from the way he gazed at Johanna, Ruth was quite sure that Peter had had his eye on her for some time now. Nobody else seemed to have noticed though, least of all Johanna. Ruth sighed again—more deeply this time. If a man ever looked at *her* like that, she would certainly notice.

"Johanna's barging about the house again like a bear with a sore head! When she finally makes it out of bed, she spends the rest of the day giving us orders," Marie said, slipping onto the edge of the bench. She was so slim that she didn't even need to push the table away as she sat down. Though Ruth was quite slim too, she envied her sister's figure. Many of the village women were funny-looking creatures with dangling bosoms and great pillows of flesh on them, but the sisters could thank the Lord that they were tall and slender, with smooth healthy skin and chestnut hair that shone like silk without needing anything more than a hundred strokes of the brush each day. Marie was smaller than the other two, more delicate and fragile looking—like a costly porcelain doll.

"At least she's made it downstairs. I was afraid I'd have to go up to wake her again," Ruth answered dryly.

Ever since their mother had died, they used the laundry shed next door for their morning wash. Joost went out there too, rather than washing in the kitchen. This way they could all have a bit of privacy, which the girls needed as much as Joost did.

"Where's Father, anyway?"

"I don't know. He got home later than usual last night. He made such a din coming up the stairs that I woke up. I couldn't fall asleep again for ages," Marie said, making a face. "I hope he's not sleeping off a hangover."

Ruth shrugged. "You know as well as I do that he doesn't drink all that much," she said indulgently, though there was no real need to spring to Joost's defense. He went to the local tavern, the Black Eagle, for a couple of hours every evening like all the other men in the village, but unlike some of them, he rarely drank more than was good for him.

The potatoes were nicely crisped and brown. Ruth picked up a slice with her fingers and popped it into her mouth. Hot! Then she poured herself a cup of the chicory coffee, and one for Marie as well. The hearty brew was just the thing for a sunny morning like this. They had a word for these sunny days after the end of summer but before fall had come; they called them "plum-cake days." All summer long the songbirds had trilled in the pear tree outside the kitchen window, but they were gone now. The only sound these days was that of a blackbird chirruping or the high piping of a lark, and soon the mists would fall and silence even these. Ruth held her cup to her nose and breathed in deeply. She hated it when the year turned cold.

"Not long now and we'll have to light the lamps in the morning," Marie said, as though reading her sister's thoughts. The sisters often found that they could chime in and speak aloud what the other was thinking.

After Anna Steinmann had died, they had found a way to cope—both with life and with their work. Of course they were always shorthanded—the Steinmann family ran as good a business as any of the other glassblowers in the village. Not bad for a household where the women "ruled the roost." They were used to friendly teasing, and to ill will as well. They specialized in pharmacy jars and test tubes, and they made them well. First-class goods. The family did every step of the work—from grinding the stoppers to size to incising the words into each jar, writing out the labels, and packing every consignment for delivery—all without outside help. It was a great advantage.

Like all the other glassblowers, they worked on commission for a wholesaler in the nearby town of Sonneberg. Friedhelm Strobel had customers all around the world and always told the Steinmanns that he would happily buy more of their jars and tubes. Joost was the only glassblower in the house, however, and they couldn't make more pieces even if they wanted to. The men at the Black Eagle were always telling Joost that a hardworking son-in-law would be a great help, but he waved them away. He loved to tell them all: "My girls don't have to marry—not for money, that's for sure!"

Ruth sighed, put down her cup, and went back to the stove. She lifted the heavy cast-iron pan effortlessly and put breakfast on the table. "Enough is enough! I'm going to see where . . ." She fell quiet when she saw that Johanna had appeared in the doorway. She was even paler than usual, and her eyes were wide with shock, as though she had seen the devil himself in the hallway. She held one hand in front of her mouth and seemed to be stifling a scream.

"Johanna! For heaven's sake! What's wrong?" Marie called out.

Ruth felt a lump in her throat. Two hands, cold as ice, gripped her heart and squeezed. She knew that something dreadful had happened. She couldn't say a word.

"It's Father . . ." Johanna said, her brow furrowed with worry. "He's just lying in bed up there. He's not moving at all."

2

Whenever Johanna recalled that morning, she always thought of the story of Sleeping Beauty. Marie sat where she was, utterly still, her mouth half open. Ruth was caught between table and bench, half standing, half sitting. And Johanna herself couldn't step away from the doorway where she stood. It was as though all three of them had turned to stone, as though they could keep the horrible truth at bay if they didn't move.

Marie was the first to break the spell. She ran up the stairs to Joost's bedside. Her scream tore through the quiet house and silenced the few birds that still sang outside. Johanna and Ruth stared at one another over the frying pan on the table. Then they rushed upstairs.

The wooden treads of the staircase were pale and polished from years of use, but that morning they blurred into thin yellow stripes before Johanna's eyes. She tasted something salty at the corner of her mouth, and only realized then that tears were streaming down her cheeks. She could do nothing to stop them—or the thoughts that crowded unbidden into her mind.

Father was dead.

Should they call the doctor from Sonneberg? No, a doctor was no use.

A priest. They needed a priest.

And they would have to wash him. Dead bodies had to be washed. And laid out.

A sob burst from Johanna's throat, so scorching hot that it hurt.

Marie folded Joost's hands together on his chest. Thank God his eyes were already closed when Johanna had found him. If one of them had had to shut his eyes . . . She couldn't bear to think about it.

Joost was not even fifty years old. And he'd been in the best of health. Other than the occasional backache, he'd been fit as a fiddle.

"He looks so peaceful," Marie whispered, smoothing out the bedclothes over him. His body looked much smaller beneath the covers than it had in life.

On tiptoe, as though not to wake him, Ruth crept across to the other side of the bed, leaned over her father, and looked at his face. There was no sign that he had felt any pain.

"Maybe he's just asleep? More deeply than usual?" Though touching Father didn't feel right, she tentatively placed a hand on his forehead. She was surprised to find that his skin was not ice-cold the way the stories said. Nor was it damp, or even dry. But the bones beneath the skin were unyielding as Ruth passed her fingers over his face.

Rigor mortis had already set in. Ruth began to cry. Marie was already in tears, and Johanna sobbed loudly.

"But why? I don't understand!" The lump in her throat swelled, and it was hard to breathe. "How can Father just die in his sleep like this?" Johanna called out plaintively.

But nothing could alter the truth of it. His heart had simply stopped beating as he slept. Johanna went next door to fetch Peter Maienbaum, who was just as shocked as Joost's daughters when he heard the news. He told them that Joost had seemed to be in fine spirits the night before and showed no sign of being the least bit sick. He'd been laughing along with everybody else at Stinnes, the local joker.

"You know what Stinnes can be like. He's a loudmouth, but he can keep the whole tavern roaring with laughter," Peter said distractedly.

Johanna waved this away. She had no time for jokers now.

"We'll have to lay Father out," Johanna said. Her voice was flat and calm, as though she were talking about setting the table.

Startled, Ruth and Marie looked at her.

"The best thing to do is clear our workbenches to one side of the room and then carry Father and his bed downstairs."

"But why would you want to do that? We can . . . lay him out . . . just as well up here," Ruth said, shuddering. Marie looked from one sister to the other.

Johanna shook her head. "No, we'll have to do it properly. It's what Father would have wanted. Once people start to come . . ." The rest of her sentence was drowned out by a sob. She turned away.

Ruth and Marie looked on helplessly as their sister's shoulders shook. Crushed by their own sorrow, neither one of them had a drop of comfort to offer her. Johanna was usually so ready to take charge, but here she was, just as helpless as they were. It made the situation even worse.

Peter cleared his throat. "I'll go and fetch some of the men. Then we can begin with the . . ."

Why is it that nobody knows what to say? Johanna thought in a flash of anger as she wiped at her eyes with both hands and her sobs slowly subsided.

Peter shook her gently by the arm. "It might be a good idea for one of you to go downstairs and put the kettle on. For when people come."

A little while later he returned with three men, who clutched their hats in their hands and uttered the customary words of condolence. Peter took charge and led the men upstairs. First they laid the dead body on the floor; then they took the bed apart and carried each piece down the narrow stairs, cursing under their breath. Then they reassembled the bed in the middle of the workshop, and carried the dead man down the stairs. Once he'd been laid out on the bed, the four men sighed with relief.

When the neighborhood women heard the news, they stopped whatever work they had in hand and came to pay their respects. One brought a dish of mashed potatoes, another a pot of soup, and a third a platter of bread that she had sliced and spread with drippings and sprinkled with salt. The wooden floorboards creaked under the steady tramp of feet while the women bustled about, looking for matches to light the candles, fetching coffee for the men, casting a wary glance at the dead man every now and then.

Widow Grün from two houses down helped Ruth wash the corpse and clothe it, while Johanna and Marie put fresh linens on the bed.

One of the neighbors had evidently already told the priest, for they had just finished laying out the corpse when the pastor showed up at the door, followed by two altar boys swinging censers.

Johanna felt numb as she joined the others in a circle around Joost's bed while the pastor uttered a few prayers. *This can't be happening,* she thought.

All day long people stopped in to offer their condolences or share the sisters' vigil for a while. None of them stayed long, for they all had work waiting for them at home. Every face showed relief that they had been spared such a tragedy. Johanna could not blame them for feeling that way. The winter before, there had been a bad outbreak of the flu in Lauscha, and Hannes the bladesmith, who had been almost ten years younger than Father, had died, along with two of the older villagers down the hill. Johanna had had the same thought at the time: *Thank God it wasn't any of us!* Every time she came back from Sonneberg and spotted the desolate house with the brass sabre hanging over the door, she always thought of poor Hannes. He had not even had time to marry, poor fellow, he died so young.

Over the course of the afternoon, Johanna began to squirm. Each hand on her shoulder, each murmured word, each clammy handshake—taken all together, they stung like a bunch of nettles. She was convinced that there was more than just sympathy in the sorrowful looks people cast at her. They were expecting something too. They were excited.

Three young women without a man to look after them.

Were people waiting for one of them to collapse in a flood of tears? Or for some other disaster to strike the household? Johanna scolded herself for such uncharitable thoughts. These people were only trying to help as best they could.

3

It was past seven o'clock when the last guests left. Peter Maienbaum was the only one who offered to share the wake. Johanna hesitated for a moment but declined his offer. It was something that they had to do themselves.

None of the sisters could even think of eating, so Ruth spread cloths over all the dishes that the neighbors had brought and put them away for later. They sat down at the kitchen table, tired to the bone.

Johanna got up again and opened the door. "It's so stuffy in here, you could cut the air with a knife."

"It's the incense." Marie's eyes were red with tears.

"Not just that. All those people . . ." Johanna was too tired to explain that she felt that the visitors had somehow tainted their house. They had left their own smell behind, and the tread of the many boots seemed to linger on the wooden floor, even if there were no prints to be seen.

"Perhaps it's . . . Father?" Ruth glanced back toward the workshop.

"Ruth!" Marie said, shuddering, and looked at Johanna with fear in her eyes.

"Everyone knows that dead bodies begin to smell when—"

"That's enough!" Johanna cut in harshly. They had the whole night's wake ahead of them. The last thing they needed was Ruth talking nonsense. She went to the cupboard and took out the rest of the candles. Light was good. Light would certainly help. "That's not a *dead body* over there, that's Father."

Ruth opened her mouth but then thought better about uttering whatever she had been about to say. Nobody wanted an argument with a dead man in the house.

Johanna gradually unclenched her jaw. Her eyes had been staring ahead like a painted puppet's, but now she looked around, and her arms relaxed as well. She hadn't realized until then that she had had them crossed in front of her almost the entire day. She leaned back in her chair. For the first time that day, there was nothing she was expected to say, no task she had to do.

One of them was gone now.

The longer the silence lasted, the more they all missed him. The way he'd clattered his spoon on the table when he had to wait too long for his supper, or if he thought Ruth had skimped on putting sausage in the soup. The methodical way he sliced bread and carved the smoked ham.

Johanna was the first to break the silence. "Father was always such a picture of health . . ." Then she pressed her lips tightly closed again.

Ruth nodded. "He was never a spindle-shanks like Bavarian Hans or Friedmar Grau. But he wasn't a fat fellow either, not like Wilhelm Heimer."

"You never needed to look and see whether Father had come into the room. You always felt that he was there." Marie was speaking Johanna's thoughts for her. "Everyone respected him." She smiled. "Do you remember the time he bought those two roosters?"

Johanna laughed a sad little laugh. "He bought them for me from Paul Marzen. He hoped that I would wake up more easily if there were two roosters crowing in the yard, not just one. And then Marzen came knocking at the door, drunk as a skunk, saying that he'd given Father the wrong birds, that these were his best breeding fowl, and he wanted them back."

"All Father had to do was square his shoulders and Marzen turned tail and fled."

"And those roosters never did turn out to be of much use."

They laughed, and then fell quiet again.

"Who will look after us now?" Marie asked.

Johanna looked over at her. She mustn't ask that. Not tonight. Nor tomorrow, either.

"When you were little, he always used to call you his princess, do you remember?" Marie had always been Joost's little girl.

"A princess whose palace was inside a soap bubble. He was always promising to tell me the whole story, but he never quite got around to making one up." Marie's eyes brimmed with tears again.

"But he always found time to mix up the soapsuds for you to blow bubbles!" said Ruth. "Oh, those bubbles of yours." She swept her hands through the air in the shape of a ball. "Pfft! They burst all over the place and leave little wet spots behind. Even when I was little, I couldn't understand what you saw in them."

"Father understood. He loved to look at the colors, just like I did." Marie looked up. "I'm sure he's in heaven now, and there are rainbow colors everywhere. He'll like that. And he'll be glad to see Mother again."

She burst into sobs, and the others followed suit. They didn't fight the tears.

A long while later, Ruth tucked a strand of hair behind her ear and made a face, sniffling.

"I just remembered when Friedhelm Strobel gave us that order from France with just two weeks' notice. Five years ago, do you remember? In 1885."

"Oh my goodness, yes!" Johanna exclaimed, clapping her hands. The candles fluttered in the gust of air. "The order for that French perfumer!" Marie looked baffled and Johanna went on. "Don't you remember? They wanted five thousand perfume bottles. And every one had to be engraved 'Eau de Paris.'"

Marie snapped her fingers. "I remember now! Father wrote it out for us. But his handwriting was so bad that we couldn't rightly read it. By the time he checked up on us, we'd put 'Roi de Paris' on a thousand bottles."

"King of Paris." Ruth shook her head. "Anybody else would have beaten us black and blue for a mistake like that, but what did Father do? Laughed and laughed till it seemed he would never stop." She glanced over her shoulder into the workshop. That wasn't just a cold dead body lying back there; it was their own dear father.

"I didn't laugh when I had to tell Strobel what we'd done, mind you," Johanna said bitterly. "It was only the third time I'd ever been into Sonneberg on my own, and I had no idea how to talk business. I was all of sixteen years old, and I stood there stammering away. I was sure he wasn't going to take those bottles."

"You talked him round somehow, though." There was a trace of awe in Marie's voice, even after all this time. "A few weeks later Strobel gave you another order, with 'Roi de Paris' on every single bottle!"

"Ha! I daresay he sold them to the French at twice the price and claimed the new name was all his own idea!" Ruth wrinkled her nose. "How I longed for a bottle of French perfume for myself! I used to dream about it. One morning I woke up and thought I could smell it in the room. Lilac and lily of the valley." She sighed.

"If Father had had his way, you would have gotten a bottle," Johanna replied. "He made me go and ask Strobel whether he could get hold of some perfume for us. I didn't think much of that idea—what does a fourteen-year-old girl need with perfume, after all?—but Father always did what he could to make you happy."

Ruth looked as though she wanted to answer back, but she bit back her words.

They each sat there with their own thoughts. There were so many stories.

Ruth's head nodded forward onto her chest, once, then twice, but when Johanna suggested that they take turns with the wake so that they could get some sleep, Ruth and Marie refused. Not long after that, however, Ruth's head sank forward onto the table, and Marie's did the same. Johanna sighed. They would have been more comfortable if they'd gone to bed.

She stood up quietly, not moving her chair. She was exhausted herself. She took a candle and went into the workshop. Her gaze lingered on her father's workbench and lamp. The tools that lay there were worn smooth with use, apart from the gleaming silver pipe that connected their house to the new gasworks. It shone in the candlelight, and Johanna felt a pang of pain in her breast. She had worked so hard to persuade Joost to have that pipe put in. Father had never liked change. If it had been up to him, he would have spent the rest of his life blowing glass over an oil lamp.

Why now? she wanted to scream out into the dark sky above. Her eyelids burned. She took a deep breath.

But once he had gotten used to the "newfangled nonsense," he had been so proud! The gas flame was hotter than the old lamp, and he could blow bottles and test tubes with much thinner walls. From then on not an evening passed down at the Black Eagle when he didn't try to persuade the last few glassblowers who were not on the gas mains that it was the only way to work.

Her father. She would miss him so. Her heart was a gaping wound.

Their mother had died when she was eleven, Ruth was nine, and Marie seven. For a whole year they hadn't been able to sleep unless Joost left a lamp burning in their room all night. Every evening he would tell them how beautiful it was up in heaven, how happy Mother was there. It became part of their bedtime routine, instead of prayers. And every night the girls took turns getting up out of bed to go check on Father. They had been so afraid that he would leave them too. He had been kind and patient with them, and at last the fear faded away. But now it was back, seeking to devour her, swallow her whole. Johanna fought it as she looked down at her father's face in the candlelight, her heart heavy with love. Joost had spent years teaching them to be strong, and his lessons would not be in vain.

Joost Steinmann. The widower whose daughters had ruled the roost. One evening at the Black Eagle one of the men had dared to tease Joost for having fathered three girls but never a boy in all those years. He had ended up with a black eye for his pains, and couldn't see straight for a week. "Why do I need sons?" Joost always said. "Steinmann girls are worth twice any boy in the village!" Johanna swallowed hard.

She looked at him and stroked his cheek. "I don't know what we'll do now," she whispered. "But I promise you one thing." Her hand felt hot against his cold skin, and she had to steel herself to keep it there. "We won't make you ashamed. When you look down from heaven at us, you'll be proud of what you see!"

By morning, Johanna had cried all the tears she had. While Ruth and Marie sat by the dead man's bedside, she went up to sleep for a few hours. She woke up a little before noon. There was still a lot to be done before Joost's funeral.

4

"Gone at last!" Ruth had been scrubbing the front step with a cloth. Now she stood up and threw it into the sink with the pile of dishes still waiting to be washed. Then she flopped down onto the bench next to Marie and Johanna.

It was late afternoon. Usually they would be bent over their workbenches at that hour, but the funeral had taken place at two o'clock that day. Although it had been pouring rain, so many mourners had come to the churchyard that Johanna had worried that all the breads and cakes in the house would not be enough for the guests. Most of them, however, had said their good-byes at the graveside and gone back to work. Only their closest neighbors came home with the sisters to drink a cup or two of coffee and reminisce about Joost. They had hung up their wet coats in the front hall, and the hooks almost gave way beneath the weight. Soon the whole house had smelled of wet cloth and great puddles spread out on the hall floor. Widow Grün had helped Ruth in the kitchen, but the two of them could hardly keep the kettle boiling fast enough to make all the coffee. A funeral was thirsty work; everyone knew that. Once all the cakes and sandwiches had been eaten and the air in the house grew fusty, the guests said good-bye, one after another.

Peter Maienbaum had been the last to leave. He stood there with his hand on the door handle, looking at the empty workshop as though he still had trouble accepting that Joost had died so unexpectedly.

"It's so quiet in here all of a sudden." Marie looked about as though she could hardly believe it was all over.

Johanna nodded. Nobody wanting another cup of coffee, nobody looking at her with concern in their eyes.

"It was so kind of Swiss Karl to bring that glass rose," Marie said.

The others nodded.

Karl Flein had spent years in the Swiss Alps as a young man, so the other glassblowers called him Swiss Karl. While the others put fresh flowers onto the coffin, he had brought a rose made of glass, which he had blown himself. Johanna couldn't help but think that a burial was no place for flowers, real or glass.

"And Wilhelm Heimer spoke from his heart," she said.

"He did," Ruth agreed. "I got a lump in my throat when he said that he always felt he shared a burden with Father because they both became widowers so young."

"I was surprised that Heimer came at all. It's not like him to let the lamp go cold." Johanna made a face. The gas flames were always burning at the Heimer family home on the hillside, long past when all the other lights in the village were out. Some thought that Wilhelm Heimer worked too hard, while others were envious that he had so many orders to fill. He could take on the extra work because he had three sons, all of them hard workers and skilled glassblowers.

"Why did it have to rain, today of all days?" Ruth complained.

"I would have liked it even less if the sun had been shining," Marie replied. "Imagine being buried under a clear blue sky with the sun blazing down. No, better to have the clouds weep along with the mourners."

None of them could think of anything more to say after that. They had talked over all the details while the guests were still there: Father's death, the burial itself, the turn that the weather had taken after weeks and weeks of sunshine, the way the priest had stumbled over his words at the graveside, so that many of the mourners thought he might have had a little too much of the communion wine. They'd had enough talk.

Johanna stared at the piles of dishes. The fire was still burning in the oven. She could put some water on to heat, and then wash the dishes. She jumped to her feet before either of her sisters had the same idea. Marie stood at her elbow and pulled each dripping plate from the water, then piled them all up on the table. Once everything was clean, Marie and Ruth dragged the tub of dishwater out into the yard and tipped it out. Johanna began to clear the shelves of the sideboard where they kept their crockery. "High time I gave this a good clean," she declared when the other two cast questioning glances at her. Ruth picked up her embroidery, and Marie took out the dress that she had begun sewing a couple of days before. Yet no sooner did they have their work on the table in front of them than they folded their hands in their laps and just sat there.

When they finally went upstairs, it was almost completely dark outside. None of them dared to look into the abandoned workshop.

◆ ◆ ◆

When Ruth woke up the next morning it was still raining. She lit the gas lamp in the kitchen and went to the pantry, just like any other morning, to take out the potatoes they had boiled the night before. She was going to peel them and slice them for the pan. Then she stopped in her tracks, her hand on the china knob of the pantry door.

They hadn't boiled the potatoes last night.

This was not a morning like any other.

Her eyes stinging, she ran from the kitchen out to the laundry shed. Her arm surged up and down as she pumped water into the basin, working the handle so hard that it clattered and jumped. The water spilled over the basin's blue enamel rim, but Ruth didn't notice. She only stopped when it splashed onto her feet. She let out a loud sob, standing there in the damp shed.

By the time she came back to the kitchen, Johanna and Marie were already sitting at the table. One of them had gotten bread from the pantry, along with a pat of butter and the honey jar. They sat there chewing their bread in silence. None of them tasted the sweetness of honey in their mouths for they each had the same bitter question on the tip of their tongue: "What shall we do now?"

◆　◆　◆

It went on raining for the next few days, and inside the house it was like Sleeping Beauty's castle once more. Each sister crept into her own quiet corner, idling the days away and hoping that it would be bedtime soon. Peter looked in from time to time, but he never stayed long. Unlike the girls, he had work to do. And though he was ashamed to admit it to himself, every time he visited the Steinmanns, he was happy to leave again and escape the gloom in that house.

◆　◆　◆

Another meal had passed in silence. Johanna suddenly looked up and cleared her throat. "I think it's best if we go and clear away Father's things now."

Ruth frowned. "I don't know . . . shouldn't we wait a little while yet?"

"I suppose it makes no difference if we do it now or in a . . ." Johanna began, her eyes darting from one to the other, as though hoping that one of them would talk her out of the idea.

Ruth realized that Johanna no more wanted to tackle such a dreary job than she did. But it would be hard no matter when they did it. Quite apart from that, she didn't know how long she could bear this dreadful silence in the house. Better a dreary job than nothing at all to do.

"You're right; it's time to tidy up a little."

◆ ◆ ◆

Ruth and Johanna were upstairs folding shirts and jackets, making neat bundles that they wrapped in linen, but downstairs the neighbors continued to come knocking. Even a week after Joost's death, they still came by with food. One woman had just brought them a pot of soup, peering over Marie's shoulder as she handed it over. How were the orphaned girls getting along? Three young women, on their own . . . that was a rarity in the village. Marie quickly realized that the old busybody would have liked to come in and look around, but she shut the door as soon as she thanked the visitor for the gift.

As Marie looked for somewhere to put the soup down, the lid of the pot slipped a little. A sharp, sour smell assailed her nose. Marie shuddered. Perhaps the soup was already spoiled? She wondered for a moment whether she should just tip it out behind the house, but then decided to put it aside for the time being. Looking for somewhere to put it down, she carried the pot through the kitchen and into the workshop, where she set it on one of the empty workbenches.

She was just about to go out again when she stopped in her tracks.

How quiet it was here!

Marie drew up a stool and sat down.

No ghosts. But it was as though the silence were haunted all the same. Day after day, the flame singing in the lamp had been the sound of their lives. "If you want the flame to sing, you have to blow hard, give it a lot of air," Father always said. Marie felt her throat tighten. She ran her fingers lovingly over the old oil lamp where it stood abandoned next to the new gas pipe. The flame would never sing here again.

She heard a sound upstairs. Tidy up, Ruth had said—but they were talking about Father's life!

When she had asked what she could do while the two of them worked up there, her sisters looked at one another in panic. What could they do? Ever since Father had died, the question had been everywhere in the house, unspoken but so loud that Marie felt almost deafened by it. Although she didn't have any idea either what they should do next, she felt hurt that Ruth and Johanna didn't even want to include her in their discussions. Just because she was the youngest, they never took her seriously. Father had treated her as a child, and now Ruth and Johanna were doing the same. But there was nothing she could do about it. She stood up with a sigh and went back to the kitchen.

Around noon, Widow Grün came calling with an apple cake. The scent of cinnamon and aniseed wafted up the stairs and drove out the smell of their father's old clothes. While other neighbors had brought pot after pot of casserole—which the sisters ate without enthusiasm—the fresh-baked cake brought back their appetite.

"We have to thank Widow Grün again for all she's done for us," Johanna declared as she sliced it.

"We really must," Ruth agreed. "The way she helped me wash Father as we laid him out—not everyone would have done that."

"It just doesn't seem like her to make herself so useful. She generally likes to mind her own business . . ."

"It is odd, isn't it . . . She only lives two doors down, but we hardly ever see her," Marie chimed in.

Everybody in Lauscha knew all about their neighbors' comings and goings, and not only because it was a small village where almost everybody was in the same line of work. It was hard to keep anything secret in a place where all the houses were lined up side by side like pearls on a string. The main street twisted and turned as it climbed the mountainside, and there were hardly any side streets at all—the steep forested slopes all around saw to that. This part of Thuringia had changed little over the years, and the houses stood huddled together the way they had for centuries.

"How do you ever expect to see Widow Grün when she's up at the Heimers' house working all day?" Ruth answered. "She probably has no time to sit down and gossip."

Johanna shook her head. "Griseldis always did keep herself to herself, even when Josef Grün was alive. I don't think he much liked it when she chatted with the neighbors. He was an old soak!"

"Whatever happened to their son?" Ruth asked, between bites of cake. "What was his name, Magnus?"

"I've no idea. He just cleared out and left one day. Nobody seems to know where he went, or why. But I was only thirteen when it happened, so . . ." There was a knock at the door, and Johanna fell quiet.

"Not more food," Ruth groaned.

But it was Peter, who asked Johanna to step outside with him. Marie and Ruth looked at one another meaningfully.

5

Peter shut the door behind them. "And? Is everything all right?"

Johanna shrugged.

"I'm sorry I haven't come to see you these past two days, but I've had a lot of visitors."

Peter Maienbaum made glass eyes. Some of his customers came from far away. When someone needed a glass eye after an accident, time was of the essence. The longer the delay, the greater the danger that the eye socket would become inflamed or even suppurate once the false eye was in. But if an eye was fitted right away, there was a good chance that the muscles would accept it, perhaps even learn to move it around.

"There's no need to apologize. After all, you've done more than anyone to look after us," Johanna reassured him.

"That was the other thing I wanted to talk to you about." Peter shuffled his feet, embarrassed. "You see . . . I'd love to buy your father's tools and his stock of raw glass . . . but the truth is, none of that's any use to me!"

Johanna tried to smile. "Oh, I know that. You get your stock when they make colored glass down at the foundry. You don't have any need for our clear and brown glass." She put a hand on his shoulder. "Don't worry about us. You can't get rid of us that easily." Gallows humor. She gave him a light shove. "We won't starve, that's for sure—you should see all the food that people have brought round. It's as though there were ten of us in the house, not just three."

He looked at her skeptically. "Food's only the half of it. You need money as well. And work. Even with all the goodwill in the world, I don't know how you're going to manage!"

Johanna sighed. "Nor do we. We were just clearing away Father's things. He'll have put some money aside for a rainy day, and we can use that for the time being." So far though they had found nothing of the sort, and she couldn't imagine where else they might look for it.

"There are still some boxes of finished wares in your workshop. Should I take them to Sonneberg for you?"

"No, I'll take care of that myself," Johanna said hastily. "To be honest with you, I'll be happy to get out of the house for a day. Anyway, what would Friedhelm Strobel say if you showed up with our wares! Even if it's raining cats and dogs tomorrow, I'll go to Sonneberg and sell what we have." She sighed. "I really should have done it last Friday. But it was so soon after Father died."

"Strobel had better not try any tricks, or he'll have me to answer to. You tell him that. And"—he put a hand under her chin—"if you have any trouble with anything at all, just come to me for help. Will you promise me that?" he asked, fixing her with his gaze.

She turned away. Something in her fought against the very idea of making such a promise, harmless though it may have been. Instead she said, "We'll manage somehow." Although it sounded vague, she didn't want Peter to feel responsible for them, for her in particular. She squeezed his arm, gave him a friendly nod, and then walked back into the house. For a moment she toyed with the idea of creeping upstairs to bed. All this talking wore her out, and she was tired of having to pretend to be in charge the whole time. Why didn't the others notice? But then she pulled herself together—she could hardly leave her sisters sitting downstairs on their own.

"What did Peter want?" Ruth burst out before Johanna had even closed the door.

All at once Johanna felt butterflies in her stomach. Strange. She had stood in the doorway just like this, back on that fateful Monday. She pulled herself together before the grief could settle on her shoulders again like a black shawl. They had to talk about their future. There was no getting around it.

"Peter said that he would like to buy Father's tools and the stock of glass, but unfortunately it's not what he needs."

"Maybe one of the other glassblowers will buy up the stock?" Marie asked.

Ruth sighed. "I don't know . . . It wouldn't seem right to me to just get rid of it all like that. It makes everything seem so final."

"But that's just what I mean!" Marie said, raising her voice. "Now that Father's gone, we won't be blowing any more glass." She put her hand to her mouth. "Whatever will become of us?"

Johanna didn't know what to say. Ever since Father had died, she had thought a good deal about how they would cope. She had put on a brave face for Peter, but in truth her confidence was as hollow as the glass beads that half the village made and sold.

Without someone in the house to blow the glass, they had nothing to live on. Without someone to blow the glass, they wouldn't grind the stoppers, paint the labels, or pack the wares. Those few skills that they had were of no use at all.

"Tomorrow I'll go to Sonneberg to sell the last few things that we have. It's just some jars and tubes, and it won't fetch much, but we can live off that for a while. We can't rely on people bringing us food forever after all." Johanna looked at Ruth, who seemed to be off in a daydream somewhere, and decided to speak plainly. There was no sense trying to soften the blow. "I've looked in every nook and cranny in Father's room, but it looks like he didn't put aside any savings. Putting in the gas pipes probably cost him everything he had." She bit her lip. It was still so hard to believe.

"Maybe the gasworks will give us that money back if we tell them we aren't using the gas?" Marie asked quietly.

Ruth frowned. That was typical of Marie. "You can't really believe that! Don't you remember that their men had to spend three days digging a trench to lay the pipes? That's where the money went. We can't just turn up and ask for it back!" She nonetheless cast a glance at Johanna with a glimmer of hope in her eyes.

Her older sister shook her head. "They won't hear of it. No, we'll just have to use whatever Friedhelm Strobel gives us to get by until something turns up."

The hope in Ruth's eyes died away. "If only we had a man about the house to help us! Someone who could take over Father's bench and lamp."

"And who would that be?" Johanna laughed bitterly. "The other glassblowers all have their own work to take care of. And anyway—how would we pay him, whoever it was?"

Marie looked as though she wanted to say something, but she kept quiet for fear of being told off again.

"We'll have to hope that someone takes us on as hired hands. If the Widow Grün can work that way, then so can we," Johanna said. They could hear in her voice how little she enjoyed the prospect of doing such a thing. Hired hands earned even less than a maid; everyone knew that. They had to work ten hours a day, even more, just to get by.

Her sisters didn't say a word, but she could hear their skepticism all the same. There were only a few workshops in the village that even took on hired help, and so far none of them had come offering work.

"There's another way we could get a glassblower into the house . . ." Ruth grinned. "Maybe we should think of marrying! It's not a bad idea given our current situation, is it?" She sat up straight, as though she were about to grab paper and pencil and draw up a list of candidates.

Johanna and Marie looked at each other, downcast. They didn't know if their sister was serious.

"And where are you going to conjure up three eligible bachelors?" Marie asked.

Ruth didn't seem to notice the sarcasm in Marie's voice. Pursing her lips, she replied, "Well, that is a problem. Father was very fierce with them all. If we don't get a move on, all the lads in the village will be spoken for, and we'll end up as old maids. All the other girls have been engaged for ages!" There was an undertow of panic in her voice.

Johanna could hardly believe her ears. "What are you blathering about?"

"I'm not blathering, it's the truth," Ruth shot back. "One or two of the men who are getting married caught my eye as well, let me tell you. And there were some good glassblowers among them. But since Father never even let us go down to the foundry square, how could we ever have caught a man's eye? I daresay they've all written us off!"

The young men of the village often gathered down on the foundry square after work. While great bursts of flame shot out from the furnaces inside the foundry, the girls sat outside on the low wall and giggled. The boys stood by the wall, digging one another in the ribs, cracking jokes, or smoking cigarettes that more often than not made their eyes water. The boys and girls traded glances—appraising, amorous or scornful, flirtatious or brazen, or even downright shameless. Some were all smiles and elegance, while others made fools of themselves.

Johanna never felt that she had missed out on anything by not going down there. Quite the opposite; she hated the way the young men gawped as she walked through the village with Ruth and Marie. And Ruth had always claimed that she would rather wait for a Polish prince or a Russian nobleman to come courting than walk out with one of the clumsy boys from the foundry square. Johanna reminded her of what she had so often said.

"Maybe those were just a young girl's daydreams," Ruth said, waving a hand dismissively. "I don't want life to pass me by. Do you think I enjoy being stuck here in the house and only ever doing chores? I want to wear pretty things the way the other girls do. And I want to sing with the choir, or join in the theater shows where they wear such splendid costumes! Or even just go to the fair one of these days. Who knows, maybe that's where I'll meet my prince. But it certainly won't happen if we just shut ourselves away like hermits!"

Johanna gazed at her sister, aghast. All of a sudden she felt she knew far too little about what Ruth wanted in life.

"But we can't just go out in the street and find a man to marry, easy as that!" Marie's skepticism broke the sudden silence. "I can't think of anyone who wants to marry us!"

Johanna sighed again. Sometimes Marie was just too naive.

"I can, but it's not me he wants to marry . . ." Ruth laughed. "Who keeps paying us neighborly calls, and wanting to talk to one of us alone?"

Marie giggled.

Johanna rolled her eyes. It was hardly news that Ruth thought that she and Peter were more than just friends. She thought of him as a big brother, someone she could talk to without having to mind her words. "Peter's a good friend. To all of us!" she said, although she didn't want to talk about it.

"Maybe *you* think he's just a friend. You think he just spends his days making false eyes for others . . ." Ruth raised her eyebrows and paused meaningfully. "But he's making real eyes at you!" she burst out, giggling.

"That's an awful joke!" Marie snapped at her. "I think Peter's very nice. But who could ever think of marrying a man whose family name means *maypole*?" And she broke into giggles as well.

"You're a pair of silly fools, both of you!" Johanna got up from the table and started to take the dishes to the basin. "For all I care you can go and find a man to marry," she told Ruth. "But when I look around the village, it hardly seems like an earthly paradise! Times are hard, and it makes no difference whether you're married or not. Do as you like though . . ." She shrugged. "While you're at it, you can make sure that whoever he is, he has a brother, and then that's Marie taken care of. As for me, I'm going to Sonneberg tomorrow!"

6

It was still dark outside when Ruth shook Johanna awake. For a moment Johanna just lay there, uncertain whether she was still dreaming, but then she remembered what she had to do that day. While Ruth went downstairs, still in her nightgown, Johanna got dressed. She had taken her clothes from the wardrobe the night before and gotten everything ready. She looked with dismay at the thick woven jacket, but it was too chilly to go in just a thin knitted cardigan.

Down in the laundry shed she scrubbed her face with a wet washcloth and combed her hair. It had gotten tangled up in the rough collar of her jacket, but she teased it out and braided it tightly. Then she wound the braid around the crown of her head and fixed it in place with several pins. She bound a headscarf over it and knotted the ends so that the corners were tucked away out of sight. If she had done her hair any other way, she would have trouble with the load of glass she had to carry. It was in a deep basket with shoulder straps, and when she hoisted it on her back, the top of the basket reached high above her head. She looked briefly at herself in the mirror, but all she could see was a pair of vast dark eyes. Every time she saw her face without its frame of hair, she was astonished at how different she looked. Her mouth looked much bigger as well.

Maybe the mirror was rippled? She opened her mouth slightly and saw that the mirror told the truth—the change was indeed in her face. Her lips curved sensually, and it almost looked as though she were blowing a kiss to her image in the mirror! Johanna frowned. Father had never liked the idea of sending her off to Sonneberg on her own. He had always insisted that she dress modestly. Not for the first time Johanna wondered whether she had achieved the effect he had in mind. Then she stuck out her tongue at the woman in the mirror, and went back into the house.

Ruth had already loaded the cardboard boxes into the wooden frame that would fit inside the basket. Four jars to each box. The two of them carried the pack out to the front step, and Johanna looked up the steep village street. She was glad to see that there was no mist today. With a practiced motion, she shouldered her pack and buckled the belt tightly. Then Ruth lifted up the wooden frame and strapped it into place at all four corners. She put her hand on Johanna's arm. "When you're in Sonneberg, keep your ears open. You may hear of someone who wants us to work for them. Perhaps Strobel knows a glassblower who would take us on."

Johanna nodded. The wooden frame was already digging into her back. She set out.

"And try to get a better price from the old skinflint this time. We need every penny!" Ruth called after her.

As if she didn't know that! Johanna grimaced. It was all very well for Ruth to give orders like that, but she never wanted to go and sell the wares herself. "Strobel gives me the shivers," she had said the year before, the only time she went along with Johanna. "I wouldn't want to see him too often." Johanna didn't much like the look of the man either, but what could be done about it? She sighed, and strode on purposefully.

It was just after half past six.

When she passed the railway station, the temptation to go in and buy a ticket to Sonneberg was as strong as ever. Ever since the rails had been laid four years ago, more and more women took the train when they ran errands from the village and delivered the wares to town. But Joost had no fondness for the train; he had always called it a "stinking black contraption." Johanna could hear his voice as clearly as if he were still alive: "It'll break down halfway, just like it did when they cut the ribbon for the maiden voyage, and then you'll have to hike the rest of the way all the same!" She wondered, however, whether he had really been so distrustful of the new technology, or whether his attitude had more to do with the fact that they just couldn't afford the fare. Just as they had never been able to afford to send one of the village women into town on their behalf.

At this time of year the sun was so low over the horizon that it almost shone through from below the treetops. The rain that had poured down during their father's funeral was long gone, and it was unusually warm for September. Johanna soon felt the heat gathering in her armpits; the thick woolen jacket made her perspire. Her back was damp, and it itched. She had tied the headscarf too tight, and she tried to ease it with her finger so that the air could get to her scalp.

Usually she would have hitched a ride with a wagon for most of the thirteen or so miles into town, but today, whenever the drivers slowed up and offered to let her ride, she waved them on. If she accepted their offer, she would have to give them a couple of pennies for the favor, and she had to be careful with what little money she had.

The rain over the last few days had made such a quagmire of the path that Johanna found herself cutting through the trees to avoid sinking up to her ankles in mud. Great clods of earth got caught in her soles all the same, and every step was an effort. She toyed with the idea of washing her boots in the Steinach brook, but it was swollen with rainwater and no longer the tame little stream she knew; it had broken its banks and foamed and thrashed wildly, throwing up fountains of spray in places that Johanna had to dodge. She carried on with the mud still clinging to her boots.

When she reached Sonneberg, she looked up at the church clock and saw to her dismay that it was already past eleven o'clock. More than four and a half hours—it had never taken her that long before. Usually she was one of Friedhelm Strobel's first callers, which was an advantage since she never had to wait long to speak to him. She looked down at her filthy boots and her heart sank further. Strobel would hardly be pleased to have her tramping mud all over his gleaming parquet floor.

Like every Friday when she came to town, she was struck by how busy it was. Johanna knew she was late and picked up her pace unconsciously as she walked. She often had to step aside to let others past, which wasn't easy with the great basket on her back.

Sonneberg was full of people this time of year, and as Johanna crossed town, she heard countless German dialects and foreign languages buzzing around her. Almost every inn and lodging house had hung up a shingle to show that there were no more free rooms. Buyers had flooded into town from far and wide to see what the craftsmen in the nearby villages had made over the summer months. Most of all, they were here to reserve stock for the Christmas season.

Rather than going from house to house and haggling over the items with the pieceworkers, the businessmen relied on local wholesalers, who had set up their networks of suppliers years before and turned the putting-out system into a fine art form in Sonneberg. There were at least twenty wholesalers in town—maybe more since their shops were sometimes hardly recognizable as such from outside—and all of them could contract any kind of piecework a customer cared to name. Not that they had storerooms full of glassware sitting on the shelves waiting for a buyer—instead, most orders were placed from the wholesaler's catalogs. These great tomes were full of pen-and-ink drawings or even photographs, with every item described in minute detail, including its dimensions and material. Each wholesaler guarded his samples book fiercely. There were no prices in the catalogs, for those were always negotiated separately for each order.

The buyers came to Sonneberg for the beautiful porcelain dolls in particular; they had real hair and glass eyes that moved, and they were dressed in finely sewn silk clothes. But they also bought toys of tin or wood, and colorful glass marbles and beads, and all the other wares that a glassblower could make. Thuringian handiwork was known and admired all over, and sold for good money in the department stores of Munich, Nuremberg, and Hamburg, and even farther afield in Saint Petersburg, Copenhagen, and Brussels.

Once a customer had made his choice from the catalog, he would work out a price, the size of the order, and the delivery date. Then the wholesaler would go to his pieceworkers with the order book under his arm. The Christmas orders were all coming in now, and a wholesaler's door had hardly swung closed before the next visitor came bustling into his shop.

Johanna could tell at a glance which people were buyers and which were pieceworkers. The buyers were far more elegantly dressed, in clothes of the best quality. What's more, they almost invariably had a secretary at their side, carrying a leather briefcase or a carpetbag, which likely held samples of their own, so that they could ask a wholesaler, "Could you make me a vase like this one?" or "What would you charge for a hundred wooden candlesticks?"

While the businessmen were fresh faced and well rested after a night in their lodgings and a leisurely breakfast, the pieceworkers had often worked through the night to have their orders ready on time. If they had had time to eat at all before they set out, then it was nothing more than a few potatoes or a slice of bread. They walked briskly through the streets, and Johanna suspected that they hurried not for the love of business but because they had a house full of children back home and a pile of work that grew bigger every minute they were away.

When Johanna opened the door to Friedhelm Strobel's showroom, she was almost choked by the thought that this would be the last time she came here. She was suddenly glad that she had to wait until the glassblower who had arrived before her had finished his business with Strobel. She sat down on the wine-red velvet sofa at the other end of the shop, her heart thumping.

It was strange that she had been here so often but had never really looked at the place before now. The shop was lined floor to ceiling with cabinets in which Strobel kept his samples and finished wares. None of the drawers were labeled, but Strobel knew even with his eyes closed what was where. At the very top of the cabinets was a shelf with baskets instead of drawers. One of the baskets was full of the balls of soap that he bought from an old woman who lived in a nearby village and who made the soap by hand with the help of her two daughters. Johanna had once been at Strobel's when a consignment of soap was delivered, so she knew it was the source of the glorious herbal smell that always filled the shop.

As she wrinkled her nose to stifle a sneeze, she heard Strobel's voice. "The bowl's much too deep," he was saying. "My client wants to use each bowl to present seven or eight pralines, but you could put a pound of chocolates in there. I made this quite clear when you were here last!"

Johanna knew all too well the expression of scornful incredulity that went with that tone of voice—as though he could hardly believe the stupidity of the world. She had been in the shop often enough when one of the other suppliers was the target of such a dressing down. Every time this happened, she had felt sorry for whoever was on the receiving end.

As Strobel spoke, he pulled over a wooden ladder and climbed three steps to open one of the drawers. "I'd like to know why I bothered to show you the sample piece at all if you're not going to stick to the model. Look here, you managed to get the radius right but this bowl is much shallower!" He held up the pale blue glass bowl.

The man took the bowl and looked at it closely. Strobel snorted impatiently. He glanced over at Johanna and tried to catch her eye, but she turned away. Surely he didn't imagine that she would take sides with him against this poor fellow! The man spoke: "You didn't make such a fuss about it last time. What happens now?" He looked worried.

Strobel shrugged. "Is it my problem that you can't listen? I have to supply what my clients order."

"But you must have some clients who want bowls this deep! What am I supposed to do with fifty of them?" A look of despair crossed his face. Johanna didn't want to think what would happen if he returned home with his pack still full of the glass bowls he had been planning to sell.

Strobel clapped his hand onto the man's shoulder. "I'll keep one here as a sample. Maybe I'll find a use for it," he said, steering him toward the door. "I'm sure we'll do business again one of these days." That was probably meant to reassure the poor soul, but the man was hardly out the door before Strobel put the bowl away in a drawer under his counter without a second glance.

"Johanna!" He held out his arms toward her. "I just heard what a dreadful misfortune has befallen your household! My deepest sympathies!"

Friedhelm Strobel's handshake was bony and always just a little too firm. The skin around his fingernails was bitten to the quick, seeping blood and even pus in places. Johanna gave him her hand unwillingly and pulled it away as soon as she could.

"I've come to sell the last jars that we have," she said, pointing to the pack. She didn't want to talk to this man about how Joost had died.

Strobel didn't seem to take the hint though. "He was such a hard worker, and an excellent glassblower. It's quite a tragedy that he should have died so young!"

He put a hand on Johanna's arm, leading her to the table where he had his catalogs laid out for his customers. The polished red wood of the tabletop reflected the chandelier that hung above them. On either side of the table, comfortable armchairs were upholstered with gold and brown brocade. The furniture made the whole room look elegant and prosperous. Johanna had never been invited to sit there before, but today Strobel practically pushed her into a seat. He gazed at her intently.

"We'll have a look at your jars later," he said offhandedly.

Johanna had to make an effort not to roll her eyes. She really didn't have time to listen to one of Strobel's little speeches. She just wanted her money.

"You barely even knew my father. I hardly think you can be much affected by his death," she said sharply.

Strobel's gaze moved from her eyes to her cheeks, then settled on her lips.

"Did I say that I was?" he asked, raising his eyebrows.

Without quite meaning to, Johanna pushed her chair back a little.

Strobel leaned forward, propped up his elbows, and folded his hands as if in prayer.

"I was mostly thinking about what his death must mean for you and your sisters."

As she noted the look in his eyes, the great sigh he heaved, and the eagerness in his face, Johanna felt her hackles rise. She was ready to snap at him again, but she held back and instead said, "It's not been an easy time for us. A great deal has changed now that he's dead." She held her breath. Perhaps he knew someone who had work for them.

"What would life be like if nothing ever changed? We can't stop such changes; that's for certain. But sometimes we can turn the screw a little and make them work for us." Strobel nodded portentously. "Which is why, my dear Johanna Steinmann, I have an offer for you."

7

"I would like you to come and work for me. As my . . . assistant."

Strobel's words echoed in her ears. *Assistant*—what a fancy word. Why not say shopgirl, or hired hand? She walked through the streets of Sonneberg as though in a daze, and a thousand thoughts crowded round her, keeping pace. Strobel's offer had given her a great deal to think about.

At the edge of town, she stopped suddenly. Should she buy a bag of coffee as she usually did? Deciding that they wouldn't starve to death for want of a few pennies, and that they all deserved a reminder of the good times, she headed for the grocer's that she visited every Friday. She ignored the silver trays piled high with tempting pastries and the barrels of salt herring. A little while later, she left the shop with a couple of ounces of coffee. The smell of freshly ground beans was an extra treat she could enjoy for free.

As soon as she reached the outskirts of town, the road began to climb gently uphill. Johanna strode on like a sleepwalker. Her thoughts kept going round and round, always returning to the conversation in Strobel's shop.

He had said that he admired the stubborn way she bargained with him, and he thought that she might turn out to have a good head for business—whatever that might mean.

Her first reaction was to say, "Me? Help you here? I can't be of any use to you!" But she had paused a moment and stroked the smooth mahogany table with the palm of her hand. Then she had asked, "What kind of work would I be doing for you?" Her voice was flat, toneless. She thought she knew the answer—indeed, she could already see herself polishing the floor. Some work!

"I would make you my right-hand woman," Strobel had replied. "As I do business with my customers, you will draw up inventory, note down their orders, and then deliver them to the suppliers. The greater part of your work would involve keeping proper records. In a business the size of mine, written records of every transaction are absolutely crucial." What a pompous tone he had! "I've been thinking for some time of hiring an assistant. Perhaps the time has come to make the thought a reality."

She had just nodded. It could hardly have been more astonishing if Strobel had offered her a job polishing the moon.

"I would pay you of course," he had added, misinterpreting her silence. "Though you understand that we would have to agree on some probationary period at a lower rate of pay. But once you have been on the job for a while—" He broke off there, leaving the rest of the sentence to dangle tantalizingly unspoken, like bait on a hook. Johanna snorted. He hardly needed to lure her in like this! His first few sentences had been enough to conjure up images in her mind's eye that were quite tempting enough in themselves: Sonneberg and all the visitors in its streets, customers from all around the world, orders that ran into the hundreds of items, the samples all sitting neatly in their drawers waiting for the right client—and in the middle of all this hustle and bustle, Johanna Steinmann from Lauscha.

Then straightaway she had felt a pang of guilt. How could she let herself be carried away so soon after Father's death?

"I don't know whether I can do all that," she had answered, brushing aside her daydreams. She had seen herself standing there, notebook in hand, elegantly coiffed and wearing a dark-blue dress, attending to the customers . . . but she couldn't ever be anyone's assistant. Although excitement bubbled up inside her, she had kept it from spilling over.

Friedhelm Strobel grasped her hand. "If *I* trust you to do all that, it should be enough. Or do you think I would make such an offer to any young lass who wandered in off the street?"

Johanna wasn't quite sure whether this was meant as a compliment or an insult. But she shook his hand—that horrible hand with the chewed flesh at the fingernails—and stood up. "I will have to consider your offer," she had said, noticing how frosty her tone was.

Oh, drat it all! She kicked at a pile of leaves. Why did that man always put her on the defensive? Was it because he wasn't from around here? Somebody had told her once that Friedhelm Strobel was from an important family of Berlin merchants. Maybe that was why he could seem so hoity-toity, even arrogant, Johanna mused. On the other hand, he had always been scrupulously polite to her, and that despite the fact that she could be stubborn, even mulish, in her dealings with him. More than once she had wondered whether, for some unknown reason, she had ended up in Strobel's good graces. Well, today's job offer certainly confirmed that.

Johanna grinned. She had been able to get a good price for the jars as well.

Now she could see the outskirts of Lauscha in the distance. The mountains all around cast their long shadows over the houses that clung to the steep slopes. When the sun shone, the wooden shingles on the rooftops glittered gray and silver, but when the village was in shadow like this, all the houses seemed to be wearing gloomy black hoods.

Johanna stopped to rest before tackling the final slope. Wouldn't Ruth and Marie be surprised? She smiled from ear to ear, and though she knew it was vain, she felt she had every reason to be pleased with herself. What had he said? "Do you think I would make such an offer to any young lass who wandered in off the street?"

"Not to any lass, but certainly to me!" Johanna said to herself, and laughed out loud.

But a moment later, she had her doubts. If she took Strobel up on his offer, she would have to live in Sonneberg. She would have to leave Ruth and Marie on their own, and only come home at weekends; there was no way she would be able to walk more than twenty-five miles every day. And if she took the train all the time, it would probably eat up most of her wages.

And another thought nagged at her: What if she couldn't live up to Strobel's expectations? What if she did something foolish?

Ever since leaving Sonneberg, she had been of two minds about the matter. She had asked to be allowed to sleep on the decision. After all, she had to talk it over with her sisters first. And with Peter. Not that he had any say in the matter, but he did have a knack for asking the right questions, which her sisters did not. Yes, she decided, she would pay him a neighborly call after supper. She set off up the hill toward home.

◆ ◆ ◆

Friedhelm Strobel was also thinking back on the conversation, his mind elsewhere as he went through the motions of showing his samples catalog to a buyer whose company was notoriously late with its payments. He grinned quietly to himself as he remembered how nonchalantly she had answered him—as though there were nothing in the least bit unusual about his offer. The little minx certainly knew how to play it cool. He passed his tongue over his lips until he found a scrap of dry skin, which he bit off greedily. Oh yes, Johanna Steinmann was far from being a frightened little mouse like most females her age. You could see that just by looking at her figure, which was wiry and firm, without an ounce of extra flesh on her anywhere and instead the muscles of a hard worker. Shoulders square, she looked ready to face the world, almost like a proud young brave except for the gentle swell of her breasts, which were such a pleasure to gaze upon. And the way she looked at him with those big eyes of hers above broad high cheekbones? Even the dreadful headscarf she always wore could not disguise her beauty. If he took away her scarf, replaced those dreadful country bumpkin boots with an elegant pair of shoes, and put her into a close-fitting dress, Johanna Steinmann would be far more attractive than many of the fine ladies who came to buy from him.

She was also far from stupid. Just now she had given further proof of her ability to cope with the unexpected. She was confident, intelligent, and adaptable—all qualities that were greatly sought after in his line of work.

And not just in the world of work.

He turned half his mind back to the current customer, naming prices for the vases and glass dishes he was looking at—full price for this buyer, no question of a discount. And all the while he felt his excitement growing.

The customer was disappointed at Strobel's stubbornness and made some disparaging remark. Strobel leafed on through the catalog, chewing at his lip as he did so. He soon tasted blood on his tongue. He had to get rid of this fellow. He could hardly wait to lock up the shop for a while and be alone.

He had always been sorry to see Johanna leave his shop on Fridays, her head held high. More than once he had imagined what might happen if he met her in other circumstances. What an opportunity that would be for him—or for them both! Well, now that Joost Steinmann was dead, his chance had come.

He could hardly wait to take Johanna under his wing. She would learn fast; he was sure of that. Under his instruction, she would be able to develop her talent, and he had no doubt that she would soon play the game better than anyone.

Then he heard a voice in his mind, speaking from somewhere far back in his memory. *"Only a fool would poach in his own forest."* It was so unexpected that for a moment Strobel couldn't recall who had said it. Father! His father had said that, back when . . .

All at once he remembered the old man's proud patrician face as though it were yesterday. He hadn't thought about him for an age, or about all that he stood for in Strobel's life. His good mood vanished in a gust of cold wind.

Why now? Why today? Strobel fumed inwardly. It was as though his father was still seeking to rule his life, even from so far away. Was it the secret envy of a man who begrudged his son even the smallest pleasure in life? Or was it perhaps a warning?

Strobel stopped turning the pages of the catalog.

God knows, this current situation was nothing like what had happened back then . . .

All at once he remembered the old story so vividly that he quite forgot his customer was there. He looked up with a start as the man cleared his throat, loudly and insistently. The buyer was pointing somewhat impatiently to the first page of the catalog.

"I said, I would like three dozen of these dessert dishes, for two marks and thirty pence each. Would you be so good as to note that down?"

8

In the end the decision that had given Johanna such trouble was taken out of her hands. While she had been away, Wilhelm Heimer had come to call on her sisters. Although he had wanted to speak to her, as the eldest, he had settled for Ruth. He had recently begun supplying a new wholesaler, and he had a number of extra commissions to fill and would need help. He told Ruth and Marie that the work would consist of painting patterns, applying the silver wash, and packing the wares. There were bowls, drinking glasses, vases, and glass beads to prepare.

"I didn't want to say anything at Joost's funeral; I hadn't shaken hands on the commission back then," he added, and then he asked them whether they would come work for him. They could start the very next day, he told them. "Your father would have wanted you to."

Ruth and Marie were almost bursting with excitement when they told Johanna about Heimer's offer. All of a sudden working as hired hands wasn't something to be ashamed of, but a goal to strive for.

Once she heard the news, Johanna never even mentioned that Strobel had offered her a job. If there was work in the village, then it made no sense to go off somewhere else. All the same, she felt a pang of regret the next morning on the way up to Heimer's workshop when she stopped one of the village women who was headed into town and handed her a note to pass on to Friedhelm Strobel, turning down his offer. Farewell then, Sonneberg. Farewell dark-blue dress, and farewell customers from far and wide.

Instead she found herself standing in Heimer's workshop a little while later with a rubberized smock around her, listening closely as Widow Grün explained how to work with the silver solvent.

"Look here, you take the goblet by its stem, and then put a couple of drops of silver nitrate into it from this tube." Griseldis Grün showed her where the bottle of solution hung, and then pointed out the hole at the base of the stem. The goblets were made with double walls, to be silvered on the inside. "Then you put in a few drops of this one as well, that's the reducing fluid. After that you can dunk the goblet in the hot water. The silver doesn't take so well unless there's a bit of heat working on it from the outside, do you see?"

Johanna nodded. She had been wondering why there was a hot plate next to their workbench.

"You have to be quick about it. You'll need to give the goblet a good hard shake, so that the solution goes all over the inside."

The clear glass goblet turned silver as Johanna watched.

"And you have to be sure that you never get any of the solution onto the outside of the goblet, or it leaves behind the most horrible marks." Griseldis held up the finished product and showed off the unblemished silver all the way around. "That's how it works."

"It looks splendid! Hardly like glass at all!" Johanna shook her head, amazed.

Griseldis smiled. "That's why they call it poor man's silver, you know. Now look, once the silver has taken to the glass, there'll be a little fluid left over. You shake it out in here." She pointed to a box, its sides covered in a thick layer of cotton wool.

Johanna frowned. "What's the good of that? If the silver nitrate's only good for one use, then surely we could just tip the rest out."

"My word, no! It's nasty-looking stuff, and you may not think so to look at it, but there's still some silver in there. It all drips down to the bottom of the box. By the end of the year there's enough to make it worthwhile, believe you me. This box is worth money." She leaned closer to Johanna.

"And just try to guess who gets the profit from it?"

Johanna shrugged. "Heimer, I should imagine."

Instead of answering, Widow Grün shook her head and grinned knowingly.

Instead of asking further, Johanna stared at the bottle of silver nitrate where it hung on the wall.

"You're in no mood for riddles, are you, my dear?" Widow Grün put a hand on Johanna's arm and shook her gently.

Johanna swallowed. "It's all so . . . strange. Father's hardly been dead two weeks and now here we are in someone else's house, working at someone else's benches . . . It's all happened so fast, I almost feel that life is a merry-go-round."

The old woman sighed. "I know what you mean. You wouldn't believe how well I know! Just be happy that you have any work at all, my child. A woman on her own has a hard time in this world, let me tell you."

Johanna looked up. "Did Heimer come and offer us work of his own accord, or did you have a hand in that?" she whispered. From the corner of her eye she could see Heimer looking over Ruth's shoulder as she packed up the finished goods. She hoped that he would have no complaints.

"I wouldn't dare try such a thing!" Griseldis laughed. "You can't change that fellow's mind, nor try to plant an idea in him. You'll see soon enough that he runs the workshop just exactly as he sees fit." She was whispering too now. "Let's get to work, or we'll have trouble."

Johanna would have liked to thank her for her help. Maybe even ask her about her son, Magnus, who had been gone from Lauscha for so long. But one look at her neighbor's face showed her that this was not the time or place for such talk.

She couldn't believe how big the workshop was. It made their workshop at home look like one in a dollhouse. The Heimer family home was the only three-story house in the village; the kitchen was upstairs on the second floor and the bedrooms were above it, right under the roof. The workshop and storerooms took up the whole of the first floor, and even that didn't seem to be enough space; every square inch was crammed full of supplies or half-finished items or products already packed into crates and waiting to be taken away. The air was foul and smelled of chemicals, unwashed bodies, and bird droppings. Johanna was disgusted to see that there were some ten bird cages in the room. The village glassblowers loved to catch songbirds in the forest in the hope that the sound of their song would cheer up the workshop, but Joost had never liked the custom and his daughters didn't either. Quite the opposite: Johanna always felt sorry for the poor little creatures in their dirty cages. She turned away from a robin redbreast that gazed at her, sad eyed.

What would Father say if he could see her here now?

Like Joost, Wilhelm Heimer had lost his wife very early, and he had raised his three sons alone. All three had become glassblowers, but unlike most of the young men in Lauscha they made no attempt to set up their own workshops. Instead, they worked in their father's house, just as the Steinmann sisters had for Joost. Despite their similarities, the two families had never had much to do with one another, not only because the Heimer household was at the top of the village but also because both houses had quite enough to do with the work that came in. Joost and Wilhelm had drunk together often enough at the Black Eagle, but otherwise each went his own way and didn't interfere in the other's business. One had three daughters and the other three sons, and naturally there had been talk around the tavern table of making a match. In the end though, everyone in Lauscha knew that the Steinmann girls kept to themselves and didn't let the boys turn their heads.

Johanna sighed. It was a mad world, for here she was now, working with Wilhelm's sons. She stole a glance to the left where three lamps were set up by their workbenches, each with its own gas pipe. She could guess what that must have cost, given the fees the gasworks charged. But judging by the mountain of raw glass rods that lay by each bench, the three Heimer lads had plenty of work. The three brothers had already been sitting there, stooped over their lamps, when Johanna and her sisters had arrived that morning. Thomas had been the only one to look up and greet them; the other two had just grunted a word or two. So far none of them had taken a break.

Thomas, the eldest of the three, was her age. Sebastian was the middle brother. He was the only one to have married, and his wife, Eva, came from the village of Steinach. She was sitting at a table with Marie, busily painting. When Johanna looked over at them, she had trouble telling them apart from behind—they both had the same slim figure. The men in Eva's family made stylus pencils for writing on slates, the kind that schoolboys used, and they were dirt poor. Johanna remembered what Ruth had said about getting married, and she smiled. The Heimer household must look like paradise on earth to Sebastian's wife. Making a slate pencil was an exhausting and dirty job, so the work she did here must seem like child's play by comparison.

"When you're done with this little lot, you can get to work with the tinsel," said a voice at her ear all of a sudden.

Johanna jumped.

Heimer had appeared as if out of nowhere and was standing behind the Widow Grün. He set down a pile of cardboard boxes and inspected a few goblets that were drying on a bed of nails. He filled two boxes, which he left standing by the workbench. Then he was gone again.

Johanna frowned. "What does that even mean?"

Widow Grün shrugged and smiled indulgently. "You'll get used to that sort of thing. Best not to ask the point of every order he gives. Come on, let's pack up the rest of them!"

Johanna looked at the last goblet she had silvered and felt a twinge of pride. No streaks and no bubbles. Good! She was beginning to enjoy the work.

◆   ◆   ◆

Ruth was enjoying herself too. Wilhelm Heimer was pleased with her work. At least, that's what she assumed his muttered words to mean when he took a jar from her hand and checked the label she had written for it. She wasn't daft! It was hardly difficult to tell the jars apart when one type was five inches tall and the other seven inches.

And it was a clean job too! She was lucky that Heimer had put her to work at this bench. Ruth glanced over her shoulder at her older sister. She felt sorry for Johanna, standing there in a beige rubberized smock that was already splashed all over with horrible gunk. By the looks of it, she must be perspiring underneath it. The ripe smell of the silver solution filled the whole room, and Ruth didn't even want to imagine what it must be like for Johanna and Widow Grün to breathe in those fumes directly.

Ruth was working at the packing table alongside Sarah, another hired hand. The table ran almost the whole length of the workshop. As she looked with growing dismay at the chaos of glassware in front of them, Ruth thought the packing itself was barely even half of what they had to do here. Someone or other was constantly coming over and putting more finished pieces on the table; either it was the glassblowers bringing dishes and plates that were to be packed away without painting, or it was Johanna and Widow Grün with the silvered pieces, or Marie and Eva with painted items. It wasn't long before Ruth began to wonder whether her job really was something to envy, as she had thought at first. Sarah, however, seemed utterly untroubled by the chaos all round as she calmly painted letters and numbers onto labels and pasted them onto the wares.

Ruth hadn't wanted to make any fuss on the first day of work, but as the mountain of glassware grew, she cautiously suggested, "Maybe we should sort things out a little first, before we write the labels."

Sarah looked up. She looked slowly down the length of table at the mounting heaps of wares, then shrugged. Although she didn't seem resistant to the idea, she didn't agree either.

Ruth was beginning to get fed up with how slowly Sarah worked. "If we don't hurry up we'll have to pile the next lot of finished wares on the floor." Then she began to sort the pieces without bothering with what Sarah would say. She didn't want Heimer thinking she was daft.

Sarah went on working at the labels. "If I got myself into a tizzy every time the table filled up . . ." She puffed out her cheeks, and then exhaled a long breath.

An hour later the table was almost empty, and Ruth calmed down. But an hour after that, the wares were piling up again so fast that they could hardly keep up. There was something to be said for Sarah's air of indifference, Ruth decided, the way she kept calm even when the table was a mess. She herself practically panicked when she saw Marie approaching with a whole tray of vases. "The two of us can't manage all this," she muttered. And the boxes that were already full had to be cleared away somewhere. Maybe she should start by—

Just then, a tall, fat woman appeared in the doorway. "Lunch is ready!" she called in a deep voice, then turned and stomped off.

Ruth had never been happier to go to lunch.

"Be our guest, and let this food to us be blessed." Wilhelm Heimer looked around the table. "Starting today, there are going to be three more mouths to feed, but no one will have to go hungry. Old Edel has taken care of that, eh?" This was directed at Edeltraud, the housekeeper, who just nodded, a sour look on her face. "Right then, dig in and don't hold back!"

The three sisters looked at one another. They didn't dare to do as Heimer said. Were they really supposed to eat from the serving dish like pigs from a trough?

The deaf old housekeeper had brought in a great platter of food and set it in the middle of the table. Everyone had a spoon set in front of them, but there were no plates. There was nothing wrong with the meal as such, the potato salad looked tasty enough and there were plenty of spicy little sausages piled on top. Ruth tried to ignore the rumbling of her stomach. The others were already digging in, and she could even hear the sausages burst as teeth bit into them. Surely they weren't going to put a sausage back into the dish with the end bitten off? Ruth wondered. Then she saw Michel, the youngest son, licking the grease off his fingers before reaching for the next sausage. Maybe she should just eat a slice of bread for the moment.

"What's the matter? Shy? Don't put on airs!" Wilhelm boomed, digging his elbow playfully into Johanna's side.

Ruth watched as her sister reached her spoon daintily into the dish, took a little of the food, and lifted it to her mouth. She pulled herself together. It was going to be a long day, and she had to eat something after all. She picked up her spoon, wiped it inconspicuously to be sure it was clean, and helped herself from the dish. There was a clank of metal as her spoon hit another. Ruth looked up—straight into the green eyes of Thomas Heimer.

"Spooning already, are we?" he said, grinning, and grabbed her hand. "Or were you just trying to rap me over the knuckles?"

"I . . ." Ruth felt herself blushing furiously. She didn't know what to say to a joke like that. Her hand burned as though she had held it in the fire.

"Don't hold back if you're hungry!" Thomas said, looking right at her. "We Heimers are used to taking what we want!" When he finally let go of her hand, it felt as though a thousand tiny ants were crawling over it.

There was laughter around the table. Ruth tried to smile as well, but her jaw muscles cramped. She peered around at the others, who were all busy eating or chatting or drinking down their beer, paying no attention to her. Though Thomas was shoveling food into his mouth, Ruth could feel him looking over at her from time to time. Slowly she raised her eyes, and met his gaze. She was right! All of a sudden a flock of birds seemed to flutter through her breast, beating their wings against her heart.

Her mouth was as dry as dust, and when she tried to lick her lips she found that her tongue almost stuck to them. Why did she suddenly feel that licking her lips was not a ladylike thing to do? She pulled herself together and put her spoon into the dish again, wondering as she did so whether she would be able to swallow even a morsel of potato.

Thomas was still watching her. "You learn fast, Ruth Steinmann," he said with a grin.

Thomas Heimer!

She had already noticed him that morning. Unlike his brothers, who took after their father and were running a little to fat, Thomas was tall and rangy. He was also the only one who had opened his mouth to utter a greeting. He wasn't like the rest of them, she had thought then. His smooth, healthy skin emphasized his even features and strong chin. And those eyes! She had never seen a man with dark-green eyes before.

She took a slice of bread and tore it in two, her fingers moist. Then she handed him half. As their eyes met again, sparks flew.

"Some things are easy to learn to like!" she said, wondering as she spoke whether that husky voice was really hers. She watched eagerly as he bit into the bread. Then she did the same, almost greedily.

Who would have thought that this new job would turn out to be so exciting!

9

As Marie dipped the brush into the pot—whose stained and smeared label bore the word "Ultramarine"—and pulled it back out again, the paint looked surprisingly lackluster, showing no sign yet of the depths of color that would emerge once she'd painted it onto the silvered vase. She began to trace the lines and curves around the lip of the vase the way Eva had showed her, her brush gliding easily along. She trailed the very tip of the brush across the smooth glass, as gentle as a breeze. This was nothing like the painting she had done for the pharmacy jars, which required writing out chemical names such as "Phenethyl Alcohol" or "Glycerin" or "Ether." Father had always insisted that the letters had to be bolt upright, so Marie had doubted at first whether she would be able to master these curves and swirls. But she had no sooner taken the horsehair brush in hand and traced the first lines than her doubts vanished. She could do this!

"Well anyway, Pa said that if there was going to be another baby he'd give it away at birth. Ma didn't even know whether she was pregnant yet, and she burst into tears and . . ."

Marie frowned a little. Eva had been gabbing away ever since they sat down at the workbench that morning. Marie was glad that Sebastian's wife was friendly, but now she just wished that the woman would keep her mouth shut for a minute or two.

"And then Ma said that she would do whatever it took to make sure she didn't have another brat, but . . ."

She had no shame at all about revealing even the most intimate family secrets! Marie looked around in alarm, but nobody seemed to be paying any attention to Eva's chatter. Johanna and the Widow Grün were busy unrolling some kind of glittering thread from a thick reel and snipping it into equal lengths, and the Heimer brothers were bent low over their lamps and could hardly hear anything anyway. Ruth didn't seem to have noticed Eva, or indeed anything around her. She looked . . . lost in thought. Was the work here becoming too much for her?

"There we go!" Eva flicked the paintbrush across the glass in a great flourish that seemed to come all the way from her wrist, linking the last swirls back into the start of the pattern. She didn't much seem to care that her lines swooped up and down all over the place. She beamed at Marie. "Now we put on the green leaves and white flowers." She pointed to two jars of paint that sat unopened. "Before you change paint you have to clean the brush thoroughly. My father-in-law's an angel really, but if he sees you treating the tools carelessly he can be the very devil. Wilhelm!"

Marie followed Eva's glance; from the look in that woman's eyes, Marie would almost have thought she was in love. Wilhelm Heimer was standing in the doorway, leafing through a sheaf of crumpled notepaper and cursing a blue streak as he did so. As soon as he looked up and saw Eva, however, his face softened.

"My Ma always says that if you can find what you're looking for straightaway, then you don't have enough to do!" Eva called over to him, grinning.

Marie could hardly agree that Heimer was an angel. Just then, he looked furious. Hoping that his bad mood had nothing to do with them, she turned hastily back to her work. Whenever Father had been ill-tempered, the best thing had been just to leave him alone. None of the sisters would ever have dreamed of teasing him the way Eva teased her father-in-law.

Painting the leaves onto the stem was a quick job. Marie didn't like this mossy-green color as much as the ultramarine, which was a lovely blue the color of a bright clear sky. But once she got around to painting the white flowers, she began to enjoy the work again. They were a simple five-petal design, the kind of flower that a child might paint, but the white paint was so translucent that if she laid it on just a little thinner, it looked as though a shadow were falling on the blossom. Perhaps she could try making them a little bit longer—just a tiny bit of course. Yes, didn't the flowers look more elegant that way? She recalled the wild lilies that blossomed up at the edge of the forest in late summer. Their petals turned outward just a touch, as though they were inviting the passing bees to stop and sip. Marie traced that same shape with her brush as she painted the next flower.

"Well then?" A booming voice called out behind her, and something soft and warm pressed up against her back. Wilhelm Heimer was standing so close behind her that his belly was touching her. She was so taken aback that the brush twitched in her hand, smearing the petal that she had just been painting. She quickly covered it with her hand to hide the mistake.

Heimer beamed down at Eva without even glancing at Marie's work. "Has my favorite daughter-in-law been showing our new girl what painting's all about?"

Was Heimer talking just to her, or to both of them? Marie nodded, just in case.

"Favorite daughter-in-law!" Eva laughed. "You've only got one, so why even call me that?" She turned around coquettishly. "Did you hear that, Sebastian? It seems your father is still pleased with your choice of bride. What do you say?"

Sebastian grunted something, though Marie couldn't quite hear what.

Wilhelm shook his head. "You young lads are very sparing with your words! When I think of the sweet nothings I used to whisper into your mother's ear, God rest her soul!"

"And how do you know that Sebastian doesn't do that?" Thomas Heimer asked over his shoulder. "At night, when you're asleep? They make enough noise in their room . . ."

The others laughed, and Eva gave her father-in-law a playful nudge. "See what you've started?" she said, feigning anger. Her eyes gleamed with amusement.

Marie held her paintbrush poised like a stylus over a slate. She didn't know what to make of such talk. She felt queasy just listening to it. Surely nobody expected her to say anything? She decided the best thing would be to just carry on with her work, but she hesitated when she realized that there were only three painted vases on Eva's side of the bench and seven on hers. Without even trying, she was working much faster than Eva.

Before she knew it, Heimer had picked up one of her vases and turned it round and round, frowning thoughtfully.

"I . . . I painted the flowers so that the petals are a little longer," she said timidly.

Eva leaned over and picked up another vase. The smile was gone from her face now. "That's not how I showed you to do it." There was an edge to her voice, with no trace of the girlish charm from earlier.

Heimer put the vase back down in front of Marie.

"I can show her again . . ." Eva began, visibly put out, but Heimer raised a hand to silence her. He smiled. "That's all right, little Evie! Every painter has her own style, and the customers know that too." Heimer turned to leave and clapped a hand on each woman's shoulder. "As long as you don't start painting ladybugs instead of the flowers they ordered, I don't mind a little artistic freedom from either of you."

Marie exhaled, relieved. She had been holding her breath without knowing it. Artistic freedom . . . There was a humming in her ears. Eva was right: Wilhelm Heimer was an angel really, if a rather big-bellied one. Glad not to have been given a dressing-down on her first day, she picked up the next vase and began to paint.

Eva followed suit, but not without first shooting Marie a look that was much less friendly than before.

10

By the time the three sisters got home that evening, it was almost dark outside. Ruth felt faint at the thought of having to lay a fire at this hour. "There's still a bit of bread. And the meat loaf that one of the neighbors brought . . . I don't even remember who. We can eat it cold." If one of her sisters wanted a hot meal, then she could fire up the oven herself.

The others just nodded. "As long as we each have a plate to ourselves . . ." Johanna said.

Ruth and Marie giggled.

"Can you believe such a thing? In one of the richest houses in the village?" Ruth shook her head as she pulled three plates from the cupboard and put three glasses on the table. "They must have enough money, so it can't be about that, can it?" she said in bemusement.

Johanna shook her head. "I think old Edel just doesn't make the effort. And the Heimers aren't used to having it any different." As she began to slice the bread, she remembered that Joost had always done that. She had to stop herself thinking such things. "Did you see her fingernails? Oof! And the potato salad platter was all sticky on the underside," she added.

"That's horrible! I didn't even notice!" Ruth replied, putting a little meat loaf on everyone's plate.

"I'm not the least bit surprised . . ." Johanna said, raising her eyebrows meaningfully. "You were only looking at one thing . . ."

Ruth frowned. "You busybody! I don't know what you mean!"

"Who was talking just the other days about getting married? About having someone to look after her?" Johanna cocked her head. "If I recall correctly, it was you, wasn't it?"

"And what if I did?" Ruth snapped at her. As always, nothing got past Johanna. "Thomas wouldn't be the worst choice of husband, you have to admit that. It's amazing as it is that only one of the three brothers is married." She held her breath, annoyed at herself for wanting Johanna's approval.

Her sister took a hearty bite of bread before speaking.

"I'll grant you he's not a grumble-guts like the other two," she said, chewing. "And he certainly has a fine singing voice." She shook her head. "But I have to say I'm surprised he still feels like singing with all that work to be done."

"I like it that he sings a little song here and there. And I like the way everyone sings along," Ruth said, almost defiantly. Then she laughed.

"I felt a bit silly at first. When was the last time we girls sang together? It must have been in school. And the others know all the words. But we'll learn them too."

Ruth waved a hand. "Tell me though: What do you think of Thomas?"

Johanna rolled her eyes. "What can I say? I hardly had time to look at him."

"Well, don't trouble yourself to look at him from now on," Ruth said firmly. "I spotted him first. Those dark-green eyes of his . . . Have you ever seen a boy with such lovely eyes?" she said dreamily.

"I didn't notice. What I did notice though was the way the work piled up on your table," Johanna answered dryly. "If you really want my advice, forget about Thomas for the time being. After all, if old Heimer isn't happy with our work . . ." She let the rest of the sentence speak for itself.

"I don't plan to fling myself at him, if that's what you mean," Ruth said pointedly. She sighed. "With all the work we have, there's hardly time for a few words. I tell you, I broke a sweat this morning at the packing table! Not everyone's lucky enough to be put to work painting flowers."

Marie didn't react. It was as though she hadn't even heard what Ruth had said. She hadn't even taken a bite of bread, but was sketching patterns in her meat loaf with the point of her knife.

Johanna elbowed her. "You're sitting there staring into space as though you've had a vision of the Virgin Mary! What's wrong with you? Don't tell me you've fallen for Michel!"

"What nonsense! Nothing's wrong with me!" Marie replied, picking up her bread and lifting it to her mouth. But then she paused before taking a bite, and her eyes lit up.

"I've been thinking about something. If we were to paint the plants twining up the length of the vase rather than round and round, they would look so different . . ."

The other two stared at her, and Ruth rolled her eyes. "Our princess is dreaming again."

"Is it any wonder?" Johanna said. "If I spent the whole day sitting next to such a chatterbox, I would daydream as well just to get away. That Eva could talk your ears off!"

Ruth leaned forward over the table. "You know, I'm surprised Sebastian married her, given that she's all the way from Steinach. And the old man's so fond of her!"

"You're right!" Johanna chimed in. "He values the glassblowing trade so highly, you'd think he'd rather have someone from the village in his house. What's that saying? Marry a glassblower's daughter and your cup will never run dry."

They laughed.

"It hasn't happened yet, but it could!" Ruth remarked airily, winking at Johanna as she did so.

After they had eaten, nobody felt like doing the dishes or getting breakfast ready for the next morning or fetching the wood. They decided to go to bed so they would be well rested for the next day. But sleep wouldn't come. Each of them had too much to think about.

"That Sarah hardly seems like a fast worker," Johanna said suddenly. "Whenever I looked over at the two of you, you were the only one doing any work."

"You can say that again!" Ruth sat up in bed. "Father would have had some words for her; she's slow as a snail."

Johanna snorted. "Well said! She even looks a bit like a snail."

"She guzzled down the beer," Marie said, shuddering. "Nasty bitter stuff! I'll ask for some water tomorrow."

"So will I," Johanna agreed. "I was surprised that the men could sit down and work at their lamps with a steady hand after drinking all that beer at lunch. But the women were drinking just as much. It was very odd, don't you think, Ruth?"

"Who cares?" Ruth grumbled. She simply wanted to lay back down in the dark and think about Thomas.

Johanna sighed. "You're right! It's no business of ours how much the Heimers drink—our business is in their workshop. But they have a funny way of running the place. If the old fellow hadn't decided halfway through the morning that we should stop the silvering and start snipping the tinsel wire, Widow Grün and I would have gotten a lot more work done."

"What's the wire for, even?" Marie asked.

Johanna shrugged in the dark.

"It's for decorating something, but we never found out what. Once we were done snipping it into pieces we had to go help with the packing, and after that it was time to leave." She thought for a moment. "It really is very odd. Heimer spends all day running around the workshop checking up on this and that, but he causes such a commotion when he does so. He really puts the cat among the pigeons."

When there was no answer from Ruth, Johanna rolled over.

"Well, we Steinmanns put in a good day's work on our first day," she mumbled, and then she fell asleep.

11

Marie painted in her dreams all night, and when she woke up the next morning, she could hardly wait to get back to work. She was all the more disappointed, then, when Wilhelm Heimer put her to work with Sarah decorating perfume bottles.

She cast an envious glance at Ruth, who was sitting next to Eva today. She probably didn't know how lucky she was! In front of Marie were thick bundles of glittering wire, the tinsel that Johanna and the Widow Grün had cut into lengths yesterday. Reluctantly she picked up a bundle. Upon closer inspection, she had to admit that the curly, shimmering wire had its own particular charm; its warm golden tint glowed or faded, depending on how the light fell on it. The perfume flasks themselves were pretty as well. They were the same shape as the ones that Father had blown for the French consignment, but they were all made of colored glass—violet, blue, and green—from the stock that Heimer had from the glass foundry. Marie had never seen this shade of violet before. The gloomy cloud that hovered over her head lifted a little. This part of the job could never give her the same pleasure as painting with those lovely colors, but decorating work had a certain appeal.

She watched cheerfully as Sarah wound the glittering wire round and round the belly of a perfume flask until it had made a kind of cage about the bottle.

"There, you see, that's how you do it," Sarah said, picking up the next bottle just as placidly as if she were chopping firewood.

Marie was horrified. Wrapped around as thickly as that, the tinsel wire lost all its delicate charm! And the bottle itself could barely be seen. The glass was no longer transparent and the colors might just as well have been the dreadful dull brown of a beer bottle.

Marie could have wept.

◆ ◆ ◆

Ruth was secretly glad when Heimer put her to work with Eva at the painting bench, for she thought it would give her the opportunity to find out more about Thomas from his sister-in-law. And she was sitting much closer to him than when she had been at the packing table on the other side of the room. So far, however, neither had been advantages; certainly Eva never stopped jabbering, but since she seemed to regard herself as the most important member of the Heimer family, most of her stories were about herself. She hadn't mentioned Thomas even once. Ruth was beginning to lose patience.

"When I found out they had a housekeeper here, I was so surprised!" Eva said, so caught up in her story that her cheeks were glowing. "Edel is an old woman, of course, but she takes care of so much of the work that there's nothing left for me to do! My mother always told me, 'My child, you must take what you can get in this life! It's little enough.'" Her eyes gleamed. "Well, I certainly made a good choice here," she went on, with unmistakable pride in her voice. "Look at this dress. Sebastian gave it to me just last week." She held up her sleeve right under Ruth's nose. "Bouclé silk—it must have been expensive!"

Ruth pursed her lips. What a silly, self-satisfied cow! All the same, she couldn't resist running her fingertips over the silky fabric. "It feels wonderful."

Eva beamed. "My mother always said, 'My child . . .'"

Ruth took a deep breath. She didn't want to hear any more of Eva's mother's wisdom. She cast a yearning glance toward the workbenches with the lamps, where Thomas looked very focused on his work.

Just like the day before, he and his brothers had been bent over their lamps already when the Steinmann sisters arrived. Thomas had only looked up briefly and nodded.

Disappointed, Ruth looked down at herself. Thomas hadn't even glanced at her blue blouse, which hugged her figure so nicely and was something she usually only wore on special occasions. She had expected Johanna to make some comment when she took the blouse from the wardrobe and was surprised when she'd said nothing.

Ruth decided to try again. "How did you meet Sebastian?" she whispered, silently hoping that Eva wouldn't include half the room in her answer.

Eva laughed. "That's quite a story. I was on my way home from the slate quarry with my father and three of my brothers when our old nag collapsed in the middle of the road. It was on its last legs, you know. Anyway it was just lying there, and we were standing around wondering how we were ever going to get all the slates back home when Sebastian came by. And . . ."

So it had been blind luck. Eva had no new insights that might help her with Thomas. Ruth switched off the stream of chatter in her ears, like switching off a gas lamp. *And . . . and . . . and . . .* she thought, rather unkindly. Nobody would call Eva a skilled storyteller. She dipped her brush into the pot so roughly that a couple of drops spilled over the side.

"Be careful, you clumsy coot!" Eva hissed at her like a scalded cat. "Wilhelm doesn't like any paint being wasted."

Ruth snorted, but then realized how unladylike that must have sounded. If Thomas had happened to have looked up from his lamp just then . . .

She forced a smile. "I'll learn soon enough. Not everyone can be as good as you with the brush."

Johanna was walking past them right at that moment with a load of new glass pipes in her arms, and she raised an eyebrow questioningly. Ruth made a face at her. Nothing got past Johanna!

Eva, however, didn't seem to have noticed the sarcasm in Ruth's remark. Instead, reassured, she favored her new workmate with a graceful smile. "Do you know what? I'll show you how to do it again. It's all in how you turn the brush."

◆ ◆ ◆

There was potato salad for lunch again, just like the day before. Edeltraud brought a second dish full of chopped herring. The heads and tails were still in there, piled up in a grotesque heap with the fleshy middle bits, and the sour smell of the pickling brine hung over the whole table. The others once again washed down their meal with plentiful helpings of beer.

Johanna found when she took a spoonful of potato salad that it had taken on the fishy taste of the herring. Perhaps if she took some from right at the edge of the platter, lower down the side . . . Before she could do anything about it, she had a whole heap of potato on her spoon.

"Oh yes, old Edel knows what she's about! Everybody likes her cooking!" Wilhelm Heimer beamed when he saw how much Johanna had on her spoon.

Not knowing what else to do, she swallowed the lot.

"Well then, what's it like joining our workshop from your house, where you girls used to rule the roost?" he asked, chewing. "Not that there was anything wrong with how Joost used to run his workshop," he added jovially.

"There's a lot to get used to, of course," Johanna answered diplomatically. Heimer looked at her expectantly, so she went on. "We used to blow far fewer shapes. Just pharmacy jars, really." She hurriedly bit into a slice of bread.

"Oh yes, there's hardly an outfit in the whole village that does as many different lines as ours. I would never have dreamed just a few years ago that I would have five pairs of hired hands." Heimer was not far from giving himself a slap on the shoulder.

Johanna made an effort to smile.

"If anybody could do it, you could!" Eva told her father-in-law with a twinkle in her eye. He laughed, and little bits of potato salad leapt about on his tongue.

Disgusted, Johanna turned away. The way Eva piled on the flattery! And then some devilish impulse made her clear her throat and say, "It's certainly impressive how many different things you do here."

Wilhelm's face was as round and happy as a balloon.

"But there are one or two changes you could make to work more efficiently."

The balloon went pop. The air escaped.

There was a deathly silence over the table. Not even a spoon clinked. Johanna felt the hairs stand up at the nape of her neck. That hadn't been a good idea, her instinct told her a moment too late.

"What do you mean?" Wilhelm Heimer asked calmly.

Perhaps Johanna should have followed Ruth's advice at that moment—her sister was gesturing as unobtrusively as she could for Johanna to pipe down. And the look in Eva's eyes—visible enjoyment at the prospect of someone ending up in Heimer's bad books—should have warned her as well.

But Johanna was so caught up in her own ideas that she didn't notice. "Of course it's only my second day here, but I did notice that we lose a lot of time carrying the finished wares from the painting bench to the packing table. Because the silvering bench is in between, you see. And every time we need new glass stock, it has to come up from the cellar—" She fell silent as she saw Heimer's face growing redder and redder.

"Let's make one thing clear, Johanna Steinmann . . ." He had narrowed his eyes so that they almost disappeared behind the puffy lids. "I took the three of you on and gave you work because it was a duty I owed your father. Not everyone would be so high-minded!"

Thomas Heimer was the only one still eating. The others sat there as though rooted to their chairs. Nobody moved.

"But if any one of you thinks that the women will ever get to rule the roost in my house, you can think again!" Heimer slammed his fist down on the table and made the dishes jump. "If you don't like the way I do things, you can leave!"

"That's not what Johanna meant," Eva broke in, her voice as smooth as silk. She stroked Heimer's arm as though she were calming a savage bull. "She only said that because she's not as quick about her work as I am, or the Widow Grün. Isn't that right, Johanna?" she asked, tilting her chin toward her.

The sparkle in Eva's eyes was more than Johanna could bear. She looked over at Ruth, but found no reassurance there either—rather, a glance of irritation.

"I didn't mean to criticize anybody," she said at last. "It just takes a while to get used to new things, that's all." She spoke much more demurely than she would have liked. For goodness' sake, she just wanted to be allowed to speak her mind! If Father had blown up at her like this every time she had made some observation, she would have left home long ago.

Wilhelm Heimer seemed to accept her apology. He grumbled something unintelligible as he took a tail from the herring dish and stuck it into his mouth.

◆　◆　◆

That evening too, the oven went unlit in the Steinmann house. The sisters had been at work for ten hours, and none of them felt like fetching the wood and building a fire.

The mood among them was just as chilly. Neither Ruth nor Marie was ready to forgive Johanna for having put their jobs on the line by speaking out of turn. Too tired to argue, they ate in silence, trading awkward glances every few bites.

They went to bed shortly after. But instead of chattering excitedly as they had the night before, each was silent with her own thoughts.

◆　◆　◆

Marie had wanted to ask Heimer to be put back on the painting bench the next day. After the squabble, however, she wouldn't dare ask such a thing. But how on earth was she going to get through the whole day so close to the pots and brushes, if she wasn't allowed to paint? The very thought was painful, and she held her belly as though she were having her menstrual pains.

◆　◆　◆

Thomas had looked over at her at least five times that afternoon! And his eyes had unmistakably—and shamelessly—fixed on her blouse. Fervently hoping not to blush, Ruth had tucked her plaits back over her shoulder in a show of nonchalance, but she saw how his eye followed the action greedily. Now she put her hands to her hair in the dark and fixed her plaits. If she kept them bound up tight like this all night, her hair would have waves in the morning. Oh, if only she could let her hair down at work! Then he would see her chestnut-brown tresses at their best.

Did Thomas really have his eye on her? Or had she been imagining things? No, she was sure she hadn't been. Perhaps he was lying in bed and thinking of her at that very moment? Ruth was overjoyed. The idea that she might have caught Thomas Heimer's eye was almost too good to be true. She was delighted that the dreadful prospect of ending up an old maid was fading a little. Maybe a happy ending awaited her after all. Thomas wasn't just handsome and a good singer; he was also the son of one of the richest men in the village. Marry one of the Heimers and you had a good life; that much was certain. After all, it looked like Eva lacked for nothing: she had such lovely clothes and a string of beads at each wrist and a necklace as well. Ruth sighed gently. Maybe Thomas would give her a present like that soon?

◆　◆　◆

That fat, self-satisfied, short-tempered old fool!

Johanna's thoughts were trained on one of the Heimer men as well, but she was thinking of Wilhelm. She asked herself for the umpteenth time why she had even opened her mouth. Her boldness had quite gone since the morning, and now she was only angry at herself. She ought to have known that not every man was as mild-mannered as Father. And looking back on it, she realized that it had been the height of folly to make her criticism at the table while everyone else was listening. She had to make an effort to unclench her jaws; she had been grinding her teeth so hard that her face hurt. She would never be able to tell Peter about this because he would fall all over himself laughing. Well, damage done need fear no mockery, as the saying went. *"That fearless tongue of yours will get you in trouble one of these days!"* Peter had said that often enough. Johanna took a deep breath. She just hadn't been thinking. She had been so angry at Eva that she had simply burst out with her thoughts, despite the fact that it was neither the time nor place for it. But tomorrow, she'd hold her tongue all day long, she promised herself.

12

Four weeks later Wilhelm Heimer paid them their first wages—a mere fifteen marks each for a full month's work!

Johanna was outraged. Neither she nor her sisters had dared to ask Heimer about the wage when they started work—though they had taken some guesses among themselves, of course.

"It'll be all right, Heimer knows what the going rate is," Ruth had said quite sharply the first time Johanna broached the topic. After all, she had been the one to talk to Heimer while Johanna had been in Sonneberg. All the same, she had tried to get Sarah to open up a little about what she was paid, but the girl was either too slow-witted or too secretive to say.

Johanna had had no more luck with the Widow Grün; apparently it wasn't proper to discuss wages.

As the three of them sat around their supper table and stared at the little pile of coins in the middle, all the euphoria of the last few weeks was quite gone. They had been so proud to be making their way in the world after fate had dealt them such a cruel blow.

"Forty-five marks—that's not even enough to buy groceries for the month. Why, I used to spend forty marks a month just on the shopping in Sonneberg," Johanna said. "And then there's Mrs.

Huber's store here in the village; I've been buying on credit from her for the past two weeks, and we have to pay our debts."

Ruth looked as though she would burst into tears. "And now? What are we going to do next? We'll need new clothes as well, from time to time. A new hairband. A cake of soap. And . . ." She broke off.

"And I had so wanted to buy more drawing paper and a few pencils! I've been looking forward to that all month," Marie said.

"You can forget all about that sort of indulgence," Johanna said brusquely.

"What do you mean?" Ruth snapped at her. "We worked for this money just the same as you did. So we get to decide as well how we spend it."

"Will you listen to yourselves?" Johanna said, shaking her head angrily. "Hairbands and colored pencils—I think you both know that there are things we need far more than that! Firewood for the winter, for instance."

As if on cue, a mouse scurried through the room.

"If the mice are already coming indoors in October, it'll be a hard winter," Marie said, her face expressionless.

"Really? Is that all you have to say?" Ruth shot at her. "If you could bestir yourself to put out a few traps from time to time, we wouldn't have mice in the house at all. But oh no, our princess is much too fine for that sort of thing. After all, I'm here to do the dirty work, aren't I?"

"Enough of that!" Johanna shouted. She wanted to burst into tears, but what good would that do?

"There's no point in our arguing like donkeys." She got up and went to the cupboard. "I'll make a pot of coffee to celebrate, and then we can calm down and think how to spend our money." The situation called for a dose of gallows humor. But when Johanna saw the miserable few coffee beans that were left, her heart sank even further. That wouldn't brew more than colored water! All the same she picked up the coffee grinder and began to turn the handle energetically.

Ruth watched as Johanna ground the coffee. "I'm getting fed up with that horrible stuff the Heimers brew. What does old Edel put in her pot?" She shrugged uncomprehendingly. "Do they just dry out any old root they can grub up in the forest and then boil it up with water?"

Johanna and Marie laughed. Ruth could be funny when she wanted to.

Johanna sighed. "Our dear father was a different kind of man entirely. 'There's more to life than just work, you need a little pleasure now and again!' he told me once. And he was right!" She put the ground beans in the pot and poured boiling water over them.

As soon as the smell filled the room, it had the effect Johanna had hoped for. Ruth's expression softened a little, but she shook her head helplessly all the same. "I don't understand all their penny-pinching. Judging by the amount of glass they sell, they must have more money than they need. Do you think he only pays us so badly, or do Sarah and the Widow Grün get just as little?"

"I don't know," Johanna replied, biting her lip. "We're going to have to find out somehow."

"But how would that help?" Marie asked. While the other two drank their coffee, she was drawing complicated knotwork patterns in a notebook. "We can't just go to Heimer and demand that he pay us more." Her tone of voice suggested that she hardly cared.

Johanna bit back a sharp reply. Marie wasn't being the slightest bit helpful, as usual. Instead she was filling up valuable paper with her sketches. "The problem is," Johanna said, turning to Ruth, "that the Heimers live so modestly themselves. Have you ever seen them indulge in anything? Fresh herring? A cake? A better cut of meat?"

"Oh, don't even talk to me about meat! That horrible tripe that was swimming in the soup today was so ghastly that it wasn't even much of a comfort that we each had our own bowl to eat from." Ruth stuck out her tongue, revolted at the memory. "But you're right. Old Heimer wouldn't care if he were just chewing on a crust of dry bread every day. All the same though, there's someone in that household who never goes short . . ."

Johanna nodded.

Eva.

Sometimes Johanna wondered which of the Heimers Eva had really married. Sebastian hardly ever seemed to look at his wife, while the old man waited on her hand and foot. Evie this and Evie that. If golden spoons had been for sale, he'd have bought her one long ago.

"Just imagine, she's the one who gets the box of leftover silver at the end of the year," Johanna said. "I would have thought that Heimer would split that up among his three sons, but no such thing. Griseldis says the old man spoils Eva because she looks so much like his dead wife. She must be the spitting image of her."

Over the last few weeks Johanna and the Widow Grün had grown a little closer. Sadly there was never enough time to talk for long while they were working. And in the evenings, she either had housework to do or was too tired to go calling. The most Johanna ever managed to do was go next door to see Peter for a while, but that hardly counted as paying a call.

"Do you really think that's the only reason?" Ruth asked. "She's his daughter-in-law after all. Maybe he thinks she's more likely to give him a grandson if he spoils her?"

"Who knows whether that skinny goat can even have children," Johanna said. She had hardly uttered the words before she glanced over at Marie, embarrassed. Her younger sister was at least as slender as Eva. But Marie either hadn't heard or didn't hold Johanna's remark against her.

Ruth grinned. "Maybe it's time for someone else to try. Someone who can marry the *oldest* son, and have his children . . ."

Johanna's face clouded over. "You've hardly known the lad a month and you're already talking about having his children! I don't like it that you spend your whole day flirting with Thomas."

Ruth exploded. "What business is that of yours? I'll flirt with whomever I like. Besides, when I'm Mrs. Heimer I can make sure that old man Wilhelm pays us better. And when Thomas gets to have his say . . ."

"You'll be old and gray before that happens," Johanna said scornfully. "Wilhelm Heimer might get out of breath from time to time, but that's just because of his big belly. Even you can't believe that he's going to let his eldest son take over the business any time soon."

Marie looked up. "Do you love Thomas so much that you want to marry him?"

Ruth stood up, clattering her chair. "I've had enough. I don't have the slightest desire to talk to you two about Thomas. I'm going out for a while. The air in the workshop was so horrid today. It's a wonder we haven't gone blind or gotten ill from all the chemicals we splash around." She put on her jacket and buttoned it up.

Johanna had a headache too, but she didn't know whether the pounding at her temples came from the stink of the silver bath or from their money worries. "You're going out for a walk? In this cold?" she asked suspiciously.

"So what? Nobody says anything when you run off to visit Peter all the time! I can go off and be on my own for a quarter of an hour, can't I?"

Before Johanna could think of a reply, Ruth had hurried out.

13

"I've never seen such a thing!" Peter said, shaking his head. "Normally a glass eye lasts about three months. But Mr. Wunsiedel wears his out so fast you can practically watch the surface cracking. It's because his tear ducts don't function. Even in the eye he has left . . ." Peter stopped when he heard Johanna sigh. He looked up from his work.

She looked tired sitting by the stove with her eyes closed, her back pressed up against the stove tiles to warm her, her shoulders drooping. The skin under her eyes was almost translucent. He wanted very much to take her in his arms and soothe away all her troubles.

"What's the . . . am I boring you with my talk?" he asked, only half joking.

She opened her eyes. "Of course not. It's just so nice to be able to sit still for a little while. And the heat's making me a bit sleepy," she said, shuffling up closer to the stove. "But do go on, why does this gentleman from Braunschweig have such dry eyes?"

Peter shook her arm gently. "You don't have to pretend you're interested. I can see that your mind is elsewhere. What's the matter, have you been arguing with Heimer again?"

Johanna snorted. "Arguing—that rather depends what you mean by it. If you're asking whether I've spoken out of turn again, then no, we haven't argued." She waved her hand dismissively. "Let's talk about something else."

"Listen, I'm your friend!" Peter said, pointing to his chest. "Instead of talking to me, you go back in your shell like a snail."

Johanna laughed. "Well, thank you for calling me a snail!" she said, but she had perked up a little.

Peter waited. You could never hurry Johanna.

"Oh, I don't know what's wrong with me!" she said at last. "Maybe it's because it's Friday, and I miss going into Sonneberg."

"Going begging to Friedhelm Strobel? God knows you're not missing much there!" Peter answered scornfully. The glassblowers took all the risk, while the wholesalers made all the profits, wasn't that it? And Strobel was the kind of man to trample his suppliers underfoot if that would get him the best prices. He didn't care whether a glassblower almost broke his back filling an order; all he cared about was keeping his customers. And he had enough of those. Word was that there was hardly a city in the world where Friedhelm Strobel didn't have at least one buyer for his Lauscha glassware or Sonneberg toys. Very few wholesalers gave as many orders to glassblowers and toymakers as Strobel did. So even though his terms were terrible, the suppliers hurried to meet them.

"You should be glad to be free of that cutthroat," Peter said when there was no response from Johanna. "I can still remember the days when your father had trouble buying the glass stock he needed to fill Strobel's orders!"

"Well, that's just how it works; the glassblowers have to take on liabilities, but the wholesalers procure the orders. And Strobel is a mastermind at that part of the business," Johanna answered crisply.

Peter went to the stove, opened the door, and put another log on the fire. "Whatever you say. All the same, I don't think that you're so out of sorts today because you miss Strobel."

She folded her hands in her lap. "To be honest, I don't know what's wrong with me. Father's been dead for five weeks now, and it seems like forever. We don't even have time to think of him. It's dark when we leave the house every morning and dark by the time we come back home in the evening. And when we get home, the clothes aren't laundered and there's no hot meal, and the whole house is dusty and cold!" She looked at Peter reproachfully, as though it were his fault that she was so miserable.

"Somehow it's not our own little home anymore. It always used to be so warm, with the smell of potatoes cooking . . . But now, we get up, we go to work, we come home, we sleep. That's all we do. And all for a handful of marks that's barely enough to keep body and soul together." Her anger dissipated, though, and she leaned up against the warm oven once more.

She didn't need to tell him that Heimer was an old miser. Peter had seen it with his own eyes; whenever Heimer paid for drinks at the Black Eagle, he never gave the barmaid so much as a single penny for a tip. And often he sat there all evening with just the one tankard of beer, as though he couldn't afford a second one. But what could he tell Johanna? Bad as it seemed, the truth was that the Steinmann girls should be glad to have any work at all, no matter how poor the wage. He felt something clench inside him. "If it's really too little, then tell old Heimer to take a running jump. Come and help me. The money I bring in is enough for two."

He'd said it at last. Now he held his breath.

When Johanna didn't answer, he added, "And I've got my work at the foundry as well."

The great ovens down at the foundry square were stoked up to full heat twice a year, and Peter put in his hours there. From

September through New Year's Eve and then March until summer, he filled his own commissions in the evenings after working down at the foundry all day. He even had a certificate granting him the title of Master Glassmaker, though it meant little since he didn't have his own booth down at the foundry or any journeymen working for him, which had once been the privilege of masters in the guild. Many years ago his family had been among the wealthiest in the village, but through the generations they had had too many sons, and Peter and his brother had inherited nothing but a small share in the foundry. Peter's brother was dead, but even so, he knew that Johanna knew how little he had.

Johanna shook her head. "Don't hold it against me, but I couldn't do the work you do. I can't even watch when you put the veins into the glass. What you do is wonderful, but it gives me the shivers!" She smiled. "I think that you really have to love your job to do it well. I would probably just get in the way."

Perhaps she was right, Peter thought to himself. The people who needed his help were usually desperate and railing against their fate. Many of them were in pain and in a state of denial about having only one eye. It wasn't always easy to get them to trust him. Nor was making the glass eyes an easy job. It was more than glassblowing; for him, it was an art. But as much as he loved his job, he knew it would never make him rich.

"I think we're just not used to working outside our own home. While Father was still with us, we could do quite a lot of our housework in between other jobs, but we can't now. The paid work isn't the real trouble." Johanna waved a hand dismissively. "It's hard work of course, but we can manage it. And it's extraordinary to see the variety of wares the Heimer lads blow at their lamps! I find quite a lot of what they make just horrible," she laughed, "but they seem to have customers for it all."

Peter still had no idea why she was so unhappy. "What's the real trouble then? Is it old Heimer?"

She nodded. "I get so worked up when he creeps up behind us and peers over our shoulders. Does he really think we would spend all day lazing about if he weren't always checking up on us?" Her eyes gleamed. "And the mess in that place! I tell you, it makes a beehive look neat and tidy. Last week we ran out of paints, this week it was glass stock. He could have sent one of his boys down to the foundry to pick up more, but oh no, the old man put all three of them to work at the packing table. Can you imagine?" She laughed, exasperated. "In the end we had nothing to paint, nothing to silver, and nothing to pack. But"—she raised an eyebrow mockingly—"Ruth was delighted! She got to spend the whole day working side by side with Thomas." Johanna frowned. "I can't understand why none of the lads opens his mouth when Wilhelm loses track. Anyone can see that there's no planning or organization in that house."

"The two young ones are too stupid, and Thomas Heimer can't win an argument with his father. What are you hoping for?" Peter asked calmly. "You'll just have to speak your mind again and take what comes." He gave her a friendly nudge and grinned.

"You're the only one who thinks that. I'd rather bite my tongue!"

"And? Is there anything new with Ruth and Thomas?"

"Have you ever seen a man with such handsome green eyes?" Johanna said, mimicking Ruth's dreamy tones. "He spends most of his time staring at her as though he's forgotten how to count to three." She made a face. "All that's missing is for him to let his tongue hang out and to start drooling! If you ask me though, Thomas isn't the kind of man who's looking to get married. Otherwise he'd be engaged by now, wouldn't he? But Ruth thinks that she's going to be Mrs. Heimer any day now. To be honest I'm not sure I would even want the two of them to get married. They don't seem suited to one another." She raised her eyebrows again and added, "At the moment she says she's gone out for a walk—just how stupid does Ruth think I am? She's meeting him, of course. I only hope that she knows what she's doing."

Peter kept quiet. He couldn't stand Thomas, not only because—unlike himself—the young Heimers had something to offer a bride, but also because he knew both sides of Wilhelm Heimer's eldest. Most of the time Thomas was a dull dog but bearable, at least. But it was another story if you came upon him when he'd had one too many at the fair or the village dance! When he was drunk, he bragged and snarled and picked fights. Since Johanna and her sisters had hardly joined in the social life of the village while Joost was alive, they knew nothing about this side of him.

"Whether you like it or not, the two of them will get together if they want to, and there's nothing you can do to stop it. Ruth will know the right thing to do, don't worry. The more you go clucking over her like a mother hen, the harder she'll fight back," he said.

Johanna turned to look at him. "You can talk! You only have yourself to look after. If I don't keep an eye on everything, things will soon go off the rails in our household."

If anyone else had said such a thing, he would have dismissed it as pompous nonsense. But Peter knew that this was exactly what Johanna believed. "It's not good for you to spend all your time worrying yourself sick about other people. Let them think for themselves."

"I can't rely on my sisters much when it comes to household matters." Her face clouded over. "And I'm just as bad! We had so much work that I forgot to get firewood for the winter while it was still cheap. Now I don't know where we'll get the money for that. You can't truly expect Ruth or Marie to be any help there."

"What about me? Don't you expect me to be of any help?"

"Expect you to? You . . . you're not responsible for me and my troubles."

Oh but I would like to be, Peter thought once more. "I can help you all the same, can't I? In any case, if it's firewood we're talking about, that's easily solved. I haven't even used my rights in the forest this year. My share of wood is still standing there on the slopes, but we can soon change that."

"Do you really think so?" Johanna asked skeptically. "Are the guild masters at the foundry going to let you just give your wood away?"

"They don't care what I do with it. The statutes were drawn up hundreds of years ago, and a master glassmaker is allowed to take a certain amount of wood from the forests each year and that's that. Those rules still apply today. The master makers have always taken a bit of the wood to use at home. "

A spark of hope flared up in Johanna's eyes.

"You girls will have to come help me get it of course," Peter said sternly. Johanna wasn't generally one to take help, but Peter knew that if he gave her a chance to work for it, she would swallow her pride. Darned if he didn't know the woman better than she knew herself.

Lo and behold, Johanna smiled at him. "When shall we go up to the forest?"

Peter laughed. "Tomorrow, if you like."

14

She'd gotten the idea from a basketful of vegetables. A red cabbage, shimmering violet; the dark-green cucumbers, which looked as though they must taste bitter; a thick bunch of carrots with earth still clinging to them; and pods full of peas waiting to be shelled. All this bounty had spilled out over the brim of the basket onto the wooden kitchen table where Edeltraud worked. Marie had only caught a glimpse of the basket on her way through to lunch, and she hadn't gotten the chance to go back for a better look. Violet and green, green and orange—although the colors clashed, they somehow went well together all the same. Once she was back at her workbench, Marie had found herself looking at a stack of plain glass platters that were to be given a band of white enamel around the rim. It was simple tableware, which Heimer said was destined for a hotel in Dresden. How would they look with a basket full of vegetables—or fruit, perhaps—painted into the bowl of the dish? Before she could give it any further thought, Wilhelm Heimer had turned up with a whole box of silvered candlesticks, and she and Eva had spent the rest of the afternoon painting them with flower motifs. But the basket of vegetables and the bare glass dishes hadn't been far from her thoughts since.

Marie looked around. It was only when she finally had some peace and quiet that she realized just how much the constant chatter in the workshop upset her. Talk, talk, talk—all day long. Even listening wore her out. She sighed.

Why couldn't everyone just do their work in silence?

It had looked as though Johanna might stay home after Ruth had gone out for a breath of fresh air—Good gracious! Did her older sister think that she always had to be around to hold Marie's hand?—but then she had headed out the door to see Peter.

Reverently, she fetched a fresh sheet of paper from the drawer and picked up a pencil. It was too sharp for her purposes, so she picked up another and tested its point with finger and thumb. This one was good, it would give her the soft lines she needed. Marie began by drawing a circle about the width of the bottom of the dish. For a while, all she did was look at the circle. This was how much space she had to work with. No more, no less. The challenge was to place the basket so that the vegetables could spill out over the brim to one side—but which side? There also had to be enough room on the other side for the cucumbers to stand upright, as it were. Even as she was still thinking about the structure of the still life, her pencil began gliding over the paper in gentle strokes.

Marie was suffused with the same warm glow that she felt every time she sat down in front of the paint pots in Heimer's workshop. Heimer must have some notion of how much it meant to her to be allowed to paint, because for the last few days he had only assigned her to the painting bench, even though the others had different jobs every day.

She held the paper up at arm's length. Good. Just to be quite sure, she stood up and took two steps away from the table. She smiled. Even from a distance, the basket and its contents were quite clear. She pulled the chair back in to the table and sat down. The next step was to choose the right colors. For some of the vegetables, she already knew exactly which color she wanted. The violet for the cabbage could be mixed together from dark blue and carmine red, and she could use the same red to make the orange by mixing just a drop into the lemon yellow they used. She could hardly wait to see how the paints would mix and mingle. But the basket would be the problem. Brown wasn't a color suited to painting onto clear or silvered glass. It just ended up looking dirty—as though the dish had been put back in the cupboard unwashed.

Marie gnawed at her lip. A blue basket would look wrong, as would a red one. Perhaps she could use the white enamel? She closed her eyes and tried to imagine how it would look. No, if she used white then the woven pattern of the basket wouldn't show; it would simply look like porcelain.

Marie sat up with a start as the clock on the wall began to strike. Nine o'clock already! It wouldn't be long before Ruth and Johanna came back. She put her sketch back into the drawer, along with the pencil. She didn't need them any more tonight. But the basket . . . Marie imagined again how it would look, enjoying the vision. And then and there she had the answer: gold! She would use the same gold that they had been using that afternoon to paint the pistils onto the wildflowers. If she laid it on thinly, it would let the light through in such a way that the shadows in the pattern were there from the start. It would look bright and appealing, and it would go well with all the other colors she had in mind.

"Just one thing: How on earth will I talk old Heimer round?" Marie asked herself aloud, then laughed at the sound of her voice.

She would paint that basket—no doubt about it. Even if she had to buy a dish to do so.

By the time she was ready for bed it was half past nine. Neither Ruth nor Johanna was home yet. Marie was a bit surprised that Ruth would want to go out walking for so long in the cold. She had probably gone to pay a call on Peter as well after her stroll. Marie snuggled down under the covers and got comfortable. She was still in a daze, thinking of the shapes and colors of her design. Marie couldn't imagine that either of her sisters had had anywhere near as much fun as she had that evening.

◆　◆　◆

"You're so beautiful! So soft. And so . . . rounded," Thomas whispered into Ruth's hair as he stroked her breast.

She moaned softly in reply as warm ripples of pleasure spread through her body.

Thomas then began circling her nipples gently with his fingers. Strangely, the ripples intensified.

"You feel so lovely. Everything about you is beautiful." He stroked her more urgently.

Ruth felt that he could set her afire just as easily as he turned up the flame on the gas lamp. She had never even dreamed that it was like this, that a man's desire could feel so wonderful. She had no name for the astonishing feelings coursing through her body, but she knew that they had changed her life forever. Did other women feel like this? She lifted her face toward him.

He kissed her so roughly that he squashed her lips unpleasantly against her teeth. Ruth turned away and broke the contact between their mouths. She had been yearning for a somewhat softer kiss, one that wasn't so greedy. The flame within her died out.

"Not like that." She gently moved his hand away as his fingers fumbled at the buttons on her blouse. Why couldn't he just carry on stroking her and muttering lovely compliments?

"Why not? You like it too. You know you do. I want to have a little bit of fun with my girl!" Thomas squirmed up against her, trying to put his right leg between her thighs as he did so.

There was an undignified tussle, and Ruth felt her back thump against something. Thomas was snorting and panting so heavily that it made her a little queasy to hear him.

"Thomas!" She forced a laugh, and managed to shuffle away from him. To soothe his pride, she turned her mouth up to him and let him kiss her. He sucked greedily at her lips, and for a while they were lost in the taste of each other's tongues.

But it wasn't long before she felt his hand on her cold thigh. The warmth inside her cooled suddenly.

Not that.

She fished around under her skirt, grabbed his hand and removed it. The blanket that Thomas had spread out on the warehouse floor was as ice-cold as the stones beneath it. Ruth shuddered.

Indifferent to her change of mood, Thomas wriggled up against her once more. "Don't be so stubborn!" he whispered into her ear.

Ruth shoved him firmly away. "In case you hadn't noticed, it's ice-cold in here! I hope I don't get sick!" she said in an accusing tone as she straightened her blouse and smoothed out her skirt.

Thomas looked at her, baffled. "I could have warmed you up. But you don't want to." He stared down at the bulge in his pants.

Ruth was close to tears. "Sometimes I think you don't care about me at all. Every time we meet you drag me in here. You've never even asked me once whether I like coming to this dingy hole!" She couldn't have said herself why she was so on edge all of a sudden.

"What are you talking about?" Thomas looked utterly perplexed. "This is a fine place to meet, not a dingy hole. Nobody else has a key, except my father, and he certainly won't be coming here at this hour. And it's not ice-cold; it's just a bit brisk."

"But . . . I just feel that we're taking things much too fast!" There, she'd said it. What was it that Joost had always told them? A woman who didn't respect herself would never find a man to respect her.

"But we love one another! How else is a man supposed to show his girl how much he loves her?"

"I could think of one or two other ways," Ruth thought bitterly. "We could do something else for a change. We could go to Sonneberg, for instance, and go window-shopping. Johanna tells me that . . ."

"I don't understand you," Thomas broke in, shaking his head. "Why would you want to go hiking the hills in the middle of winter?"

Seething, he folded up the blanket and hid it on a lower shelf. He had brought it here a few days ago in preparation, but he found that Ruth was far harder to please than other women. Too cold here and too dingy there, and once she had even complained that his shirt was scratching her cheek! Sometimes he thought he couldn't do anything right with her. And that was a problem, because he had never wanted a woman the way he wanted Ruth. The very idea that he was with one of the prettiest girls in the village fired up his desire. The fact that she was a virgin only made him want her that much more. How often had he and the other village lads fantasized about showing one of the Steinmann girls a good time? Well, so much for that. The way she fought to protect her virtue, you'd think she had a pot of gold between her legs. He felt a stirring in his pants at the thought.

The silence stretched out between them as each waited for the other to apologize.

"I have to go," Ruth said at last. She felt disheartened at the thought that there would be no fire in the oven back home, no hot brick to wrap in flannel and take to bed with her. She wound her scarf twice around her neck and already had her hand on the door handle when Thomas put his arms around her from behind.

"Come along now, don't be such a sulk. How about we meet again tomorrow?" He grinned at her.

She took his hand off her arm. "Tomorrow's a Saturday. I don't think I'll have the time." Even if she had to spend all day scrubbing the floor on her hands and knees, with Johanna and Marie, Thomas mustn't get the idea that Ruth Steinmann was easy.

But she had hardly stepped outside into the alleyway before she felt herself overcome with longing for Thomas once more. Maybe she had been too harsh with him? She would have liked to turn around and throw herself into his arms. After all, she loved him too.

If only he weren't so insistent!

15

Indeed, Ruth spent all of Saturday hard at work. Instead of scrubbing the floor, however, she learned that they were off to gather wood.

Peter had come knocking early that morning, and they set off. They had hardly buttoned up their jackets before he was handing out the tools: a few saws, large shears for cutting branches, stout twine for binding up the wood, and a half dozen baskets. He had a knapsack with him as well. "Lunch," he said. "We'll need it when the sweat begins running down our brows!" Ruth and the others had laughed. Peter and his jokes! The baskets weren't heavy; the sun was shining down through a thin layer of clouds, and they were almost in a holiday mood as they set out.

Neither Ruth nor her sisters had ever gone out to the forest to gather firewood. Joost Steinmann hadn't been a master maker, and therefore hadn't had the right to go gather his own wood, and besides, it was men's work. Up until then, the Steinmanns had always bought their household wood from Ugly Paul. Not that he was really ugly, but the wood seller was known for the ghastly faces he could make to scare children or just for fun. He went around the village from house to house, his basket of wood stuck fast to his back—nobody had ever seen him without the pack on his shoulders. When they had been little, the girls used to hide behind the wardrobe when Ugly Paul sat down at the kitchen table with their father to settle up the bill for the wood he brought them.

This year, however, Ruth would have happily sat down at the table with the funny old man, all on her own if need be. She quickly learned that gathering firewood was hard work. The little patch of forest where Peter was allowed to gather firewood was on a steep, almost inaccessible slope overgrown with knee-high saplings. Anything would have been better than scrambling around and trying to keep her footing like a mountain goat. Endlessly slipping and sliding, she desperately dug her heels into the earth, scarring the ground with her boots. Before she could even recover her balance, she heard a call of "Timber!" from above, and a branch as thick as her arm landed just a couple of feet away. And then another. And then another.

Ruth clung to the steep slope as tightly as she could. Earlier that morning she had been hit by a branch, and ever since then her elbow hurt every time she stretched her arm. On top of that, she had to put up with Johanna scolding her for not paying attention when they called out. Ha! Ruth knew that they hadn't called out at all. They had probably been canoodling up there in the trees, rather than thinking to warn her. Johanna didn't need to make such a show of concern. She hadn't even climbed down to look at Ruth's arm.

When no more wood came flying down, Ruth hobbled out cautiously to gather the freshly fallen wood into a single pile.

It was just like Johanna to go up there with Peter! Probably she was having an easy time of it while he did all the work.

"I'm throwing down some more wood!" Ruth called down to Marie, who was a good two hundred yards below. "Did you hear me?" she called again when there was no answer. She waited until Marie answered, then swung the first bundle down the slope. She felt a sharp stab in her elbow and yelped with pain. She watched as Marie crawled uphill to fetch it. It had only gone halfway down the hill again. When Peter had shown her how to swing the bundles out and down, it had looked like child's play. The only difficulty was in making sure they didn't get tangled up in the underbrush on the way down. The first few throws had gone smoothly enough, and the wood had landed right at Marie's feet. All her sister had to do was bend down and gather it into the baskets. It wasn't long, however, before her arms began to ache and her strength deserted her.

She flung the next lot of wood down, trying not to stretch out her arm all the way as she threw. This time it landed where it was supposed to, but Ruth still felt like crying. It was too much! After all, it wasn't as though they had been well rested before setting out. They had been at work all week, and had spent the evenings doing laundry or cleaning the house or cooking or doing a thousand other things that had practically taken care of themselves in the old days. They had hardly had time to stop and breathe.

Whenever she wanted to meet Thomas she had to sneak away like a thief in the night. She felt even sorrier for herself when she recalled the way they had squabbled last night. But then she remembered some of the flattering compliments he had paid her. He was the son of one of the richest glassmakers in all of Lauscha, and he thought she was beautiful. Desirable. She looked down at herself. Were her breasts really that much prettier than other women's? Thomas had said they were. She asked herself in a fit of jealousy how many breasts he had seen. She shut her eyes for a moment and ran her cold hands over her jacket. What would it be like when he ran his fingers over her naked skin? Maybe she should let him next time they met?

"Timber!" she heard from above.

Before she knew it, half a dozen branches crashed down right by her.

"Watch what you're doing! I can't manage this on my own! Why can't one of you come down here and help!" she called, tucking back a strand of hair. This was another fine mess that Johanna had gotten them into. She was quite sure there must have been a simpler way of getting firewood for the winter.

Neither Peter nor Johanna said a word. Instead Marie called up, "What was that you said?"

Ruth cast a sullen glance downhill. "I wasn't talking to you! Don't worry!" When it came to carrying heavy loads, they really couldn't ask much of Marie; she was simply too delicate. Ruth found herself thinking of Eva. She was a slim little thing as well, but her forearms were corded with muscle, and her whole body was as tough and lean as that of a boy who spent his days climbing trees. Born into a family that worked with slate, she had gotten used to hard work even as a little girl, and her fingers were strong and bony from all the filing, slicing, and sharpening that it took to make a stylus. Ruth would never want to trade places with someone in that line of work. But Eva's life these days more than made up for her difficult childhood: she may have been on a bed of thorns before, but her life was certainly a bed of roses now. Ruth rubbed her sore back and asked herself for the umpteenth time how the woman had managed that particular trick.

◆ ◆ ◆

As soon as they had reached the forest, Peter had set Johanna to work gathering the branches that he cut and tying the smaller ones into handy bundles. But Johanna soon grew tired of waiting for the branches to fall. Without being too obvious about it, she peered over his shoulder. Then she picked up a saw of her own.

The handle sat snugly in her hand as she set the saw blade against a branch. Instead of sinking smoothly all the way through the way it did when Peter cut though, the blade's teeth snagged in the wood.

She expected him to burst out laughing. Or to tell her to put the saw down. But Peter just kept on working, as though what she did was no concern of his. She watched, and saw that he pulled his arm back farther than she had. And he kept his wrist quite still, while hers had wobbled from side to side like a cow flapping its tail. She tried again. This time she managed five strokes of the saw before the blade got snagged again. Peter looked over at her as she cursed softly, but said nothing. She stared at the crooked line her blade had made. She had to saw straighter. When she got to work on the next branch, she steered the blade a little with the thumb of her other hand. And there it was! "It's working! I can do it!" she announced, beaming with pride.

Peter nodded at her. "You should only saw branches that are at least an inch thick. I'll do the rest later with the shears." Then he fell quiet again.

For the first time in ages, Johanna felt that she could breathe freely. It wasn't just the air up in the forest that smelled of herbs; it was because there was nobody telling her how to go about doing her job.

She set the saw blade onto another branch, placed the thumb of her other hand against it, then started to saw in smooth, even strokes. Soon she had taken the branch clear off the fallen trunk and set it on top of the heap with the others. Then she moved on to the next one. The rasp of the saw reminded her a little of the hissing of the gas flame, and the rhythmic sound of the blade was soothing.

They worked in silence for a while. Once they had gathered a little heap of branches, Peter threw it downhill to Ruth with a practiced swing of his arm. It would have been impossible to drag all the wood downhill, but even throwing it took effort. Johanna tried to throw down the branches that she had sawed, and it wasn't long before she was bathed in her own sweat. Saw, throw, saw, throw; soon she had worked out the rhythm that worked best for her.

She was so absorbed in her work that she jumped when she unexpectedly felt Peter's hand on her shoulder. The saw blade wobbled, snagged in the sappy heartwood of the branch, and got stuck.

"Sorry!" He gave her a wry grin. "But I called you three times already. Are you looking to set a record here?"

Johanna tugged the blade free of the branch. Only then did she realize that her forearms were trembling. "I thought we came here to work," she said stubbornly and was just about to resume sawing when Peter put a hand on her arm and stopped her.

"Haven't you looked down the hill? Ruth and Marie can't keep up with gathering all that wood." He led her over to a tree trunk that was already cleared of all its branches, and gently pushed her until she sat down.

Johanna admitted to herself that it was good to sit and rest for a few minutes.

As she sat there, she realized how dry her throat was. When she passed her tongue over her lips, it stuck. A moment later, Peter passed her a flask of apple juice.

"Can you read my mind?" She took a long swallow. The juice was so sweet that it tickled her gums. "You really have thought of everything," she said, sighing.

He shrugged. "Something to drink, bread and ham—it's the least I can do. I would do so much more for you if I could!"

Johanna turned and looked at him. As always when he was upset about something, there was a long furrow of worry on his brow, right down to the bridge of his nose.

"Oh, Peter, don't keep blaming yourself and thinking you're responsible for us. And as for the food, heaven knows we're not fussy. You should see the stuff they serve up at the Heimers' table."

He was silent.

"You know," she said after a moment, "the worst of it is that Wilhelm's workshop could be a tidy little business. All it needs is a bit of care and attention."

"Johanna," Peter said suddenly. All at once his face was right next to hers. His normally placid features were like a mountain stream after a rainstorm. "Forget Heimer and that mess he calls a workshop! Come to me! You can see how well we work together! I—"

Before Johanna quite knew what was happening, he had his arms around her and was pressing her to him. "You and me," he whispered, "wouldn't that be something?"

Johanna felt her cheek burning where his jacket rubbed against it. Her head was at an awkward angle and her neck hurt. She felt as though the ground had been snatched away from beneath her feet. Peter was her neighbor. Her friend. What should she do?

"Peter . . ." she scolded him.

Luckily he let her go a moment later.

As they sat there against the tree trunk, an awkward silence descended.

"I . . ." Johanna began.

At the same moment Peter said, "I'm sorry . . ."

They both laughed, disconcerted. "You don't need to say sorry," Johanna said softly. "I'm fond of you too."

But not like that, she thought.

She squeezed his arm, overwhelmed by the feeling that somehow she had failed. The question *What now?* pounded through her head. What could she say or do to let him keep his dignity intact?

As the silence dragged on, Johanna listened with one ear for what was going on down the hill. Why wasn't Ruth calling to ask where the next bundle of wood was?

"Well then, let's get on with it before this thin air up here turns my head again," Peter said, getting up. He took a deep breath to stop himself from smiling awkwardly. "What is it? Are you going to sit there until you put down roots?" He gave her a wry grin, and stretched his hand out to Johanna. She took it.

He pulled her to her feet. "Once we're finished with this tree here, we'll deserve a bite to eat. The others must be hungry too," Peter said as though nothing had happened.

As she leaned into her saw, Johanna cast furtive glances in Peter's direction. He'd accepted her rebuff so graciously. He didn't seem the least ashamed that his feelings had gotten the better of him, but somehow just rose above it all. Johanna felt stupid for having ruined someone's day again.

Before she could look away, his gaze met hers. Peter shrugged. "About just now . . ." A roguish grin spread over his face. "I can't promise you that something of the kind won't happen again. Knowing myself the way I do, I reckon that's not the last time I'll push my luck."

She shook her head and smiled. "You're impossible!"

They worked on, side by side, with not a trace of ill feeling between them. They were friends, and nothing had changed that.

16

The next few weeks flew by in a flurry of work. It was pitch dark when the three sisters left the house in the morning, and had been dark for hours by the time they got home in the evening. Johanna yearned to be able to hang out the laundry in the sunshine, or to be able to dust the house by daylight. But the housework lay unattended, and with good reason. In every house in Lauscha the only job to do so close to Christmas was blowing glass and preparing the wares, until they were all so tired they were fit to drop. It was no different in Heimer's workshop.

Buyers arrived from all over the country. They may have hemmed and hawed in the fall, but now they thronged the doorways of the Sonneberg wholesalers to be well supplied for the Christmas sales. The haggling now was not over prices but over delivery times and deadlines, for every client wanted his orders delivered as soon as possible. The wholesalers passed on the deadlines to their piece-workers, pushing them to deliver toys and wood carvings and glass as quickly as they could—all while pocketing the profits themselves.

Thomas and his brothers sat at their lamps without a break from morning till night, while the hired hands painted, silvered, labeled, and packed. In addition to the two women he normally paid to take the wares into Sonneberg, Wilhelm Heimer hired a farmer from a nearby village to take a delivery into town every day.

As Johanna sat there stringing twenty glass beads each onto lengths of string and knotting the ends, she forbade herself even to think of her Friday visits to Sonneberg during the Christmas season in years past. But threading the strings was tedious work, and as the heap of glittering trinkets grew ever higher, Johanna could no longer keep the memories at bay.

The taverns and cafés were all lit up, and the town's narrow streets were filled with crowds. There were few foreign buyers in Sonneberg that time of year, as it was impossible for them to get their orders across the borders so soon before Christmas. But dialects from all over Germany flowed through the streets. And the air was filled with scents so intense that the memory of them started Johanna's mouth watering. On these cold, short days, old ladies stood in front of their houses with a pot of mulled wine spiced with cinnamon, aniseed, pepper, and secret ingredients. Others sold gingerbread—much to the disapproval of the bakers of Sonneberg, who could do little to stop their competitors from breaking the guild monopoly just once a year. Still others toasted almonds or grilled the famous Thuringian sausages. And all of these treats sold quickly, since there was a hardly a visitor to town who would refuse a snack along the way. Johanna always had liked to soak up the hustle and bustle, and she always returned to Lauscha energized.

She let her hands drop onto the workbench. The gleaming silver beads swam before her eyes. Ruth and Marie had always been so pleased when she brought back a bag of almonds or an elaborate gingerbread biscuit. Father had never objected to the extra expense. He never even counted the money that Johanna handed over from the sale of the glass.

She glanced over at Wilhelm Heimer, who was upbraiding Sebastian about something. Her new employer hardly knew the meaning of the word trust, and took an inventory every evening. She would never want to steal any of his ugly products—the ones Marie designed being the only exception. "Cheap, gimcrack stuff," she muttered under her breath.

This year there would be no gingerbread, nor any other treats. Instead they would sit staring at Father's empty chair, and the Christmas carols would sound thin and feeble without his voice booming out the words. Johanna was beginning to understand why those who had suffered a death in the family always hated Christmas so much; the hole that their loved one left behind seemed bigger in the light of the Christmas candles.

But it wasn't just grief over Joost's death that made her so miserable. She was also worried sick about money. She had to plan the budget down to the last penny every month to make their wages last. So far they had not gone to bed hungry, but it had been close at the end of last month. It was true that Heimer paid them a mere pittance, but there was another problem too: everything from bread to soup cost more now that they were working outside their home. Before, Ruth had spent every Wednesday morning kneading a huge batch of dough, which she then took to the bakehouse to bake into six loaves that would last the family through the week. But now they no longer had time to bake, so they had to buy bread instead, which cost much more. Since they didn't have time to go to the butcher to buy a bag of bones or to stand by the stove boiling them for soup, they had to rely on a can of Liebig's Extract of Meat from the pantry.

Johanna looked down with hatred at the heap of beads in front of her. She couldn't understand why anyone would spend good money on that sort of thing. Money, money, money—that was all she thought about these days. But neither Ruth nor Marie ever gave her a word of thanks for keeping accounts and sticking to a budget. Instead Ruth always complained that she couldn't bear to see another meal of potatoes or bread and drippings, that she wanted a nice juicy roast or a dish of herring. As though it were her fault that they were short of money, Johanna had to explain to them again and again why it was out of the question to spend a little extra on a drawing pad or colored pencils, a hair clasp or comb. Though Johanna had to admit that her sisters had stopped making such extravagant demands recently. Maybe they finally understood that she couldn't just snap her fingers and make these things appear. Johanna sighed again. Perhaps old Heimer would give them a couple of extra marks for Christmas. She toyed with the idea of asking Griseldis if Heimer might do this, but she dismissed the thought immediately. She didn't want to sound too bold, especially since Griseldis was always telling her how grateful she should be to have a job at all as a woman. As a woman—sometimes Johanna wondered whether being a woman was like having some ghastly disease.

The impulse to shove all the beads off the workbench with one sweep of her hand was so strong that Johanna stood up. Confound it all, she didn't want to spend another moment thinking about the Christmas that lay ahead.

◆　◆　◆

Unlike Johanna, Ruth was always able to find some room for optimism. Thomas had hinted that he had a present for her. And so Ruth spent most of her time thinking about what it could be. She wouldn't say no to a bead necklace, even if Johanna thought that they were tawdry old things. But she would quite like one of those perfume bottles that they had spent the last few days packing away by the hundreds . . . though she had no idea what she would put in it.

The very best present Thomas could give her would be to propose, but Ruth was realistic enough not to hope for too much. Even at this busy time of year Thomas begged and pleaded to meet her in the warehouse as often as possible, and when they did meet he was never short of compliments and declarations of love. He was always telling her how beautiful her body was, her hair, her skin—everything. In front of the others, however, he acted as though he had no feelings at all for her. If she tried to take his hand over the table at lunch, he pulled it back. And he'd never taken her out, not even to the Black Eagle, much less Sonneberg. Ruth didn't budge an inch: as long as Thomas insisted on hiding the fact that they were in love, she wouldn't let him under her skirts. He got angry about that every time they met, and she could partly understand his frustrations. She liked it too, to feel his hands on her, to hear his breath come faster. Kissing and petting was much better than the awkward silences that fell whenever they tried to have a conversation. "We've got all day to gab at one another," he said dismissively if she tried to tell him what was on her mind.

Maybe it was time to take the next step? Wouldn't Thomas be surprised if she suddenly stopped putting up a fight? Or perhaps she could think of a Christmas present she could give him instead? But how was that supposed to work, when she didn't have a penny to call her own?

17

Two days before Christmas Eve, Wilhelm Heimer beckoned Ruth over to him. Eva watched suspiciously as Ruth followed him up to the family's front parlor on the second floor, which they kept for special occasions.

Heimer shut the door behind them. Because the room was hardly ever used, it smelled heavily of dust. Ruth sneezed.

"I need you to do me a favor, but I'll pay you just as if you were still at work," Heimer said, wheezing a little from the exertion of climbing the stairs.

Ruth felt flattered and waved away his offer. "Of course I'll help you!" Maybe it meant something that he had chosen her, in particular, to lend him a hand.

Heimer pointed to the table behind him. "These presents are for Evie and a few of the others. Now that there's a woman in the household again I want Christmas to be really special. Like it was when my wife was still alive, God rest her soul. But I can't let Evie wrap her own presents." He pointed to a few sheets of wine-red paper printed with golden angels. "I didn't skimp. It was the most expensive wrapping paper I could find."

Ruth nodded, keeping her face neutral. Heimer certainly shouldn't see her eyes pop out at the sight of such extravagance. She stole a glance at the table. There was a round case of some kind, a woolen garment, and a few little bottles. She looked at Heimer. "You've even bought name tags and gold ribbon!" She couldn't entirely conceal her surprise. She never would have expected him to go for such luxuries.

Heimer beamed. "Only the best for Evie!" He told Ruth to put the presents on the dresser once she had wrapped them, and then he trotted back downstairs.

Evie, Evie, all day long! Ruth rolled her eyes. All the same, she couldn't wait to see what Heimer had bought his daughter-in-law.

As soon as she was alone, she rushed over to the table. A powder compact! Decorated with red and gold roses and—Ruth fiddled with the catch until the case opened—a mirror inside the lid. Ruth gazed at her reflection and pretended she was powdering her face. She closed her eyes and tried to imagine the powder settling on her skin like silk.

The garment was a knitted jacket in hunter green. Ruth grinned. Eva would look as pale as a milkmaid wearing that. But she sighed when she saw the next gift: a piece close to six feet long of the finest Plauen lace. Ruth ran her fingers along the stiff edges of the lace, estimating enviously as she felt the quality of the handiwork. It would be enough to edge a blouse and then some—enough for one bodice at least, maybe two. A lump formed in her throat. All for Eva. It was so unfair. Ruth pushed aside the cardboard box that held the lace. When she saw that there were no more presents with Eva's name on the tag, she was almost relieved. She picked up one of the little bottles. Aha, a liqueur for old Edeltraud. Not that she'd be able to pour herself more than two glasses. How stingy he was! Ruth put the bottle aside and picked up the next. Another liqueur, this time with Sarah's name on the tag. So at least there was something for the hired hands. She picked up the third. This one was for Griseldis. Ruth looked up and down the table but saw no presents for Thomas and his brothers, nor for herself and her sisters. She tried not to be too disappointed. It could only mean one of two things, she thought as she wrapped the lace in the wine-red paper: either Wilhelm Heimer had some special gifts for his sons and Joost's daughters, or . . . they would get no presents at all. But surely that wouldn't be the case, Ruth told herself as she smoothed the paper flat.

Though it was only two o'clock in the afternoon, it was so gloomy that she had to turn the light on. The dark heavy furniture made the room even dimmer. Ruth put down Edeltraud's present. If her voice ever came to count for something in the Heimer family home, the first thing she would do would be to put this room in order. Striped wallpaper would look good in here. And new curtains. Maybe she'd even be allowed to choose some new furniture. Once she was Mrs. Heimer, she would get to work making it a room they could be proud of. After all, not many houses in the village even had a front parlor like this.

Maybe she wouldn't even live here, though, but in the empty rooms above the warehouse instead? Just a few days before, Thomas had said in passing that the whole house belonged to his father. Perhaps he'd mentioned it for a reason?

Ruth could hardly wait for that time to come.

◆ ◆ ◆

The only one who wasn't thinking about the coming holiday was Marie. That was because every day was like Christmas for her at the moment. Since she had gathered up the courage to show Heimer her design for the basket bowl, she had been given the go-ahead to paint that one and three more new designs. To suit the season, one of her suggestions was a silver goblet with a pattern of frost and snow. She also found inspiration in the tinsel wire that she had disliked so much at first; if she wound it around the glasses in a thin web rather than by the fistful, the result was enchanting. Marie had endless variations of glass and colors and ornamental detail to work with.

By now she didn't even have to wait for the right moment to go to Heimer with one of her designs; he had fallen into the habit of coming over to Marie's workbench at least once a day to watch her paint. "Well now, what kind of egg is my girl artist brooding on today?" he would ask. The joke soon grew old, but he expected her to laugh at it each time. If she did, then when Marie suggested some little refinement or showed him one of her new designs, he never said much about it. In this, he was like her father, whose motto had always been that silence was praise enough. Marie cared little for flowery praise—all she wanted was for Wilhelm Heimer to let her carry on with her work.

"As long as you keep up with the orders we have, I don't mind if you try something new from time to time," he had assured her, patting her shoulder. Eva had watched jealously and then not said a word to her for the rest of the day, which Marie found very welcome indeed.

There were words of praise for Marie all the same—from an unexpected source. Heimer's wholesaler had liked the basket bowl so much that the very day he received it, he offered it to every customer who came in. That evening, when Heimer's hired woman had come back to the village with an order for three hundred pieces, Wilhelm's eyes had almost popped out of his head. Over the following week, Thomas and his brothers had to take turns sitting at the lamp for an extra hour in the evenings to make enough bowls to fulfill the order. Marie realized that what she had painted for her own amusement, on a whim, would now brighten the day for hundreds of people.

From that moment on she could not shake the thought that her artistic talent might be more than just a pleasant way to pass the time.

18

Two days before Christmas, Friedhelm Strobel could no longer bear to be trapped in the narrow confines of his shop with the shelves all the way up to the ceiling. He felt like a wild animal, torn from its natural habitat and wasting its life in captivity. *What am I doing here?* he asked himself with a sudden rage that startled him. *What on earth am I doing in this provincial backwater?*

The catalyst for this anger was the letter that the postman had brought that morning. Strobel stared at the unassuming gray envelope, seething with hatred. He could smell the scent of the perfumed writing paper through it. The words themselves might have left him cold, but that scent! Oh, how well he knew that scent. For as long as he lived, it would always bring back the same bittersweet memories. Greedily, reluctantly, he breathed in the aroma of old times. He could not banish the images conjured in his mind. He heard himself sob. Why did they have to get in touch now? After all these years?

The old unease seized hold of him again. Pacing restlessly up and down, he wondered what the arrival of this letter might mean for him. What it *could* mean. Was there any way back?

He gnawed at his lips until they began to bleed once more.

He had tried so hard to leave the past behind him, and for a few years, he had even succeeded. He had been so relieved to escape unscathed that leaving B., despite all its temptations, had been easy. Of course he had known right from the start that the forests of Thuringia had few suitable opportunities for a man of his caliber. At the time, however, he had accepted that. Wanting to make a clean break with *everything*, he had made no move to keep in touch with . . . old acquaintances.

By now he knew the letter by heart: just ten lines, no letterhead, not even a complete signature. It began with an insincere inquiry about how he was, and then went straight to the point: they had plans that would outdo everything that had gone before and they were looking for investors. Perhaps, they asked, Friedhelm Strobel would be interested in renewing those old ties that had once pleased him so well.

For years nobody had even taken the trouble to find out where he had vanished to so hastily. Once he had left B., they simply lost interest in him. Only now that they wanted something from him did they suddenly remember who he was. He gave a wry grin, mocking the memories. Wasn't that just like them?

He had trouble recalling some of their faces. A great deal of time had passed since then, and in all that time his only ambition had been to expose his family's bourgeois moral standards, to show them that there was far more to him than . . . He still felt sick when he recalled all the insults they had hurled at him back then.

And the truth was that in the ten years he had been working in Sonneberg as a wholesaler, he had made more money than his father had in his whole respectable lifetime. But was anybody interested? No. As far as his family was concerned, he no longer existed. Since nobody had made any inquiries about him, they didn't know what a brilliant businessman he had become, hidden away here. But what had all this money brought him?

He had become a shopkeeper.

He had lost his freedom.

He looked around wildly at the walls that threatened to collapse and bury him. He was a prisoner among all the wooden toys, glasswork, and useless knickknacks. His clients were the prison wardens, and they made it impossible for him to escape even for a day.

A bitter smile crept across his bloody lips. *They* had no way of knowing that though. In *their* world he had a reputation as a man who always got whatever he wanted.

A desire that he had thought long dead stirred within him. In his mind's eye he saw himself walking along the winding path, between the tall box hedges, to the great wooden door. Three knocks, pause, two knocks, pause, one final knock, and then the door to his heart's desires was open. Strobel put a hand to his throat as though this could stop the feeling that the walls were closing in on him.

Was it still all as it had been back then? The letter said that the building work proceeded apace. It also mentioned other investors. Might these include anyone he knew?

He need not dwell on that question, he told himself sternly. Certainly he had the money; that had never been an issue! But he couldn't simply walk away from his wholesale business and risk having his customers turn their backs on him for the competition.

Something warm was dripping onto his hand. Startled, Strobel looked down. Blood. He had bitten his lower lip so hard that it was truly bleeding.

He hurried to the bathroom and dabbed at his mouth with a towel. Then he reached for a comb. He stopped in the middle of tidying the severe part in his hair.

What were their plans, exactly?

He couldn't imagine anything that could surpass what they had. On the other hand, *they* certainly had ideas and ambition, he knew that much . . .

He sobbed as he realized that he would have done anything for another visit to B. just then.

19

"I still can't believe it!" Johanna said, practically in tears. "A bowl of apples and a lot of smarmy words!" She shook her head. "The work itself is your present this year," she scoffed, mimicking Wilhelm Heimer. "Maybe we were supposed to give him something, from sheer gratitude?"

"But even so, we should be glad to have jobs and wages!"

Johanna shot a glance at Marie. "So now you're singing from the same sheet as Griseldis! She's always going on about being grateful. I don't understand either of you!" She slammed her fist on the table. "It's not as though Heimer is doing us any favors! He gets our work and our time, doesn't he? And all for just a few marks!" she spat disdainfully. "He's earning a pretty penny from Marie's basket bowls. And he doesn't even think we deserve a little something for Christmas?" Her voice was wavering again.

It was six o'clock on Christmas Eve. The church bells were ringing for the service, and the three of them should already have put their coats on and left for church. But ever since they had gotten back from work an hour ago, not one of them had stood up from the table. There was only a single candle burning since they hadn't lit the lamps or made up a fire. Merry Christmas!

"A bowl of apples. To share among the three of us."

"How many times are you going to say that?" Ruth asked sourly. "He's our employer, nothing more than that. He's not obliged to give us any presents. Christmas or no Christmas!" There was an edge to her voice that sharply contradicted her words.

"If that's the case, then why are you so upset?" Marie asked.

Ruth spat out, "I get tired of listening to Johanna moan on and on!"

"She's probably upset because her darling turns out to be just as much of an old skinflint as his father!" Johanna said in an uncharacteristically sharp tone. "Haven't you chosen a lovely family to marry into?"

"When it comes to family, old Heimer isn't the least bit mean— you should have seen all the things he bought for Eva! We . . . it's just that we're not family. But I did get something from Thomas, something very nice even," Ruth said, making a face at her sister.

"And where is this present? Why don't you show it to us?" Johanna challenged her.

Marie looked from one to the other. "Must we squabble like this? It's Christmas after all. If Ruth doesn't want to show us her present, then"—she raised her hands helplessly—"then that's fine! I can understand that she might want to have something to keep for herself, just for once."

Ashamed, Johanna looked down at the table. Marie was right. She sighed. All of this was only happening because she was so upset.

"I'm sorry," she said in a small voice, and reached out to take Ruth's hand.

"Leave me alone!" Ruth snatched her hand away, and then began sobbing loudly.

"What is it? For heaven's sake, Ruth, I didn't mean to upset you." Johanna looked aghast at the miserable, huddled figure beside her. *Merry Christmas one and all,* she thought. If only Peter would come and visit.

"I . . . it's got nothing to do with you, and nothing to do with the Heimers," Ruth sobbed.

Johanna and Marie looked at one another. They thought they knew what Ruth was feeling. This was the first Christmas without Father.

"We miss Father too," Marie whispered. "I miss him so much I sometimes get chest pains."

Ruth looked up, her eyes heavy with tears. She went over to her bag and fumbled about inside it. Then she came back to the table and put something down with a clatter.

"My bowl!" Marie called out. "How did that get here? What does that have to do with Father?"

Then she added incredulously, "Is that your Christmas present from Thomas?"

It was dead quiet for a moment.

Ruth nodded and buried her face in her hands again. "Pretty, isn't it?" she asked, her shoulders shaking.

It took a moment for Marie and Johanna to realize that the tears running down Ruth's cheeks were tears of laughter. And, her laughter was contagious—hysterical, out of control, liberating. They laughed until they could taste salty tears on their lips and only stopped when they were out of breath.

Ruth picked up the bowl and turned it around in the candlelight. "He whispers one endearment after another in my ear, and then he's so thoughtless he just picks up one of a hundred pieces in the workshop! 'I'm sure you'll especially like this, your sister painted it after all,'" she said, imitating his tone as she repeated his words. "I didn't know what to say! Not that I don't like your painting, please don't misunderstand me," she said, turning to Marie.

Marie waved a hand.

"It's just that . . . somehow I was expecting more. Something just for me. A token of his love, so to speak." Ruth was fighting back tears again. "He couldn't understand why I wasn't jumping for joy! By the time we said good-bye, he even looked offended."

"Men!" Johanna said dismissively. Why couldn't Ruth work out for herself that this dumb cluck wasn't the man for her? That he wasn't in the least bit like the knight in shining armor she used to dream of?

Marie added, "Men from the Heimer family in particular!"

And because they didn't want to cry, they laughed again until their sides hurt.

◆　◆　◆

When they got home from church, Johanna marched over to the stove and built a fire. Then she put everything she could find from the pantry onto the table: bread, butter, a jar of honey, and some plum jam that Griseldis had given them. And finally, too, the apples that Wilhelm Heimer had presented with such a flourish, as though they were worth their weight in gold.

"Now don't sit about like a pair of moaning minnies!" she said to her sisters. "We'll get through the evening somehow." Then she shook flour into a bowl. She cracked a couple of eggs into it, added some milk, and stirred up the batter.

"We can have pancakes with honey or plum jam," she said as brightly as she could.

"No Christmas tree. Not even a bough." Ruth was staring at the stool where they had put the tree every year.

"Where were we going to get a tree? Ugly Paul always gave it to us along with our winter wood."

"We never even cut a bough on St. Barbara's Day. And we could have done that for free," Marie said.

"True." Johanna sighed. They had been so busy with work that they hadn't even thought to go out on December 4 to cut a few boughs from the apple or cherry trees for Christmas Eve. She watched as the pancake began to crisp at the edges. Once it smelled done, she flipped it over.

"A tree! St. Barbara's boughs!" Ruth spat disdainfully. "What good would a tree do us if we've nothing to put on it? Look at us: no nuts, no gingerbread, no candy canes—we're poor, poor, poor!" And she burst into tears again.

It wasn't long before Marie joined in. Johanna looked up helplessly from the pancakes. She would have liked to pay a call on Peter, but she couldn't leave the two of them alone in this state.

As if reading her thoughts, Marie sobbed, "Why isn't Peter coming over? He's always been here for Christmas."

"I don't know where he is. He wasn't in church either, although that doesn't mean anything. He's never been much of a churchgoer," Johanna said. "Maybe he doesn't feel comfortable around us. As the only man among three women . . ."

"You mean because Father's gone." Marie shook her head. "Peter was never one to spend all his time with other men. If he were, he'd spend his evenings with the Heimer brothers and all the others at the Black Eagle."

Johanna silently agreed. She couldn't remember a time when Peter hadn't been there for them.

"He'll come."

With a flourish, she dished up the first pancake. "So, let's eat until we get stomachaches. And I don't want any more talk of men this evening, except perhaps for baby Jesus."

Ruth looked up, her eyes wet with tears.

"You're right. We Steinmann girls won't give up so easily." She took a handkerchief from her pocket and blew her nose loudly.

The fire crackled.

They could hear singing from one of the neighbors' houses, and the sound of a flute.

Joost's chair was empty, as was the stool for the Christmas tree.

There was no cracking of nuts and no gingerbread crumbs on the table.

"At least it's warm," said Johanna, spreading plum jam onto another pancake.

20

None of the sisters were sorry when Christmas Eve was over.

It had begun to snow thick, feathery flakes that melted as soon as they hit the ground. Instead of mantling the landscape in a coat of virgin white, the wet snow turned the streets into a morass. After a hard night's frost, the ground had become dangerously slippery underfoot. For Johanna and her sisters, the miserable weather was further proof that this Christmas was not like ones past.

Tottering and holding onto each other, the three sisters braved the bitter cold and walked up the steep street to Wilhelm Heimer's house midmorning on Christmas Day. Sheets of ice had formed on the foundry square, which was empty and abandoned at that time of year. "Careful!" Johanna said, grabbing Ruth by the elbow right as she began to slip.

Marie cast a yearning glance over at the furnaces, which stood neglected in the glass foundry. "If only they would build up the fire again!" she sighed. "I think it's dreadful when it's abandoned like this."

Johanna was longing for spring as well, when the square would be stacked high with wood for the master glassmakers' fires. The stokers would be calling loudly for more wood to keep the furnaces burning at the high temperatures needed to melt glass, and Peter Maienbaum and his fellow masters would be working night and day in shifts to keep the foundry going. The masters themselves would be working at the melt, each in his own mixing room, fussing over the best possible recipe for each batch, while outside the journeymen would be stretching the viscous lumps of glass into long, thin rods with their tongs. The rods would then be snipped into lengths to make the glass stock that Peter and all the other glassblowers used for their work—and she could watch it all happen, exactly the way it had been done since the glass foundry was opened in 1597 almost three hundred years ago. Johanna was suddenly immensely comforted by the thought that they were all part of this enduring rhythm.

Peter. He had stopped by the previous evening after helping Widow Grün fix a hole in her stovepipe.

"That was a good idea Peter had with the glass animals, wasn't it?" Johanna said, her words muffled by her scarf.

Children who needed a glass eye fitted often found the procedure very trying. To make the ordeal a little easier for them, Peter had started to blow toy animals out of glass for his younger patients. With a little bird or a dog or a monkey in their hands, they didn't mind sitting still so much, and Peter could get on with his work. He had brought along three of these animals for Johanna, Ruth, and Marie. Now they stood on the windowsill, where the light showed off the colored glass wonderfully.

"It was. I still don't know whether I like the elephant best or the lion," Marie answered. "The way he made that elephant coil its trunk . . ."

"I just love the curls in the lion's mane—such a pretty yellow. I never even knew that the foundry sold stock in that color," Johanna replied.

"I think what he did was melt together a bit of yellow rod with some orange," Marie said thoughtfully. "Apparently it's not easy to mingle the colors like that. When old Heimer got that order for the striped drinking glasses, they all cursed up a storm."

Johanna's sigh hung in the air like a little white cloud. "Those glass animals would certainly sell well. Friedhelm Strobel . . ."

Ruth laughed. "Save your breath. Peter makes eyes because that's his passion, and there's nothing you can do to change that. He doesn't care about earning money. Which is unfortunate," she giggled. "If our dear neighbor were a little more business minded, you might have become Mrs. Maypole long ago!" She nudged Marie.

"The things you say! How often do I have to tell you that Peter and I are just good friends? Mrs. Maienbaum—why, it would be like marrying my own brother." Johanna grimaced. "Anyway, who cares about marrying money? I certainly don't. I just want Peter to do well. If he made his business in glass animals, he'd make money much more easily than he does with his wounded soldiers and those poor children who've had accidents."

As soon as they opened the door to the workshop, Johanna felt her hackles rise. She wanted to turn right round and . . . well, do anything but this. Anything but stand in this ill-ventilated workshop, working on Christmas Day itself because old Heimer couldn't organize the business well enough for even a day's holiday, putting ugly glassware through the silver bath or packing it into boxes. Marie went in first and made a beeline for the painting bench. Johanna shook her head as she saw Marie take off her jacket while striding across the room, as though she could hardly wait to get back to work.

As Ruth walked past the glassblowers at their lamps, her chin held high, she said nothing beyond "Good morning." Johanna was pleased to note that her sister still didn't seem to have forgiven Thomas for putting so little thought into his gift to her. She scanned the room for Griseldis, but Widow Grün was nowhere to be seen. Peter had said that her house had been ice-cold; perhaps she'd caught a cold when her stove stopped working.

There was no sign of Wilhelm Heimer either. Johanna felt strangely at a loss. *What am I doing here?* she thought. By now Marie had opened all the paint pots in front of her as though it were the most natural thing in the world. Ruth was caught up in conversation with Eva and seemed to be admiring her new hair clasp. Sarah came in from the storeroom at her usual snail's pace, her arms full of flattened cardboard boxes. And the three Heimer boys were hunched over their lamps—she had heard the flames hissing as soon as she opened the door. Everyone had a job to do but her.

Thomas Heimer turned round. "Father will be in later. He's in Sonneberg this morning," he said, looking past Johanna. When he saw Ruth standing with Eva, he got up and walked over to her, without giving Johanna any indication of what work there was to do.

So Johanna joined Sarah and began folding cardboard boxes. Sarah told her that Widow Grün was in bed with a high temperature, and then fell back into sullen silence. After folding boxes until there was no more room on the table, Johanna said, "That's certainly enough for now. There must be more urgent work to be done."

But Sarah carried on folding boxes as though she hadn't heard.

Was the girl really as simpleminded as she acted? Exasperated, Johanna walked over to the silvering bench, where at least three dozen glass goblets were waiting to be silvered. Here was something for her to do.

She found she had a new appetite for work as she picked up the first goblet and held the opening in the base up to the stopcock on the silver fluid bottle. It was only then that she noticed there was no more silver solution in the bottle on the wall. The flask of reducing fluid was full, but that was no good on its own. She stared helplessly at the flasks of ammonia, spirit vinegar, and silver-nitrate salts. Heimer always made a great secret of the exact proportions. Griseldis was the only one who knew how much to take from each bottle before she mixed them together with water and a pinch of grape sugar as a reducing agent. Granted, Heimer's silvered wares were especially smooth and shiny. Other masters didn't use such pure ingredients, or they used the wrong reducing agent, and their silver didn't wash evenly over the glass, leaving bare spots here and there. But the drawback of Heimer's appetite for secrecy was clear: without Griseldis there to mix the fluid, the whole workflow ground to a halt.

"Why are you standing there like an ox staring at the barn door?"

Johanna spun round. Heimer. How could such a heavyset man appear as if from nowhere?

"I . . . there isn't any silver bath," she said rather feebly.

"What about over there?" Heimer pointed to where Sarah's head could just be seen above a wall of cardboard boxes. "Didn't you think to go and help her instead of standing there gawping at the empty silver bottle? It seems to me that there's plenty to do!" And with that, he stomped off, shaking his head. "You girls may be used to ruling the roost at home, but you're not paid to stand around here," he said, wagging his finger at her.

Johanna stood there sheepishly, feeling the eyes of the others upon her as they stole glances over their shoulders. How could he reprimand her so—and for no good reason at all?

"Better to rule the roost than let you run the place like a pig-sty!" she muttered to herself.

Heimer stopped in his tracks. "What did you say?"

Of course, at this point Johanna could have said something like, "Nothing, it's all right." She could have hurried over to Sarah at the packing table and carried on folding boxes that nobody had any use for. But she didn't.

21

Peter turned off the gas tap. Without the singing of the flame, the room instantly fell quiet. As he sat down to join Johanna at the table, he cast a glance at the pair of glass eyes that still needed the veins painted on. A courier would come to collect them the next morning. The patient would surely be anxiously awaiting them. He would probably have to work through the night to have them ready, but he didn't care—Johanna needed him now. Even if the stubborn woman would never admit it.

"Well don't expect me to drag every word out of you like I'm pulling teeth. Did you say that to his face, about the pigsty?"

Johanna nodded, her expression a mixture of stubbornness and pride that only she could manage. "I don't let anyone call me lazy. After all, it was his fault there was nothing for me to do. Gracious me—I only told him the truth, but you should have seen the way he exploded! He turned so red in the face that for a moment I thought he might drop dead on the spot."

Peter had no trouble imagining it. "And then?"

"Then he began calling me all sorts of names. Going on about how ungrateful I was, and so on." She shrugged. "Ungrateful fiddlesticks! I told him that he wasn't giving me anything out of the goodness of his heart. In fact I told him that I was giving him my work and my time for next to nothing! And that I had no reason at all to be grateful to him because he was just taking advantage of the hard times we were going through to get himself a few hired hands on the cheap."

Peter raised his eyebrows. She hadn't minced words. He wasn't surprised that Heimer had slung her out on her ear. "You sound like that Karl Marx. He was always going on about the workers being exploited."

Johanna looked askance at him, not sure whether he was pulling her leg.

"I don't know anybody called Marx. But damn it all, I'm not going to stand there and be called names. What would you have done in my place?"

Peter looked at her across the table. "I don't know, to be honest. Maybe I would have kept my mouth shut. Maybe I wouldn't. But I can say that I'm happy to be my own boss and won't ever find myself in a scrape like that."

"But you can understand why I did what I did, can't you? A little bit?" she asked woefully.

Peter had to laugh. "What do you want me to say? I can hardly tell you it's a good thing that you got Wilhelm Heimer to give you the boot, can I now?" Johanna didn't need to know that deep down inside, he was actually rather proud of her. But he also wondered what it would mean for both of them that Johanna was out of a job.

She stood up. "If you're siding against me as well, then I might just as well go home!" she said, going to the window. She stared over at her own house.

"The moment my sisters got home, they tore into me! Ruth told me that I was putting all our jobs in jeopardy. And Marie called me a quarrelsome know-it-all." Johanna was standing straight as could be. "What a horrid thing to say—when all I did was speak the truth!"

"Come back and sit down," Peter said as he went to the stove and fetched a pot he had put on to warm. "Let's eat first, and then we'll think about what to do next."

Johanna was about to wave away his offer when the scent rising from the pot reached her nose. Her mouth started to water. She hadn't had a bite to eat all day. When Peter put a bowl of soup in front of her, she realized how hungry she was. She dipped her spoon in before he even sat down with his own bowl. There were green beans, meat, and potatoes, all chopped up and swimming in a rich golden broth. He had everything he needed here—unlike her.

She put her spoon down so suddenly that the soup splashed over the edge.

Peter looked at her, his eyebrows raised. "What's bothering you now?" When she didn't answer, he said, "To be honest, I don't think it's all bad. I never liked to think of you working your fingers to the bone for Heimer. A woman like you, working for a blockhead like him. That was never going to end well."

"Maybe you're right." Johanna looked at him, still tense. "I think the argument was just waiting to happen. If it hadn't broken out today, it would have by the new year."

Her expression grew more cheerful, and she picked up her spoon and carried on eating.

Now! Now was the time to ask her again.

"Sometimes a storm clears the air . . ." he heard himself saying instead of what he wanted to ask. "Who knows? Perhaps you'll find some way to make peace with the old fellow." He held his breath.

Johanna looked up. "Make peace with him?" she asked uncomprehendingly. "You don't really believe that I would go crawling back to him. I'd rather starve!" She pushed the bowl away.

He leaned across the table and took her hand. "Johanna, come to me, to my workshop!"

Her arm went rigid.

"You and me . . . we work well together, you have to admit that." But she didn't respond. He let go of her hand.

"Oh, Peter!" Johanna looked at him with despair and amusement in her eyes. "I know you mean well, but you don't really need me around. You've got everything just as you like it."

Peter looked around his home, seeing it through her eyes; the narrow room with windows at each end. The simple workbench and the racks of glass eyes staring out of their sockets. The table in the kitchen corner where he consulted his patients. And in the back, his bed with the old patchwork quilt his mother had made flung carelessly over it. *Damn it all, why didn't he have more to offer her?* "Just as I like it? This is the messy, untended household of a bachelor. A woman's touch would work wonders here." *And a woman's love . . .*

"Oh, so I'm supposed to help you keep your home looking nice," she answered sarcastically. "Do you think that's all I'm good for?" She laughed bitterly. "It seems our father was the only man who didn't think that we girls were stupid!"

"Nonsense!" Peter felt himself losing his temper. Why did she always have to make things so hard for him?

"Maybe that came out wrong. You know quite well that I think the world of you. But that's not what we're talking about. What I wanted to say was—me and you . . ." He looked at her and fell quiet.

It was pointless. Johanna looked like someone who had made up her mind long ago. He didn't know what she was thinking about, but it wasn't him.

"Just forget I spoke," he said, dismissing his own suggestion with a wave of his hand. "You're quite right; I can rearrange the workshop all on my own. And when I start making a new line of glass animals in the new year, I'll be able to do that on my own as well, at least at first." He saw Johanna prick up her ears. For a moment the throb of disappointment faded in his chest. Yes, she'd sit up and look twice when he began to make good money with the glass animals.

"I'll manage on my own. And I'm sure you will too." He didn't let it show just how much it cost him to say these words, which he didn't even believe himself. How on earth was a single woman without a job going to manage on her own? But Peter knew when he'd lost a battle. And he also knew there was no point in trying to force Johanna into anything. Either she would come to him one day of her own accord . . . or she wouldn't.

He tried to ignore the dull throb in his chest and went over to the pantry. He came back to the table with two glasses and a bottle of cherry schnapps.

"We can't drink to the new year quite yet, but let's drink to better times ahead," he said, pouring Johanna a generous glass and handing it to her. Ignoring her startled look, he lifted his own glass just as though he were drinking with a buddy down at the pub.

For the first time that day, Johanna smiled. As they raised their glasses in a toast and looked each other in the eye, any awkwardness between them fled.

22

"You could not have chosen a better time to come to me," Friedhelm Strobel said, smiling down at Johanna from the ladder. "The year-end inventory will help you get to know every item we have in stock, without my having to take it down from the shelves for that purpose."

Johanna nodded. When she had gone to Sonneberg on the Monday after Christmas and knocked on the wholesaler's door, hoping with all her heart that his offer from the fall still stood, she had never expected that she would start the very same day. But she had come to realize that it made sense to join in the inventory. They had spent three days on it already, and she had a good grasp of Strobel's business now. Not wanting to sound too full of herself, however, she simply replied, "I hope I don't forget where everything is kept." Even as she spoke she knew perfectly well that she could see every drawer and shelf in her mind's eye; she knew just where the vases were kept and where to find the candlesticks.

"We can make sure that doesn't happen," Strobel said as he climbed down from the ladder. "With the next set of shelves, I'll check the list and you can inventory what's there. I'm sure you'll remember it all much better that way. And you'll also learn how to climb that ladder." He chuckled. "The ladies sometimes have trouble with that, so I'm told."

Johanna shoved the list and pencil into his hands and pulled the ladder toward the next set of shelves. "I don't get dizzy easily, if that's what you mean." As she climbed the rungs, she trembled a little nevertheless. He wasn't going to try to peer up her skirts, was he? Cautiously, she glanced behind her. Strobel seemed absorbed in his list, although he had an odd smirk on his face. She tried to breathe deeply and evenly. If she were honest with herself, she was really quite high up. She fumbled for the shelf.

"Good. Let's move on to the porcelain pots." Strobel's tone was businesslike once more, which Johanna greatly preferred to the affected tone he so often used. She pulled open a drawer and was surprised to find how heavy it was. When she peered inside, she could see why: the drawer was full to the brim with little porcelain jars. "They're beautiful!" she said without thinking. The first one she picked up was made of porcelain so thin it was almost transparent. A hunting scene was painted on the lid, and the sides were decorated with vine leaves and ivy. She wished Marie could see it.

"And? How many?" an impatient voice asked from below.

Johanna put down the pot and began her count. "Three of number six-eight-nine, five of number six-nine-zero." She shut the compartment and opened the next. More pots, these featuring pierced porcelain. "Two number six-nine-one. Four number six-nine-two."

Once Johanna had gotten used to being up on the tall ladder, the inventory went as quickly as it had when Strobel had been up there.

Once she was done with the jars, Johanna turned, as far as she could, to look down at him. "What if you took on more kinds of porcelain jars? What would the numbering look like?" She knew that the seven hundreds were reserved for glass carafes, since they'd counted them that morning.

Strobel looked up from his list. "You think ahead, I like that . . ." he said absentmindedly. He had that odd little smile on his lips again that Johanna couldn't quite read. She tried to convince herself that it was a smile of approval. Or was he mocking her? Strobel's reply interrupted her thoughts.

"If we take on more porcelain pots, then we start again with six-eight-zero but we add another number on the end, starting at zero." He clapped his hands. "Well, that's enough for New Year's Eve. We'll do the rest on Monday. Then we'll have to have the full inventory ready for our clients."

Johanna followed his glance to the clock on the wall. "It can't be three o'clock already. Time flies when you're busy." *And when the work is as interesting as this,* she thought. She congratulated herself silently as she climbed down from the ladder and untied her apron strings.

"And you're sure you want to go home? As I have said, you may use your room on the weekends and holidays as well . . . especially now, in the depths of winter," Strobel called over his shoulder. Just as he did every day, he was putting the inventory lists into the safe. He always carried the key with him on a long chain.

"I have to get back to my sisters," Johanna said. She was hardly going to spend New Year's Eve alone in her room. Or did he imagine that she was going to join him for the occasion? She could hardly wait to get back to Lauscha. She had only had the chance to send Ruth and Marie a quick note with one of the messenger women, and by now they would certainly be eager to know how the first few days in Sonneberg had been. And Peter! Wouldn't he be surprised to hear how well she had done for herself? Besides, if she didn't get to tell someone about all she'd seen and done, she would burst—she knew that much.

Strobel was just about to shut the heavy safe door when Johanna cleared her throat.

"Yes?" He turned to look at her.

"My wages," she forced herself to say. She was mortified at having to ask, but she had made up her mind that from now on she would have what was her due.

Strobel laughed. "Good gracious me! I might have clean forgotten that most important detail." His knees cracked audibly as he squatted down to rummage in the depths of the safe.

Johanna stood there awkwardly and wrung her hands. This was the moment of truth. Although she had made Strobel agree on Monday that she could have her wages weekly rather than just once a month, she hadn't been bold enough to ask him how much she would be getting. And he hadn't said anything of his own accord. Now that it was too late, she was angry at herself for having been so shy. If she was in for another disappointment like with Wilhelm Heimer, then she had only herself to blame.

"Here." Friedhelm Strobel stood up, and put a pile of coins into her hand. "That's six marks for these first three days. It would have been ten, if the New Year's holiday had not intervened. Ten marks a week, for forty marks a month as wages." Seeing that she was dumbstruck, he added, "You'll get a bit more after you've served your probation. Always assuming we still get on." There was that curious smile again.

Johanna swallowed. Ten marks a week. Forty marks a month. More after the probation. Nobody at home would believe it! She bit the inside of her lip to stop herself from squealing with delight. Strobel mustn't imagine that she would fall at his feet from sheer gratitude just because she was a country girl. Although she very nearly felt like doing just that.

"How long am I on probation?" she asked instead.

Strobel went over to his shop counter and found the calendar for the coming year. "If we agree on half a year, then your probation will be over on the twenty-ninth of June exactly!" He pointed to the date.

Johanna nodded, feeling stupid. "I wish you a happy New Year," she said, making sure her voice sounded friendly. She wanted to be absolutely sure that her first week ended on a harmonious note. She put her hand on the door handle, and then turned round once more. Strobel was just turning down the flame in the gas lamps, and she had trouble making out his figure in the darkness. "Thank you for taking me on," she said quickly, and then vanished.

◆　◆　◆

Smiling, Strobel watched her go.

Johanna Steinmann.

He would never have expected the old year to drop such a gift in his lap. A gift? No, it was a twist of fate.

Instead of locking up and going back to his own apartment, he sat down on the sofa reserved for clients. He didn't usually see the room from this angle, but now he ran his eye around the place, feeling the pride of ownership. He had to admit it was impressive: not just planks on frames like most of his competitors had, but fitted shelving of mahogany and rosewood. And no shabby old floorboards squeaking at every step. Instead he had the finest parquet flooring, which he had ordered specially from southern Germany. He found himself thinking of the letter from B. and of all the spiteful thoughts he had had about his beautiful business when he read it. He'd called it a shackle on his freedom, a ball-and-chain around his leg. But no longer! Now that he was well on his way to training Johanna up to be a skilled shop assistant, it was only a matter of time. Perhaps he would even be able to travel for a couple of weeks in the spring, knowing that he'd left his business in good hands?

Even if not, he would be able to take B. up on their invitation no later than the coming summer.

So far Johanna turned out to be a quick learner. He had never expected otherwise. She had a sharp mind and was a hard worker. Everything else—elegance, self-confidence, and a certain worldliness—would come with time, he would make sure of that. Once Johanna had learned what he had to teach her, she would be able to cope with any kind of customer whether arrogant, hesitant, or simply difficult. The fact that she knew no foreign languages would be a problem, but she would surely be able to learn a few words of English and French—enough at least to greet customers.

Johanna Steinmann.

She was simply not like the others. He moistened his lips. Perhaps he should train her up to be *more* than just his shop assistant. Lost in thought, he bit off a little scrap of skin. Johanna Steinmann was a diamond in the rough. Good raw material, perhaps the very best. But that was only the beginning. It was up to him to make of her what he could. He could cut and shape her to perfection. He giggled at the thought, and the sound filled the silent shop. He was a gem cutter, and Johanna was his diamond. The world might think he wanted to make her shine. But any street-corner jeweler could cut rhinestones to a high gleam. Friedhelm Strobel wanted something else; he wanted sharp edges, clean facets.

If he wanted it, Johanna would be a sweet little something on the side, in between his visits to B.

But was that what he wanted?

Like a connoisseur rolling a drop of wine across his tongue, testing the bouquet, he played with the thought, still unsure whether he could stick to whatever decision he made.

23

It was so good to be home.

Johanna found herself thinking of the parable of the Prodigal Son as Ruth brought dish after dish to the table and even conjured a bottle of wine from somewhere. Johanna had no idea when her sister had found time to cook all the food.

"I don't want you to go to all this trouble just for me. You may not believe it, but we do have food in Sonneberg as well!"

"Yes, but you must be hungry after the long walk home, and cold as well. And Peter certainly is!" Ruth squeezed onto the bench next to Marie and held out the bread basket to their guest.

"I caught a ride most of the way. A slate-maker took me on his cart as far as Steinach. He didn't ask nearly as much as the railway does for a ticket. And he said that I can ride with him every Friday," Johanna told them. "But it was a lovely surprise to see you waiting there for me," she said to Peter, who was sitting next to her. "How did you even know when I would be coming home?"

He shrugged. "A day's work in Sonneberg can't last any longer than it does in Lauscha, can it?" He had actually spent well over an hour standing waiting at the edge of the village, but he kept that to himself.

"Oh, I almost forgot," Johanna said, getting up again to fetch her bag. "I brought you something."

"Salted herring!" Ruth clapped her hands, almost snatching the jar from Johanna. "And you only tell us now?" She took her fork and fished a herring out onto her plate, and then another. "It's almost like old times . . ."

For a moment her comment hung in the air like an icy breath. There was an awkward silence. It still hurt to think of Joost Steinmann.

Peter cleared his throat. "So go on and tell us. How have you been doing in Sonneberg?"

Johanna grinned. She looked from Peter to her sisters. "I'm doing well." She didn't know where to start.

"We want to know everything!" Marie said. "Where do you live? What's Strobel like? What do you do all day? And and and . . ." She leaned across the table to Johanna.

Johanna held up both hands to fend off the questions. "All right then, all right. Well, it's like this: I get up at seven o'clock. Then . . ."

"You get up at seven o'clock," Ruth broke in. "And who wakes you up?" She winked at Marie.

"Nobody! Believe it or not, now that I don't have anybody to rely on in the mornings, I somehow manage to wake up on my own. Though it's still dreadfully hard." She made a face.

"It almost sounds as though it was my fault that you were always so groggy in the mornings," Ruth said sharply.

"Nonsense," Johanna said, smiling to placate her.

Marie waved this all away; it was all water under the bridge. "So? What next? What's your room like?"

"My room's small but very pretty. There's a bed with a real feather duvet. And a window looking out onto the yard, with a table and chair by it. It has wallpaper with a sort of blue-and-white pattern. There's a mirror as well, and the housekeeper brings me a basin of hot water every morning, which means I can wash in my room."

"So there's a housekeeper," Ruth declared enviously.

Johanna decided not to mention the lavender soap for the moment, even if it did smell wonderful. "Her name's Sybille Stein and she's everything that Edeltraud isn't. She's as skinny as a goat and not much older than I am. She's a neighbor's wife. She doesn't live in the house of course, but she comes round every morning at six o'clock. She makes up the fire in the kitchen, heats the water, and gets breakfast. And while we're eating she goes off to the stockroom and opens the shutters and lights the lamps so that it's nice and bright when we get in."

"And Strobel? Where does he sleep?"

"His apartment is up on the second floor, but I've never been in there. My room's right behind the shop, next to the kitchen."

"That's good. I still don't like the idea that you spend your nights sleeping in a strange man's house," Peter said, his eyes blazing.

Ruth smiled. "Are you jealous? To be honest I wouldn't like the idea either."

"I certainly felt a little odd the first two nights. After all, I've never spent the night on my own before. I pricked up my ears at every strange sound," Johanna admitted. "But really, there's nothing to it. Every parlor maid and scullery maid has to spend the night in her master's house as well." She shrugged. She would never have believed that she could get used to a strange room so quickly, with all its strange sounds and smells.

"And many a maid has been sent home from work in the family way."

"Peter!" Marie turned scarlet. Ruth giggled.

"But it's the truth! And better to talk about it out in the open now than regret it later. Joost cosseted you girls for years so that nothing happened to you. It's no surprise that you know less about life than other women. Johanna, you probably wouldn't even notice if Strobel had some kind of mischief in mind with you."

Johanna shook her head. "Nonsense. How naive do you think we are? If Friedhelm Strobel had any untoward designs upon me, I should certainly notice. But he is as correct and honorable as a man can be." Johanna didn't mention that she still felt a little uneasy around him. "Quite apart from which, I have my own key, and I always lock my door at night. Strobel told me to do that himself. He said that some villains broke into his stockroom once. And that he didn't want me to be in any danger if it happened again." She looked around at each of them in turn to see how they reacted to the news. Surely that was proof enough of Strobel's honorable conduct?

"Anyway," she went on. "Strobel always reads the newspaper at breakfast and pays me no attention at all. Not that I mind."

The others laughed.

"When the clock strikes half past seven, he folds the newspaper. That's the sign that we must start the day's work. The shop has been closed to customers this week, but we've been working all day every day despite that." She began to tell them about stocktaking. "Hand-carved combs and hair clasps made of horn, powder compacts . . ."

Once Johanna started listing all that was hidden away in the drawers, Ruth's eyes began to sparkle. "Strobel's shop sounds like a treasure chest! What I wouldn't give to be allowed to borrow just one of those lovely things!" Ruth said.

Johanna decided that as soon as she had saved a bit of money she would buy something for Ruth. Maybe Strobel would give her some kind of discount?

"You would be amazed if you could see all the lovely painted porcelain and glass," Johanna said, turning to Marie. "This is the first time I've gotten to see what all the other glassblowers spend their days making. Some of it is quite gorgeous!" She sat up straight and squared her shoulders. "But now it's your turn: What have you all been up to?"

Ruth and Marie looked at one another.

"Heimer doesn't seem to hold it against us that he had such a blazing row with you. Or at least he behaves just the same as he ever did. And the work's the same as well!" Ruth shrugged. "And apart from that? There's nothing really to tell."

Ruth wouldn't say a word about Thomas with Peter sitting there. "And how's Griseldis?" Johanna asked.

"She's still sick. She's certain to miss the money after not working all week."

"Widow Grün is well accustomed to getting by on not very much," Peter said. "When Josef Grün was still alive, there was never any money in the house. He spent it all down at the Black Eagle."

"A husband who boozes instead of looking after his family—I don't think I could live with that," Ruth replied.

Peter opened his mouth and then shut it again, biting back whatever he was going to say.

"If you ask me, your Thomas is hardly moderate in his drinking," Marie said sharply.

"That's different! Working at the lamp just makes him thirsty, he says. How can you compare him to a drunkard?" Ruth almost shrieked.

"As far as I can see the Heimers are all drunkards," Marie replied disdainfully. "Father never used to drink so much as a drop of beer while he was working. And in the evenings, he drank half of what the Heimers put away. The way they sometimes stink of beer even first thing in the morning is dreadful!"

"I don't think it's right that Griseldis doesn't get any wages just because she's ill. It's hardly her fault that she's sick," Johanna said, changing the subject before her sisters' squabbling could become a full-blown argument. "It wouldn't hurt Heimer to pay her at least some of her wages for this week."

"What an idea! What good does she do him when she's ill? None at all. So there's no need to pay her," Ruth replied vehemently, as if it were her own money at stake.

"It could very well be that she didn't fall ill because her stove was broken, but because of the work," Johanna replied. "I know that I came home with a headache often enough from the stench of that silver solution."

"Just wait. You'll soon be getting headaches from doing sums all day long," Peter teased her.

Marie clapped her hands. "That's enough, all of you! The old year may not have been the best we've ever had, but let's not spend the last few hours squabbling. That only brings bad luck for the new year!" She pointedly picked up a slice of bread and offered it to Johanna.

While she spread butter on the bread, Johanna tried desperately to think of some topic of conversation that wasn't so divisive.

24

The first lesson that Johanna learned from Friedhelm Strobel was "Salesmanship is an art!"

Even on her first day at work in the new year, she had an inkling that there was more to it than just "give the man what he wants." However, it took some time for her to realize that Strobel was a master in his profession.

He knew every one of his customers by name, and he knew what kind of business each had and what he would be looking for. He tailored his behavior so perfectly to each of his customers that he knew just the words they wanted to hear, even the tone of voice in which to speak them. For some customers, he described the wares in such extravagantly flowery language that Johanna had to bite the inside of her cheek to stifle a giggle. With others, he hardly mentioned an item's decorative features, but talked instead about its market appeal and price. When customers knew what they wanted, he let them have all the time in the world picking out the wares, but if a customer was hesitant, he harried him into making a decision. By the end of the process, every customer had ordered exactly what the wholesaler had chosen for him, felt pleased with their choices, and believed they had been given the best possible advice.

It would have been quite enough for her to spend the first few weeks simply peering inconspicuously over his shoulder, memorizing names and faces. She was astonished at how skillfully he handled the clients and wondered how she was ever supposed to be able to help in this regard. Whenever the bell over the door rang, she faded into the background as best she could to draw up lists or dust the shelves, only coming forward if Strobel called for her, which he often did. Every time, her heart leapt into her mouth.

"What is the meaning of all this? Have you some reason to creep into hiding like a mouse?" he asked irritably on the third day, when she had once again emerged timidly from behind the counter. "You are my assistant, so kindly behave like one!"

Johanna felt her hackles rise like a hedgehog's quills, in a mixture of stubbornness, fear, and uncertainty.

"And how exactly does an assistant behave?" she asked almost venomously.

Strobel smiled that baffling smile of his. "She assists."

He looked at her with condescension in his eyes, but Johanna did not turn away. Instead she tilted her chin and pressed her lips together. She would rather drop dead than ask him what "assisting" was supposed to mean. Instead, the next time the bell rang, she hurried forward to greet the customers with an obsequious "Good morning." They were merchants from Hamburg, she soon learned. While Strobel shook their hands, she took up a position by the samples table and held the chairs for the men to sit down. She wondered for a moment whether small talk about the weather was also part of an assistant's duties but decided against it. She didn't want to appear foolish. When Strobel gestured for it, she fetched the catalog of glassware and put it in front of the older merchant, assuming that he was the senior of the two. She also took care to smile the whole time. That was the hardest part, because it made her feel ridiculous. But the customers seemed to like it, which became clear when they reached the pages showing the gold-rimmed glass bonbon dishes and the older gentleman turned to her and asked her opinion. Johanna wasn't sure whether this was out of mere politeness or whether he was genuinely interested—or indeed whether she was expected to answer at all. She looked over at Strobel uncertainly, but instead of giving her any kind of sign, he gazed pointedly down at his gnawed fingernails. Had she really expected otherwise?

Rather than shooting venomous glances at her employer, she tried to concentrate on what the customers had just said. "We have certainly had several orders so far for the gold-rimmed dishes; it seems they are very much in demand. However . . ." she hesitated for a moment. "If I may make a suggestion . . . ?" The younger man had mentioned earlier that during the past Christmas season shoppers had disliked a particular vase that was too ornate for their tastes, and it had simply gathered dust on the shelves. "I would recommend this simpler style here." She pointed with her pen at a picture in the catalog. "Although very elegant, they are not as . . . ostentatious as the gold-rimmed dishes." It was all she could do to stop her voice from trembling.

"Miss . . ." The younger man was looking at Johanna with a question in his eyes.

"Johanna," she said quietly.

"Miss Johanna is right. Given the new taste for plain designs that our clientele have developed, we should steer clear of baroque golden ornamentation," the younger man suggested. "I believe that simplicity will be *en mode* this season."

The older man nodded.

"Good. Then we shall make it three dozen of these simple *bonbonnières* with lids, undecorated, the tall model on a slim stem," Strobel said, noting it down on his form. As he turned to the next page in the catalog, he glanced approvingly at Johanna.

She returned his look, her lips curling mockingly at the corners, and hoped that no one could hear how her anxiously hammering heart finally began to slow down.

◆　◆　◆

The next few weeks seemed to fly by. Johanna was soon so settled into her new routine that she could hardly remember a time when she had not lived in Sonneberg and worked for Strobel. She always looked forward to the weekends in Lauscha and to every minute she spent with Marie and Ruth, but she was equally eager to get back to work on Mondays. Every day with Strobel was different. Though she often still felt like an ignorant village girl—which she did her best to hide—she was learning new things every day. Perhaps it was because she put up such a show of confidence that Friedhelm Strobel seemed to assume that she could take any task in her stride. At first Johanna had broken out into a cold sweat every time he threw her in at the deep end the way he had with the Hamburg merchants, but in the weeks that followed her doubts died down. Strobel encouraged her newfound self-confidence, though the way he went about it often made Johanna queasy.

"Customers are like whores," he told her once. "They're there to be taken. And if you don't take them, then someone else will come along and do so." He peered at Johanna as he spoke. "You can do whatever you like with a customer, anything at all—except one thing: never let him leave without closing a deal." He spoke the words so vehemently that Johanna didn't dare ask what would happen if she ever did such a thing. It wasn't that she never asked questions. Quite the opposite in fact: whenever something struck her as out of the ordinary in his sales talk, she always asked Strobel about it afterward.

"If Mr. Hallweger liked those carved wooden spoons so much, why did you just put them aside? Wouldn't he have bought at least two dozen of those without needing to be talked into it?" she asked when a merchant from Konstanz had just left the shop. Strobel seemed pleased by her question and said, "Salesmanship is a constant give and"—he paused dramatically—"take!" Johanna looked baffled, so he added, "A customer must never get the impression we're only waiting for him to come spend his money." He grinned. "If I can make him think that my wares are worth more than his money, then he's like a batch of dough in my hands: I can knead and shape him at will." He gave her a sly look. "Why should I sell him those silly wooden spoons when he'll just as happily spend more on the more expensive model with the mother-of-pearl inlay?"

Whores! A batch of dough! Brrr! Johanna couldn't help but wish that Strobel wouldn't always use such horrid analogies. She didn't know whether it was the result of his expert salesmanship or his coarse comparisons, but from then on she always tried to size up a customer as soon as he walked through the door. Would he make up his mind quickly? Or was he more the dithering type? Did he want cheap goods or costly one-offs? Would he include her in the conversation or snobbishly ignore her? The longer she played the game, the more often she was right in her judgments.

Though the work was not physically demanding, in the evenings Johanna was as tired as if she had been hauling stones all day long. They generally shut up shop at seven o'clock and then ate supper together in the kitchen. Sybille Stein served up a meal before she left the house. Cold dishes, bread, and wine. At first Johanna always declined whenever Friedhelm Strobel tipped the wine carafe toward her glass. She wasn't used to drinking wine and was worried about getting tipsy. But since he kept on offering it, one evening she eventually let him pour her half a glass.

"So? How do you like it?" Strobel asked as soon as she had taken the first sip.

"It's sour," Johanna said, deciding that honesty was the best policy. When Strobel reacted with neither anger nor scorn, she added, "And it somehow tastes of wood." She took another sip. "Other than that, it's a good wine," she said lamely, hoping that she had not offended him.

Strobel bit at a hangnail. "The only way to appreciate some things, my dear Johanna, is to try them over and over again." He passed the carafe of water across the table to her.

Johanna took it gratefully. She didn't believe that she would come to like the wine any better if she kept on drinking it, but she kept this to herself.

From then on, Strobel made a habit of pouring her half a glass of red wine every day. And indeed: without even noticing it, Johanna got used to the taste of it.

The wine was not the only new taste. Instead of the simple fare she had eaten at home—bread and drippings or potatoes in all their variations—she was served unfamiliar pâtés and cheeses that looked anything but appetizing. Although Strobel explained that there were truffles in the liver pâté and that the goat's milk cheese looked like it did because of the blue mold, that hardly helped. What on earth were truffles? And why would she want to eat moldy cheese? More than once she was reminded of the grubby platters at Wilhelm Heimer's table, where everyone had to dig in with their own spoon. She had managed to overcome her misgivings about the food there, and she would do the same here. The surprise was all the greater whenever she found she liked the unfamiliar dishes.

"The wine goes well with this game terrine," she remarked one evening. "The woody notes suit the way the meat's been marinated. It tastes of the forest! Of wild berries and herbs, if you see what I mean . . ." She trailed off uncertainly.

Strobel smiled. "Those woody notes, my dear Johanna, come from the oak barrels that the wine is aged in before it is fit to be drunk. But yes, you're quite right, taken together they do taste of the forest."

Johanna didn't like the way he looked at her, nor did she like it that he called her "my dear Johanna." But that was just the way Strobel was.

Supper never took long. Once they had eaten, Johanna put the dishes in the kitchen sink and cleared the food into the pantry, which was a room all to itself. Strobel always protested that the housekeeper would do it the next morning, but Johanna couldn't bring herself to leave the table cluttered. By the time she went to her room, her eyes were drooping and her feet hurt from standing all day long.

It wasn't long before she turned out the light and dropped off to sleep. She told herself that she could explore Sonneberg when spring came, and then she would get to know the people and the shops.

25

Strobel was finally the one who made her get out and about. "What do you do every evening after supper?" he asked her one evening.

Johanna looked up from her smoked trout. "Nothing," she replied, taking another forkful of grated horseradish. She decided that she would buy some smoked fish for Ruth and Marie the following Friday. "Do you have more work for me to do? It would be no problem to—"

Strobel interrupted her. "No, I was asking rather more generally. You have a key to the back door after all. Why not use it every now and then? There's more to Sonneberg than just my house, as you know," he added, sweeping his arm around as though showing off the town. "It's about time you got out to see a little more of the world. Sonneberg is small enough, believe me! Why not go out to the café sometime? Or buy yourself a new dress? Or some other little treat? Some of the shops are still open in the evenings after we close. Or won't your wages allow that? Oh my, maybe *that's* the reason!" He struck his forehead theatrically.

Johanna looked on, perplexed, as Strobel got up and went over to the kitchen cabinet. When he came back, he had a banknote in his hand. "Go on, take it. Half of your probation is already over, so you deserve a little bonus. But only"—he drew back his hand—"if you use it to buy something for yourself and don't take it straight to your sisters in Lauscha."

◆ ◆ ◆

Strobel didn't stop at insisting she take the money. He also gave her the following Wednesday afternoon off. And so Johanna had no choice but to set out, her heart pounding.

"A good salesman must also know how to shop. It's only by understanding the customer's desires that we can satisfy them. Consider this afternoon off to be a continuation of your training." Strobel's words echoed in her ears as she left his shop. Straightaway two pedestrians barged right into her, talking heatedly to one another and hardly looking where they were going. It was March and the first foreign buyers of the season were in town. Uncertain where to go, Johanna stopped. Should she go to the grocery that she always went to on Fridays on her way home? No, Strobel wanted her to get to know new shops.

She felt nervous at the very idea of walking into a strange shop. What was she supposed to say? She knew nothing about shopping. She had always bought whatever she and her sisters needed—from groceries to the dark linens they used to sew their own clothes—in Lauscha's only general store. Mrs. Huber, the shopkeeper, knew that the Steinmann girls had little in the way of money, and she always showed them her bargains, not even bothering to fetch the more expensive goods down from the shelves. Ruth and Johanna had never even thought to ask Mrs. Huber what else she had in the shop.

Strobel had told her to buy herself a dress. Johanna made a face. She didn't even know how much a dress cost. Although she had made a habit of putting aside some of her earnings, she didn't want to break into her savings to buy a dress. Every penny saved felt like a measure of safety in a harsh world. She never wanted to be left with nothing again, as they had been after Father died.

Worried that Strobel might be watching from the shopwindow, she set off at last. Once she reached the marketplace, Johanna looked all around. Over on the other side of the square, she spotted a shopwindow with white blouses, skirts, and . . . wasn't that a blue dress hanging there, the very kind she had always dreamed of? Johanna found herself thinking of Ruth, who surely wouldn't hold back if she were here. She would go into the shop with her eyes shining, impatient to look at all the lovely things.

A couple of hours later, Johanna had a new blue velvet dress that fit her like a glove, and she also had a new insight: Strobel was right. Salesmanship was fun, but so was shopping. The salesgirl had been so polite!

She had fetched item after item from the stockroom and shown them all to Johanna. And she hadn't merely helped her try on the dresses, but described the merits and drawbacks of every piece she tried. Johanna was quite certain that she had chosen well in buying the blue dress. She could hardly wait to get back to her room and try it on again. The lady in the perfumer's had been just as friendly, even though Johanna only bought two little cakes of soap for Ruth and Marie. Only the old gentleman in the stationery shop had been rather rude, which was why she hadn't bought anything there. Ruefully she thought of how much she'd eaten into her savings in the last couple of hours. On the other hand she certainly wouldn't go shopping on such a scale very often.

Grinning broadly, Johanna set off back to Strobel's. What a shame that Ruth and Marie hadn't been here with her.

"So? How was your first trip to the emporia?" Strobel asked her that evening.

"Very nice," Johanna answered noncommittally. She had almost put the new dress on to wear at supper. But Strobel might think she was doing it on his account.

Strobel chuckled. "I admire your ability to dissemble, my dear! But you can't fool an old fox like me. There's a sparkle in your eyes that tells me you were unable to resist temptation."

Johanna frowned, but when she saw his grin, she found herself smiling as well.

"All right then, you've found me out. I really enjoyed my little outing."

Strobel looked as pleased as if he'd just closed a sale.

Johanna thought for a moment, then asked, "Why do you find it so important that I go shopping?" When he didn't answer at once, she thought aloud. "I mean, you're my employer. There's no reason for you to be so generous with your time and money . . ."

"No, no, no! You don't seriously imagine that I care whether you had a nice time?"

Johanna swallowed, suddenly afraid that she would make herself look ridiculous, or that Strobel would poke fun at her.

Friedhelm Strobel leaned across the table. "You are a beautiful woman. And you are also clever. What you lack—I will speak bluntly here—is a certain finesse. Not just in how you approach my clients, but also in how you carry yourself." He stood up and walked around her chair, looking her up and down as he did. "Just look at yourself! Your dress looks as though a cobbler made it in his spare moments. The material is so rough that I shudder to think what it must feel like on your skin." He shivered in exaggerated disgust. Then he pointed a finger at Johanna's head.

"And there—not a comb, not a clasp, not a sparkle to be seen! And it would do you no harm to visit a hairdresser. After all, your hair has a natural shine. God knows, we can't compare Sonneberg to such fashionable cities as Paris or Milan, but there is no need for our womenfolk to walk around in sackcloth and ashes."

"Well thank you for all this!" Johanna shot back. "And there I was thinking you had employed me for my *looks*." For all the sarcasm in her remark, she swallowed hard nevertheless. She took a sip of red wine and tried not to let her irritation show. She couldn't appreciate just then that Strobel was simply giving her his usual sales pitch—a mix of give and take. She could hear only his criticism and not his compliments. No finesse and a clumsily sewn dress—Ruth would have been livid! Her sister was fiercely proud of her skill with the needle.

Strobel took Johanna's hand almost as soon as she put her glass down. "I apologize if I have hurt you with my remarks. That was not my intention."

Johanna sat frozen, waiting for the opportunity to snatch her hand away, while Strobel talked on. "I am expecting some important customers in the coming weeks. Businessmen who are at home in the world's greatest cities. The competition does not sleep, not even here in Sonneberg. If the other wholesalers are not to knock me off my perch, I must always be on the alert. And in this regard, an elegant and worldly assistant can be of great help." He fell silent.

Johanna stared sullenly ahead. Despite herself, she saw the same image in her mind's eye that she had seen when Strobel first made his offer after Father died; herself, elegantly dressed in blue velvet, a pencil in one hand and a leather notebook in the other. A smile crept into the corners of her mouth. Well, she was a little closer to that picture now that she had bought the new dress.

Strobel was watching her carefully. "How others perceive us is entirely up to us. A man is what he makes of himself. He can be treated with respect and goodwill, or he can be crushed underfoot like a worm. If you want to be successful in the world of trade and commerce, then you must look successful. It rests in your hands. Do you understand what I mean?" he asked insistently.

Johanna nodded. In fact she only understood part of what he was saying. She—Johanna Steinmann from Lauscha—successful? But even if she couldn't quite say what Strobel was going on about, she had begun to glimpse the bigger picture. His criticism had woken something inside her for which she had no name.

Others would call it ambition.

◆ ◆ ◆

From then on Johanna went shopping in Sonneberg at least once a week. She decided that this new habit of hers had much less to do with Strobel's urgings than with the fact that she liked to look around the shops and admire the window displays. Of course she didn't always buy something; she was far too frugal for that. But most weekends she brought a little something home with her, a bag of coffee for Ruth or a few colored pencils for Marie. She bought Peter a thick notebook so that he could keep a record of how many glass animals he had sold, and although he grumbled something about "not needing that sort of thing" Johanna knew that she saw a gleam of pleasure in his eye.

Inspired by her experiences as a customer, she began to develop her own way of dealing personally with Strobel's clients. She greeted them with a self-assurance she had never shown before, recommending a purchase or pointing out its drawbacks, praising their decisions or occasionally even voicing criticism. The right words seemed to come easily to her tongue. More and more often, a customer with questions turned not to Strobel but directly to his assistant, who wasn't just good-looking but also showed a good grasp of what would sell. And more and more often, Johanna's suggestions ended up on their orders.

This growing self-confidence showed in her appearance as well. As she was treating herself to a violet-scented hair powder, the lady in the shop suggested that she might try parting her hair rather than scraping it back into a bun. Well, why not try something new for once, Johanna decided. She hadn't realized that the new style would better emphasize her even features. And when she chose a small rhinestone clasp, it was not because she had consciously thought about how it would offset the shine in her hair but simply because she liked it. She bought one for Ruth and one for Marie as well.

On another occasion she noticed that most of the skirts in the shopwindows no longer had crinolines. They still used yards and yards of material, but they were pinned and gathered up into artfully draped styles. She also noticed that the new dresses had more modest necklines. They were made with finer fabrics, designed to emphasize a lady's silhouette rather than show her skin. Johanna tried to copy the new fashion by pinning a swath of silk inside the neckline of her old dress and pinning its skirt in closer as well. Even if it was a clumsy piece of sewing, she had turned it into something she could wear for a while longer. For the first time in her life Johanna was paying attention to her looks. Her natural grace blossomed into an elegant simplicity that would be her trademark style from then on. But she was far too modest even to realize what had happened.

There were others, however, who watched Johanna's transformation with sharp eyes. Ruth and Marie noticed every new hairstyle and accessory. But it wasn't envy that made them tease their sister and sometimes even make cutting remarks—far from it. Rather it was a deep though unconscious fear that, having already lost their parents, they might now lose Johanna as well.

Even Peter found it harder each week to recognize the Johanna he had grown up with behind this new and elegant façade. He felt that she drifted further away from him with every scrap of fine clothing she put on. For the first time in his life, his steadfast belief that he and Johanna were meant for one another began to waver.

◆　◆　◆

Strobel congratulated himself on every sign of progress he saw in his assistant, for he did not miss the slightest change in her either. Friedhelm Strobel was in a springtime mood and decided to see her as a butterfly that must first spin a cocoon before revealing itself in its true splendor. Any interruption to the process would be dangerous for the butterfly, which would need large wings to be able to soar high above the humdrum world. In short: it needed time to grow.

And so Strobel waited for his moment. Waited, and watched. In the meantime the letters flew back and forth between Sonneberg and B.

26

The winter had overstayed its welcome like an ill-mannered guest, but in the third week of April it finally said good-bye. Bushels of yellow cowslips and blue squill blooming among the old grass heralded the coming spring, and virgin green buds were on the verge of bursting into leaf on every branch and treetop. Lovesick tomcats crept through the alleyways, keeping the good folk of Sonneberg awake at night with their serenades. Spring was on its way and Nature almost outdid herself in preparing the world for its arrival. It was simply inevitable that this unrest would spread to humanity as well.

◆　◆　◆

Though it was warm enough now to walk through the village without a jacket by day, it was still cold after the sun went down. And so—for want of any better place—Ruth and Thomas continued to meet in old Heimer's warehouse.

Ruth ran her tongue quickly over her teeth to be quite sure that she didn't have a breadcrumb still lurking there from supper. Then she began to nibble gently on Thomas's lip. She didn't know where she had gotten the idea; she was simply doing what felt right. She nipped at his upper lip. Then sank her teeth more firmly into his lower lip. The skin at the corners of his mouth was dry, almost cracked. Spontaneously, she ran her tongue over it and Thomas moaned. His desire was overwhelming. A glow of pleasure spread through Ruth's belly. She could have kept up with these games forever . . . unlike Thomas.

He pulled her head toward his quite suddenly. "Now we'll kiss for real," he whispered hoarsely.

His mouth clamped down on hers, and for a moment she was choked by the beery gust of his breath, which had only been a gentle spicy scent in the air before. His tongue prodded around in her mouth like a red-hot poker and swept roughly against her gums. Ruth tried to tip her head back a bit, but he held her tight. The delight she had just felt drained clean away.

Thomas's hands were busy with the buttons of her blouse. Ruth shuffled backward as far as she could. When the rough stonework of the wall pressed up hard against her spine, she shoved Thomas away with all her strength.

He looked at her in utter shock. "What is it now? Come back here!"

Ruth's heart was hammering. "You know very well that that's not what I want!" she said reproachfully, and began to button her blouse back up.

It was the same every time; she gave him a bit, and he only wanted more and more. But her anger vanished a moment later, and she felt miserable. Joost's warnings echoed in her ears again. "In this world, once a girl loses her honor she has nothing left to call her own!"

Thomas stood up and straightened his pants. "This is the last time I let you make a fool of me!" His voice was trembling. He stood before her with his legs wide apart.

Ruth found she couldn't stop looking at the great bulge between them.

"You shove your breasts at me week in and week out, but if I want to touch them I have to beg like a dog. You show off your legs but won't even let me set eyes on what you have between them. Let alone put my hand there. I've had enough!" He slammed his fist against the wall. The nearby shelves shuddered.

"If everyone else knew that you'd been leading me up the garden path like this, I'd never live it down! They all believe we've been at it for ages by now."

"What has everyone else got to do with us? I hope you don't talk to your buddies about what we do! This has nothing to do with anyone but you and me!" Ruth said heatedly. She toyed fleetingly with the thought of getting up and leaving—it might be better to have this conversation when Thomas wasn't in quite such a rage—but the moment passed and Ruth stayed where she was.

He went on as though she hadn't spoken. "They'll say you've got me whipped. They'll call me a gelding. If you plan to keep your maidenhead right down to Judgment Day, then just tell me now!"

Ruth flinched as though she'd been punched in the gut. Thomas had never spoken to her so coarsely before.

She was even a little afraid as she saw how greedily he was looking at her. Like a snarling beast that had fought long and hard for its prey. She tried to clamber to her feet, but all of a sudden he was on his knees in front of her.

"What do I have to do to show you that I love you? Tell me and I'll do it!" he pleaded. "I don't know how to treat a woman right. How am I supposed to know?" He shrugged convulsively. His blustering manner had melted away, and now he just looked helpless. "If you like, we can meet somewhere else from now on. I'll think of something," he said in a defeated tone. "Just tell me: What can I do to make you happy?"

Ruth looked at him, astonished. He had certainly changed his tune! Unsure as to how to answer him, she took a moment to shake out her skirt as though to free it of all the dust and grime. Should she use the opportunity she'd been given? Or should she wait for Thomas to come to the idea on his own . . . She would probably have to wait until Judgment Day herself before *that* would happen.

She went to him and put her arms around his shoulders. "Do you want to have me?" she asked, choosing her words carefully.

Thomas nodded. There was hunger in his eyes.

Ruth smiled quietly to herself. He must think he got where he wanted. Ha!

"I'll let you have me. And you don't even have to do anything to 'make me happy,'" she said, her voice as smooth and sweet as syrup.

She ran her hands along his forearms. Her lips drifted up his cheek to his right ear. "I love you, Thomas Heimer. And I want you to be my man." She pressed herself up against his bulging loins. Her legs were trembling, and she wondered whether she was going too far. On no account did she want to send him back into a fury. Then she slipped out of his embrace, gently but firmly, before it could turn into anything more.

Thomas could hardly believe his ears. "Ruth! Ruth! Ruth!" he whispered over and over again. He buried his hands in her hair and breathed in the vanilla scent of her hair powder. "You don't know how much I've wanted to hear those words!" He still had no idea how to read her mood, and he tried to push her down to the floor.

"Not here!" Ruth's voice sounded like the crack of a whip, stopping him instantly. "You don't really think I want to lose my virginity in this ghastly dust-filled room!" She took a step back.

"I'll sleep with you." And now *she* was looking at *him* like long-awaited prey. "But it will have to be in some lovely, romantic spot that suits the occasion."

He looked at her, baffled.

166

"And I have one more condition: I want you to tell everybody that we are engaged, at the village dance in May. You know quite well that I will only give my virginity to the man who's going to marry me." She raised a hand to fend him off. "There's no need to say anything now. You have more than a week to think it over, and I don't want your answer until then."

27

The sun was still shining weakly as Johanna set out for Lauscha. Just as he did every Friday, the slate-maker was waiting with his cart at the outskirts of Sonneberg to take her as far as Steinach. The man might even have agreed to take her all the way to Lauscha, but Johanna liked to walk the rest of the way; it took barely an hour and gave her a chance to enjoy the warm April air, which already held a breath of sweet summer temptation. And though she could easily have afforded it, she didn't use the railway either.

Strangely enough, she also needed time to get herself ready for Lauscha. Though they were only thirteen miles apart, the distance in her mind was much greater than that. More and more often these days, it felt to her like a journey from one world to another. Sonneberg meant something new every day—foreigners and new faces, interesting encounters and commerce. Lauscha was home. The same dear old place, day in and day out. Johanna loved them both and could hardly wait to be back with her sisters. But all the same her thoughts kept returning to her last conversation with Strobel.

"It might be that you will have to stay in Sonneberg next weekend," he had told her as she was leaving. "I am expecting some important clients from America. A gentleman by the name of Mr.

Woolworth will be visiting us for the second time. Last year he told me that he wanted to stop in Sonneberg for at least two days on this coming visit, and his assistant has confirmed this by letter."

Johanna had nodded. She had seen the letter with its faded American postmark.

"Unfortunately Steven Miles could not tell me in advance when exactly he and Woolworth would be coming."

Was it just her imagination, or had Strobel actually seemed a little nervous? "Of course I'll stay in Sonneberg next weekend," Johanna had answered. "But only if you tell me what's so special about this Mr. Woolworth."

So Strobel had done just that. "Well, first of all, I confidently expect to do a tidy bit of business with him," he had admitted, grinning. "Last year he bought hundreds of dolls, glass dishes, and glass candlesticks. All of them from the bottom of our price range, admittedly, but it adds up. Especially in the numbers that Mr. Woolworth orders. But that's not all. The man himself is something of a phenomenon. There is even a name for someone like him in the American language; he's called a 'self-made man.' The story goes that his parents had a potato farm and that he never learned a trade himself. He worked his way up from the very humblest beginnings with nothing more than ambition, and perhaps a certain hunger for power." Strobel had shaken his head, marveling. "You have to wonder at a story like that; he started with absolutely nothing and now he owns a whole chain of stores. It sounds like a fairy tale but it's the truth. Who knows what the man will do next?"

Johanna had never seen Strobel so carried away and he only very rarely expressed admiration for others. Next week was sure to be another interesting week, she told herself with delight.

From a ways off, Johanna saw Peter up ahead. He was waiting on the last hilltop before the descent into Lauscha, just as he did every

Friday. She waved at him. Then she stopped for a moment and rubbed her sore feet. The dainty new ankle boots she had bought were certainly elegant, and the black leather fitted her as snugly as a glove, but they were not particularly well suited to long walks. She walked on toward Peter, half hobbling, half hopping.

"So? How was your week?" they both asked at the same time and had to laugh. It was the same every Friday.

"*Chacun à son goût,*" Johanna said.

"I beg your pardon?" Peter asked, frowning.

"It's French, *monsieur*!" Johanna said, grinning. "We had the first French buyers in this week," she explained. "It seems that the roads are clear again."

"Just wait until we get a few more railways. Then the foreigners will be visiting all year round," he grumbled.

"I'm happy about every new line they add. How else are we going to get Lauscha glassware out into the big wide world?" Johanna replied. Then she told him about her meeting with the French clients.

"You've never see a married couple like the Molières. He must be at least eighty years old. It took him an age to get from the shop door over to the table. And guess how old Madame Molière is? All of twenty-five! Blonde as an angel and absolutely beautiful!" She looked expectantly at Peter.

"I daresay she didn't marry him for his blue eyes," he said dryly.

Johanna laughed. "I thought at first that it had to have been for the money, as well. But you should have seen the two of them! They spent the whole time billing and cooing. Strobel and I didn't know where to look. And then when they left, Strobel said, '*Chacun à son goût!*' which more or less means 'There's something for everyone.'"

"You and Strobel seem to get along well." The note of jealousy in Peter's voice was impossible to miss.

"That's putting it rather too strongly," Johanna said, struggling to give an honest reply. "I still find him a very odd man. Not that I want to change him to make him more to my tastes," she added hastily when she saw Peter's face cloud over.

"How exactly can you find Strobel odd when you spend all day, every day with him?" he asked suspiciously.

She gave him a friendly nudge. "I'll never know anyone as well as I know you. Now, let's get going before these shoes kill me. I can hardly wait to get the things off my feet."

She listened halfheartedly as Peter told her about an eight-year-old boy who had come that week to have a glass eye fitted.

"When I asked the parents why they hadn't gone to a glass-blower in the Black Forest—that would have been much closer for them in Freiburg, after all—they told me that they came all the way to Lauscha because of my good reputation!" Peter sounded as though he could hardly believe it.

Johanna looked askance at him. "Why are you always so ridiculously modest?" she asked mercilessly. By now every step she took was torture. *"If you want to be successful . . . then you must look successful,"* she heard in her head like an echo.

"What do you mean modest? Of course I feel proud when word gets around that I'm good at my job. But that doesn't mean that I have to boast about it like some people do. Or do you like braggarts these days? There are certainly enough of those in town."

Johanna had to hold back from making a sharp reply. Instead, keeping her voice soft and calm, she asked, "So? What is the latest news on your glass animals?"

Instead of taking up her offer of a truce, Peter snapped back, "You don't really care. What do a couple dozen glass critters mean compared to your commercial conquests?"

Johanna looked away. After a full week of hard work, the last thing she needed was to argue with Peter about his provincial views.

28

"Where's Peter?" Ruth asked Johanna as soon as the door shut behind her.

"He didn't want to come in," Johanna said offhandedly.

"You haven't argued with him, have you? You only see him on weekends, after all, and he . . ." Ruth's eyes followed Johanna as she bent down to unlace her boots. "New boots!" Peter was forgotten. "What lovely leather. And the heels!"

"Thank you for such a warm welcome home," Johanna answered dryly. "These things very nearly killed me," she said as she reached into her bag for the presents that she had brought. She didn't want her sisters to think she had forgotten about them.

While Marie opened her box of colored chalks with delight, Ruth looked skeptically at the little package that Johanna had brought for her. "Henna," she read aloud from the label. "What's this supposed to be?"

Johanna smiled as she explained.

"It's a powder that gives brown hair a wonderful red tint. The lady in the perfumer's told me that it comes from India. Apparently the women there use it. You put it into a bucket of water and then wash your hair with it."

Once the gifts had been admired, Ruth began to get supper ready. Johanna put her feet up and watched her sister work.

"Oh, it's good to be home again," she said, sighing pleasurably. Then she began to tell what had happened that week.

"Strobel said that although it was very sad of course that Sybille Stein's husband is at home with a broken leg, he simply can't allow her to leave the house every half hour to go and look in on him. Lunch has to be on the table when we shut the shop at twelve o'clock sharp." Quite without her noticing it, Johanna's voice had taken on a chiding tone.

"What if Heimer had said a thing like that? You would have spat fire at him," Ruth said from where she stood by the stove.

"That's different," Johanna said indignantly. "Strobel was quite right to scold her. After all, it's not as though I could take care of lunch."

"And would that really be so bad?" Ruth replied. "Are you too fine for that sort of thing now?"

"Nonsense! It's just . . . that isn't part of my job!"

"And what is your job exactly?" Ruth asked, standing on tiptoe as she moved around the oven. "Doing the chores, my goodness no!" Then she turned to Johanna and went on. "I've had to give old Edel a hand in the kitchen from time to time. I didn't think that was beneath me."

Marie looked up. "But if I remember right, you wouldn't say a word to Thomas the next day because he hadn't sprung to your defense about doing the kitchen work."

"That was for other reasons," Ruth spat out, her chin held high.

Johanna was too tired to carry on the argument, so she turned to Marie. "What are you drawing these days?" she asked.

"It's a design for a decorated vase," Marie replied. "Heimer said this week that we have to change with the times. And the taste these days is for glass that's painted like porcelain."

"So it is," Johanna said, relieved to have something she could agree with her sister about. "Though Heimer's wrong if he thinks that he's ahead of the times. Strobel says that frosted glass is old hat by now. Apparently the glassblowers were making it a hundred years ago—can you believe it? So Strobel says that it's more of a *renaissance*."

Marie looked blank, and Johanna realized that the word meant nothing to her. Hastily she kept on talking, trying not to sound like a know-it-all. "At any rate, painted glass is very much in fashion. Especially hunting scenes but anything with human figures as well. Sometimes I'm amazed what people spend their hard-earned money on. And I wonder where in the world all the glassware from Lauscha really ends up." She laughed.

"Let's have a look!" she said, moving Marie's arm aside to get a good look at the drawing. Two doves sat on a branch, their beaks together; beneath them was a curving, twining frame around the word "Inseparable."

"That's really lovely," Johanna said, impressed. "They look just like real doves!"

Ruth put down the teapot and sat down at the table.

"It's certainly a lovely design. But Madame isn't considering how hard it will be to paint these fine lines onto glass," Ruth said, pointing to the feathers.

Marie let the criticism bounce off her. "Maybe you'll be doing the silvering or the packing when we get round to making these vases."

"Oh, and wouldn't it suit you perfectly if you were the only one who ever got to paint."

Listening to the good-natured squabbling of the other two, Johanna suddenly felt strangely excluded.

"Thomas invited me to the May dance next week," Ruth suddenly burst out. Her cheeks flushed as she scooted closer to Johanna.

"Just think, we spinsters are finally going to get to see the May dancing! And that's not all. There's some other news as well—" She stopped abruptly, as though having second thoughts. "Oh, I'm so excited I can hardly sleep at night!"

Johanna raised her eyebrows. "It can't be all *that* exciting. And you?" she asked, turning to Marie. "Are you going to the dance as well?" She quietly congratulated herself on having bought new blouses for her sisters. They would be just right for the occasion.

"Of course she's coming," Ruth answered. "All three of us must go." She looked at the door. "I was expecting Peter to stop in. He . . ." She bit her lip. "I don't know whether I'm supposed to say, but he wants to invite you to the dance. He even asked me what kind of flowers you like." She giggled. "I can hardly wait to see what bouquet Thomas will give me!"

Marie smiled and gave Ruth a nudge. "As if it's the flowers you care about!"

Johanna looked from one to the other. Something was going on. What were these two making such a big secret of?

"I'm sorry to say that you mustn't depend on me to come to the May dance." When she saw her sisters' smiles freeze on their lips, she went on to explain about the American businessman, Woolworth, and the importance of his visit.

"I really am very sorry," she repeated, though in truth, she didn't feel she'd miss very much. Of course the May dance would be a fine opportunity to show off her new dress and let Wilhelm Heimer know that she was getting on very well without him. But annoyed as she was with Peter, she didn't want him asking her to the dance. Besides, this was the first time that Strobel had asked her to do anything out of the ordinary, and she was glad of the chance to repay some of his generosity.

She began to spread soft cheese with chives onto a thick slice of black bread. After a week of dainty dishes, she always longed for

Ruth's simple home fare on Fridays. She took a hearty bite of bread, savoring the cool, fresh taste of the white cheese on her tongue. After a couple more bites, she realized that the sound of her chewing was the only sound in the room. When she looked up, her eyes met Ruth's.

"You've certainly changed, Johanna Steinmann!" her sister said icily. "And you don't need to go kicking me under the table," she snapped at Marie, then turned back to Johanna.

"For the first time in ages we've got a reason to celebrate, and what do you do? Turn your nose up at it."

"But it's just a perfectly ordinary village dance!" Johanna said, feeling hurt. "None of us would have even thought of going while Father was alive. Don't you remember? It was quite enough for us to see all the drunken souls lying in the streets still sleeping it off the next morning while we walked to church for the May service. We used to have a good laugh at them!" Her smile faded as she saw Ruth's stony expression. Johanna sighed.

"If it wasn't such an important customer coming to visit . . ." She stopped when she noticed tears in Ruth's eyes. "Goodness gracious, what's the matter?"

Instead of answering, Ruth shook her head stubbornly.

"She and Thomas are going to announce their engagement at the dance," Marie told Johanna.

Blast it, so things were getting serious between those two. She put her hand on Ruth's arm.

"Then why didn't you say so? There was no way I could have known. I . . ." Before she could continue, Ruth shook off her hand.

"I don't even want you there. It's just a *perfectly ordinary village dance* after all. And Strobel's clients are so much more important, aren't they?" Now she was yelling at Johanna.

"Besides, just look at yourself!" She pointed at Johanna's head. "Your hairdo. Your dress. Your shoes. All new! We can't keep up, of course, oh no. You must have much better friends in Sonneberg, all running around dressed to the nines. What do you care whether or not I get engaged?" Her hand trembled as she poured herself a cup of chamomile tea.

The room was filled with the gentle calming scent of chamomile, but their argument was bitter. For a moment Johanna thought of the smell of incense in Strobel's shop. Tears pricked at her eyelids. It was all going wrong. They should be chatting about the engagement and what it would mean for them, but instead they were at one another's throats for no reason at all.

"How can you say such silly things? You know perfectly well that the two of you mean more to me than anyone in the world. And that I'll always want to know what's going on in your lives. And as for making new friends—do you really think I'm in Sonneberg to have fun? I have to work. Or do you think that Strobel pays me all that money for nothing?"

Ruth turned away.

Oh, her sister didn't want to hear about that, Johanna thought bitterly. No more than she wanted to acknowledge all the presents, though she was always happy enough to have them.

"You really could have said earlier that Thomas was going to make you his betrothed at the dance. It's an important step, isn't it? You can't have just decided it in passing. If you had given me a bit more time to—"

"Stop it, both of you. It's like listening to chickens henpecking each other in the farmyard!" Marie broke in. "Why don't you just say that you'll come?" she said, turning to Johanna. "It's sure to be a wonderful evening for all of us!" Her pleading gaze spoke volumes.

Johanna forced a smile. "Of course I'll come! I wouldn't miss Ruth's engagement for anything in the world! I'll think of something to tell Strobel." Helpless, she clapped her hands. "It's just . . . why does it have to be that weekend of all weekends?"

"Because you can't have a May dance except the first weekend in May," Ruth answered dryly.

They had to laugh at that. And then, luckily, the rest of the evening passed without further squabbles.

That night Johanna lay awake for a long time, listening to her two sisters breathing. Ruth's recriminations echoed in her mind. Had she really changed? She didn't think so. Deep down she was still the same old Johanna she had always been. The others simply didn't want to believe it.

Johanna rolled over onto her side and plumped up the pillow beneath her cheek. Why did nobody ask her how she really felt? How it felt to spend her nights sleeping in a strange room in a strange house? All on her own with no one to talk to. Neither Ruth nor Peter seemed interested in hearing that if she had changed at all, it was only because Strobel had mocked her for looking like a country bumpkin. And they never acknowledged that she came home faithfully every weekend even though she would have liked to stay in Sonneberg now and again. Instead they made a great fuss about how she was away all week. They only saw what they wanted to see, and she was gradually getting fed up with the way they took offense at every little thing.

29

The Heimer brothers were up in the forest with all the other young men from the village, felling a great tall pine tree with much yelling and laughter. The sounds carried down into the village on the warm spring wind, where the women were just as busy preparing for the festivities. Up in the woods, the men took turns swinging the ax at the tree, stopping after every few strokes to pass round the schnapps bottle. Thomas took a hearty swig before handing the bottle to the next man in line. He looked appraisingly around this patch of forest. Ruth was expecting him to come up with some idea or other. He wrinkled his nose. How had she put it? *"When I lose my maidenhood, it will have to be somewhere warm, clean, and dry. And romantic!"* Though she'd been looking at him with lovestruck eyes as she spoke, he hadn't been quite sure whether she was pulling his leg. But Ruth had meant every word. His gaze settled on a bench. The ground all around it was covered with a thick growth of moss and relatively few lumpy roots running through it. It was a beautiful spot where villagers and visitors liked to sit and look out at the landscape. Surely that would be *romantic* enough for her ladyship?

He furtively reached a hand around to his back. Once the other lads were all on their way downhill with the May-tree, he would put his rucksack with the blanket inside underneath the bench. He'd even thought to bring a couple of candles and some matches—after all, he wanted to see what he was getting.

He was caught unawares when the bottle came around to him again. The schnapps burned his throat as he tipped it down.

If it had been up to him, they could have gone right ahead in the warehouse. But if Ruth wanted romantic, then romantic she would have. He knew that many of the village lads would have long ago taken by force what he felt was long overdue. But that wasn't his style. Wasn't there an old saying that a horse bears its rider better when you take the trouble to break it in gently? Nobody wanted an old nag that shied in the saddle on every ride because of a bad first experience.

Thomas made a face. She was a sly little minx, though. Not only had she managed to put him off one more time last week in the warehouse, but she'd even gotten him to promise to marry her. He didn't know why he let Ruth run rings round him like that, but every man had to take the plunge at some point. And there were worse women to marry than Ruth Steinmann. She was something special for sure. She was like the first prize in the shooting match. He liked the image—both were hard to get, at least in his experience. Every year the village had a competition for all the men who fancied themselves to be marksmen, and every year he was always just a few points short for the grand prize. Well, never mind all that, for soon enough the prettiest girl in Lauscha would be his!

Somebody dug him in the ribs, interrupting his reverie, and Sebastian put the ax in his hands. He took one more swig of schnapps and then began to peel off the bark from the May-tree with short, shallow swipes of the blade. Ha! Short, shallow strikes! Things would be different tonight, of that he was certain!

◆ ◆ ◆

Ruth buttoned up her new blouse with trembling fingers. She was ready at last.

It had taken her much longer than usual today to bathe, powder her skin, wash her hair, and choose her clothes, but she was delighted with the result. She turned this way and that in front of the mirror, admiring herself and enjoying the way the mother-of-pearl buttons caught the lamplight. Thank heavens Marie and Johanna hadn't squabbled with her over whose turn it was to have the bathtub and the mirror. Both knew that today was her special day.

Neither one of them knew, however, about what else was planned for the night ahead. After the dance, which she and Thomas planned to leave at some suitable moment. Ruth passed her tongue over her lips. She could hardly wait to see what Thomas had prepared. Perhaps he had taken a room in one of the guest houses up in Neuhaus?

The fluttering in her belly intensified and her heart pounded. She forced herself to think about what would happen first, how that night he would finally tell the world he loved her. She could already see the looks on people's faces—the astonishment, the envy, the surprise!—when Thomas asked for her hand in marriage at the festival. Old Heimer would certainly be in for a shock. As would Eva, who would hardly be too pleased at the news that she'd be getting a sister-in-law. She would no longer be queen bee in the family hive.

Ruth pulled the door open to let a little more light into the bathroom. She took one last appraising look at herself in the mirror and was pleased with what she saw. Johanna had chosen the blouse well: the light shade of apple green went wonderfully with the red tint that the henna had given her hair. She blew a flirtatious kiss at her image in the mirror and then walked back toward the house, her head held high.

Wouldn't Lauscha have a surprise when the May dance turned into an engagement ball!

◆　◆　◆

As every year, the May dance took place on the foundry square. The May-tree was placed not in the middle of the square but off to one side so that it wouldn't get in the way of the masters pulling molten glass the next day. The bare trunk gleamed silvery pale in the hazy evening sunshine. Colored ribbons were wrapped all around the tree, their ends fluttering in the breeze. All the tables and benches were full and the beer flowed freely. The Steinmann girls were the only ones drinking water.

While Johanna and Marie sat at one end of a long table with Peter, Griseldis Grün, Sarah, and some others from the village, Ruth was squeezed in with Thomas and his brothers. At the head of the table sat Wilhelm Heimer, lording it over them all as head of the family.

Everybody seemed to be having a wonderful time.

Almost everybody.

Ruth looked around in a huff. Everyone at the other tables was already eating, but none of the Heimers had given any sign of wanting to go fetch the grilled sausages and potato salad that the landlord of the Black Eagle was selling behind the May-tree. Weber the baker had set out his stall next to him, and the smell of his leek tarts reminded Ruth that she had hardly had a bite to eat all day. At long last, Peter stood up and fetched food for everyone. But as soon as Ruth saw it in front of her, she couldn't swallow a thing.

"Oh, bratwurst! If you don't want those, I'll eat them." Before she knew what was happening Thomas had pulled her plate over and was biting into a sausage with every sign of enjoyment.

"Maybe there's something else Ruth wants instead," said the youngest Heimer brother as he grasped the fly of his pants.

Ruth shot a furious glance at Michel. Even though coarse language was the order of the day in the Heimer workshop, she still hadn't gotten used to it. Nor could she laugh at such crude jokes—the way Eva was laughing right now. Most of the jokes were aimed against the womenfolk, and were about breasts or backsides or other more intimate matters.

She gave Thomas a gentle dig in the ribs.

"When are you finally going to say it?" she whispered.

He looked at her as though he had no idea what she was talking about, but then seemed to remember.

"There's still time for that," he said, waving a hand. "The fun's only just starting."

By then the band had started to play. The instruments all seemed to be engaged in a battle over which one could drown out all the rest, and it soon grew so loud that nobody could hear a word anybody was saying. This didn't seem to bother anybody, however—they simply raised their voices and yelled louder. Ruth didn't know how in the world Thomas expected anybody to hear him. And soon nobody would even be sober enough to grasp the news when he gave it. One or the other of them was always getting up to fetch more beer. Even the women were drinking, although less than the men. Turned off by the bitter taste, Ruth hadn't taken so much as a single sip from the stein that Thomas had pushed across the table at her.

It was already nine o'clock by the time Thomas finally made a move to announce the news.

Ruth was shocked when she saw that he struggled to keep his balance as he got to his feet. Surely he hadn't drunk that much already, had he?

"Quiet, you lot. Thomas has something to say!" Michel called out, unexpectedly coming to his brother's aid.

Thomas took Ruth's arm and pulled her up to her feet beside him. "It's like this . . ." Tongue-tied, he pushed back a hank of hair from his forehead.

Ruth lifted her chin proudly. Now they would all hear it.

"Well spit it out and then leave it at that!" Sebastian yelled, lifting up his beer stein. "We're not here to make speeches after all!"

The others grunted their agreement. Ruth's smile turned sour.

Thomas glared at his brothers. "It's like this," he repeated. "Ruth and I, we . . ."

Now he'd gotten the attention of most of the table. Her sisters and the others at the end of the table were looking their way, Ruth realized. She beamed at Johanna and Marie.

"You all know the proverb, I'm sure: a cobbler should stick to his last. Which is why glassblowers should marry the daughters of glassblowers. Uh, that's to say . . ." His face flushed when he saw Sebastian and Eva glowering at him. "There are exceptions that prove the rule of course."

Everybody else joined in the laughter, and the awkward moment passed.

Ruth smiled indulgently. She had never imagined that Thomas would be so nervous!

"Anyway . . . We're not getting married, not today anyway, but engaged. This is it, today, this is our engagement." Thomas had hardly stopped talking before he began to sit down again, but Ruth held him firmly by the sleeve. Smiling, she glanced all around while Thomas's friends, astonished, began to call out congratulations. His brothers didn't say a word, but instead looked fixedly at their father, who rose heavily to his feet.

"My son and, eh, dear Ruth . . . Although as a rule I don't like it when something's decided without my say-so"—he wagged his finger as an exaggerated caution—"you have my blessing! And that means that I would like to welcome you, Ruth, as a member of our family here and now!" He raised his beer stein toward her.

"You two work well together, as we see every day in the workshop," he continued. "And although we're not there yet, after you get married, I wish you every success in another line of work. I'm an old man, and I wouldn't say no to a grandson or two!"

He basked in the laughter that followed his little speech, while Ruth hoped fervently that she wasn't blushing.

"You're getting married? When?" Eva asked in a voice like a pistol shot as soon as they sat down again. She was the only one who hadn't congratulated them yet.

Ruth held her breath. She was just as curious about Thomas's answer as all the rest of them. They hadn't talked about fixing a date for the wedding yet; she hadn't wanted to push him too hard.

Thomas looked at Ruth as though he'd never even thought about it. At last he said, "We'll see. Not today anyway." He laughed at his own joke, but when he saw Ruth frown in dismay he hastily added, "Let's drink to the prettiest girl in the village. My betrothed, and my bride-to-be, Ruth!" He held her hand up in the air as if she'd just won an arm-wrestling match.

Ruth beamed.

Wilhelm Heimer boomed out, "If only Joost could be here today!" and then her sisters and Peter, too, came over and hugged her.

Eva sat there with an icy look on her face as more and more people came across to the table to congratulate the newly engaged couple.

But soon the news seemed to lose its sparkle, and so did Ruth's mood. The men became ever more drunk with each hour that passed, their jokes ever more shameless. While Peter danced with

Johanna and Marie by turns, it never even crossed Thomas's mind to invite her for a dance. When she looked at the dance floor, Ruth tried to convince herself she was glad to have nothing to do with it; the planks were so roughly hewn that anybody dancing there had to be careful not to get a splinter in the soles of their feet. As for the music, Ruth wanted to clap her hands over her ears to shut out the monotonous blare of the trumpets. She had thought it would all be so different. And definitely more romantic. She had seen herself in Thomas's arms, a scented bouquet in her hand. He would make a beautiful speech about how much he loved her. There would be candlelight and violins. But who in this village had a violin? Nobody. She had to laugh at her own naïveté.

"So you're enjoying yourself at last! I thought I'd never see a smile." Thomas's breath stank of beer and the hand he cupped around her chin was unsteady.

"I'm tired. I want to go home," Ruth yelled in his ear. "Home," she said again, seeing that he couldn't hear her.

At last he seemed to catch on, but as he got up, he staggered so wildly that Ruth had to catch hold of him. She drew him aside.

"I think we should put off our little plan for another time!" she yelled in his ear. But when she turned to leave, Thomas grabbed her by the arm.

"A deal's a deal. Don't you go thinking you can talk me out of it again," he slurred. He stumbled and Ruth staggered a little. "You'll see. I've got everything ready. It'll be so *rrr*omantic!" Cackling, he rolled the *r* the way the Italian migrant workers on the railroad used to do.

"You're hurting me," Ruth said, digging her fingers into his hand to free herself. He couldn't possibly believe that she was going anywhere with him tonight. Not when he was as drunk as this.

"Maybe you need to treat her right for a moment!" Sebastian called out. "Some women want that sort of thing."

"I can give it a try." Instead of letting her go, Thomas put his other arm around Ruth's waist and began to dance about in the narrow space between the table and the bench.

Ruth realized that he no longer even knew what he was doing.

"Let me go this instant," she hissed, still trying to avoid making a scene. Thomas stumbled again, this time backward onto the table, almost pulling Ruth down with him.

Ruth felt a surge of panic rising within her.

"Hey, Thomas Heimer," came a voice from behind her.

It was Peter. He looked down contemptuously at the man sprawled backward on the table.

"Even if you and Ruth are engaged now, that doesn't give you the right to mistreat her. If she wants to go, you let her go. And you do it right now!" Peter looked as though he meant every word. Thomas released Ruth's arm.

She didn't know where to look. There was such eager anticipation on the faces all around. As though they were enjoying the spectacle.

Ruth had never felt so humiliated in her whole life. But all the same, she wanted everyone to see how well suited she and Thomas were to each other. She wanted the other women to envy the future Mrs. Heimer.

After that it all happened much too fast: Thomas swung his fist and hit Peter. Later, Ruth would still wonder how he had even managed to do such a thing in his condition. Peter hesitated for only a moment and then hit back. The women leapt aside, shrieking. The other men's eyes gleamed, and suddenly they decided that someone had knocked over a beer, or jostled them, or simply looked at them wrong—and those became reasons enough for a brawl. Without any warning, it was in full swing.

30

"So how was your sister's engagement? Or rather, I should ask: How was the May dance?"

Johanna had hardly taken off her jacket and Strobel was already hurling questions at her. Usually he wasn't the least bit interested in what she did in her free time in Lauscha, so she was not ready for his interrogation.

Strobel sniggered. "Let me guess," he said, putting his finger to his lips in an exaggerated gesture. "The music was awful, the dance itself was provincial, and everyone was horribly drunk by the end. I wouldn't be surprised to hear that the engagement was a fiasco because the groom-to-be was drunk!"

Johanna's cheeks flushed.

"If you really must know, it was absolutely horrid! I'm sorry I even went," she said vehemently, as though Strobel had talked her into it. She tried to ignore the look on his face, which unmistakably said *I told you so*. The best thing was to forget the whole weekend as quickly as possible.

"Did Mr. Woolworth come in the end?"

Strobel nodded. He had the look of a cat that'd gotten into the herring tub on the sly.

"Here's his order. It must be dealt with today."

Johanna reached unsuspectingly for the list, a standard form that detailed the articles a client wanted, the suppliers, prices, and delivery deadlines. She found herself holding not one sheet of paper but three, and one more had dropped to the floor.

There was no way that all this could be just one order.

She picked up the sheet that had fallen and gazed at the pages incredulously. Dolls, toys, glassware, wood carvings—this man Woolworth seemed to want everything they had to offer. She swallowed when she saw what was written on one line.

"Five *hundred* Parisian dolls?"

Strobel grinned in response to her astonishment.

Johanna leafed through the list, reading each item silently to herself. When she looked up again, her face showed a whole range of conflicting emotions; she was speechless at the quantities involved, baffled by some of the wares on the list, and shocked at the final cost. She had to check three times before she could accept the sum involved. Holding the sheets in her hand, she went across to the catalog table and sat down.

Strobel followed her and sat down too.

For a moment Johanna struggled to collect herself. When she looked up and said, "Why wasn't I here? Woolworth must really be a man of great standing. Who else could be sure of selling such quantities?" She pointed quite at random at a line of the order.

"Two hundred Sonneberg dolls, the 'babe-in-arms' model. Heinrich Stier will weep tears of joy when we give him the order."

"I told him from the start that he'd score a success with that style of doll," Strobel said dismissively. "Where else in the world do dolls have that same rosy glow on their little faces? Nowhere!" he said, answering his own question.

"His visit must have lasted for hours. Did Sybille Stein manage to come by and look after you? And his assistant? Did he . . ." She flushed at the thought that it should have been her job to make coffee for the American customers.

Strobel interrupted her with that odd laugh of his. "If I were to tell you every detail of my client's visit, which I will grant you was certainly quite remarkable, then we would be sitting here just as long as Woolworth and I sat together." He took her hand with his bony one.

She was just about ready to let him call her "My dearest Johanna," thinking that she would get to hear one or two anecdotes, but then Strobel said, "You never get a second chance in life!" He sighed, then clapped his hands together theatrically. "If I had not considered your presence in Sonneberg . . ."

Johanna wished fleetingly that Strobel had simply ordered her to stay, rather than letting her take the time off. Then she scolded herself for such childish thoughts. She had no choice but to sit there and hear him preach about missed opportunities and making the wrong decision. But she consoled herself with the fact that at least he had let go of her hand.

"Oh and by the way, I will be gone for two weeks at the beginning of June—that is, if my travel plans do not conflict with your own calendar," he added, with more than just a touch of sarcasm. "You will deputize for me while I am away. We will discuss all further details when the time comes."

Johanna's first impulse was to say, "I can't. I don't know nearly enough about the business. And besides, I don't dare!" Instead she nodded obediently. She wouldn't be so quick to refuse any more of the chances he offered.

While Strobel welcomed new clients and helped them with their orders, Johanna was busy all day with the Woolworth order. All of the pieceworkers and suppliers whose articles Woolworth wanted had to be notified. Strobel had a system for this, and Johanna entered how many pieces of every style each supplier had to deliver with the prices and the deadlines. She had to be absolutely sure not to mix up any names or item numbers. To her, this work was pleasure rather than business. Every form she filled came with a name, a family, a story of its own. By the time she had finished, she had written out one hundred and thirty individual commission sheets. That would give a lot of families work for the next few months, she told herself happily. She could hardly wait to give the sheets to the messenger women to take round to the villages.

While almost every household in Lauscha made money by blowing glass, in Sonneberg they earned their daily bread by making dolls. And just as with the glassblowing, here, too, there were specialists for every step in the process: One man would spend his days fitting the glass eyes into dolls, though the eyes themselves were made in Lauscha. The next man painted lips in just the right shade, while another painted eyelashes and eyebrows on the bare faces. There were also seamstresses, knitters, shoemakers, and handbag makers—all for the dolls. Though Strobel insisted that Sonneberg dolls were world famous, the doll-makers hadn't had an easy time of it in recent years. The French were pushing their way into the market by ordering porcelain heads from Sonneberg and then having female convicts finish the dolls for no wages. The foreign competition made an order of this size all the more important for the local doll-makers.

There was plenty of Lauscha glassware in the Woolworth order too. Not for the first time, Johanna thought what might happen if only she could persuade Peter to put his glass animals into Friedhelm Strobel's hands. They would very likely be setting off for America as well. But no, Peter had dug in his heels. "Your Mr. Strobel is far too fine for a raw beginner like me. No, no, I'll take them to another wholesaler," he had answered, ignoring Johanna's argument that Strobel had already helped more than one unknown artisan get his start in the business.

But then she realized that there was another name missing from the list. Johanna's mood brightened. "At least old Heimer won't be cluttering up foreign shelves with his gimcrack," she muttered to herself somewhat spitefully.

◆　◆　◆

The day's customers had brought him a good deal more business, and Strobel was in an expansive mood at supper. He had ordered the housekeeper to serve fish in a green herb sauce. Then he opened a bottle of champagne to go with it. If he were to be believed, rich people all over the world drank practically nothing else. He had sent Johanna down to the cellar on occasion to fetch a bottle when there were important clients visiting, but she herself had never tasted this luxury before.

Cheered by her long day's work and relieved that Strobel was not angry at her, she took a long sip. The champagne tasted a lot like white wine, though much . . . bubblier. Feeling the thousands of bubbles bursting on her tongue, she laughed.

"Ruth would certainly like this! She's always had a taste for the out of the ordinary."

Strobel laughed too, but a moment later, he said, "My dear Johanna, you really must stop comparing yourself to your sisters all the time. You are not like them. I am quite sure that this past weekend was ample proof of that." And with that, he went about skillfully filleting his fish.

Embarrassed, Johanna took another sip, but the bubbly suddenly tasted sour. Had Strobel already heard rumors about the fistfight? Or was he perhaps clairvoyant?

Strobel lifted the backbone out of the fish and set it on the side of his plate, then went on, paying no attention to her evident disquiet. "Often enough we allow a sense of obligation to force us to do things we have no desire to do on our own. In your case, I am of the opinion that you should gradually stop playing nursemaid to Ruth and Marie."

Johanna looked up. *What would Peter say if he ever found out that he and Strobel actually agreed on something?*

"But who's to say that isn't my purpose in life? I'm the eldest, after all, and that means I am responsible for my younger sisters."

"There are other ways to accept responsibility," Strobel retorted, raising his eyebrows. As always when he wanted to make a point, he leaned over the table. His breath smelled of fish and parsley sauce.

"Your purpose in life is not to serve others. Your purpose is to lead. You should not run around after your sisters all the time—rather *they* should run after *you!* Just look at yourself: you are a strong woman. But if you jump to attention every time Ruth or Marie or anyone else whistles for your help, you simply make yourself ridiculous."

What did Strobel think he was doing, shoving his nose into her affairs like this? She didn't like the way he talked about her sisters either. But if she were honest with herself, she often felt silly for scurrying faithfully off to Lauscha every weekend. She said, "Perhaps you find it ridiculous that I love my family. But I can't change that. After all, I'm just a simple village girl. And I'm not as strong as you say. If I were, your clients wouldn't like it. Men prefer women who smile nicely and agree to everything, do they not?"

"That may be true for the common herd," Strobel said dismissively. "However, there are also true connoisseurs who are man enough to want to take on a strong woman. And I'm not just talking about business here . . ." he added, drawing out his words.

The conversation had taken an unpleasant turn. At the very least, it was becoming personal. Embarrassed, Johanna picked at her fish, which lay untouched on her plate. There were a thousand questions she wanted to ask about his travel plans, but she didn't know how to change the subject. "Most men don't care for it when a woman has opinions of her own. Never mind a strong will," she replied sharply.

Strobel shrugged.

"As I have said, there are men, and there are men. I like it very well indeed when a woman shows her dominance. In my experience, a man may even find great"—he hesitated for a moment, as if looking for the right word—"pleasure in submitting to such a woman. Putting himself into her hands. Of course both the man and the woman must show certain qualities, but this is not quite so rare as you may think. The phenomenon can even be found in many works of world literature. Perhaps I should give you one such work to read."

His mood brightened suddenly. "Yes, that's an excellent idea," he said, greatly pleased with himself.

Johanna frowned. What on earth was Strobel talking about? She cleared her throat and pointed at the fish with her fork.

"Perhaps you could show me again how to get the bones out? Otherwise I'll be sitting here till midnight with this plaice!"

◆ ◆ ◆

Strobel watched thoughtfully as Johanna vanished into the dark hallway.

She had shied away so quickly when the conversation became personal that he had no doubt that she was still a virgin. All the same, he was certain that she had at least an idea of what he had been talking about.

He poured himself more champagne but did not drink it. His thoughts were so tantalizing that he needed no further stimulation.

Johanna, his assistant. And his key to freedom.

In less than three weeks it would be done; he would travel to B. while his business thrived under her care. He shifted about on his chair in a fever of anticipation. A kaleidoscope of gruesome yet gorgeous visions unfolded before his mind's eye. In his eagerness he didn't even notice at first that some of these images were of Johanna and no one else. Then he heard himself laugh.

Why not, after all?

Why shouldn't he mix business with pleasure? Had that not been his intention from the start? Which he had only discarded—at least until today—because the matter of B. had arisen in the meantime? Could he not initiate Johanna into the game, at least a little ways? The risks were great, he had to admit; in the worst case, she would be shocked by the suggestion and give notice, and then he would have lost a capable assistant.

All the same, the thought of introducing a woman whose sensual appetites still slumbered into his kind of pleasure was ever more enticing. It was something he had done only once before, but at this moment, he didn't want to remember the catastrophe that had resulted. As a rule, the women he played with were all more experienced at the game than he was. Perhaps that was another reason he did not know how to shift what was—so far—a business relationship to the next level. He gnawed at his lower lip until he tasted the familiar metallic flavor. Should he take her out on the town? Whisper sweet words in her ear? Shower her with gifts?

Strobel leaned back in his chair. The problem was that he had never been interested in such conventional flirtations. He saw no appeal in charming Johanna with flattery. He had no desire to see her eyes light up as he presented her with a gift. He had no interest in Johanna as a woman with feminine feelings. It was her stubbornness and contrary ways that made her desirable. Her fearlessness, coupled with a natural arrogance that was seldom found in a woman. Of course he knew that part of this arrogance was simply a show. That Johanna wanted to mask her insecurities. But that was quite permissible. More than that, it was precisely what made the whole matter appealing.

His eyes drifted down the hallway toward Johanna's room.

He stood up abruptly before he could lose himself entirely in such fantasies. On his way back into the shop, he scolded himself for having wasted even a moment on such thoughts.

"Only a fool plays with fire in his own house!"

He had already lost his self-control once, back in his old life—and lost everything else as well. Did he want to risk the same thing happening again? It was not difficult to answer that question—only fools made the same mistake twice.

31

At last the house was empty. Sometimes her sisters could be hard work. Especially Ruth. The way she had been flapping about just now! As though she had some important meeting to attend. Not that it made any difference whether she went out for her stroll with Thomas a few minutes earlier or later. It was still a mystery to Marie what Ruth saw in him—or rather, after the dance and the engagement, it was even *more* of a mystery. It was lucky that the fistfight hadn't led to anything worse.

But enough of that, Marie told herself. She didn't want to waste a valuable evening alone thinking about what happened when people drank too much beer. All the same her thoughts drifted back to the May dance. She couldn't stop thinking about the way the women's skirts had swung as they danced. Like bluebells in the breeze. Their layers of petticoats formed waves—sometimes around their knees, sometimes all the way up to their hips, depending on how fast the women spun. There was such grace and joy in that image. Marie chewed on the end of her pencil. There had to be some way to capture those swinging, curving shapes in glass. For a while she let her pencil wander over the paper as if it had a will of its own. The result could sometimes be extraordinary but not today. Neither she nor her pencil knew what the final shape should be. A drinking goblet with a curved rim? A dish made of fused layers of glass, with the pattern carved through from one layer to the next? A compact?

Marie briefly considered going over to visit Peter. When he made one of his glass animals, he didn't always know at the outset what shape the end result would be. But she didn't even know how to phrase her question. "How do I capture the shape of swinging?" Marie had to laugh. Shaking her head, she put down her pencil and got up.

A moment later, she was in Father's workshop. Hesitantly, as though worried she might see a ghost by their light, she lit the lamps. Scolding herself for her overactive imagination, she went over to Joost's bench and lamp.

The glass rods, tools, and gas burner were still in place. The only indication that his workbench had been abandoned was the dust that lay over everything like a silken cloth. Marie sighed and wiped away the worst of it with the sleeve of her dress. Ever since they had started working for Heimer, there had been simply no time to keep the house clean.

Obeying an impulse, she fetched her sketching things and sat down at Joost's bench. Straightaway she felt better than she had at her improvised place at the kitchen table.

For a while she simply sat there enjoying the silence. She dearly missed working in this room. How different it was from the Heimer workshop, with the din of the three lamps burning, all the people, Eva's chatter, the loud singing, the hurrying and scurrying. She shook her head. The work was different too. Heimer had more and more orders coming in. The lists that he handed out to his three sons and the hired hands every morning described what the customers wanted down to the last detail. And in the evenings the old man checked whether it had been done properly, again down to the last detail. If not, they would work late. There was no time left for Marie's own designs.

Perhaps that was why her imagination was letting her down now? It was like an old door that nobody ever opened; the lock would gradually rust over until it was jammed tight shut. It was up to her to make sure that didn't happen.

She shut her eyes and let her thoughts roam free.

In the Heimer workshop, everything was aimed at making products. And everything he produced—no matter how ornately decorated the drinking glasses or dishes or goblets were—was expressly made to serve a purpose.

Maybe that was it! Maybe she had to free herself from the idea of use and function. Marie's eyes widened. Suddenly her mouth was watering, so much that she had to swallow hard. What was the opposite of useful? Not useless, surely? No, she mustn't be discouraged, she had to keep thinking.

She wanted to capture a curve, a swing. A movement that had made her smile, that made her feel joyful. Perhaps there was no way to do this on the base of a dish. Perhaps the only way to capture feelings was to create something with no function in mind. Something that existed for no other reason than to please the eye and lift the heart. The idea of blowing glass as a work of art, for its own sake, with no practical purpose was risky, however.

If she were to ask the glassblowers of Lauscha whether they saw what they did as a craft or an art, the overwhelming majority would say the former. Marie knew of one man in the village who called himself an artist. His name was George Silber—he insisted that people pronounce his name with a soft *g* in the English manner—and he traveled a great deal. On the rare occasions when he was back in Lauscha he held forth about all the international exhibitions where he showed his pieces to a select audience. The rest of Lauscha laughed at him and his shapeless glass figures, which he gave odd names like *Venus Awakening* or *Zeus at Daybreak*. Art? Well, if there were any such thing as art, it meant something quite different to them. A drinking glass painted with a wreath of lily of the valley—that was art. Or a figure of a stag made using the free-blowing technique.

Anything else was just a waste of time.

So what if it was? Marie decided that as long as she liked whatever she drew or dreamt up, nobody could laugh at her for it. Nobody had to agree to call it art.

Thoughtfully, she opened her sketchpad. Now she was ready to let her pencil go wherever it wanted. This time she felt even after the first few strokes that her pencil was guided not by the hand that held it but by some power deep within her. The feeling was not entirely new, but she had never known it to be so strong before. She gave herself up to it entirely, trusting its strength.

She drew and drew. Her hand picked up the pencils, color after color, without conscious thought. Instead of putting each one back into the box, she let them drop where they would. Soon the workbench looked like a battlefield, strewn with colorful spears. Marie shaded and crosshatched, blurred the lines or drew them in more strongly.

All the while she was thinking of the gas flame and the glass rods. Glass was difficult to work with, perhaps more difficult than any other substance. Joost had said this over and over again, even when they were children; if a glassblower didn't hold the rod over the flame for long enough it was sluggish and recalcitrant. Heat it up too much though and it flowed and dripped like honey. Its transparency was unique—Marie couldn't think of any other material that could match it in this respect—but that very quality tested a glassblower's skills anew every day, for every little mistake was clear to see. There was no way to hide even the least little bubble or knot or bump. A wood carver could cut away here and there. Iron could be filed down or wrought anew, but glass had to be perfect. And as Marie saw it, a sketch was worth nothing if it could not be made at the lamp.

By the time she finished, her fingers were trembling and then some. She put her hand to her mouth as though she wanted to hide even from herself that she was so awestruck. But the shape she saw on the page in front of her was easily described. She had drawn a spiral. A spiral in all the colors of the rainbow, growing ever brighter and fresher as her eye followed it upward. At the very top was a dainty little loop from which it could be hung. In a window for instance. Or from the ceiling.

A glassblower would have to know his trade well to blow and shape such a spiral.

A glassblower would also have to know how to make the rods of differently colored raw glass melt cleanly into each other.

But all that was just tricks of the trade. Technique.

Marie was captivated by something else, however, something that could not be put into words; she could imagine the colorful light that this spiral would beam into a room when it caught the sunlight. She could almost feel the movement, turning and turning, that the spiral would make when tapped with a fingertip. Images and emotions showered down upon her like a warm summer rain. Marie leaned back on her chair and savored it all.

She saw a housewife, tired from the day's never-ending chores and work. A couple of children clung to her skirts as she elbowed the door open, a basket of laundry in her hands. And then she would catch sight of Marie's spiral hanging in the window of the room. Even this first glance would lighten her mood a little. Perhaps it would be enough for her just to look at the spiral. Perhaps she would run her finger over its smooth, cold curves. A smile would flit across her lips. And when she left the room, there would be a new lightness in her step. Perhaps the smile would even stay with her for a while.

Marie opened her eyes again.

She shivered.

A warm summer rain might be refreshing, but it still left you wet and cold. They were daydreams, nothing but daydreams!

Wilhelm Heimer would laugh if she were to show him her spiral. One of his sons or Eva might even make an indecent joke out of it—Marie believed them entirely capable of it. There was not a glassblower in Lauscha—not one—who would take a chance on making her design a reality. The best thing would be to shut it away in a drawer. Marie laboriously collected all her pencils and packed them away.

She put out the light in the workshop, then stood in the doorway for a moment and looked longingly over at Joost's gas burner. That flame had the power to breathe life into her pictures. But she, Marie Steinmann, had no such power.

If only she knew how to blow glass!

32

Once all the roads outside of town were open for travelers again, the buyers came to Sonneberg in droves. Over the next few weeks, the bell over the shop door tinkled so often that Johanna wondered how it could ever have startled her back when she was new in the job. There was still a mountain of paperwork to get through for the Woolworth order, but she kept having to put it aside to help Strobel. Though she delighted in being part of the hurly-burly of business life, she had to admit that she had rarely worked so hard in her life. In addition to the workload itself, Strobel was visibly on edge. As the date of his departure drew nearer, he grew increasingly irritable. Johanna would never have thought such a self-possessed and worldly man could lose his composure so easily.

When he finally marched off to the railway station one Monday morning, Johanna heaved a secret sigh of relief. If he had tried to tell her one more time what to do while he was away, then *she* would probably have left town. He warned her at least half a dozen times to keep a close eye on the cash till. And the catalog. He was practically sick with worry that his competitors might find some way to spy on his samples book while he was away. In the end he had put Johanna herself so much on edge that she took the cash and the catalog with her into her room every night and hid them under her bed.

Over the next few days, however, Johanna realized just how different it was to have to shoulder all the decisions herself, great or small, rather than just carrying out orders. Should she let Monsieur Blatt from Lyon have that discount he wanted, even though it was more than Strobel had told her to allow? Which glassblower should have the order for five hundred silvered goblets now that Bavarian Hans had sprained his wrist and couldn't take it on? Was it her place to tell off Sybille Stein for neglecting the housekeeping ever since Strobel had left?

All in all, though, the first week passed without any major disasters, and Johanna was pleased with how she had handled her new role. All the same, by Friday she was exhausted, so she spontaneously decided to stay the weekend in Sonneberg for the first time. She scribbled down a quick note for her sisters and gave it to one of the messenger women who came by the shop every day at noon.

When she went to bed that evening at eight o'clock instead of setting off for the long trip home, it was an unfamiliar but pleasant feeling. That she didn't have to get up at any particular hour the next morning was a great relief.

By the time Johanna finally awoke the following day, it was noon. She staggered to her washstand and looked at herself in the mirror incredulously, shocked that she had slept so late. Sybille Stein did not come in on weekends, so there was no hot water either. She splashed her face with cold water until she was well and truly awake. Then she put up her hair, chose a cream lace collar for her blue dress, and got dressed. It was a strange and seductive feeling to have a whole day ahead of her and no need to hurry or fret.

She was just on her way to the kitchen when a knock at the door made her jump. She thought of the money and the catalog under her bed—thieves!—but came to her senses a moment later. Thieves would hardly come knocking. Annoyed at her own fearfulness, she went to the door and pulled it open.

"Ruth!" She felt a chill in her bones. "What's wrong? Is it Marie? Did something—"

"Everything's fine," Ruth hurried to reassure her. "We got your message. And I thought, if you're not coming to us, then I'll just come to you."

Johanna's heart slowly stopped hammering.

"You certainly wouldn't come to visit me out of sheer affection," she said suspiciously. "There's another reason, isn't there?"

Ruth raised her eyebrows. "And what if there is? Do I have to tell you out here in the street?"

◆　◆　◆

"You're going to have a baby?"

Johanna couldn't believe what she had just heard. She didn't *want* to believe it.

"But how could that happen? You're not even married yet!"

Ruth laughed bitterly. "Do you think that not being married can protect a woman from pregnancy?" It was just like her high-minded sister to make such a remark.

Johanna shook her head brusquely.

"Rubbish. But . . ." She didn't even know herself what she had meant by that. "What does Thomas say about it?"

Ruth sat up straight. "He's pleased as Punch," she said. Seeing the skepticism in Johanna's face, she added, "No, he really is! If I hadn't sworn him to silence, he'd be going round telling the world right now that he's going to be a father."

Ruth decided to keep to herself just how Thomas had taken the news of impending fatherhood. *"Jackpot, first shot!"* he had said, strutting like a cockerel. Instead she said, "Sebastian and Eva have been trying to have children for years now without any luck, so you can see why he's so pleased. There's going to be a little Heimer at last! And Thomas has even been to see the pastor. He decided that we should get married at the end of June. Which suits me. The sooner the better. He can hardly wait to tell his father the good news."

"Old Heimer will have some idea what's coming when you suddenly rush to get married so soon after the engagement. The old fellow can put two and two together."

"I don't know about that." Ruth shrugged. She didn't care what the old man thought. "Anyway, I don't want to stand in church with my bump showing. Nobody needs to know that we've already . . ."

Johanna got up and went to the calendar that hung next to the kitchen dresser. She leafed through it quickly and then said with relief, "What luck—Strobel will be back by then. Otherwise I would have missed your wedding."

"You'd have me to answer to if you did," Ruth said, then she clapped her hands. "So now we're going shopping. I'm going to buy myself a dress, and Thomas says he doesn't care how much it costs."

Johanna looked at her askance. "Well, he really does seem pleased."

If Johanna had ever thought that she was a fussy shopper, she soon learned better; it took several hours for her sister to select a dress in wine-red taffeta, and during that time not a single item in the shop escaped her scrutiny. Red was the usual color for a bride to wear in Germany, but she only came back to the dress after looking at almost everything else as well.

It wasn't difficult to persuade Ruth to go out to one of the town's many restaurants after that. Tired but happy, they sat at a table by the window and enjoyed the warm sunshine that filtered through the lace curtains. Ordering coffee and the day's special—a kohlrabi bake with sausage and potato—they felt like women of the world. Three other tables were occupied by women, two of whom were messengers Johanna regularly sent to the villages. They waved at her from their table. While Johanna was relieved to realize it was not unusual for women to eat out at a restaurant, Ruth simply assumed that her sister did this every day.

When their food came, they ate hungrily. Because it was a special day, they also ordered a slice of the chocolate cake, which had tempted them from its stand. But once the cake was in front of them, neither of them touched it for a while. It was Ruth who spoke aloud what they both were thinking.

"Isn't it odd? Just six months ago, we didn't know where our next meal was coming from. Simple village girls, we were. And now we're sitting in a restaurant in Sonneberg planning my wedding."

"Things certainly do change—sometimes even for the better," Johanna said, digging her fork into the cake happily. "So? What's it like, sleeping with a man?" she asked.

Ruth looked at her incredulously. Had Johanna really asked such a question?

"If you'd rather not talk about it . . ."

Did she want to talk about it? Ruth was torn. She wanted very much to tell *someone* what it had been like. But was Johanna the right person to talk to?

Her hesitation made Johanna waver too. "I only ask because of the pregnancy . . . Couldn't you have put Thomas off a little?"

"Putting a man off isn't so easy. When you're in love, the moment will eventually come when it really gets difficult. But you wouldn't understand such things," Ruth replied rather condescendingly.

"No, you're right, I really can't imagine that sort of thing," Johanna agreed. She threw up her hands in an almost comical gesture. "Mind you, I can fill out order forms and keep the books."

Ruth laughed at Johanna's disarming honesty.

"Well that's certainly going to come in handy in affairs of the heart!"

They ate their cake in silence. While Johanna gazed fixedly down at her plate, Ruth's thoughts wandered back to her first night with Thomas.

After the May dance had ended in such disarray, they had made their way up to the forest the following evening instead. Thomas hadn't gotten anything ready but a blanket and a couple of candles. Though it was far from the magical, romantic setting Ruth had hoped for, she had let him pull her down onto the blanket. Thomas had kept his part of the bargain by announcing their engagement at the village dance, so she couldn't back out now. His compliments that evening had been oddly halfhearted. He told her that he thought of her night and day and that she was beautiful, but he stumbled through the words as though they were a poem he had been forced to learn by rote. Straight after that, his hands were hunting around under her skirt. Greedily. Possessively.

Ruth's mouth was dry. She swallowed a bite of cake.

After that it all had happened very fast. He had shoved her legs apart with his calloused hands and pressed her body down onto the blanket. The mossy forest floor beneath was lumpy; there was something digging painfully into her back—a root or a stone or a pinecone; and she felt cold, though she hadn't dared complain. The last thing she had wanted to hear just then was some remark about how overly sensitive she was.

And then?

She had squeezed her eyes shut and tried to conjure up some of the romance she had so desperately wanted for the occasion. Groaning and breathing heavily into her ear, he thrust into the chill of her body—and it hurt. Ruth had been relieved when he finally let go.

Involuntarily she pressed her legs together. The sudden movement made Johanna look up. Ruth smiled at her and took a sip of coffee.

She had been so shocked by the nasty dampness between her legs!

When Thomas had seen her dismay, he had simply laughed. "That's the elixir of life! You'll have to get used to that." Then he had taken her in his arms and they had looked up at the night sky to search for stars together. But it was overcast that night. All the same, these were, for Ruth, the most beautiful minutes of the evening.

She sighed and looked across at Johanna.

"Mrs. Heimer—it'll take me a while to get used to that."

"How do you think I'll manage?" Johanna asked.

They both had to laugh.

"Is he really Prince Charming, like you used to dream about when you were a girl?" Johanna asked quietly.

Ruth was quiet. It was an important question. Not for Johanna, she realized, but for her.

She certainly couldn't claim that he catered to her every whim. But it wasn't stinginess that made Thomas treat her so . . . unimaginatively. That was just the way he was. If she enthused to him about something she had seen in one of the magazines that Johanna brought home, he merely looked at her with blank incomprehension. "You and your silly ideas," he would say. But was that any surprise? Thomas had grown up in a household that sneered at sophistication.

At last she answered, "No, he's not Prince Charming. But what would I do with someone like that in Lauscha?" She smiled coquettishly. "I'd rather have the son of the richest glassblower in the village. After all I'm no princess myself; I'm just a perfectly ordinary girl."

"No you're not," Johanna replied decisively. "Thomas couldn't find a woman anywhere in Lauscha or beyond who's prettier than you or cleverer or works harder! Don't you hide your light under a bushel, not even for a moment!"

Ruth was deeply affected but popped the last piece of cake into her mouth to hide it. "Sometimes I have my doubts," she admitted. "Marie has her painting; you've got your work here in town and earn a good wage. But me . . . ?"

"You'll soon be the mother of a curly-haired little blond angel, and we'll all be wildly envious of you," Johanna said, grinning. "But before that you'll be the prettiest bride Lauscha has ever seen."

"The dress is wonderful, isn't it?" When Ruth thought of the big packet under the table, her melancholy vanished. "Eva will be so jealous she'll burst!"

The two sisters hugged good-bye in the doorway of Strobel's shop. Ruth was already outside when she turned around one more time.

"Where has Strobel gone anyway?" Though she wasn't really interested, she felt a twinge of guilt after talking about herself and Thomas all afternoon.

"I have no idea," Johanna answered darkly. "But given the fuss he made about it you'd have thought he were setting off for a trip around the world."

"That's odd," Ruth declared. "Don't you talk to one another, then?"

"Of course we do. But to be honest, I prefer knowing as little as possible about him. He can be a rather odd duck."

33

On Monday Johanna was so swamped with work that she had no time to think about Ruth's wedding. She had just unlocked the shop and was putting the key in a drawer under the counter when the door opened and Swiss Karl walked in. He must have set out from Lauscha in the middle of the night to get there so early.

"You've got young swallows up under the eaves," he said instead of hello, and pointed his chin toward the door.

Johanna smiled. This was typical of Karl Flein. The glassblower had a better eye for the beauties of nature than almost anyone else in the village.

"I know," she answered. "If I let Strobel have his way, I'd have to clear that nest away. He's worried that the little beasts might drop something on our customers as they come in. But they do say that a house where swallows build their nest will have health and wealth." Johanna leaned over the counter. "Now then, Swiss Karl, what can I do for you? Are you thirsty? Shall I get you a glass of water? It's warm for June, isn't it?"

She'd always liked Karl Flein, a quiet, polite man, even before he had come to Father's grave with the handblown glass rose as a final gift to a fellow craftsman. She was happy that Mr. Woolworth had ordered several items from him.

Flein waved the offer away. "I shan't need anything, thank you."

Johanna waited while he ceremoniously took a sheet of paper from his breast pocket and unfolded it. It was the order sheet she had given to a messenger woman for him last week. For a moment Johanna flushed hot and cold. Had she made a mistake?

"There's something I don't understand on your order. What's this mean?" he asked, pointing to one line.

"We'll soon sort this out," she said, taking the sheet from his hand. But the next instant her confident smile faded. "Twenty dozen balls with eyelets for hanging, silvered within, diameter two inches," she read, furrowing her brow. "What does it mean?"

"At first I thought it was the bead necklaces, since you've bought plenty of those from me," Flein said. "But that can't be it, not at that size."

Johanna put her hand to her mouth to disguise her own confusion.

"Two inches in diameter—they'd certainly be very big beads!" she said, trying to laugh. "Mr. Strobel isn't here at the moment. Let me fetch his notebook. Perhaps he's written down something that might clarify things a little." She went to the back of the shop.

She hadn't noticed anything odd as she was filling out the order sheet. She had simply copied out every item on the Woolworth order that Strobel had written under number 386, which was the number for Karl Flein in the books. Perhaps Strobel had made a mistake about the size of the balls? Johanna bit her lip. Drat it all; it was her job to make sure of details like this. Now she couldn't even ask him.

Strobel's notebook didn't tell her much though. He'd jotted down a comment in the margin for this item, as he often did, but Johanna had trouble deciphering his handwriting.

"New product/ add to catalog/ globes for hanging: as Christmas tree decorations," she read out loud, frowning.

"Christmas tree decorations?" Flein repeated.

"Glass globes? On a Christmas tree?" Johanna asked, baffled, while outside the young swallows chirped hungrily.

The glassblower shrugged. "Why not? For all I care, your clients can hang themselves on the tree if they want to," he said with a laugh. "When you get right down to it, these are nothing more than big glass beads then. The only difference is that instead of drawing the tail off the bead, I'll blow a little hook into it. So that it can be hung." He smiled confidently. "I can do that, of course, now that I know what the globes are supposed to be for . . . Well then, I'm off to get back to work." He pulled his cap down over his brow.

"Anyway, let that wholesaler of yours know that next time he should be a bit clearer about what he wants." Karl winked and left.

◆ ◆ ◆

Three weeks later Ruth Steinmann became Mrs. Heimer.

The wedding banquet was such a magnificent affair that it was almost as though Ruth really was marrying Prince Charming. Nearly a hundred guests had been invited, mostly glassblowers and their families but also the Sonneberg wholesalers who did business with the Heimer workshop. For once Wilhelm Heimer hadn't skimped on costs and had rented the Black Eagle outright. It wasn't Lauscha's largest tavern, but it had always been a popular gathering place for the glassblowers.

There were eight waitresses at the reception to serve coffee and fancy cakes. The sweet treats were hardly finished before they brought out potato dumplings with a goulash of venison and wild boar, and both red and white cabbage. The beer flowed freely, and though red wine was also offered, only the Sonneberg businessmen drank it. Glassblowers were beer drinkers and always had been, and the bridegroom was among the staunchest upholders of this tradition—and, at least to start with, his bride watched indulgently. His friends followed his example faithfully, and the celebration grew louder and merrier as the hours went by.

But the food and drink, good though it was, was not the high point of the occasion. That was the table itself and the decorations; Marie had spent days wreathing box branches into lengths of tracery and adorning them with rosettes of gold paper that she had cut into delicate patterns. She wound one length around the chairs of the bride and groom, joining them together so that they looked like one royal throne. Another length was placed around the tables that bore the wedding gifts.

And there were plenty of gifts: the glassblowers gave them all kinds of glassware of course—from drinking glasses, dishes, and plates to perfume bottles, vases, and little lidded pots. Swiss Karl had given the couple a whole bouquet of glass roses blown from the orange and red rods in his stock, complete with green leaves and thorns along the stem. The whole piece was so lifelike that Edeltraud came hurrying up with a vase full of water for the roses. When the guests standing around noticed her mistake, they laughed until their sides ached.

Thomas's brothers gave the couple two goose-feather quilts and pillows, which they handed over with much ado and several off-color remarks. The gifts from the Sonneberg wholesalers included a two-way mirror, a five-armed porcelain candelabrum, and a set of silver flatware for fish. Johanna got the impression that all of Heimer's business partners were trying to outdo one another with their gifts. She found herself thinking ungraciously that the newly-weds might have liked some more practical presents for day-to-day use, perhaps some cooking pots.

Ruth received all the gifts with a dignity befitting a queen. Having always dreamed of having some luxury in her life, she was visibly overjoyed by all the expensive, unusual presents. And she was equally effusive in thanking the guests who brought only a few towels or a single glass dish, like Widow Grün. All day long Ruth had a kind word for everybody, tirelessly shaking hands and receiving their congratulations.

"If only Father could see her now," Johanna said quietly.

Marie nodded. "Somehow I feel that he's here anyway," she confessed. "I have to stop myself from looking up to heaven all the time."

"You too?" Johanna and Marie traded awkward smiles. Then Johanna sighed. "But I don't like the thought that you'll be living on your own from now on."

"Well, look who's talking! Who's been living with a strange man for more than six months now?" Marie countered, then added, "You don't have to worry about me. I don't mind being on my own."

"I'm just next door after all," Peter said. "All Marie has to do is knock on the wall if there's anything she needs. Besides . . ." he said, pulling Johanna gently to her feet. "I think you've had enough worries for today. Come on, let's go join the fun."

The newlyweds had just finished the first dance and were beckoning for everyone else to join them on the dance floor. Ruth's pregnancy didn't show at all. In fact the dress that she had chosen in Sonneberg rather emphasized her tall, slender figure. She had decided against an elaborate coiffure and instead wore her hair in one thick plait all the way down her back.

"Ruth looks beautiful," Johanna whispered to Peter as they joined the other dancing couples.

"And you look just as lovely," he whispered back. His breath tickled the hairs at the back of her neck.

Johanna felt clumsy as she fended off the compliment. "Nonsense," she said. "I'm nothing special."

"You are to me," Peter said emphatically.

Johanna looked up at him, on her mettle. "Don't you ever give up?"

He shook his head. "I never will. I'm still quite convinced that we belong together."

"Oh, Peter!" she said, nudging him gently. "And what if you have to wait for me until you're old and gray?" It was only half in jest. While she found it flattering that he was so insistent, she didn't want to raise any false hopes. It didn't matter how Peter felt about her; she saw him as a brother, nothing more.

"I'll take the risk," Peter replied cheerfully. "Look at those two." He nodded toward Ruth and Thomas. "A year ago nobody would have thought that they would be married."

"Well I have to agree with you there at least; nobody knows what time may bring," Johanna said vaguely, to end the conversation on a friendly note.

Once they had danced enough, they went to the bar and ordered two steins of beer. Then they sat down at a little table where the waitresses put their drinks. It gave them a good view of the crowd while they weren't noticed themselves.

"I think I'll stay here for the rest of the party," Johanna said, her cheeks glowing. The beer was cool and refreshing. "I can't take any more of Wilhelm Heimer's speeches today. There's a way he always looks at me out of the corner of his eye as he talks . . . brrr! As if he always wants to remind me what a good catch our Ruth has made." She sighed. "Though I must admit it's very generous of him to give them the apartment over his warehouse. I didn't even know he owned that building."

Peter laughed. "Well there you have it. Thomas really is a good catch."

"There we have it indeed!" Johanna scoffed, jutting her chin toward the dance floor, where Thomas and his buddies were making fools of themselves, clucking like hens and prancing about. Johanna raised her eyebrows as the women tried to drag their men off the dance floor. She was relieved to see that Ruth was not among them.

"Do you think it'll work out?" she asked Peter, nodding toward the newlyweds.

Peter shrugged.

Johanna knew that the happiness she felt today was just an exception: the dancing, the easy chatter, none of Strobel's odd remarks, no worries about how Marie would get by on her own. Everything would be quite different again tomorrow.

All at once Johanna felt sick at heart. She changed her mind about sitting and led Peter back onto the dance floor, hoping that her worries would go away.

34

And then summer was over. Up on the forest heights where the wind was strong, deciduous trees shed their leaves, exposing the grim dark pines behind them. The sun was soon barely visible behind the steep mountains, and the shadows stayed in the village longer each day. When Johanna set off for home on Fridays, it was already dark as the slate-maker's cart rattled on its way.

◆ ◆ ◆

There were days when Ruth felt unwell as her belly grew rounder, but she turned up for work right on time all the same. And a good thing too, since the workload at Heimer's workshop never ebbed. Thomas and his two brothers sat at their lamps and blew glass from morning till night, while Ruth, Marie, and the other women painted and finished the wares.

◆ ◆ ◆

Although Marie often had a backache after the long hours up at Heimer's, she frequently sat up half the night at the kitchen table with her sketchpad. She felt invigorated by the peace and quiet in the house now that Ruth had moved out. At last she could put her sketches and her colored pencils wherever she liked, could draw and experiment and cross out without anyone looking over her shoulder and squealing with delight. Her sisters' interest in her art had always felt like rather a burden. They were bound to praise her, whatever she did. If anyone was going to pass comment on her work, then Marie would have much preferred that it be someone who really knew about art, someone with whom she could exchange ideas. Despite the fact that she had no such expert guidance, her designs became clearer and more considered over time. All the same, Marie constantly found herself drawing circles and spheres rather than the dishes or bowls she had intended and which she ended up crossing out in frustration.

The ideas had started with a passing remark many months before. Something that Johanna had said shortly after Ruth's wedding had put those shapes into Marie's head, and now they simply wouldn't go away.

"You can't imagine all the new things I get to see at Strobel's shop," Johanna had said. "There I am thinking I know every kind of glass made in Lauscha and then a glassblower comes along and surprises me with some new design."

Marie had asked her sister what exactly she got to see, even though she would have liked to put her hands over her ears. She didn't want to hear about all the wonderful things—or even the ugly things—that the glassblowers brought to Strobel. Not when Wilhelm Heimer had just turned down another of her designs.

"You have good ideas, girl, I'll give you that," he had said. "But as long as we still have commissions to work through, we don't need to go trying anything new." He clapped a friendly hand on her shoulder, but it did nothing to lessen the disappointment. So Marie had only listened with half an ear while Johanna talked about Karl

Flein and his order from an American buyer. "We've seen people hang glass beads on their trees of course, but glass *globes*—can you imagine?" Johanna had laughed.

And all of a sudden Marie had pricked up her ears. She had nodded impatiently at Johanna. *Tell me more!*

Taking the hint, Johanna had explained, "When Strobel got back from his trip, I asked him how on earth Mr. Woolworth had gotten the idea of ordering glass globes for Christmas trees— whether that was what they usually hung on their trees in America. Strobel said it wasn't, but that Mr. Woolworth had told him he'd bought a small consignment of clear glass globes from a dealer in Penn . . . Pennsylvania"—she had stumbled over the name a little— "and only because the man had been so insistent about it. If nobody had bought the globes, he'd have sent them back to the dealer. But apparently they sold like hotcakes.

"Woolworth's a businessman and saw there was a tidy profit to be made. And now Swiss Karl's working away on them. I'm glad that Strobel picked him for the order. His family can certainly use the work."

Marie had asked for an exact description of the globes. There really wasn't much to them, she realized. But the idea itself was fascinating.

When Johanna had gone back to Sonneberg shortly thereafter, she had no idea that her remarks had planted the seed of a new idea in her sister. Marie had tossed and turned sleeplessly in bed that night, fighting to hold back the flood of images in her head: glittering globes, their colors standing out against a green pine. The candlelight playing across the silver sheen. She wanted to get out of bed and put the pictures safely down in her sketchbook. But then she scolded herself for the thought—Wilhelm Heimer would never want to bother with these globes, any more than he did with the rest of her designs.

But she nonetheless came back again and again over the following weeks and months to the thought that Karl Flein's glass globes would soon be on their way to America to glitter and shine as Christmas tree ornaments. She was full of pride that glass blown in her home village was cherished all over the world.

◆　◆　◆

Once again, Marie couldn't sleep even though she was dead tired. Christmas was fast approaching, and she didn't know whether to look forward to it or dread the day. Ruth would spend Christmas Eve with the Heimers, but she had promised to visit Marie and Johanna for a while.

On her last visit, Johanna had said, "I've thought up a few nice surprises." Marie could well imagine what that meant; Johanna would probably come home with a whole trunk full of gifts. But that was hardly unexpected given how much she earned.

If only she could think of something that would *really* surprise her sisters.

In the end Marie gave up on getting to sleep. She found her socks in the dark, put them on, and went downstairs. She lit the kitchen lamp and sat down at the table with a cup of tea. She hadn't taken the trouble to light the stove earlier that evening, so it was unpleasantly cold. She went to the window, checking for drafts. Though the pane sat snugly in its frame, the cold seemed to be seeping through the glass all the same. Marie's gaze fell on the frost flowers that had spread themselves across the window like the finest Plauen lace. She traced their delicate tracery thoughtfully with her finger. Nature still shows us the best designs, she reflected, the most beautiful works of art. And then she thought, *There must be some way for me to capture this wintry beauty.*

She fetched a shawl and threw it over her shoulders, then hurried into the workshop.

Should she decorate a Christmas tree, the way they used to do when she was a little girl? She could weave some stars out of straw and then paint them white perhaps, to make them look like ice crystals. That was not exactly an original idea though.

But a tree with glass globes like the ones Karl Flein made—that would be a real surprise!

Deep in thought, she began to wipe down Father's workbench with a damp cloth.

She had gotten into the habit of dusting the abandoned workbench and all his tools once a week, no matter how much other work she had. Her father had worked at this bench all his life, day in and day out. The ritual was important to her, just as Ruth felt it important to clear the moss away from Joost's gravestone regularly.

Everything was still just as he had left it: the gas pipe to the left with the box of matches that had a picture of an orange flame on the label; the air hose to the right, which connected to the treadle-operated bellows under the table; and in between there were the glass rods, neatly lined up by color and length. Marie carefully picked up each one and wiped the dust away. Then she put aside the cloth and sat down.

She gazed into the darkness for a while. Dusting the bench had just been an excuse, she realized, a pretext for sitting here. She reached for the matchbox and took out a match. Her hand was trembling a little at the audacity of what she was about to do. She hesitated. Then she looked over the workbench, checking that all was in place.

And then she did what she had to.

She turned the gas tap counterclockwise, once round, twice, until the gas began to flow invisibly. Marie couldn't see it, could hardly even smell it.

And with that, Joost's workbench awoke to new life.

Her right foot found the bellows and her leg settled into the rhythm of its own accord. Up, down. Up, down. Marie bent down and held the hose to her cheek, testing the flow. She seemed to feel every little hair in the gentle stream of air.

"You have to blow hard to make the flame sing!" she heard her father say. She choked back a sob. Then she lit the match and held it to the flame. A bluish-red flame shot up.

Marie sat up straight, took a deep breath, and tried to shake some of the tension from her shoulders. There was no reason to be nervous. She had the gas under control. She wouldn't open the tap any more than she knew was safe. She needn't be afraid.

Once she had calmed down a little, she took the air hose, which had been blowing off to one side, and brought it closer to the gas tap. Very soon the flame would turn blue, and then it would burn ever more fiercely until it was hot enough to melt glass.

But nothing happened.

Marie was taken aback. Not enough gas? Or not enough air?

She began to work the bellows faster. Still nothing. Not enough gas, then. She put the air hose into its clip so that her hands were free. Then she turned the valve on the gas tap all the way around. When she turned the air hose back onto the flame, it flickered for a moment, but Marie could see at a glance that the temperature was still far too low to heat up one of the glass rods.

She struggled to recall just how far Thomas and his brothers opened their gas pipes. Even though she was at the workshop every day, she never paid attention to such details. She was a woman and had nothing to do with the glassblowing. Women just finished the wares.

Marie stared at the gas tap as though it would tell her what to do. She had turned the valve three times by now—did she need to turn it ten times, or twenty, to get a good flame?

It was no use, Marie decided. Either she plucked up her nerve and used more gas, or she could give up right now. She swallowed. Then she turned the gas tap round and round until she heard it hiss. She knew that sound! She brought in the air.

The next moment a burst of flame shot up toward the ceiling.

35

Marie couldn't believe how easy it was to explain away her singed eyelashes to Ruth. And her eyebrows, which were charred almost beyond recognition. Never mind the way her right index finger and middle finger were puffy and swollen. She had thrown away the singed shawl first thing. She had stammered out something about being careless as she lit the gas lamps in the house, expecting Ruth not to believe a word. But her older sister had just looked at her a little skeptically and asked no more questions. Marie heaved a sigh of relief. For a moment there she had considered telling the truth— "I burned myself because I thought I could blow glass like a man"— but didn't they say that pregnant women should avoid shocks? And Ruth would certainly have been shocked. She would have shouted something like, "You—blow glass? Are you mad? What the devil got into you? The whole house could have burned down! You could have been burned alive!"

A few nights later, Marie was back at the workbench, smiling. Perhaps some devil really had gotten into her. But if so, she was going to grab him by the horns!

Granted, after her first attempt had gone so wrong, she had tasted fear. The flame was dangerous—every child in Lauscha knew that. But in the end, her desire had been stronger than her fear.

This time she had taken off her shawl and put her hair up in a tight braid. She also didn't turn the gas valve all the way, but only as far as she had seen Thomas and his brothers open it when she'd watched them these last few days. Four turns, no more. She was rewarded with a blue flame that looked a lot like what the other glassblowers used. A smile flitted across her face.

Her hand trembling, she picked up one of the rods of clear glass that Joost had used to blow pharmacy jars. It felt smooth and cold. She turned it carefully in the flame, keeping it in one position, until it began to glow in the middle. That was the moment when the glass became soft. Marie put the air hose down and pulled the two ends of the rod apart until she was holding two pieces. She put one of these aside and looked critically at the other. In pulling the rod apart, she had made a long thin shape that the glassblowers called a tail, and it looked just like the ones Thomas and his brothers made. So much for this being men's work. She knew just what she had to do next from watching the Heimer brothers over their shoulders. She was excited as she put the shortened glass rod back into the flame until the end melted closed. She did the same with the second piece. Then she put both pieces down to cool off in a pail.

Only then did Marie allow herself to draw a deep breath.

So far, so good.

She did the same thing to another dozen rods. Now everything was ready.

"You can do it, Marie Steinmann," she told herself in a whisper. She took one of the shortened rods from the pail and held it to the flame until the middle was heated through. Once it was glowing red, she took the rod from the flame and put the open end to her mouth. It felt cool, even though immensely high temperatures were at work on the glass just a hand span away from her lips. She blew into it.

Dear God, please let this work, she prayed as a bubble appeared in the glass before her eyes. A large, transparent bubble.

Marie kept blowing.

A little more.

The pounding at her temples intensified.

And a little more.

That was it. She had to stop, or the bubble would burst.

There was now a perfectly round ball where the tail had been. Marie gazed at it, hardly believing what she saw. She had managed it. She was so surprised that she forgot to work the bellows for a moment.

The flame promptly went out.

◆　◆　◆

The next few weeks were the most exciting in Marie's life—largely because nobody else knew what happened every night at Joost's old bench.

Every evening she learned more about how to work with the lamp, how to calibrate the gas pipe and the air hose, and how to blow the glass. After creating ten almost perfectly round globes, she began to experiment with shapes. One time she stretched the bubble as she blew so that the result was egg shaped; another time she blew a shape like a pear. She was always careful not to let the glass walls become too thick or too thin or poorly proportioned. However, when she tried blowing a shape like a pinecone, she found the end result far too long and thin. Though she had to laugh at her creation, which looked not the least bit like a pinecone but rather like a long thin sausage, she was unhappy at the thought that she had wasted half a rod.

Marie turned the thing around and around. If she used a little imagination, it looked rather like one of the icicles hanging from the eaves outside, but it wasn't a pretty sight. She put it aside.

From then on, she only blew globes and eggs. She hid all of them in the wardrobe in Joost's old bedroom, where neither Ruth nor Johanna would happen across them.

A seasoned glassblower like Thomas Heimer could blow up to ten dozen of such a simple shape in a single day, but Marie never managed more than a dozen in one night. Her flame went out more than once, and she had to work hard to coax it back to life. Once she cut herself and had to look all over the house for a bit of clean cloth to wrap around the ball of her thumb. Another time she thought she heard Ruth coming and hastily put everything away, but it was only the wind at the door.

Marie had decided to finish four dozen globes by Christmas. It was December 18 by the time they were all blown, which didn't leave her much time for the rest of what she wanted to do.

She took the knife that she had found in Joost's tool kit and with trembling hands began to shear off the stems of glass as close to the globes as she could. Then she took a pair of pliers and a bale of wire that she had bought in the village store over the weekend, and cut lengths as long as her hand. She wound them around what was left of the stem at the base of the globes until each one had a loop. She held up a globe at arm's length and examined it. Not bad. These would hang nicely on a tree.

Finally the moment she longed for had come—it was time to paint the globes.

Marie eagerly took the bottle of white enamel paint out of the drawer, then rooted around until she found the black paint as well. Black and white was all they had needed for writing the words on pharmacy jars, and they would be enough for what Marie had in mind. She gave both bottles a vigorous shake and then dipped her brush into the white paint. She began to paint one of the globes with clear, decisive strokes and only stopped when the whole globe was covered with frost crystals—large and small, some simple and others elaborately curled like the ones she had seen on the windowpane.

Shivering with anticipation Marie picked up the next bauble, which was pear-shaped. She painted the bottom half almost completely white and then dabbed tiny white dots all over the top half. A wintry landscape took shape before her eyes. When she had finished with the snowflakes, she dipped her brush into the black jar and painted the outlines of houses and rooftops.

Marie sighed with pleasure as she put the finished decorations aside. Everything looked exactly as she had imagined; the contrast between light and dark, so typical for winter, went beautifully with the cloudy glass globes. She thought regretfully of how lovely the painted designs would look against a silver background. But she couldn't just walk into Heimer's workshop and take over his silver bottle for her own globes.

She reached for the misshapen icicle, but a moment later she stood up abruptly and went out to the hall. She fetched a small bag from her coat pocket.

Even in a well-run workshop there were always breakages and failures. A glassblower might stop paying attention for a moment and the glass would run like honey. Or it fell off the painting bench, or shattered as it was being packed. Anything with only a minor crack was taken to the wholesaler to be sold at a discount, but whatever was too badly broken went into the waste bin.

A couple of days before, Marie had asked Wilhelm Heimer whether she could take some glass home from the waste. Though he had shrugged and allowed her request, he had also peered over her shoulder as she sorted through the bin, to be quite sure that a usable piece hadn't slipped through. "Old skinflint!" Marie muttered to herself now.

Instead of taking the shards of glass out of the bag, she broke them up with a hammer wrapped in old rags, pounding away until there was not a sharp edge left anywhere. Then, smiling, she sifted the glittering powder from the bag into the palm of her hand.

Stardust! The glitter of snow!

She poured the tiny particles back into the bag as carefully as if they were gold dust. She dipped a wide brush into the white paint and then put a layer all along the icicle she had blown. Before the paint could dry she sifted the powdered glass onto it until there was an even layer all around. Now her icicle was perfect.

After that she picked out a few globes that had only the black outlines of stars on them. She filled in the shapes with white paint and sifted the powdered glass onto these as well.

As if on cue, it had begun to snow outside—thick fluffy flakes that tumbled down through the night air. Marie gazed out the window with concern. She hoped it wouldn't snow for days on end. If it did, the roads would be impassable and Johanna would not be able to get home. Marie bit her lip. She didn't want to think about that. Instead she closed her eyes and tried to imagine what the Christmas tree would look like in its full glory. She wished she could afford a few more candles, but she had only had enough money for half a dozen from the store.

"A tree!" she suddenly yelped. "Marie Steinmann, just how stupid can you be?"

In her eagerness she thought she had taken care of every detail, but she hadn't asked Ugly Paul to cut a Christmas tree for her. She would have to stop by and ask the firewood man the very next morning.

Thank heavens there were still six days until Christmas Eve.

36

Johanna had thought that Strobel's shop would be bustling with visitors on Christmas Eve. But by ten o'clock, the shop bell hadn't rung even once, and Johanna went to the door to check that she had actually unlocked it. They hadn't had a single customer by noon.

At twelve o'clock sharp, Strobel turned the key in the lock.

"So, that was that," he said. He walked over to the sales counter and produced a bottle of champagne. He opened it with a flourish, poured two glasses, and handed one to Johanna.

"Champagne at noon? Does that mean you were pleased with the Christmas orders?" she asked mockingly.

"We will each be going our own ways shortly, so let's drink to the season!" Although their glasses barely touched, the crystalline chime hung in the air for a long time.

"And as for your second question, yes, I'm pleased. More than pleased, in fact." Strobel raised his glass to Johanna once more.

After taking a few sips from her glass, she said, "If there will be nothing else . . . then I wish you a pleasant journey and . . ."

She was just about to fetch her coat—her traveling bag with the presents was ready and waiting in the hall—when the wholesaler blocked her path.

"Don't be in such a hurry, my dear! You haven't gotten your Christmas present yet."

"Oh, but I have!" She smiled, confused. "Or was the extra five marks in my wage packet not a present?"

Strobel waved it away. "Money! A small token of my appreciation, nothing more. But a real present is worth more than money alone. It can be a symbol, it has a power of its own—or can give you power. It can open the way to new worlds, or destroy an old one—it all depends."

Chuckling, he handed her a packet that unmistakably contained a book. "I see that my words mean nothing to you. But I think that my present will speak for itself once you look at it. By the way, this is the book that I promised you some time ago. You will remember our conversation about dominant women and the men who adore them."

Johanna remembered nothing of the kind.

"Allow me to say just a few more words . . ."

What a lot of fuss about a book, Johanna thought ungraciously.

"I thought your present would speak for itself?"

Johanna glowered at Strobel. The slate-maker was setting off earlier than usual today. If she missed him because Strobel was being so self-important . . .

He smiled in that curious way he had. "You are right; there is no need for more words. Only that my book is certain to be a revelation for you."

◆　◆　◆

Strobel was in good spirits as he locked the shop after Johanna had left. He still had more than two hours before the coach he had ordered would come to pick him up. Enough time to look back on the year that was just coming to a close. He poured himself another glass of champagne and drank to his own health. He had every cause for celebration; his business was flourishing more than ever and he could travel to B. whenever he liked, knowing that the shop was in Johanna's capable hands.

He drank some more champagne and smiled. Yes, ever since Johanna had joined him, his life had changed very much for the better. He congratulated himself once more on his wise decision not to mix business with pleasure. Not that he found her any less enticing than before. But it was enough to toy with her a little. Which is why he had given her the memoirs of the Marquis de Sade as a Christmas present. He giggled. He could hardly wait to hear what she thought of it. But that was all the interest he had in her as a person. And a good thing too—as he knew better than anyone.

The old proverb put it so well. Best to work up an appetite at home and then sate it elsewhere. Or was it the other way around? Whichever it was, he would save up his appetites for his visits to B. He could hardly wait to see the progress on the renovation work; after all, he had put a great deal of money into it. To judge by the plans he had received in the mail a few weeks before, the dilapidated old house had been turned into a real gem of a building. Yes, the right setting would make his visits to B. even more enjoyable . . . if such a thing were even possible!

◆ ◆ ◆

The fir tree that Marie had ordered from Ugly Paul filled the whole room with its glittering light on Christmas Eve. Marie had distributed the forty-eight globes evenly all around the tree, placed the candles between them, and then sprinkled the rest of the powdered glass over the branches like snowflakes. The result was overwhelming. The scent of the beeswax candles that hung in the air added to the magic.

"It's simply magnificent. I've never seen anything so lovely in my life!" Johanna said with tears in her eyes. She went to Marie and put her arms around her.

"But I really ought to give you a good telling off!" she added. "When I think of everything that could have gone wrong . . ."

She turned to Peter, who was also admiring Marie's creations. "Go on, say something!"

"I'm still speechless. You could knock me down with a feather," Peter said, smiling. "There's only one thing about the whole story that makes me unhappy—the fact that you didn't come to me for help. Sitting down at the lamp like that without serving an apprenticeship! So much could have gone wrong, I must agree with Johanna there."

"But you see, that's precisely why I kept quiet. Because I knew that you'd find fault with my plans," Marie answered bitterly. "I could have guessed that you'd be like all the other men. You don't like the idea of a woman daring to work with that sacred flame of yours!"

Peter made a face. "I've never seen you so worked up. But you're wrong—I would never have stopped you from sitting down at the lamp. Why would I? Why shouldn't women blow glass? And if you're so dead keen to do it, I could at least have given you a lesson or two."

Marie gritted her teeth and conceded his point. "Next time I'll come straight to you if there's something I'm unsure about," she promised solemnly.

"Next time?" Peter asked.

"Next time?" Johanna echoed. "Do you really plan to blow more glass?"

Marie laughed. "I do indeed. This was just the beginning!"

◆ ◆ ◆

They had gathered in the seldom-used parlor on the second floor to celebrate the occasion. Everybody was wearing their Sunday best, which in the Heimer family meant that they were all wearing black as though in mourning. Ruth, who was wearing an emerald-green dress that Johanna had bought her, felt like a bird of paradise that had strayed into a flock of crows. For a moment she didn't want to go in. Nobody thought to air the room out beforehand, so it smelled old and dusty. The smell brought back memories and she felt strange. She had entered this room for the first time exactly one year ago, when Wilhelm had asked her to wrap the Christmas presents for Eva and the others. How she had envied Eva that powder compact! And how disappointed she and her sisters had been when the old man had given them nothing but a bowl of apples.

This year the presents were already wrapped, though it had been done carelessly. They lay in a row on the varnished dresser. Ruth saw at a glance that again most of the labels had Eva's name on them. So what if they did, she thought stubbornly. She had the best present herself, and she carried it around with her all the time. She passed a loving hand over her pregnant belly.

While Thomas sat down on the sofa right away with the others to join in a game of dice, Ruth sat in an armchair. The back of the chair was hard and pressed into her back, making her sit bolt upright. Her back had been giving her trouble for a few days now. She wouldn't manage to sit here for long but she consoled herself with the thought that the family would be going down to the kitchen to eat soon, after which she hoped to be able to go join her sisters for a little while.

While the others called out their bets at the top of their voices, Ruth rubbed her back. As she did so she looked around the room. There was no point looking for a Christmas tree here, or even a couple of green boughs—somebody would have had to take the trouble to fetch them. Ruth was dismayed to realize that the Heimer family's lack of imagination had already rubbed off on her; thinking back, she couldn't believe that she had ever planned to redecorate this room. Even the idea of living in this house and having the family around at the end of a long workday was dreadful. The apartment over the warehouse was not as pretty as she would have liked, not by a mile—Thomas had no use for what he called "pointless prettification"—but at least they had the place to themselves.

She watched as Sebastian made a great show of counting out a few coins on the table, which Michel swiftly pocketed. After that the game started again. Even the old man had joined in with childlike enthusiasm though Ruth couldn't say whether the flush in his cheeks was because of the game or the mulled wine that the men were drinking in such generous quantities.

"Well, what are you brooding over now, my chicken?" Thomas asked, laying a hand on her belly and making her jump. "She's probably still thinking about what we should call him," he told the room at large, grinning. "But we decided long ago! He'll be called Wilhelm, like his grandfather." He looked across at his father, eager for approval.

"Thomas!" She didn't like it when he put his hand on her belly in front of everybody. "You keep talking about a boy. But we don't know that for sure."

"What else could it be?" her husband answered uncomprehendingly, then turned back to the others. "For a while I even thought our son would be born on Christmas, but it doesn't look like it now."

Ruth tried to nudge him in the ribs, but she was too big and clumsy these days to do so discreetly. He could hardly tell them any more clearly that the child had been conceived before the wedding!

"When's it due then?" Eva asked, pursing her lips.

Ruth smiled. "I don't really know exactly, but not before the middle of February."

"Oh, we'll likely find there's two of them!" Thomas laughed at his own joke and the other men joined in. "Last year a woman had twins over in Rudolstadt, I hear. And the two of them—"

"Thomas, as if it isn't enough that you talk about having a son all the time, but now you want two at once!" Ruth interrupted, half in jest but half in earnest too. "I think I'd better go downstairs and see how Edel's getting on with the meal."

They had hardly finished the Christmas roast when the men resumed their game of dice. While Eva helped the old housekeeper with the dishes, Ruth fetched her coat. "I'm going down to see Johanna and Marie for a while," she said, kissing Thomas on the cheek.

"Do you have to?" he asked disapprovingly.

"I'll be back soon," she promised, and hurried from the room before he could say anything more.

Eva was standing in the hallway. "Let's get one thing straight," she hissed at Ruth. "Once that brat of yours is born, all your shirking is over and done with! You'll do your share of the work!"

Ruth didn't bother to answer. Eva's accusation was completely unfounded, for she'd never missed a day in the workshop however much she might have wanted to sometimes. Besides, Eva was so envious of Ruth's pregnancy that she took every opportunity to snap at her. Fortunately, she rarely had the chance. Eva would never say a word in front of Thomas; if he ever heard her say something nasty to the mother of his son . . . well, Ruth didn't know what would happen. *The mother of his son*—now she was making the same mistake she so often chided Thomas for.

While she walked slowly through the quiet streets, she wondered anxiously what would happen if she had a daughter instead of the son that he wanted so much.

37

Christmas last year had been a dreary occasion, but this year there were a good number of parcels piled up under Marie's splendid Christmas tree. The three of them had waited for Ruth to arrive before opening any presents. But once she did and they all sat down, they didn't want to wait any longer. The presents from Peter were the first to be opened.

For a moment nothing could be heard but the rustle of wrapping paper.

"This must be something for the baby," Ruth said as she unwrapped hers.

Johanna put her parcel down in her lap.

"And what if it is?" she asked, as she thought of the presents that she had chosen for Ruth, all baby clothes. "Wouldn't you like that?"

"Peter!" Ruth gave a little cry of pleasure and seemed not to have heard Johanna's question at all.

"I can't accept this. Have you suddenly become rich overnight?" She was holding up a small case; lined with red silk, it held a brush, a comb, and a nail buffer. Johanna could see at a glance that they all had real silver handles, finely incised. "I've always wanted something like this. However did you know?"

Peter shrugged. "I know my Steinmann girls. And I thought that the others would probably give you enough baby things."

"Thank you ever so much!" Ruth was beaming. "Just wait till Thomas sees this! The poor lamb was so unhappy; he really had no idea what to give me for Christmas!"

"So what did he get you in the end?" Johanna asked. She knew all too well just how unimaginative Thomas could be.

"A woolen shawl. In brown!" Ruth made a funny face. "Not exactly the color I would have chosen." She shrugged.

"Peter!" Another cry of pleasure. Marie couldn't say anything more than that. She was leafing through a thick leather-bound book, and she was spellbound. Reluctantly she closed the cover and held it up so that the others could read the title. *A Handbook of Art and Design.*

"You could hardly have picked a better present for Marie," Johanna said, amazed. Peter's presents were not only expensive but also had been chosen with a great deal of care. It couldn't have been easy to find that book; she had never seen anything of the sort in the Sonneberg bookshops.

"Your turn!" Peter gave her a gentle nudge.

Johanna's fingers trembled as she untied the ribbon on her gift. She was suddenly excited. Ruth's present and Marie's had been very personal. She couldn't for the life of her guess what Peter had chosen for her. The shape of the package was no help at all. It was rectangular, and the thought that it might be a penholder or a notebook for the shop suddenly filled her with inexplicable dread. At last the paper fell away.

"An atlas?" She looked up, astonished.

"An atlas?" Ruth echoed. "What's that?" Johanna held up the book.

"This book has . . . well, it has the whole world between its covers. Look at this: there are maps for every continent. And then more maps for individual countries. And look, it's even been colored by hand. What a lovely, lovely book!" Realizing it rather too late, she added a hasty "Thank you!"

"I thought you might like an atlas. After all, it seems that Lauscha's too small to hold you . . ."

Johanna raised her eyebrows. Did she hear a note of mockery in his voice? She looked over at him appraisingly, but the look on his face was guileless.

"And just in case Sonneberg turns out to be too small as well, I should go out into the big wide world?" she asked with a grin.

"I never said that. But if you let people go off roaming, I've always found they come back of their own accord." Though he spoke easily and confidently, he couldn't disguise the note of longing in his voice.

Johanna smiled back at him. "You didn't even put in a bookmark to show where the Thuringian Forest is!"

Peter lowered the book in her hands so that he could look her in the eye. "Do you want me to make it that easy for you?" he said hoarsely. "You have to find out for yourself where you really belong."

Johanna swallowed. *Please say something inconsequential now,* her eyes pleaded. She didn't want to end up feeling guilty for having rebuffed him yet again. She wanted to enjoy herself. To be happy. This evening of all evenings.

Peter did as she asked. He clapped his hands. "So, wasn't I promised a bowl of good strong punch this evening? Or was that just empty chatter?"

Relieved, Johanna stood up and put another log on the fire. She put some water on to boil then added some rum, a stick of cinnamon, and a whole cup of sugar.

Once she sat down again, she cleared her throat. She took Marie's hand and Peter's, and she nodded to Ruth to join and asked that they all hold hands. They looked surprised and she felt embarrassed. "This Christmas Eve is . . . a very special day for us," she said, stumbling over her words. When she looked up, Ruth was smiling at her in encouragement. "A great deal has happened in the last twelve months. Some wishes have come true that even a few months ago we would hardly have dared to speak aloud. And some wishes will wait and keep us company for a while longer. But all in all, it's been a good year for us." She swallowed. "You may think it a bit silly . . . But I'd like it if we could hold this moment in our hearts forever."

38

Peter insisted on being allowed to go part of the way back with Johanna to Sonneberg after Christmas, even if it was only as far as the spot where the slate-maker would pick her up with his cart. He appeared at the door of her house, wrapped up warm in a jacket and scarf. It was still dark as they set out through the quiet streets together. The snow was frozen over so hard that shards of ice crackled beneath their feet at every step.

Johanna wrapped her scarf more snugly about her head.

"Do you know what one of Strobel's clients said to me recently? 'I get the feeling there are only two seasons here in Thuringia: winter and harsh winter.' Ha! He certainly has a point." Little white clouds puffed out into the air as she spoke.

A short while later Johanna stopped and looked back at her village. Even at this early hour, the glassblowers' flames were burning in the windows of the houses, warming the chill of the night. Little flickering lights, brighter than a torch, shining with strength and purpose.

"Is there another village anywhere in the world where almost everyone makes a living from glassblowing?" Her eyes were shining.

"Not that I know of. I think Lauscha is unique in that respect."

"Every time I see it I'm spellbound," she admitted. "When I think that there's a whole family working around every lamp! It's a fine thought that they're all working together on one commission, isn't it?"

Peter's heart leapt. Did he hear a note of yearning in her voice? Maybe she would have liked to turn around right here, and was just too proud to admit it? He made an attempt.

"Are you sure you still want to work for Strobel in the new year?" He felt her look of surprise more than he saw it.

"Of course! Who else is going to stand in for him while he's away? What kind of question is that?"

He paused.

"Don't pretend my question is such a surprise. Damn it all, I don't like it that you work for that . . . creep. He's not quite right in the head. Doesn't his present prove that, if nothing else did?" The very thought of it put him in a rage.

Johanna had suspected nothing when she opened Strobel's present with Marie and Ruth peering curiously over her shoulder, but they had all been deeply shocked by those horrible pictures. Strobel's disgusting book had shattered the festive mood, and they had spent the rest of Christmas Eve trying hard to regain their good cheer.

Johanna linked arms and made him walk on. "Don't get so worked up. I know quite well that he's an odd fellow. The only explanation I can think of for that book is that maybe he didn't look at it himself beforehand. Maybe someone gave it to him as a present and he simply passed it on to me? That would be just like him. It wouldn't be the first time that he's given me a sample he had no use for."

Peter didn't think much of Johanna's explanation. "A sample!" he snorted. "The whole book is nothing but a parade of perversions! You don't just happen to have a book like that!"

Johanna sighed and quickened her pace as though she wanted to get away from him.

He hurried to keep up.

"Johanna, come to me! My glass animals are bringing in a tidy little sum these days; I'm not the poor beggar I used to be. It would be easy enough for me to look after you and your family. Your sisters would like it too if you were back in Lauscha . . ."

She turned around so suddenly that he almost bumped into her.

"So you want me to give up my job at the drop of a hat just because my employer gave me an odd Christmas present?"

"It's not that and you know it!" Peter protested. "I've wanted you to come and join me for a long time now."

"And that means you'll use whatever excuse you can find to haul me back to Lauscha!" Johanna shot back. "Do you know what your problem is? You just don't want to look beyond the borders of your cozy little world. Lauscha! If you could see a little further you might realize that people can still be friends even when they're not treading on one another's toes the whole time." Giving him no chance to reply, she stomped off through the hard-packed snow.

Johanna was fuming as she climbed up onto the slate-maker's cart. She handed over the money for the ride, and the horse trotted off. How dare Peter always try to make decisions on her behalf? The way he behaved anyone might think they were married!

But as they rode along through the cold, her anger vanished even more quickly than it had come. He just wanted to take care of her. And that was nothing to complain about, was it? But his worries were unfounded; she knew how to deal with Strobel. Despite what she'd said to Peter, it was quite clear that he had given her the book deliberately. After all his talk on Christmas Eve! Perhaps it was his idea of a joke? If so, there was one thing he hadn't counted on.

She would be hanged if she ever even mentioned it to him. As for opening new worlds, what an idea!

That was quite enough brooding over Peter. There was something else that needed all her concentration. She carefully shifted the bag next to her, making sure it was upright. It held six of Marie's Christmas baubles and a bulky object wrapped carefully in woolen blankets. She wanted to show them to Strobel as soon as he got back. She was quite sure that his American client Mr. Woolworth would like these globes. And perhaps he wouldn't be the only one? Without telling Marie, she had packed away six of the best pieces into her bag. Now Johanna wondered how best to broach the topic. Should she claim that she'd been given the globes by a glassblower who didn't want his name mentioned? That sounded unlikely even to her. Mr. Woolworth certainly wouldn't care whether the baubles were blown by a man or a woman. What did the Americans care about Lauscha's traditions?

Her hand felt for the other object. In for a penny, in for a mark, she told herself, smiling. As well as the Christmas baubles, she wanted to show Strobel the bouquet of glass roses that Ruth had received as a wedding gift.

It had taken a good deal of persuasion, but at last Ruth had agreed to let her have them for a week. Of course Johanna could have gone to Swiss Karl and suggested that he blow another bouquet for her to show to Friedhelm Strobel. But she had decided against it. Wouldn't Karl Flein be surprised if Johanna managed to win him a new commission?

39

By the time Strobel finally returned from his trip, Johanna had begun to have doubts. What if he didn't like the baubles? Perhaps the best thing was to test the waters with the glass roses first.

So Marie's baubles stayed packed away, waiting for their moment, while Strobel turned the bouquet of roses around in his hands. Then he put the bouquet into cardboard boxes of different sizes, to see whether it could be easily packed for shipping. Johanna knew that this was the main drawback of the roses; she had practically sweated blood to get them from Lauscha to Sonneberg in one piece.

Without a word, Strobel swiftly sketched a picture in his notebook. Johanna smiled to herself. When he had finished, he looked up at her. "Who did you say made the bouquet?"

"Swiss Karl Flein."

"And he doesn't know that you've brought the flowers here?"

Johanna didn't let her exasperation show. She had already told him that Flein knew nothing of the matter. She kept her voice level as she said, "This is one of a kind. But I'm quite sure that Swiss Karl would be willing to make more of them for the right price. I should imagine that some of our customers would be very pleased with a fine piece of work like this, especially the ones in the big cities."

He nodded silently. "You may be right . . ." Then he looked at her sharply. "There is a problem, however . . ."

Johanna held her breath. She didn't like Strobel's tone. She knew him too well; it was just the tone he used when he was about to browbeat some poor glassblower into agreeing to a desperately low price for his wares. She was therefore all the more surprised when he turned away from her and said, "I've reconsidered. I don't have any use for roses like this. The packaging would be far too much trouble." He put a finger to his lips and frowned irritably. "Besides . . . now that I really look at them, I find them rather kitschy. Tasteless. Not elegant. Take them away!"

Johanna felt as though she'd been hit with a brick. She fumbled for the bouquet, wishing she could think of a clever retort.

"Whatever you say," she croaked as she wrapped the bouquet back up in its blankets and put it back into the bag with Marie's baubles. She would be hanged if she was going to let him sneer at those as well.

Perhaps Strobel had just had a bad day. Perhaps he really didn't like the roses.

But . . . Johanna frowned. She could have sworn that at first he had been struggling not to let his excitement show.

Over the next few days, she had no time to ponder Strobel's odd behavior, for shortly after New Year's a thick envelope with American postmarks arrived at the shop. Johanna peered over Strobel's shoulder as he opened it and immediately recognized the thin unbleached writing paper with the green diamond letterhead. Inside the diamond was a large W— the letter was from Mr. Woolworth.

Strobel grinned. "He writes that Lauscha glass practically sells itself and that he did a roaring trade over the Christmas season.

Damn it all . . ." He frowned deeply as he read on. "He plans to come late summer this year, instead of in May. So he's asking us to send him the documents to place his order in writing instead." Strobel shook his head. "That's just like him. I don't have these documents lying around by the dozen. Don't they know in America what a lot of work it is to get this sort of thing ready?"

Johanna laughed. "From all you've said about the gentleman, I imagine that he couldn't care less."

Strobel sat down at the table, grumbling, and began copying out long passages from his samples books. He wrote out the descriptions in perfect English and added his own remarks and recommendations in the margin, or highlighted certain items by outlining them in red. Johanna helped him by drawing up price lists and applicable discounts. Strobel fretted about putting the documents into the mail since they contained sensitive information that mustn't be allowed to fall into the hands of his competitors. All the wholesalers in the cutthroat business of toys and glassware made a great secret of their prices, and most discounts and bulk orders were negotiated in person with buyers. But what else could Strobel do? Woolworth was an important customer, and his wishes couldn't simply be ignored.

A lively correspondence ensued between Sonneberg and Hamburg, where Woolworth's company had an office by the great harbor, and from where Sonneberg wares were shipped all around the world. The Hamburg office gathered all the necessary documents and then sent them on to Woolworth himself.

Johanna was astonished by how quickly the tycoon answered their letters until Strobel explained that only the sketches and photographs were actually sent by sea, and that ocean transport took only a fraction of the time it had taken even a few years ago because the new steamships had improved propellers. Anything in writing and all the numbers and prices could be sent to America by telegraph. Strobel told her about an undersea cable laid all the way across the Atlantic from Europe to America that carried electrical impulses—whatever they were.

The whole thing sounded too far-fetched to be true, but it evidently worked, since in late January a thick brown envelope arrived at Strobel's shop containing the order. Not a quarter of an hour later the champagne cork popped. Though Johanna was surprised to find herself a little tipsy at that early hour, she was just as pleased as Strobel. He carried the thick sheaf of paper around in his vest pocket for the rest of the day, humming to himself and cheerfully greeting people he usually wouldn't even nod at.

40

The next few weeks were turbulent, in Lauscha as well as Sonneberg.

Ruth gave birth to a healthy daughter and baptized her Wanda, Marie spent half her nights at the lamp, and Johanna felt like a fairy godmother.

Thanks to the Woolworth order, she had a whole stack of orders for the glassblowers in Lauscha, the doll-makers in Sonneberg, and various other suppliers. After working for Strobel for more than a year, she knew every family by name, and she knew that many of them lived hand-to-mouth. It gave her a warm glow to think that she helped improve their fate a little. A few months before, she had still been annoyed to find that there was one name that was never on the books: Peter Maienbaum. Peter was as stubborn as a mule and insisted on taking his glass animals to a smaller wholesaler who didn't have half the contacts that Strobel did. But she was well accustomed to his stubbornness by now.

Johanna was utterly unprepared for the discovery that would shatter all her good cheer in an instant.

She still had about a dozen order sheets to fill in when she came across a line in Woolworth's order that floored her completely. *Glass roses. Three dozen bouquets @ seven roses each. Crimson red. Retail 3 marks 80*, she read in the neat typewritten list, to which Strobel had added in his own writing *Number 345 and cost 0 marks 40.*

That was odd. Johanna frowned. Strobel hadn't mentioned that he changed his mind and was going to add Swiss Karl's roses to the product line. Why hadn't Karl ever said anything to her about it? And then there was the unit cost! Forty pence for such a detailed piece of work? There must be some mistake, but whose? She shook her head as she pushed back her chair and stood up to go look for Strobel. Then she sat down again. *Number 345—that isn't Karl Flein at all!*

A moment later, she discovered that number 345 was Tobias Neuner, one of the few glassblowers who didn't yet have a gas main and still worked with the old-style lamp. He hardly had enough money to feed his family, much less to spend on technical innovation. Fate had not been kind to his family. Tobias's parents were bedridden and looking after them took up a good deal of his wife Sieglind's time. They had eight children, two of whom were not quite right in the head and a burden on the family. Of the other six, only one was a boy. Tobias had a great many mouths to feed and nobody to help him do it. As far as Johanna knew he had never taken a commission that needed colored glass rods, for the simple reason that he could not afford to put down the money for expensive stock. Most of the time Tobias didn't even work directly for a wholesaler, but rather for Wilhelm Heimer and other suppliers who had more work than they could handle. He was a very good glassblower, and there were always enough crumbs from other people's tables to keep his family from starving, but he never had much more than that.

And Tobias was suddenly supposed to blow these elaborate glass roses? For just a few pence each? Besides, the rose bouquet was Karl Flein's invention!

Johanna's blood was boiling when she found Strobel and confronted him with her questions.

He wasn't in the least bit perturbed.

"I simply changed my mind and decided to take the roses after all. Three dozen pieces—it's chicken feed."

But Johanna didn't see it that way at all.

"You can't just take a glassblower's invention and give the order to someone else without asking him! That's a swindle!"

"Be careful using words like that, Johanna Steinmann," Strobel replied, picking up an item at random from the counter. "Here, have a look at this vase. Is there a name on it anywhere? Or here"— he held up a drinking glass—"is there a name on this?"

Johanna didn't bother to answer, knowing that Strobel didn't expect her to anyway.

"Anyone can blow glass once they've learned how. There's no law that says that only one glassblower can use a particular design. Oh, wouldn't that be a lovely world to live in! No, my esteemed Johanna, that's not how business works."

Johanna glared at him, bitterly upset. "You're quite right that there's no law that states who blew what first," she answered coldly. "But the way I see it, there are such things as unwritten laws. And they're just as important as whatever's in the law books!"

"Unwritten laws?" Strobel wouldn't hear of such a thing. "Look at your precious glassblowers: they would cut the very ground out from each other's feet! Every one of them blows to meet the orders he gets. Nobody worries his head over whether someone else might have blown such and such a piece before he did. They all spend their time plotting how to get a glimpse of their rivals' workshops—after all, you never know what you may see there. And you're blathering about some kind of honor code?"

Johanna stubbornly held her tongue. He wasn't entirely wrong.

"Besides, if you are really so concerned about the good folk of Lauscha, you should be glad I gave this job to one of the poorest of the poor. And just so that you understand I'm not the heartless devil you take me for, I'll tell you something else: I've advanced Neuner the money he needs to buy the color rods. So what do you say to that?" Strobel seemed to be reveling in her disapproval. His tongue was loosened now. "And another thing: Karl Flein hasn't been left empty-handed. He's making good money with his Christmas tree globes!"

Of course Johanna could have told him then and there precisely what motivated his so-called generosity: he was exploiting Neuner, nothing more. No glassblower who could afford otherwise would ever have agreed to blow such an elaborate design for a laughable forty pence apiece. Only someone desperate would do such a thing—someone like Thomas Neuner. And just as importantly, Johanna knew that not everyone would be able to make the delicate roses. But she said nothing. Friedhelm Strobel had laid out his arguments, and she knew him well enough to realize that he would not back down.

From that day forward she watched the way Strobel did business with a more critical eye.

She had always known of course, even before she went to work for him, that Strobel was a hard bargainer and always ready to trample on suppliers in his price war against the other wholesalers. She had always told herself that this was just the price of success. After all, the glassblowers didn't come out of it all that badly, did they? Without the wholesaler's far-flung networks, most of the glassblowers would be sitting and watching their wares gather dust. She had used such arguments again and again with Peter. And although he never tired of telling her that she worked for a cutthroat, she had admired Strobel. Over the course of the year her appreciation had only grown as she observed his eye for a deal, his knowledge of English and French, his worldly manner, and salesmanship.

Her only consolation after this unpleasant discovery was the thought that she hadn't let him sneer at Marie's baubles too. He would probably have stolen that idea as well and . . . The very idea was so dreadful that Johanna didn't dwell upon it. Marie would have wanted to kill her; that much was certain!

PART TWO

LATE SPRING, 1892

Glass, glass,
What is glass?
A thing that is nothing
where light may pass.
It is air and not air,
it is there and nowhere.
And yet it is hard
and the dazed bird
as it flies through the land
strikes the glass and cannot understand.

—Gerhart Hauptmann

1

With tired motions, Ruth pounded and kneaded the heavy bread dough on the tabletop, over and over again. Then she listlessly formed four loaves, placed them on a wooden board sprinkled with flour, and covered them with a clean cloth. Tomorrow at the crack of dawn she would take the bread to the bakehouse and hope that one of the other women would put it in with her batch. Ruth didn't have time to put the loaves into the great stone oven and then wait around and chat while they baked. With her job in the workshop, her chores at home, and caring for Wanda, her days were more than full. She would have given anything to have old Edeltraud's help one day a week.

"You'll manage the little bit of housework we have here. Just think how it would look if I had to ask Father for help," Thomas had said, shaking his head uncomprehendingly when Ruth suggested the idea.

"But Eva never has to ask for anything!" she hissed now, not that there was anyone around to hear her.

There was still a cup of lukewarm tea left over from the pot she had made at supper. Ruth looked down into the pale green fluid with disgust. What she wouldn't give for a cup of real coffee. She still had a few beans left—Johanna brought her a little bag from time to time—but she wanted to save them for another day, when she was in a better mood. The bitter tea was just right for today, she decided in a moment of self-mortification.

She glanced over toward the cot and then drew up one of the chairs that Thomas had dragged out from some dusty corner of Wilhelm's attic. She would far rather have had a corner bench put in for the kitchen table. "We can sit on chairs just as well. And we're up at Father's house most of the time anyway," Thomas had said when she mentioned it. When it came to spending money, he was just as stingy as his father.

It was shortly before eight o'clock in the evening and still light outside as the days were growing longer. It could be hours before Thomas came back from the Black Eagle, but Ruth nonetheless kept her ears open for any sound at the door. She didn't want to revisit their argument from earlier that evening, and she knew that Thomas's mood would not have improved after a few beers.

Once again, he had worked himself up into a rage at the smallest provocation. Wanda was almost four months old, and she had grown so big that she had been kicking her feet up against the end of the cradle for weeks, so Ruth had ordered a little cot for her from Zurr the carpenter—she didn't want her child to grow up bow-legged after all. Zurr had brought it round that evening and as bad luck would have it, Thomas had been at the door to take delivery. Zurr had hardly said good-bye before Thomas had let fly at her, accusing her of all kinds of things—spendthrift was the very least of his insults. He had hurled one recrimination at her after another. And that wasn't all.

Why hadn't she told him before that she had ordered the bed, Ruth chided herself. He didn't like it when she went behind his back, and he always wanted to be kept informed. Heaven forbid that she not let him know what she was doing and why. But damn it all. She wasn't his prisoner! Did a married woman have no rights at all?

She wanted to go to bed. Her arms ached from carrying heavy cardboard boxes full of glassware back and forth all day, and her head pounded with a dull leaden pain. But instead she reached for her knitting basket. For a moment she hesitated over the three pieces she had already started, wondering which to carry on with, but then she settled on a little jacket. By the time she finished, Wanda would probably have long outgrown it.

"Moaning minnie!" she chided herself. Then she rummaged around in the basket for the most colorful piece of wool she could find. Perhaps there would be enough of the yellow to put two narrow stripes up the sleeves?

Her knitting needles clicked in an unsteady rhythm—as unsteady as her thoughts, which were chasing around in her head now that there was finally time after a long and strenuous day of work. Struggling helplessly to clear her mind, she looked around the apartment that was now her home. They had moved into these rooms above the Heimer warehouse straight after the wedding. It seemed a hundred years ago now.

Was that what people meant when they talked about the way of the world? The days trundling by, one day blurring into the next, unnoticed, uneventful? Going to work, coming home, looking after the child, cooking, cleaning, sleeping. Arguing. Going to work.

"What do you want, child?" Griseldis had asked her with a sigh, when Ruth once ventured to talk about how unhappy she was. "That's life after all. Be glad of what you have: a husband, a healthy child, and God knows you don't have to worry about keeping the wolf from the door. You have it a lot better than many others! And believe me, I know what I'm talking about."

Ruth had only felt worse after this little sermon. Widow Grün was right: on the surface at least, she had a good life.

Her knitting needles stopped clattering for a moment. Ruth frowned. What did they say about superficial appearances? All that glitters is not gold. Scratch the shiny surface and underneath there will be bumps and scrapes or even great gaping holes.

"Be glad of what you have!"

Ruth looked lovingly over at the cradle. Wanda had been a ray of sunshine from the moment she was born. Everybody said so. She almost never cried, she smiled cheerfully at everybody who had time for her, and she had slept through the night when she was only a few weeks old. And she was so pretty! Like her mother. Everybody said that too.

There was only one problem with Wanda. Ruth felt a lump forming in her throat.

She wasn't a boy.

The knitting needles blurred in front of her eyes. *Don't be a crybaby,* Ruth thought but she couldn't hold back the tears. Soon her shoulders shook with tiny, powerful sobs. She didn't even care.

When could she give way to the tears otherwise? During the day, in the workshop? Under Eva's venomous gaze? Eva, who was just waiting for something like this to happen? While Thomas was around? He would enjoy it; that was certain. Or should she cry while she was changing Wanda's diaper, dripping tears onto her rosy-pink skin?

Thomas had been so looking forward to the child. He'd been bragging all around the village about what a great strong lad he would be, the best of the Heimer and Steinmann lineages. Night after night he and his buddies had drunk toasts to the health of his unborn son.

And then it had happened. The baby that had given her not the least bit of trouble during the whole pregnancy had been born with the worst possible defect that a Heimer man could imagine: it was a girl. He didn't care one bit that she was healthy, that she had beautiful smooth skin, that her fluffy hair was so soft and blonde that Ruth couldn't help stroking it all the time. Thomas had taken one look at the child and then turned and left the nursery without a word. He hadn't come home at all that night. Ruth had tried to convince herself that he was celebrating the birth. But deep down she knew better. When that viper Eva had visited her the next morning—under the pretext of wanting to see the child—she hadn't even said "What a pretty thing!" but launched straightaway into a hypocritical outpouring of sympathy for her and Thomas. "Not an heir after all, then . . . and Thomas was so looking forward to having a son! And Wilhelm wanted a grandson too. If only the rest of them hadn't teased him so down at the Black Eagle! They said that Thomas was just like your father and soon the women would be ruling the roost . . . No wonder that a man might drink one or two beers too many, after a disappointment like *that*! Sebastian tells me that Thomas was so drunk he couldn't even find his way home. So he brought him over to us. Oh, I wouldn't like to have his hangover! Wilhelm even gave him the day off work. You can imagine what *that* must mean."

Yes, Ruth could well imagine it, even without Eva rolling her eyes and casting meaningful glances her way. Since then, Thomas had been knocking back the booze worse than ever. She tried not to let Eva's needling remarks get to her, and she told herself that Eva was just jealous because she and Sebastian still couldn't manage to conceive.

When Thomas had finally come home that night, he didn't speak a dozen words together, never mind offer her an apology for staying out all night. She had been waiting for him to look into the cradle, or at least to ask how the child was doing, but he had done nothing of the kind.

His brothers were no better, nor was the old man. For them, Ruth's daughter didn't seem to exist. It hadn't helped that Ruth had suggested the name Wanda in the hope that Wilhelm would be happy with the *W*. Nobody seemed to care in the least what the child would be called.

And then . . .

Thomas had hit her for the first time a week after Wanda was born. And that wasn't all. Even now, months later, Ruth shuddered when she thought of that evening.

That day her left nipple had been inflamed, and breast-feeding was so painful that tears had sprung to her eyes. Thomas hadn't offered a single word of comfort, hadn't taken her in his arms and told her that he loved her. No, he had looked right past Wanda's tiny body and stared at Ruth's bare breast as though he had never seen it before. When she had gone to bed at seven o'clock that evening, tired to the bone, he had followed her into the bedroom.

"Now there's no more big belly to get in the way!" he said as he undid his trousers. For a moment Ruth didn't understand what he wanted of her. He couldn't possibly mean to sleep with her? Today of all days, when she felt so miserable?

But that was exactly what he meant to do. And Ruth had been too weak to put up a fight. He had been enraged by the way she just lay there. "Are you my wife or a lifeless doll?" he had shouted as he thrust away.

Ruth had closed her eyes and gritted her teeth, hoping that he would be done soon, crying a thousand tears inside.

She hadn't expected him to hit her. First across the right cheek, then the left. Slap. Slap. With no warning at all. She had opened her eyes in shock, and, for a moment, she sensed that he was at least as surprised as she was.

"You brought that upon yourself," he had shouted in her face. "Next time you look your husband in the eye when he takes what's his by right of marriage. You can keep your airs and graces for outside!"

From that day forward, he hit her again and again. Never so hard that the marks were visible—God forbid Thomas Heimer would become known as a man who beat his wife.

Unconsciously Ruth put a hand behind her ear, to the bruised spot where he had drawn blood earlier that evening.

She hadn't even had a chance to explain to him about the new bed when he gave her a clip on the ear.

"Where do you even get these crazy ideas?" he had yelled, as if she were a naughty schoolchild.

She still couldn't believe this was happening to her. To her, Joost's daughter. Her father had always treated women with such respect.

She was so ashamed that she couldn't bring herself to tell Johanna or Marie about it. What good would it have done? Nobody had forced her to marry Thomas. She had accepted him of her own free will, with all her heart. And that meant she had accepted the Heimer family as well, none of whom had even bothered to come to Wanda's baptism. There had been some "important business" to take care of, that day of all days. If it hadn't been for her sisters, she would have been alone with Wanda and the pastor.

She still hadn't gotten over the disappointment, but whenever she looked into the cradle or put Wanda to her breast, she felt a warm wave of happiness. She loved this child. How she loved this child! The baby was a Steinmann, like her and her sisters.

When she thought of Johanna and Marie she had to smile. Her sisters made up for all of the Heimers' neglect. Wanda was hardly a week old when Marie drew the first of many portraits of her, and she had captured every important moment in Wanda's young life from that point on. Ruth didn't dare hang Marie's beautiful drawings up around the house, but she took them out of the drawer to admire them time and time again. And Johanna! Not a weekend went by that she didn't come home with some darling little dress. Only last week she had brought a solid silver teething ring, and the little one hadn't even begun teething yet!

Ruth's features grew hard. As far as she was concerned, Johanna could spoil the baby rotten. Very soon after Wanda was born, she had resolved that she would be proud of her daughter, as proud as Joost had been of her and her sisters. Wanda should lack for nothing. She was her little princess.

2

Sketches and drawings lay everywhere: on the floor, on Joost's workbench, on the other benches where the girls had once worked. There were winter landscapes, angels, a Christmas crib in miniature—all themes that would go well on Christmas baubles. But instead of being pleased at all that she had accomplished, Marie felt disgusted as she looked at the mess in the workshop. Did she call this progress? It was laughable.

Her gaze fell on the book that Peter had given her for Christmas. *A Handbook of Art and Design*. Sometimes she wished she had never looked inside. It had become her bible, her best friend. And her enemy. Especially that, just recently. She couldn't help but wonder whether art could really be understood the way this book prescribed. Could an artist simply carve up a drawing like a Christmas goose, lay bare its bones, and then revel in its naked details? Was that what art was really about?

Marie had her doubts.

Of course there was a certain appeal in how the book described the logic of shapes. A circle was simply a point, enlarged. Several points next to one another yielded a line. Four lines of equal length yielded a square and the center of the square could also be used as the center of a cross whose arms would divide the sides of the square . . . *everything* could be broken down into shapes, lines, and angles. It was a whole new experience for Marie to see how art could be described with such precision. She had begun to check all her designs using the rules laid out in the book, but she hadn't gotten far since it didn't mention spheres at all. A sphere had no beginning and no end, no corners and no angles. It couldn't be divided up with rectangles or points. She couldn't even say, "This is up and that is down" or "This part is rounder than that part." Like the soap bubbles Joost used to blow for her, a glass ball was a world unto itself. The fact that it was self-contained was exactly what had fired Marie's imagination.

To her mind, the globes were the perfect shape. The ideal form by which all her designs must be judged. If an image could not be painted onto a globe, it was no good to her.

She set the book aside, her mind made up. She wasn't getting anywhere like this. She had to talk to someone who knew about glass. And who knew about globes.

The problem was: there was no such person.

There was no point even trying to approach old Heimer with new designs anymore. His sons were busy morning till night finishing orders for the wholesalers. And Marie very much doubted anyway that he would share her love of glass globes.

And Ruth and Johanna thought that her drawing was nothing more than a pleasant hobby. Besides, they were both so busy with their own lives that they had no time to see what strides Marie had made with her art. Even if they had been peering over her shoulder at every new bauble she created, Marie wouldn't have been happy. If anyone was going to watch her, it needed to be someone who really understood art.

Apart from them, there was only Peter. He had kept his promise from Christmas and told her, "If it will help, the two of us can spend one evening a week together at the bench and lamp. I make eyes, of course, so I only know about that one little area of glass-blowing, but I'll gladly share whatever I know. And I can give you one or two practical bits of advice as well. I didn't start blowing glass yesterday, after all."

It took some time before Marie noticed just how helpful Peter's lessons were. It wasn't just the practical advice he gave but above all the feeling that he took her seriously.

But even after serving this "apprenticeship" with Peter for the past six months, Marie still couldn't shake the feeling that she was still a mere amateur at her craft. Would she ever become a skilled glassblower? How was such a thing even possible when she didn't even have enough rods of raw glass to practice properly? Johanna earned enough to be generous when it came to buying her sketch-books and pencils, but she couldn't just conjure up rods of glass out of nowhere. They were only on sale at the foundry. Although Johanna would probably have thought nothing of walking into the foundry and buying them if her sister had asked her to, Marie didn't want to even think of the gossip that would go round the village if she did. She had no choice but to ask Peter to bring her some rods from time to time.

Once Johanna had offered to get some oil paint for her—"Don't all the great artists paint in oils?" she had asked, which was prob-ably meant as a compliment—but Marie had thanked her for the offer and declined. Oil paints were not her medium; they were too sluggish. They didn't *flow*. Glass was what she wanted to work with. It was a hard taskmaster, for sure: it could burst or dribble away or crack into a thousand shards. A glassblower could cut himself or be burned—and Marie had faced all these dangers by now. But the more she worked with glass, the more obsessed she became.

Marie looked up at the clock. It would be eight o'clock soon. Peter's patient would have left by now, and it was almost time for her lesson. She gathered up her latest designs in a sheaf, put on a light jacket, and left the house.

He was scowling as he opened the door. "I have work to do," he said instead of welcoming her.

Hesitantly, Marie took her jacket off all the same. Work? She couldn't see any work waiting for him on the table, though there was a glass and a bottle of schnapps.

"If today's not good, I'll leave," she said, trying to hide the sketches behind her back. But Peter waved her over to the table.

"You're here now. Perhaps it would do me good to take my mind off things."

"I'd like to try something new. It's still Christmas decorations, but it's nothing that I've ever tried before," she said, spreading out the drawings on the table.

"Walnuts, hazelnuts, acorns. And pinecones." Peter looked at her. "I don't understand. This isn't new. Practically everyone gathers them in the woods and gilds them to hang on their Christmas tree."

Marie grinned. "But not everyone has nuts made of glass hanging on their tree."

"Nuts made of glass?" He looked at her appraisingly.

She grew more excited as she explained her idea to him. She could see every detail in her mind's eye, could feel the nuts' smooth curves in the palm of her hand, could run her fingertips over the pinecones. She looked at Peter, expecting him to be just as enthusiastic.

But he merely shrugged. "If you want to do more than free-blowing, if balls aren't enough, then you'll have to go to Strupp and have him cast you some molds."

Was it just that he was in a bad temper, Marie wondered, or was Peter really so much less taken by the idea?

"Go to see Strupp in his molding shop? What am I supposed to say to him? And where would I get the money for the molds?"

Although Marie tried to sound indignant, Peter's suggestion was not altogether unexpected. Whenever she had pondered the matter in recent weeks, she had come to the same conclusion: there was no way to free-blow a glass nut or pinecone and have the result look at all realistic. They had to be blown into a form. And the only man in Lauscha who made forms was Emanuel Strupp.

"Then make some yourself. Your sketches are detailed enough that you could make a clay model. Then you could use the clay to make a plaster-of-Paris form. I could get you a few chunks of clay and plaster without any trouble. I imagine that your forms won't last as long as Strupp's—nobody knows what he puts into his mixture—but they shouldn't shatter the first time you use them at the lamp. It's got to be worth a try, hasn't it?"

Marie's lips curved up in a triumphant smile. "To be honest, I was thinking along the very same lines. If *you* think I can do it, that's all the encouragement I need." She shrugged. "After all, what have I got to lose?" Impulsively, she squeezed Peter's arm. "If I didn't have you . . . You really are a good man!"

Peter stared down at his glass. "You're the only woman who thinks so."

Marie kept quiet. She knew perfectly well who his remark was directed at; only last week Johanna had rebuffed him rather brusquely. All he had done was ask whether she intended to come home the following weekend. Marie thought the question quite justified, given that her sister had spent the last two weekends in Sonneberg, but Johanna had almost exploded and accused him of treating her like a child.

"You know Johanna," she said rather lamely.

"Why is that woman so headstrong?" Peter asked, raising his hands helplessly. "Who's she trying to convince that she can get by alone? We all know that by now."

Marie struggled to find a suitable answer. But she wasn't used to such outpourings of feeling, and she didn't feel she was good at this sort of thing. She wasn't the kind of person who would run to tell someone else her troubles. Whenever she felt sad, she sat down with her sketchpad and drew something. And she did the same when she was feeling happy.

"Nobody can claim that I'm pushing her into anything. I still remember what your father used to tell me. I can practically hear his voice. 'Give the girl time,' he said. 'Johanna's not nearly so grown-up as she pretends to be.' That's all very well but how long do I have to wait for her to realize where she belongs?" Peter's shoulders drooped.

So Father had known all about Peter's feelings for Johanna. And apparently he had approved.

"But you can hardly force her to love you," she said, surprised to hear a note of aggression creep into her voice. Where had he gotten the idea that he and Johanna were meant for one another? Why was he so firmly convinced of it?

Peter collapsed like a bellows at rest. "I know that," he said quietly. "But I still hope that she'll come to me one day. Of her own free will. It's just that sometimes"—he laughed awkwardly—"some days are harder than others. I'm only human after all. I have desires, I have needs . . ." He broke off. "But why am I telling you all this? You're not like other women. You seem to just float above these things."

"I'm not sure what you mean by that, but it doesn't exactly sound like a compliment," Marie said, rather put out. What had gotten into Peter today, when he was usually so cheerful?

"Do you know, for a while I even thought that you and the youngest Heimer boy . . ." he said, looking askance at her.

"Michel and I?" Now she truly was offended. "How on earth did you get that idea?" She very nearly shook herself like a cat caught out in the rain.

Peter shrugged. "Well, back in the spring he was calling on you quite often. So I thought that you and he . . . What's so odd about the idea that you might marry a Heimer boy as well?"

"Well thank you very much!" Marie said, outraged. "Perhaps he did have some hopes in that direction. But there's nothing I can do about that. I simply didn't have the heart to send him away. You know, he's not such a bad lad." She didn't mention that she had made him show her one or two tricks at the lamp when he visited. Looking back, she was rather ashamed of having taken advantage of him like that. Perhaps he had felt encouraged by her words of praise? Marie decided that it was time to change the topic.

"If we're talking about having callers . . . Am I wrong, or have I seen Rita Strupp dropping in on you?"

Peter nodded.

"So?" It was just like a man, to clam up at the decisive moment.

"She likes me." He made a face. "She even gets quite insistent sometimes. I don't think I'd even have to make much of an effort if I wanted to . . ." He broke off when he noticed that the conversation was beginning to get rather personal. "But what would I want with Rita?"

Marie had to laugh.

"Other men wouldn't ask such a silly question. She's a very pretty girl, after all."

"So what if she is," Peter said dismissively. "I prefer a girl with a good head on her shoulders. But I don't think it's anything to do with Rita, really. It's just that *any* other woman would only be second best for me. There's nothing I can do about that, but I won't settle for second best. Look at it this way: if someone forbade you from blowing glass all of a sudden, would you say, 'Never mind, I'll just take up crocheting'?"

"It's rather an odd comparison, but I see what you mean. Poor Peter . . ." She gave him a friendly pinch. "Given how wrapped up Johanna is in her work, I can see how you might be having rather a lonely time of it."

He nodded gloomily. "You're right of course. If Johanna doesn't come back to Lauscha by some miracle, I may as well become a monk."

3

"Isn't she the prettiest child you've ever seen?" Ruth held Wanda up. The only answer was the baby's giggling. "Here! I'm sure Aunt Marie wants to hold you for a while."

Before Marie knew it, she had the child in her arms. Wanda promptly stopped laughing and began to cry.

"She doesn't want to come to me, can't you see that?" Marie held the baby out, as though she were infectious.

Wanda took the opportunity to pick up one of Marie's pencils and put it in her mouth.

"Leave that alone, it's poisonous!" Marie said as flecks of apple-green drool fell onto the delicate lace collar of Wanda's dress.

"Give her to me," Johanna said, smiling "Your aunt Marie doesn't have the patience for a little scrap like you."

As soon as her hands were free, Marie tried to restore order on her worktable. She soon realized, however, that it was pointless, given all the bits and bobs that Ruth had scattered about since coming in. How could a little baby need so much stuff?

It was late on Sunday afternoon, and Marie had been planning to try to make a second clay model. The first—a long, thin pine-cone—hadn't turned out badly for a first attempt, and she wanted to see whether she would improve with practice. But by the look of things, she wouldn't be getting any work done today.

"Where does she get the silvery-blonde hair from?" Ruth asked, stroking her daughter's head adoringly. "Not from Thomas's side of the family, that's for sure. Mind you, her hair doesn't shine the way it does on its own. I give it thirty strokes of the brush every night before bed. With very soft bristles, of course. And I only ever wash it with the lavender soap that you gave me." She smiled. "When Wanda's a little bit older she'll get a silver clasp for her hair. Just like I always wanted when I was a child."

"Don't you remember? Mother's hair was blonde, not as fair as Wanda's of course, but much lighter than Father's or ours." Johanna closed her eyes. "I can still feel how silky smooth her hair was. She used to braid it every evening."

"That's right," Ruth burst out. "We always used to squabble over who got to brush it and plait it for her. Once, I . . ."

Marie cleared her throat. "Could you go into the kitchen to talk, please? I'd really like to spend some time drawing, and . . ."

"You want to draw right now? When we hardly have any time together as it is?" Ruth replied.

"You have all week long for your sketches," Johanna put in reproachfully.

"All week!" Marie pursed her lips. "Don't make me laugh!"

Ruth called in every evening, claiming that it was "just for a little while" and always stayed for hours. Talking to Wanda. Talking about Wanda. Saying how pretty she was, how clever. Marie glanced irritably at her niece, who was chattering away to herself. Why did children have to be so loud?

"Why don't you make some coffee, and I'll join you in half an hour?" she suggested, doing her best to sound friendly.

She uttered a quick prayer of thanks once the two of them did as she had asked and the room was finally quiet once more.

◆ ◆ ◆

"I don't know what's wrong with Marie," Ruth declared as she watched Johanna grind the coffee beans. "I almost feel we're not welcome here. Hmm . . . that smell. I could happily die with that smell in my nostrils."

"I brought you a bag of coffee last time I came. Is it all gone?" asked Johanna.

"Long gone. It's been three weeks since then. And I have to have my little treats, don't I? Eh, don't I, Wanda?"

She jogged the baby up and down on her knee. Then she added in a deliberately casual tone, "Oh by the way . . . I'll be coming along with you to Sonneberg tomorrow!"

"Tomorrow? That doesn't really suit me very well," Johanna responded, frowning. "Strobel's coming back tomorrow, so I have to be in the shop right on time. And I can't leave early since he always wants an update on all that happened in his absence."

"All I ever hear is Strobel this and Strobel that! Isn't this the second time this year he's taken one of his trips?" Why didn't Johanna ask what she wanted to do in Sonneberg? Nobody in this house seemed to care what she had to say.

"The third time," Johanna corrected her dryly. "But as far as I'm concerned, he can take as many trips as he likes, and for as long as he likes."

"Ha, I can well understand that. You probably have a high old time when he's not there."

"Not at all. Some days there's so much work to get through that I'm in a flat spin by noon. But tell me: Why do you want to go to Sonneberg tomorrow?"

At last! Ruth gave a secretive smile. "I have a little idea. Actually I wasn't planning to tell you, but . . . well, why not! You're my sisters after all."

She looked indulgently at Marie, who had joined them at the table. Then she fetched one of Johanna's magazines from her bag next to her chair. It was called the *Arbor* and its subtitle proclaimed it to be a journal for the entertainment and edification of ladies. Johanna only ever leafed through it, but Ruth read every line of every page, looked intently at every picture, and absorbed every scrap of information like a sponge.

Ruth turned to the page she wanted and pointed to a picture of a little baby swaddled in fine lace and lying on a bearskin.

The others looked at it uncomprehendingly.

"The newest scion of the Russian Imperial house," Johanna read the caption under the photograph. "I don't understand. What's that got to do with your trip to Sonneberg?" Johanna asked.

Ruth rolled her eyes. "Sometimes you can be rather slow on the uptake. Isn't it obvious: I want to have a photograph taken of Wanda! Like the tsar's baby. On a bearskin. After all she's at least as pretty as the little girl in the picture."

"A photograph of Wanda?" Johanna's skepticism was written all over her face. "What does Thomas have to say about it?"

"Thomas!" Ruth waved her hand dismissively. "He doesn't need to know everything. Once the picture's ready, I'm sure he'll like it."

She probably wouldn't even tell him why she wanted to go to Sonneberg but instead claim that she had to go to the doctor. In all likelihood, she would never show him the picture. Even more likely, he would beat her black and blue if he ever found out what "fripperies" she was wasting their hard-earned money on. Money that she had scraped together, penny by penny, from the housekeeping fund. But her sisters didn't need to know any of that.

"A photograph like this is a lasting memory, we'll have it forever," she said. "Wanda can hang it up on her wall when she's older."

"Isn't that terribly expensive? Wouldn't you like me to just draw you another portrait of Wanda? That would be free, after all," Marie offered.

"I don't know. I've heard of newlyweds being photographed, but a baby?" Johanna shook her head. "Isn't it all a bit too much? And don't go telling me it's the way the tsar's family does it!"

"Don't you want Wanda to have anything nice?" Ruth spat out. "If that's the case, then I might just as well have stayed with the Heimers, where I can listen to Eva making spiteful remarks." Ruth felt herself choking up. She had been feeling very weepy lately. To stop herself from bursting into tears, she went on the attack again. "If Father were alive now, at least he'd love his grandchild! He didn't find fault all the time like you do!"

"Not so fast," Johanna replied. "You know very well that we would do anything for your daughter. But that doesn't mean that we're not allowed to voice our doubts when we have them, does it?"

Ruth looked away stubbornly. She hadn't come here to be lectured.

"Don't you think that sometimes you spoil Wanda just a little too much?" Marie remarked.

"And what if I do?" Ruth shot back. "Would that be so bad?" She didn't wait for an answer but carried on, "Look at her, the little treasure! You can't compare Wanda to other babies. She's something special, and she deserves the very best!"

By the time Ruth left that evening, Johanna agreed that if they could leave earlier than she'd planned they could head to Sonneberg together the next morning.

4

As Strobel's coach drew closer to Sonneberg, his mood grew darker. For the first time, he felt not the least twinge of anticipation at the thought of returning to Sonneberg and his shop. As he gazed fixedly out the window at the pine forests rolling past, he felt stifled. A heavy stench of old sweat hung in the interior of the coach, which he had been forced to take when his train was cancelled due to work on the line.

A backwater. Nothing but a backwater.

The thought of having to spend weeks on end in this dreary wilderness before he could even think of taking another trip to B. was more than he could bear.

He shut his eyes and let his mind drift to the time he had just spent there. That was life at its fullest! He had felt every sinew in his body.

It had been a special visit, meant to celebrate the end of the renovations. The Countess P. had found just the right words for it: "Let us celebrate the resurrection of a temple of delight." Count Z. had even compared it to a palace. Well, really . . . a slight exaggeration perhaps. But the designs had indeed lived up to all their promises.

His money had been well invested. They had made something truly extraordinary.

The décor alone would have justified the expense: black and red everywhere, with great swaths of velvet, even more silk, and plain tough leather for contrast. Beyond that, there was music, champagne, and, above all, a select circle of kindred spirits. All this was reserved for a chosen few.

Strobel sat up straight. Money couldn't buy everything, even if some people believed that it could. No, those who had a key to this temple of delight had the utmost refinement and education. Doctors, lawyers, city fathers, and heirs to great commercial fortunes—the highest of society—all with one thing in common: a strict upbringing in which rigor and discipline had been prized above all else. The capacity to abase oneself, to accept punishment—or, in turn, to show harshness and punish the submissive for their faults—this had to be learned from early childhood if it were later to be celebrated as art.

Strobel's gaze was fixed now on the bench opposite. There was a long rip in the shabby imitation leather, and the brown stuffing that burst out smelled moldy. He traced the ragged edge of the rip with his finger. The material left a sharp, white line on his skin where it scratched him, but Strobel felt nothing.

Now the memory of these delights would have to last him for a while to come. No thrilling pleasures awaited him in Sonneberg. Consultations with clients. Keeping the accounts. Bargaining down the glassblowers and doll-makers—that would be his daily bread. There would be no more fine dinners, but instead, hasty meals, taken with no one but Johanna. Hardly an appealing prospect. To put it bluntly, what did she have to offer him? Pitiably little, even though he had spent more than a year now striving to broaden her horizons and open her eyes to life's pleasures. Granted, she listened to what he had to say and occasionally made a mocking retort as was her habit—a habit that had once given him hope that she might develop as a more astute and assertive conversationalist—but deep down she was nothing but a country girl. Instead of keeping pace with his flights of fancy, with his sometimes startling verbal pyrotechnics, she always brought the conversation back to Lauscha. And he couldn't care less about the blasted place, miles from anywhere in the mountains. How did the English put it? "You can take the girl out of the village, but you can't take the village out of the girl."

As for the other matter, here, too, his efforts turned out to have been fruitless. She had not uttered a single word about the frightfully expensive edition of the Marquis de Sade's memoirs he had chosen as a Christmas present. Ever since then, he had made no further effort in that direction. Perhaps the old adage was true: there was no point in trying to make a silk purse out of a sow's ear, or—ha!—trying to cut a diamond from a lump of mountain stone.

On the other hand, hadn't Count G.—or was it Baron von Z.?—claimed that in his experience it was often the simple village lads and lasses who had the greatest natural gift for submission and dominance? This certainly didn't seem to be the case with Johanna Steinmann, for she would have given him some sign by now.

The coach stopped so suddenly that Strobel lost his balance and tumbled to the floor. "Can't you pay a little attention! Bumpkin! *Putain!*" he swore at the coachman.

He looked down at the dust on his knee as the coachman unloaded his luggage. Then he paid precisely what he owed for the journey, without so much as a penny more as tip. Why would that clod deserve a tip? he asked himself as he heaved his bag up the steps to the shop door. For bringing him back down to earth with a bump?

Irritated, he turned the handle of the shop door and moved to push it open.

Locked.

Strobel looked at his watch incredulously: ten past nine. On a Monday morning.

What was going on?

He opened his traveling bag and rummaged around for the key.

Where was Johanna?

5

"Get ready, *mesdames*, don't be startled! There will be a bright flash!" The photographer twiddled the ends of his moustache, rubbed his hands together, and disappeared under the black cloth that hung behind the bulky box.

"Isn't she good? Just look at how pretty she is!" Ruth was almost bursting with pride.

Johanna looked around restlessly as though planning her escape.

"I really must go now!" she said. The grandfather clock in the photographer's salon already showed quarter past nine. Drat it all! Why had she ever allowed Ruth to persuade her to come along?

"I'm sure it'll be over soon," Ruth whispered soothingly.

Monsieur looked at her reproachfully.

"I cannot work like this, *mesdames*! I need quiet. And the *bébé* must also be quiet. Lie still!" He nodded toward Wanda, who was whimpering insistently.

Ruth hurried over to her daughter, put her back in the middle of the blanket—the photographer had not been able to find them a bearskin, much as he may have liked to—and was back at Johanna's side a moment later.

"What a self-important fellow! Are all Frenchmen like that? I think I would hardly have dared come in here without you."

You've certainly changed your tune, Johanna thought. "You and your ideas—you're going to get me in trouble! If Strobel comes back before me and the shop's not open . . ."

"Oh, he shouldn't be such a fusspot. What difference does half an hour make? The customers won't be standing in line at this hour of the morning."

While Johanna grew more restless with each passing minute, the photographer took another photograph, this time of mother and daughter together, with a great deal of hocus-pocus. When at last they were done, Ruth paid the man, and it was agreed that Johanna would pick up the photographs on Friday.

◆　◆　◆

Twenty past nine.

Strobel looked for the umpteenth time from his pocket watch back to the window.

Where was she? Was she ill? He simply couldn't imagine anything else that would keep her from work. After all, dependability was one of her greatest virtues. It had to be something serious, he told himself. If she had come down with something harmless, she would have sent him a message. He put down his pencil and the list he was holding and went to the kitchen, where he found a message in Sybille Stein's spidery handwriting on the table: she was ill, she wrote, and couldn't come in. He threw the notepaper onto the floor in disgust. Had everybody in the house gone mad? Things couldn't go on like this; he would have to find himself a new housekeeper right away.

He stood at the kitchen window like a spy. Without the clatter of pots and other kitchen sounds in the background, he felt the strain mounting.

Nine twenty-five.

No sign of Johanna.

Nine thirty.

Perhaps it wasn't Johanna who was sick but one of her sisters. Or that brat that one of them had. Strobel gnawed angrily at a hangnail on his right thumb. Why hadn't he thought of that before? All anyone in Lauscha needed to do was whistle and Johanna would come running. Though he had gone to great lengths to show her how insignificant all those country bumpkins were, when it came to her family, she was stubborn as a mule.

Come to think of it, Johanna was stubbornness personified.

Nine thirty-five.

Too much stubbornness wasn't good for a person. A stubborn person failed to see the essentials.

Nine forty-one.

Perhaps it was time to teach her a lesson. Yes, perhaps that was just what she needed. He found himself growing excited by the thought and shifted forward impatiently on his chair.

Where was she, damn it all?

It was a quarter to ten when he saw Johanna coming around the corner, arm in arm with Ruth.

6

When the door handle gave way under her hand, Johanna's heart sank. Strobel's train must have arrived early, today of all days! Hastily Johanna took off her coat and hung it up in the hall. All was quiet. He did not seem to waiting for her with his accusations. And a good thing too, since she still hadn't thought up a suitable excuse for her delay. She was still hoping something would come to her as she ran her hand over her hair and tucked back a strand that Wanda had mussed. She took a deep breath and was just about to go into the shop when a hand grabbed her arm roughly from behind.

"Where have you been?" As if out of nowhere, Strobel was suddenly standing beside her.

"I . . ." Startled, Johanna put a hand to her throat. "I had to take care of something," she said lamely.

Strobel took a step closer. "So I see!" He nodded toward the window. His breast heaved. "Taking care of things with your sister!" He shoved her back, took a few steps, and was at the door, putting down the bolt.

Strobel didn't want anybody watching while he scolded her. Johanna rubbed her arm.

"I can hardly believe it. I come back, suspecting nothing, and I find that you . . ."

"I really am very sorry. If I had known that I would be held up so long, I would never have . . . I'll work late tonight, I'll . . ."

Deciding that the best thing to do was to steer clear of Strobel and his temper until he had calmed down a little, she took a few steps toward the kitchen.

But he leapt after her.

"I leave my business in your hands in the belief that it will be well looked after. And what do you do? Abuse my trust at the first opportunity!" As he spoke, a fleck of spittle in the corner of his mouth puffed out with every breath like a spiderweb in the wind.

Johanna turned away, disgusted. She was ready to admit that she had made a mistake, but she didn't have to stand here and allow his insults.

"As I said, I am very sorry!" she repeated. With more courage than she really felt, she put her hands on her hips. "I can't believe you're making such a fuss about half an hour! This is ridiculous!"

"Ridiculous, is it? I'll show you who is ridiculous here!" And with that, Strobel grabbed her arm, pushed her into the kitchen, spun her around so that she was facing him, and shoved her up against the table until her spine bent backward.

It all happened so fast that Johanna had no chance to put up a fight.

What is going on? This wasn't how an angry employer behaved. This was the behavior of a man who had something quite different in mind, she thought in a panic.

"This is how you wanted it!" he whispered hoarsely. His bony fingers were digging through the fabric into her flesh. "This is all your fault, no one else's."

Johanna wanted to scream but not a sound crossed her lips. She tried to look him in the eyes, but he wouldn't meet her gaze.

This can't be happening. Not Strobel. Not me.

Her brain was so busy trying to grasp the situation that at first she didn't even realize what was happening. And so it took her a moment to associate the sound of cloth tearing loudly with what Strobel's hands were doing; pressing her up against the table with his hips and legs, he had reached inside the collar of her dress and yanked at it until the velvet tore. His eyes gleamed at the sight of naked skin.

"A lesson . . ."

Johanna came to her senses at last. She began to scream, tried to tear her hands free where he had them clamped in a grip of iron with his left hand—all in vain. He grabbed her breasts and squeezed them together so hard that the pain clouded her vision for a moment, and she saw black.

"This is how you wanted it. Come on, tell me this is what you want. Tell me you need it!"

She tried in vain to push his arms away and to kick him. But she could do nothing against his fanatical strength, and he simply laughed at her helplessness.

Where was Sybille Stein? Why was nobody helping her?

She was like an animal caught in a trap; the more she struggled, the harder Strobel dug his claws into her. He was muttering something to himself, but she couldn't understand what. Laughing. Raucously. Then he kneed her in the belly.

For a moment she didn't recognize the sound of her own scream in her ears, echoing off the kitchen shelves. She couldn't double over because he was holding her.

Her breasts, her belly—the pain was so fierce that the world blazed yellow before her eyes.

Just before she could faint, the pain ebbed away. As the tears streamed down her cheeks, she realized how finely tuned was the pain he administered. And upon realizing this, she grew truly terrified.

Do something, put up a fight.

I can't.

He had already torn away her skirt and petticoats. Before she knew what was happening one of his thighs was between her legs, and he was fumbling at his pants. He pushed up against her. Hot. Moist. Disgusting.

No, not that! Not that, anything but that.

"I'll teach you to lead your master up the garden path." He shook her head between his hands. Flecks of spittle landed on her cheek, her neck, and her mouth. She clamped her lips together.

No kisses, please. Please no kisses!

Given what Strobel was doing to her at that very moment, the thought struck Johanna as so crazy that she had to laugh. Panic-stricken laughter. Her eyes were wide open, wide with fear.

At some point it was over. Johanna's body was slick with Strobel's sweat. He shoved her to the floor, and she lay there, curled up, her eyes closed. Her mind was empty, her body a shell riddled with holes, dead. Her clothes were torn rags that no longer clothed her nakedness. And she still did not dare believe that it was really over. When he kicked her, it wasn't entirely unexpected.

"Get up and do as you're told!"

As the voice came nearer, Johanna tried to shrink even smaller.

"And don't you dare breathe a word about this to a soul. Remember: you have only yourself to blame for what happened here."

◆　◆　◆

Johanna was still in her room at the back of the house when Strobel came to his senses.

"What have I done?" he whispered hoarsely, looking at the blood on the palms of his hands, on the open fly of his pants. "Whatever have I done?" His heart was hammering wildly. How could he, the connoisseur, lose control like this? How could he run wild like a raging bull, when he was such a sensitive soul?

A punishment.

Johanna.

His shirt, soaked in blood.

His shop, closed all day.

Were there customers waiting at the door?

Johanna! Should he go to her?

Apologize?

His head was buzzing with pointless thoughts.

"Only a fool would poach in his own forest," he heard a voice say in disgust from a long way off. That well-known voice, humiliating him. Strobel put his hands over his ears.

"I didn't mean to."

Had he said that aloud? He bit at the knuckle of his index finger till the skin split and the blood began to flow.

Money! He would offer Johanna money. A great deal of money! Enough to make her keep quiet and . . .

"Is it not enough that your sins dishonor your Maker?"

And now Strobel saw his father's face, the fine patrician features twisted in disgust at his offspring. Next to him was the hunched figure of his cousin Clara. The old hatred boiled up in him again. Clara, that Polish whore! A poor relation who had sought refuge with his family and had been taken in. In thanks she had brought disaster down on his head. And how she had enjoyed his downfall! With her brooding, despondent manner, she could hardly have made her point more clearly if she had hung a placard around her neck with the words "Fallen Woman." And all this after she had spent months provoking him, making eyes at him all over the house.

"How could you bring your brutish habits into this house and dishonor your ancestors so?"

Until that moment he had never seen his father tremble with rage.

Strobel overturned the table and flung it to the floor. Then a chair. Another. Damn it, she had wanted it to happen! Just like Johanna.

"I condemn you for all eternity."

Strobel's stomach twisted into a hard knot.

No, no more damnation.

He had been young then, and easily browbeaten by his father. That was the only reason he could think of for why he had allowed himself to be chased away like a dog. Today nobody would be able to chase him away; that was certain!

He heard a door slam shut out in the hall. When he looked out the window he could not help but admire how Johanna held her head high as she walked away. She had two large bags and a suitcase with her.

She's going!

Leaving me, and my shop!

He had to do something, he had to. It wasn't so bad after all, a mere misdemeanor. Nothing more than that. A lapse. Insignificant.

He ran to the door, hurled it open, and . . .

She was gone.

"I will see to it with everything in my power that not a door in Berlin will be open to you!"

A smile crept back over Strobel's face. A sardonic smile.

His father had been wrong! Not all doors had remained closed to him. Quite the opposite.

Disgusted, he looked at the chaos he had made in the kitchen. Then he laughed dismissively.

A loss of self-control, no more than that. A momentary lapse, though if he wasted his time standing around here listening to the voices of the past it might still have the potential to ruin his reputation a second time.

He could not allow that to happen.

He bent down shakily and picked up the chairs. He shoved the table back into the middle of the room. Fetched a cloth and wiped down the sticky tabletop.

He had to think.

Find a solution.

He would not be condemned again.

Strobel's shop stayed closed the rest of the day.

It was five o'clock in the afternoon when he finally left the house. Carefully dressed, with not a trace of Johanna's blood left on him, his back bowed as though under a heavy burden, he walked through the streets with a worried look on his face. He looked even more worried as he went into the Golden Ox, his hostelry of choice whenever he wanted to eat out. Instead of taking a table by the window as he usually did, he chose the table where Sonneberg's businessmen gathered, and he ordered a schnapps. Everything about his behavior was utterly uncharacteristic: coming to the tavern in broad daylight, choosing a different table, ordering schnapps when he usually drank wine. It didn't take long for the first of his colleagues to sit down and ask whether anything was the matter.

At least half a dozen times, all through the afternoon and evening, he told his story, his voice trembling, his eyes downcast. He spoke of the bitter disappointment he had suffered that day. All of his Sonneberg business partners or rivals who sat down across the table from him were equally shocked and horrified—it must have been awful to find that his own assistant was stealing from him! The breach of trust was inexcusable!

7

Even before she warmed up the soup left over from the previous day, Griseldis Grün took the letter from its envelope one more time. The cheap paper was crumpled by much handling and did not unfold easily. Though she already knew the few lines written there by heart, her eyes took in every word as though she were reading them for the first time; Magnus was coming home. That's what he had written. The postmark was blurred but Griseldis was fairly sure she had read the date right; the letter had been posted two weeks before. She didn't know how long it took to get from Rostock to Lauscha, but she was expecting him home any day now. She glanced out the window.

Before she put down the letter, she ran her hand over the table-top to see that it was clean. The wood was as rough as her skin, but there were no splashes of soup. She put the letter down almost reverently. She had thought that the postman must have made a mistake when he had stopped in front of her house. A letter, for her? That was impossible, she had never had a letter in her life.

Her boy was alive. And he was coming back. Griseldis didn't know whether that was anything to look forward to.

Unable to settle down, she stood up, picked up her sewing basket, then put it down again.

It had been a long time since she had last seen Magnus. Shortly before Josef died, he had packed up his things and left. Though he had been only sixteen years old, Griseldis hadn't tried to stop him, hadn't wept or pleaded. He had not been a good son to her. Like father, like son—wasn't that how the saying went?

In the years since Josef died, Griseldis had finally been able to live in peace.

And suddenly here was this letter. Why had Magnus even written to her? There was no hint of an explanation in those few brief lines. Why now, and not once in all the years before?

It took some effort for her to remember his face; six years was a long time. There had never been anything childlike about it; it had always been a smaller copy of his father's face—plain, and wearing a sullen expression, as though he were constantly squabbling with his Creator about why he had been born at all. Griseldis couldn't remember a single occasion when Magnus had taken her side. Whenever Josef beat her, he had simply looked on, unmoved. Never once had he called out, "Stop, Father!" and run the risk of being beaten himself. He would only come out of hiding once his father disappeared off to the tavern, and she was busy soothing her bruises with a cold compress or a salve. Griseldis could still remember exactly how he would look at her; the contempt in his eyes hurt as much as Josef's blows. *He doesn't know any better,* she had told herself back then, *he's still a child.* But even a child would have realized that Griseldis was not to blame for Josef's brutality. It was the drink that was to blame, the schnapps that Josef tipped down his throat every evening at the Old Jug. It was like an acid, whittling away at Josef's wits. The only thing that she had ever had to thank God for in those days was that Josef had never turned on his son.

The memory of those wretched times made Griseldis shiver. She shut the window, though not before looking out into the warm June night one last time.

Why was Magnus coming back to Lauscha? Why not stay where he was?

He had never belonged here. Truth be told, none of the family ever had. Although the fact that Josef was not a glassblower shouldn't have been a problem—nobody shunned Weber the baker or Huber the storekeeper for not being glassblowers; Lauscha needed people to take care of the day-to-day necessities after all—Josef's nature had made him an outsider. He hadn't had a single friend. And no wonder! He was so envious and suspicious of others that he managed to make enemies of everyone he spoke to, even the best-intentioned. Magnus had hardly been any better, and none of the glassblowers' children ever wanted to play with him. *But how could he have been better?* Griseldis wondered with a heavy heart.

She was quite sure that Magnus had long ago followed his father's example and become a drunkard himself.

The solitude that gave her such peace, the lonely life that she had grown so accustomed to by now, suddenly made her shudder. There was nobody she could talk to. Not a single neighbor she could visit for a chat. For a while she had thought that she might befriend the eldest of the Steinmann sisters. But once Johanna had lost her job at Heimer's, it had come to nothing. And even if Johanna had stayed in Lauscha, she would hardly have had much time for an old woman. She had her sisters to take care of. Griseldis's thoughts turned to Ruth. Why hadn't she turned up to work today? She knew all too well what Ruth's life was like, and she didn't envy her for it. It was cold comfort that other women were as stupid as she had once been, and chose drunkards for husbands. It made no difference whether the family was rich or poor: men who beat their wives were all the same.

The thought that she had at least escaped that misery was such a consolation that Griseldis suddenly felt guilty. She looked down at her sewing basket. Perhaps she should sew a dress for little Wanda. Or crochet her a vest. Ruth would be pleased.

A little more cheerful now, Griseldis got up and went to the bench with the chest beneath it to see whether there was any wool she could use. She was so absorbed in her task that she forgot Magnus's letter for the first time in days. She had just pulled out a tangled skein of yarn and a crochet hook, shut the chest, and stood up when she glanced out the window.

There was a shadow on the road below her house.

Griseldis put a hand to her throat, and her heart began to pound.

Magnus?

No, there were two people. She squinted, trying to make out more details.

A man and a woman. They were moving very strangely.

Why were they so slow?

It looked as though the man could hardly keep the woman upright, as though her legs collapsed beneath her every few yards. Or were her old eyes deceiving her? Was there some other reason the woman was dragging her feet like that? Perhaps she was just drunk.

Griseldis's hands clutched the hank of yarn. Should she go out and ask them whether they needed help?

She hesitated. The woman had a scarf around her head that hid her face. Perhaps they were vagabonds, thieves traveling the roads under cover of darkness.

Griseldis took a step back from the window. There was no doubt about it; the woman needed help and could not walk any farther. Maybe they were travelers who had been attacked on the road to Sonneberg?

She dashed out of her house and ran toward them.

The man looked like Magnus. Not very much, but for a moment . . . Griseldis stopped abruptly. Wasn't that . . .

"Johanna!" She clapped her hand to her mouth. "Magnus!" Griseldis crossed herself.

For a terrible, long moment, time seemed to stand still. The only sound was Johanna's whimpering.

Griseldis stared at the young woman, utterly at a loss. Then her eyes bored into her son.

"Magnus—for heaven's sake—what have you done?"

8

Marie sat at her workbench, utterly worn out.

She looked at the front door to check again that it was closed and locked. Shouldn't she head back upstairs to look after Johanna? To tend the wounds all over her body, even those parts that should have been hers and hers alone? When she thought of Johanna's bruised breasts, Marie felt a current of panic surge through her all over again. She had never seen anything like it. She would have felt better if they had called the doctor, but Johanna wouldn't allow it. She didn't even want Marie to fetch Ruth. Or Peter.

"Not Peter, he mustn't find out." Johanna had spoken with difficulty, spitting out each word. Her lower lip was split and bloody.

"But Peter's our friend. He . . . he can help," Marie had answered. Even his mere presence would have been a comfort for her, but Johanna had shaken her head vehemently. "He mustn't find out."

Marie swallowed. How did Johanna imagine that was going to work? Griseldis and her son had eyes in their heads after all. Griseldis had taken Marie aside and whispered something about rape before Marie had even had a chance to see what had happened to her sister. By tomorrow morning, half the village would know. The thought of the shame it would bring on their house made Marie curl up inside.

She strained her ears to hear what she could upstairs, but it was all quiet. No whimpers, no voice calling her name.

Griseldis had offered to stay the night but Marie had declined. "If I can't manage on my own, I can always fetch Ruth," she had said, and the Widow Grün had nodded.

Undressing Johanna on her own, she had been horrified by what she saw. Both of them wept, and Marie knew that she would never forget the sight, not for the rest of her life. After washing the wounds with a chamomile infusion and applying a salve, she had dressed Johanna in the softest nightgown she could find. All the while, the look in her sister's eyes had been as vacant as if she were no longer of this world. Though her every touch must have stung, Johanna had lain there lifeless as a doll as Marie tended to the wounds. Nor had she uttered a word about who had done this to her or when and where it had happened. Marie had finally stopped asking.

For a while she had sat next to Johanna's bed, holding her hand. When Johanna finally drifted off into a restless sleep, Marie had gone downstairs. She needed a few minutes to herself or she would lose her mind.

Who was the man who had attacked her sister so brutally? The question went round and round in her head.

Helplessly she stared at Joost's tools, which over the last few months she had made her own. What would Father have done in her place? Would he have fetched Peter? Or would he have respected Johanna's wish that he must never find out?

She was clearly terribly ashamed, and Peter was a man, which was another problem. But hadn't Johanna always claimed that he was like a brother to her? Would she be less ashamed in front of a brother? Marie wondered. She didn't know.

But she knew that she couldn't cope with the situation on her own.

◆ ◆ ◆

"Johanna's been . . . what?"

Peter made a move to rush out the door, but Marie blocked his way.

"Stay here, damn it! She's asleep. Besides, she doesn't know I'm here. She . . . didn't want you to know."

"What are you talking about?" He ran his hands frantically through his hair. "I have to go to her, don't you see? She needs me now!" He was shouting.

Marie nodded wordlessly, but she did not move out of the doorway.

He very nearly shoved Marie aside. Dreadful images flashed through his mind. His Johanna . . . defiled? Strange hands—violent hands—laid upon that lovely, proud body that he dared not even embrace?

He paced from stove to doorway like a caged beast. He would kill the man who had done this!

"When did it happen? Why didn't you come to me straight-away? Tell me: Was it Strobel, the swine?" He shook Marie roughly by the shoulders.

"I don't know. She hasn't uttered ten words together since Magnus brought her to us. And I can understand that she doesn't want to talk about it. It would be like living through it all over again." Marie pressed a hand to her mouth.

"She didn't even say his name? Is she trying to defend a despoiler of women? He'll get what's coming to him, you can be sure of that. Johanna doesn't need to say anything; I'll get the truth out of him all the same!"

"Peter! You're scaring me, talking like that!" Marie sobbed. She clutched at her sides as though she too had been beaten.

When he looked over at her, he saw the same helplessness in her eyes that tormented him. Marie couldn't help that this had happened. It wasn't fair of him to take out his anger on her.

"I'm sorry," he whispered hoarsely. He put an arm around her shoulder and was horrified to realize that she was trembling. "The thought that something like that could happen to Johanna almost kills me." His throat was so tight that every word he spoke hurt.

"I feel just the same way," Marie said, tears coursing down her cheeks. "What kind of monster does something like that?" she sobbed helplessly. She put up no resistance as Peter led her over to the kitchen corner and sat her on the bench.

He fetched two glasses and a bottle of schnapps and sat down next to her. He pressed one of the glasses into her hand. "Drink!" he said, then gulped down the contents of his own glass. The burning sensation as it went down his throat was familiar, comforting.

Peter's eyes narrowed to slits. "Magnus turned up out of the blue, today of all days. Isn't that suspicious?"

"It wasn't Magnus," Marie replied. "He would hardly have brought her back to her own home. You should have seen how upset he was. He looked like he might burst into tears as well." Marie looked at Peter, the tears stinging her eyes. "It was just so horrible seeing her like that . . . For a moment I thought she might die. It was Johanna, but so weak, so . . ." Her shoulders quaked.

Peter didn't know how much more he could take. Helplessly he slammed his fist down on the table.

"I knew from the very start that something wasn't right about Strobel! Damn it all, why did I ever allow her to go work for him?" The thought that he might have been able to prevent Johanna's suffering almost drove him mad.

"Do you think it was really him?"

Peter's face was a mask of grim determination.

"Who else?"

◆ ◆ ◆

Nobody got much sleep that night, including Griseldis Grün. Fretting about Johanna, bafflement as to who could have done such an unspeakable thing, and the way that Magnus of all people had found her injured on the roadside—all this made sleep impossible. She ached in every limb as she got ready for work at six o'clock the next morning, even more exhausted than she had been the night before. She wanted to look in on Magnus quickly, but then stopped in the doorway as a wave of motherly love washed over her.

Her son.

A good lad.

Even a hero.

He had saved Johanna. If he had not found her, if he had not taken care of her . . . who knows what might have become of her?

His cheeks were pale even in his sleep. Though there wasn't much flesh on his bones, he looked good. Back when he had left home, he had been chubby, his eyes almost invisible between his fat cheeks and broad nose. Now, however, his eyes with their long lashes were his most noticeable feature.

Griseldis swallowed. She had never considered the possibility that Magnus would stop looking like his father. Now she even thought she could see a little of herself in his face.

Her son.

For a moment she had believed that he had been the one who . . . She heaved a deep sigh.

When Peter knocked on the door a little later, wanting to speak to Magnus, her heart lurched.

Her son, the hero—for Griseldis, the idea was as fragile as glass.

◆ ◆ ◆

"You're Peter the eye-maker, aren't you? Have you found the swine?" Magnus asked immediately.

"Has Johanna still not said who did it?" Griseldis asked.

Peter shook his head. These two didn't need to know whom he suspected. He was surprised that Magnus recognized him straightaway; he wouldn't have known the lad without some help.

Magnus could tell him little. He had found Johanna cowering by the roadside at the edge of Sonneberg; he couldn't say what time of day exactly but he guessed sometime around five o'clock. She had been nearly in a faint. And she was clearly scared, so he had spoken to her gently. He hadn't realized at first what had happened to her, but thought perhaps that she had been attacked on the road. When he had asked if he should take her to a doctor, she said no, that she wanted to go home to Lauscha. So he had helped her walk as best he could, letting her lean on him, even carrying her part of the way. He hadn't had the money for train tickets, but in her condition he could hardly have sat with her in a carriage anyway. At that point Magnus broke off and looked down at the floor.

"You were away for quite a while. Why have you come back?" Peter asked.

"Why have I come back?" Magnus repeated thoughtfully. "I don't quite know myself." He smiled disarmingly. "Perhaps it's time for me to think about what I'm doing with my life."

As Peter walked to the door, Griseldis and Magnus agreed not to say a word. "And that still holds true even after I come back from Sonneberg," Peter warned. He swallowed hard. "If all Lauscha started gossiping about her, it would only make her suffer more!"

"But people will wonder why she turned her back on the Sonneberg job from one day to the next," Griseldis replied, concerned. "What will you tell them then?"

Peter had no answer.

He took his leave and headed to Sonneberg to do what he had to do. Although it took all his self-control, he waited until noon before he went to Strobel's shop. Only when he was sure that all the customers had left did he go in himself.

When he came out a little while later, there was not an inch of the wholesaler's body that Peter had not beaten black and blue.

9

When Marie didn't turn up for work, Ruth went by at lunchtime to see what the matter was. When Marie told her the news, Ruth could hardly control herself. She sobbed and howled and little Wanda did the same. Marie had trouble calming them both down.

"Why didn't you fetch me last night?" she asked again and again. "Why didn't Griseldis tell me first thing this morning?" Ruth refused to leave Johanna's bedside. That afternoon she hurried up to the Heimer house with Wanda in her arms and told everyone that Johanna had come home from Sonneberg with a bad case of pneumonia, and that she and Marie would be taking turns looking after their sister. The old man made a face and muttered something about "No work means no pay," but by then Ruth was already halfway down the stairs.

Johanna spent most of her time staring at the wall. Marie and Ruth sat by her bedside, whispering a few words to one another every now and then. Even Wanda seemed to sense that she should keep quiet.

Though Ruth tried several times to ask Johanna about what had happened, she simply shut her eyes in reply.

She didn't utter a word all day. When Marie brought a bowl of soup up to her late in the afternoon, she shook her head. The look on her face was almost furious as she stared fixedly at the wall. She refused to eat or drink. She didn't sneeze or cough or cry. She didn't even use the chamber pot. She made not a sound, not even a whimper.

As the hours passed, Ruth and Marie exchanged worried glances. It was as though Johanna had left her body.

Neither Ruth nor Marie nor Peter had imagined that Johanna would begin to talk that same evening. The three of them were sitting around her bed when Johanna suddenly turned to look at them.

"He's mad," she said, her voice curiously childlike. She looked at each of them in turn with an astonished expression on her face.

None of them dared say a word—or even breathe too loudly—for fear that she would fall silent again.

"Strobel went mad. Just like that." She laughed hysterically. "From one day to the next." Her eyelids fluttered as though she had a lash trapped in her eye.

The others looked at her.

In plain language, in just a few hastily uttered sentences—as though she wanted to get it over and done with as quickly as possible—she told them what had happened. She didn't go into detail, but nor did she conceal anything essential.

"Strobel went mad. There's no other way I can explain it," she repeated, plucking hectically at the bedclothes. "So? Why don't you say anything?" she asked them, almost accusingly.

Ruth flung her arms around her neck, sobbing. "Oh, Johanna, it's all my fault," she whimpered. "I'm to blame that you got in late. I'll never, ever forgive myself . . ."

"What are you talking about?" Peter said, dragging her forcibly away from the bed.

Johanna stared at her sister. "You're not to blame. Nobody but Strobel is to blame, nobody at all. There's no explanation for something like this. Is there?" Her gaze drifted over to Peter. "What is it? Why are you looking so angry?"

"Because I could practically burst with rage," he said harshly.

Marie plucked at his sleeve.

"I'm not angry at you, God forbid," he added more gently, squeezing Johanna's hand. Nobody failed to notice that she accepted it. "But I don't think Strobel's mad. I think he's dangerous. He's a defiler of women. Perhaps more! I think he's capable of almost anything. The callous look on his face when I . . ."

"You were there?" Johanna sat up straight in bed. "What? When? Why? But you couldn't have known for sure that it was him!"

"Who else?" Peter retorted. "He didn't even bother to deny it. He just said that it was his word against yours."

Johanna clamped her lips shut. They were bloodless and thin.

"Peter," Marie said in a warning tone, "Johanna's tired, can't you see that?"

"Then I'll say just one more thing: the bastard got what was coming to him."

"What have you done? Peter, have you committed a sin?" Johanna asked with a touch of hysteria in her voice.

"He tanned Strobel's hide for him so he won't be able to sit down for a week," Ruth answered in his place. Tears shone in her eyes. "If I could, I'd do it to him all over again."

"And I'd pass you the stick," Marie said just as forcefully. At that, a sad smile flitted across Johanna's pale face.

◆ ◆ ◆

The next few weeks were a time of healing. Their routine never varied: while Marie and Ruth were at work, Johanna spent the day alone at home. Now and then Magnus came by. He seemed to have developed protective feelings for Johanna, which Ruth and Marie found touching but which Johanna found burdensome. Sometimes she went over to visit Peter, sat at his kitchen table, and watched him work. Most of the time though, she did nothing. For the first time in her life, her days were filled not with work but with calm. And it did her good. For it was not just her physical injuries that needed time to heal; so too did the wounds that were not visible to the eye.

"You have only yourself to blame for what happened here!" Strobel had shouted in her face, the spittle flying. But the more Johanna thought about it, the more certain she became that she could *not* have prevented it. There hadn't been any sign in the days before Strobel left town that he would undergo such a tremendous change of character. Quite the contrary: he had even made a point of mentioning how pleased he was that she was there so that he could travel. He hadn't looked at her strangely, or no more strangely than before. Nor was the fact that she had turned up late that morning a real explanation for his brutal attack. There could only be one reason: Strobel had gone mad, irredeemably mad, during his trip. She told herself this again and again. If she were honest—and during this time she was more honest with herself than ever before—deep down she had known right from the start that there was something wrong with him. And she had taken the job all the same. If anything *that* had been her mistake.

"If we had to go round suspecting every odd fellow of criminal tendencies, there wouldn't be many people left we would want to have dealings with," Marie responded when Johanna mentioned her thoughts aloud.

When she looked at it like that, Johanna had to admit that her sister was right. Wilhelm Heimer had his little ways, and people said the most extraordinary things about Griseldis's son. Even Ruth's husband raised Johanna's hackles. But did that mean that all of these men were dangerous? Surely not. Despite that, from then on, there was always a spark of mistrust in Johanna's eyes when she talked to a man, and she never quite lost it for the rest of her days.

As well as all these painful questions about why it had happened, there was also the fear of possible consequences. When her period started, she felt a great weight fall from her heart.

Of course it wasn't long before the rumors that Strobel had started about Johanna spread to Lauscha. As tongues began wagging, nobody quite knew what to make of it. People never went so far as to say out loud that they thought Johanna was a thief. The Steinmann girls were not like other women, certainly, but that didn't mean that they were criminals. The villagers were much more inclined to believe that the rumors from town were all about making one of their number look bad.

Thomas Heimer needled his wife to tell him more, but she remained steadfastly silent. Eventually most people chose to believe the Steinmann version, which was that Johanna had come home because of a serious illness. Nobody was much surprised when she chose to stay. Lauscha folk liked to stay close to home. Hardly any of them had ever left, and of the handful who did, most came back again, as Magnus Grün's return confirmed.

At first neither Ruth and Marie nor Peter had believed that Johanna would be able to find her way back to normalcy. But gradually, day by day, she grew more like her old self; every time Johanna laughed at one of Ruth's jokes, made some sarcastic remark about a neighbor, or left the house to fetch butter from the store, the others breathed a sigh of relief. Only then did they realize how tense they had been. Instead of tiptoeing around the house, they resumed their daily tasks. Johanna took on the housekeeping that had been so badly neglected. Ruth began to come by only once a day, and no longer stayed for hours on end. Peter got to work on his backlog of orders. And Marie finally dared to sit down with her sketchpad in the evenings after work.

10

"I'm off then," Ruth said, poking her head round the kitchen door.

Thomas had been lying on the kitchen bench after a long day at work, but now he sat up.

"Where?"

Ruth switched Wanda over to her other hip. "To see Johanna, of course!" She tried to keep her voice light and easy.

"Have you forgotten that we're supposed to join the others? Father has some business he wants to discuss with us," he said.

"No, I haven't forgotten," Ruth answered. "But Wilhelm and Sebastian will be smoking their disgusting pipes, and that would just make Wanda's cough worse. I don't know what to do about it as it is. A cough like this in the middle of summer, it's just not normal. Why can't Wilhelm talk to you while you're working?"

"You're coming," Thomas said, so quietly that for a moment Ruth didn't understand him.

She stood in the doorway, indecisive.

"I can come later," she offered. She didn't want yet another argument. "It won't take long. I just want to take them a pot of . . ."

"Damn it, are you deaf?" Thomas took two steps and struck a short, sharp blow across the back of Ruth's head. Wanda whimpered softly.

Please, child, don't cry!

Thomas hated it when Wanda cried.

"I don't like the way you spend all your time with your sisters. Eva doesn't run off to Steinach every day; she knows where she belongs. But I have to keep on reminding you that you're a Heimer now!" He was shouting by now. "I want to know what the three of you get up to all the time!"

His face was just a handsbreadth from hers, his too-big eyes boring into hers.

"I asked you a question, woman! What do you get up to? That busybody Johanna isn't normal!"

"I don't know what you mean," Ruth replied, her eyes downcast. "If you came to call on them sometime, you could see for yourself that there's nothing out of the ordinary going on." She put more courage into the words than she really felt.

"You'd like that, wouldn't you?" Thomas retorted. "And you'll stop taking your sisters food and who knows what else! From now on you'll look after my family." He gripped her wrist and twisted.

Ruth howled with pain.

"So, *where* are you going this evening?"

The pain shot up toward her elbow, then higher and higher and . . . "To your family," she said between clenched teeth. She hated herself.

Thomas let go of her wrist.

They had no sooner arrived at the Heimer house than the trouble started again.

Thomas sat down with the other men at the table, ignoring Ruth altogether. Eva gave him a stein of beer, then nodded curtly at Ruth.

"Come and help me with supper! The bread still needs to be sliced, and the butter fetched up from the cellar. And the dishes from lunch still need to be washed as well," she declared as she set to work slicing a ham.

Though it was a warm evening, the kitchen window was closed. The dirty dishes were piled high in the sink and a sour smell filled the air. Ever since Edeltraud had died earlier in the year, the housekeeping in the Heimer household had gone from bad to worse.

After she'd put in a full day in the workshop and got Thomas's supper for him at home, Ruth was expected to carry on working here as well.

"And what shall I do with Wanda? Should I just put her on the floor?" Ruth answered venomously. As she spoke, the cat leapt up onto the windowsill and made himself comfortable. Ruth nodded toward him and said, "The tomcat has a better time of it in this house than the grandchild. At least the beast has a place to call his own."

Eva shrugged. "Nobody's stopping you from putting Wanda in one of the beds."

"So that she can almost fall out like she did last time," Ruth spat. She had only just caught the baby in time when she happened to look in on her. "A baby needs a safe bed."

She hugged her little girl protectively to her breast. Wanda had started to cough. Her little body felt warm. "This horrid smoke is the last thing that Wanda needs."

Suddenly everyone was looking at Ruth and her daughter. Sebastian took a good long draw at his pipe, as if to say, *Well here we go.*

"A cot, my word! As though you would leave it at that!" Eva snarled. "It has to be the finest silk and goose down before your sort are happy. " She looked around, certain of approval.

Thomas glared at Ruth. "Do you really have to ask for the moon on a string like this?"

By now Wanda was coughing so hard that tears were streaming down her face. Ruth looked down at her helplessly, at a loss as to how to help her little girl.

"A fellow can hardly hear himself think with her hacking away like that," Sebastian grumbled. "Tell her to quiet down!"

"If you want my opinion, a bit of discipline never did a brat any harm. I think we all know what happens when you spoil the little beggars too much . . ." Wilhelm Heimer shook his head as though he simply couldn't believe his bad luck in having Ruth for a daughter-in-law.

Ruth looked at Thomas, who was busy opening another bottle of beer. He wasn't going to sit there and let his father insult her, was he?

Eva made a great show of placing the dish of ham on the table.

"Don't get angry, Wilhelm! Nobody can help their parentage," Eva purred.

The others muttered in agreement.

"Am I supposed to be ashamed to be Joost's daughter now?" Ruth snorted in astonishment. "You can hardly say I'm spoiling the child when she's sick and I want to look after her. But I know what you're all thinking—you all wish Wanda had never been born because she's just a girl!" She spat out the last few words.

She felt like bursting into tears on the spot, but she didn't want to give Eva—or any of them—the satisfaction. She stood up, her head held high.

"I'm going home. The baby has a fever and ought to be in bed. You can carry on talking *business* in peace and quiet," she said, staring pointedly at the beer steins as she spoke.

It was long after midnight by the time Thomas got home. Even the way he opened the door told Ruth that he was drunk again. She knew she was right when he crashed into something in the hallway and began cursing loudly. She pulled the covers up over her chin and prayed that he would not wake the little one with his racket.

Wanda had fallen asleep almost as soon as she was back in her own bed, the cough vanishing instantly. Ruth had looked in on her again and again and put a damp cloth on her brow. Her forehead was still warm, but her breathing was regular again. Ruth wondered if it could be that her daughter felt sick when she was around the Heimers. Wanda probably felt how unwelcome she was.

The light went on. "Good evening, my dear!" Thomas came to the end of the bed and leaned against the bedframe. The wooden slats creaked.

Fool! Ruth shut her eyes more tightly. Why didn't he just get undressed and go to bed? She wouldn't be able to sleep a wink with him snoring drunkenly away, but at least she would avoid another argument. Ruth felt Thomas staring at her, puzzling over whether she was asleep or just pretending. She was sweating from every pore beneath the blankets.

He stumbled unsteadily over to the chair where he put his clothes every evening. Humming, he began to undress.

Ruth sighed with relief. It seemed there would be no more trouble tonight. But right at that moment, Wanda began to cough again.

Ruth held her breath. *Stop. Please, please stop.*

Thomas spun round so fast that it seemed he had only been waiting for the least sign of life from Wanda or Ruth. "There she is, yapping away again! Haven't you done enough to annoy me tonight?" he slurred.

Ruth sat bolt upright. There was no point pretending to be asleep now.

"I'll take care of her. Don't worry, she'll quiet down again in a moment, won't you, Wanda?" She was so eager to please that her voice sounded shrill and panicky. She would take the little one and go into the kitchen.

Thomas was blocking her way.

"You, taking care." The fight was in him now; she could see it in his eyes. "You're too bloody stupid for that. Can't even take care of a kid. But you can make me look like a fool in front of my father, oh yes! You can nag at me and answer back—in fact that's the *only* thing you know how to do!"

"Thomas!" She hated it when her voice took on this craven, wheedling tone, but sometimes it calmed him down.

Keeping her eyes downcast, Ruth tried to get past Thomas, but he grabbed her arm and shoved her back with such force that she landed on the floor.

"Not answering back *now*, Ruth Steinmann, are you?" Thomas looked down at her and sniggered. "You wanted to show me up! Like a fool. The way you always do. What do you think the others had to say after you flounced out like that? They told me I was letting you lead me around by the nose. But they're wrong about that, the lot of them!" He towered over her, his legs straddling her, a bulge in his pants showing how he had worked himself up.

For a moment Ruth was scared. It wouldn't be the first time he had come home in this condition and . . .

But Thomas seemed satisfied with the situation as it was. "So? Where are your snappy answers now? All your fine ideas?"

Perhaps he would have been content just to hurl insults at her if Wanda had not begun coughing again at that very moment. Which reminded him that as well as a willful wife, he had a useless daughter.

"Like mother, like daughter, isn't that what they say? Lead me around by the nose—you'll do that too someday, won't you, you little brat!" Slowly, threateningly, he turned toward the cot.

When Ruth realized what he was about to do, her scream tore through the night air.

11

Marie had often wished she could live inside one of her baubles. Life would be so much simpler there. No hard corners and edges to knock up against. No beginning and no ending. Instead, the light shining through and all the colors of the rainbow playing across the round walls. A paradise of glass.

She had never longed for it so much as in that moment—though her reasons were different now. These days, she wished she could spirit herself away because life outside had become so intolerable, a nightmare that she could only rarely escape.

Her weekly lessons with Peter were an exception, which is why she could hardly wait for eight o'clock.

"I know that it makes me the worst person on earth, but I can't help it . . . I really feel put upon."

Instead of blowing glass and talking about designs as she usually did, Marie began pouring her heart out. She felt guilty and helpless, and her feelings were written all over her face.

"Ever since Ruth and Wanda moved in with us, there's not a quiet corner anywhere in the house. There's always someone fussing about the place. And I had grown so used to living on my own."

Peter put a glass of water in front of her. "And there's still no sign of those two making peace?"

Marie waved a hand. "None at all! Thomas comes over every couple of days, but Ruth won't even let him in the house. They have words in the doorway—never loud enough that we can hear what they're saying—then off he stomps. He either looks as though he's about to burst into tears or he flies into such a rage that he calls her all sorts of names. Johanna and I still have no idea why Ruth suddenly turned up at our house in the middle of the night three days ago. She won't say a word about it." She frowned. "He even asked me once whether Wanda is all right. I still don't know what to make of that. And I have to stay in the Heimers' good graces. If the old fellow throws me out, then we're all three of us out of a job. It's a good thing Johanna saved up a little . . ."

"That's the last thing you need to worry about," Peter answered. "Wilhelm Heimer knows very well that he's not going to find a better painter or a faster worker than you. He even boasts of your skills down at the tavern."

"Really? He's never said a kind word to me. He always looks at me as though he can't wait to get rid of me. As he sees it, the Steinmann sisters have been nothing but trouble to him. All the same . . ." She waved a hand. "Somehow I get along with the old fellow. And Thomas isn't my problem."

"So what *is* your problem?" Peter asked patiently.

Marie heaved a deep sigh before she answered. "If you must know, it's Johanna."

Peter frowned.

Should she really tell him? Or would Peter just take Johanna's side? Marie decided at least to try.

"The trouble is that Johanna has nothing to do. Ruth's busy with Wanda all day long, combing her hair, giving her a bath, crocheting a new dress. I think it's all a bit much. But at least the two of them leave me alone. When Wanda's not playing with my paints, that is," she added. "But Johanna? She runs around the house like a caged animal. She's so bored that she's already tidied up my desk and sorted all my papers—though if you ask me she actually just made a mess of everything—and I can hardly sit down at the bench without her peering over my shoulder. Asking questions and wanting explanations. She's driving me mad!" Marie threw her hands up helplessly.

"I understand what you're saying, but how can I help?" Peter asked, looking at her in resignation. "I've asked Johanna at least three times to come and work for me. I could pay, of course. But she won't hear of it." He pointed to a stack of cardboard boxes with blue, red, and green glass gleaming inside.

"I'll grant you that packing these animals of mine isn't half as exciting as working in a big shop. But at least she would have something to do." There was no mistaking the frustration in his voice.

"Oh, Peter! Here I am, telling you my tale of woe, and you have troubles enough of your own." She gave him a nudge.

"Do you remember our conversation earlier this year? When I said that some miracle might bring Johanna back to Lauscha?" He laughed a bitter, joyless laugh. "Now she's here indeed, but she's further away from me than ever. At best, I'm her big brother. At worst, I'm a *man* so she can't trust me. The way she looks at me sometimes—as though she's worried I'll lay a hand on her." He shook his head sadly. "After what that swine did to her, I can understand her reservations. Is she ever going to feel like a normal woman again?"

Neither of them spoke for a while. Then Marie said quietly, "Can't you talk to Johanna, even so? If she doesn't have something to do soon, she'll drive me up the wall. And who knows? Maybe once you two are working together side by side . . ." She tried to sound encouraging.

Peter laughed. "Yes, yes, and this year Christmas will come at Easter!" Then he became serious once more.

"All right then. I'll talk to her again, though I'll feel pretty stupid doing so. But I suppose it hardly matters if she turns me down one more time."

◆　◆　◆

Peter didn't need to wait long for his chance. Johanna stuck her head in his doorway the very next day.

"I've made buttermilk—shall I bring you a glass? It's ice-cold, good, and refreshing," she called over the hissing of the gas flame.

Peter would rather have had a beer, but he agreed all the same. He turned off the gas and they walked out behind Peter's house and sat down. For a few minutes they talked of this and that, then Johanna lay back in the grass. She drew up the hem of her dress as far as her knees and sighed aloud.

"Oh, the sun feels good! For the first time in my life I can sunbathe just as long as I like. Ruth says I'll end up with skin like a farmer's wife, but she spends half her days herself sitting on the bench in front of the house and soaking up the sun."

Peter had to fight hard to resist the urge to reach out and wipe away the milk moustache on her upper lip. If possible, Johanna had become even more beautiful in the past year. He admired the way her hair gleamed, falling in gentle waves over her shoulders and arms in her sleeveless dress.

He was so lost in thought that he almost missed the opening that her remark gave him.

"Does that mean the two of you spend your days lazing in the sunshine?" he asked, grinning.

Johanna sat up.

"You're quite right. I can't go on idling my days away."

Peter was delighted.

"It's just that I don't know what to do with myself." Johanna went on. "Ruth still won't say a word about what happened. She's dug her heels in though, and I'm beginning to think she'll never make peace with Thomas. And the two of them are married!"

"To be honest, I don't really feel like talking about Ruth," Peter said somewhat irritably. "But while we're on the subject, she's not the first woman to run away from her husband, and she won't be the last."

Johanna looked at him in consternation. "And that's all you have to say about it? I'm trying to find some way to understand her behavior though. And I can only think of one explanation: Thomas must have hit her. And more than once. And Ruth . . ."

That was quite enough. Peter sat up too.

"Now you listen to me," he said as forcefully as he dared, taking her hand. "You don't have to worry yourself sick over Ruth day in, day out. Even if you don't believe it, she's a grown woman. She knows what she's doing."

"I'm not so sure about that. She cries at night when she thinks nobody can hear," Johanna said, as tears sprung into her own eyes. "Her world must have fallen apart. She was madly in love with him."

"I never said it was easy for her. But perhaps what she's going through right now is easier than living with Thomas. Have you ever thought of that?"

A ladybug settled on Johanna's hand, and she fixed her gaze upon it.

"Johanna," Peter scolded her gently. "Let's talk about you for a change."

"What is there to talk about?" she asked, with a pained expression on her face. "You're just going to make the same offer again." She shook the bug off her hand. "I . . . please don't be angry with me, Peter, but it wouldn't work."

But why not? he wanted to ask her. *If you want it, it will work!*

Instead he said, "You can't sit at home all day either though. Quite apart from the fact that your savings will all be gone at some point, that's not who you are. Sitting about doing nothing doesn't suit you. Marie agrees with me, by the way. We're worried about you."

"Marie . . ." Johanna cocked her head. "Do you know that she's really quite a good glassblower? And I don't mean her ideas and designs, I'm talking about her craft skills. The last batch of baubles she blew in her forms is practically perfect."

"You don't need to tell me that. But why even mention it? First you talk about Ruth, and then about Marie—you're just trying to change the subject."

"Oh, tosh," she answered cheerfully.

There was a faint smile on her lips.

"I can hardly sit down at the bench without her peering over my shoulder. Asking questions and wanting explanations." Marie's words came back to Peter. And all of a sudden he thought he knew.

"Johanna, are you planning something?" he asked, with a note of warning in his voice.

She drew up her legs and kneeled opposite him.

"I know what you all think: Johanna's just sitting at home moping," she said accusingly. "But that's not it. In fact I've been thinking for quite a while about what to do next. And my plans *include* Marie," she added significantly.

Peter looked at her. Could it be that he already knew what this wonderful, impossible, infuriating woman was thinking?

"Marie's Christmas baubles—you want to sell them," he said.

She looked at him in astonishment.

So he was right!

"And stubborn as you are, you're not just going to give them to me so that I can show them to my wholesaler, but you want to find a wholesaler of your own."

"You really know how to spoil a lady's fun!" Johanna said, pretending to be angry at him.

"Does Marie know about your plans? After all, they are her baubles."

"No, I . . . until I'm certain that what I want to do will actually work, I'd rather not tell her anything. I want to go to Sonneberg on my own and . . ."

"Oh no, Johanna Steinmann, you'll do no such thing," he replied gruffly. "Not until you've talked to Marie and Ruth at least. I can see that you want to prove to us all over again that you can look after yourself. But this isn't just about you."

12

That same evening Peter sat down at the table with the three sisters, as he had insisted they do, and Johanna laid out her plan.

Once the initial excitement had died down, the objections followed. Although Marie had long dreamed of the day when she would no longer have to hide the glass she blew, she didn't have the confidence to take the next step.

"What will people say when they find out that *I've* been sitting at the lamp? What if nobody wants to buy glass blown by a woman?" she asked.

They would have to expect a certain amount of hostility of course, Johanna conceded. Many glassblowers and wholesalers would find it unforgivable that a woman had dared to try her hand at men's work. So she would have to go in search of a forward-looking wholesaler who didn't care whether a man or a woman had blown the baubles.

Ruth's objections were rather more practical. "If you actually manage to find a wholesaler for Marie's globes, when is she going to fill his orders?"

"At night of course," Marie answered. "That's the way I've always done it. Or what do you think?" she said, turning to Peter.

All he did was nod heavily in agreement, whereupon she made a face at him.

"You'll have to do it that way at first," Johanna conceded. "But if more orders come in—and I'm counting on it that they will— then you'll have to stop working for Heimer."

Two pairs of eyes stared at her in horror while Peter sat back, watching without saying a word, just as he had from the start. Johanna shot him a glance, unsure whether she was glad that he was staying out of it or whether she would have preferred his support after all.

Ruth was the first to recover.

"I could help with the painting," she offered. "I know that nobody can paint as well as you can," she said to Marie with a hint of sarcasm in her voice, "but I could manage your ice crystals and winter landscapes. And I can pack the globes of course. We've still got a whole pile of cardboard boxes left over from before. The globes must be about the same size as the pharmacy bottles, don't you think?"

"Slow down," Marie said. "What Johanna is suggesting here would mean opening our own glassworks. I don't know . . . three women, running a business. Can something like that even work?"

"Why not?" Ruth replied. "It would mean that we were working for ourselves. We wouldn't have to answer to anybody else."

Peter cleared his throat. "When are you thinking of going to Sonneberg?"

Johanna looked at him in surprise. "Perhaps next week? Or the week after? I haven't really thought about it."

"But you ought to, if your plans aren't going to run aground. Or have you forgotten that the American, Mr. Woolworth, is coming to Sonneberg in August? He's arriving in two weeks."

"Woolworth? What's he got to do with my plan? He only visits . . ."

Peter laughed. "Oh no he doesn't! It looks like Strobel's only getting a small slice of the pie this year. Almost every wholesaler in Sonneberg has had a letter from Woolworth announcing his arrival. They're talking about nothing else in town right now. Everybody's wondering what special deals they can offer the man, and they're all hoping for nice fat order books by the time he leaves."

It took Johanna a moment to digest the news.

"That means I'll have to go to Sonneberg as soon as possible. Once Woolworth's in town, nobody will have any time for me. I'll have to get to them before the American does. And then"—she gave them all a grin—"our wholesaler, whoever it is, can show Marie's baubles to dear old Woolworth when he comes!"

"In that case, you should go this week. Shall I come along with you? I could help you carry the samples and then wait for you with Wanda while you visit their shops," Ruth put in.

Johanna's grin faded. A wave of nausea passed over her at the thought of Sonneberg. All the same she said, "No, I think I'd rather go on my own. I don't think Wanda would like it in town in this heat."

"Magnus could go with you," Marie suggested. "He has the time, and I know he'd be happy to . . ."

"Magnus! What's Magnus got to do with it?" Peter asked, frowning. "If anybody goes with Johanna, then I will."

Johanna looked from face to face, irritated.

"Are you quite finished? I don't need anybody to go with me," she said, rather more loudly than she had meant to. "I've been going to Sonneberg on my own since I was seventeen years old. And I'll do it again. I don't need a nanny." She swallowed. "I'll set off first thing in the morning—even if it's raining cats and dogs. If it would make you feel better, I'll take the train; then I'll be in town in next to no time."

The other three looked at one another. There was nothing they could say to that.

"But I'll decide which globes you take along," Marie said. "I'd best go choose which ones are fit to be seen."

"And I'll find that crate of cardboard boxes. Then we can pack up the best bits this evening." They left the room arm in arm. Shortly thereafter there was the sound of footsteps and furniture being moved up in Joost's old room.

As Johanna poured a glass of water for herself and for Peter, she said quietly, "Thank you."

"What for?"

Johanna wasn't quite sure what she meant. All she knew was that there was not a man in the world she was fonder of. Perhaps she even loved Peter. In her way. "For not trying to talk me out of this." And then, because she couldn't help it, she added, "Given that you'd much rather have me come and work for you."

"Well," he replied, "life doesn't always work out the way we'd like it to." He sighed, deep in thought. "It looks as though I'll just have to get used to the idea of eventually marrying a business-woman." He shrugged expressively, comical and resigned all at once.

"Peter!" Johanna gasped. "I can't believe my ears. Do you never give up?"

He just looked at her. "No, not where we're concerned. I never give up."

◆　◆　◆

The next morning Ruth made breakfast and then went upstairs to wake Johanna. All of a sudden the memory of old times was so strong that for a moment she believed she would hear Joost clattering around in the washhouse. What would he make of their plans? She stopped for a moment at the dormer window and looked out into the cloudless sky. He would approve, she decided, then walked into the bedroom.

"Time to get up! Today's the big day!" As Ruth swept open the faded curtain, Johanna mumbled, "I'm already awake." But Ruth, not entirely convinced, shook her sister's shoulder just to be sure.

"Train's leaving in half an hour. Don't you dare go back to sleep!" How had her sister ever managed in Sonneberg, she wondered, not for the first time. Then she glanced into the little room next door, where Wanda was sleeping peacefully in Marie's old cot. With any luck she would stay that way until Johanna was safely out of the house.

By the time she went back downstairs, Marie had already finished her coffee. She was standing at the sink, washing out her cup.

"I'm so nervous! I probably won't manage to paint a single flower stalk today, everything will turn out zigzags."

"Don't let anyone notice. Otherwise Thomas will come round again wanting to know what's going on. He doesn't like it one bit that I can get by without him," Ruth answered, pouring a cup of coffee for herself. "There's no need for him to know what we're up to yet." *"Not answering back now, Ruth Steinmann, are you?"* She could hardly wait to see his silly face once they had their contract in the bag. She savored a mouthful of coffee.

"You're right," Marie agreed. "It's probably nothing more than a pipe dream anyway." But her face was flushed with excitement and her eyes gleamed with expectation.

◆ ◆ ◆

Ruth had no patience even for Wanda that day, and Marie felt the hours drag by in the Heimer workshop. They could think of nothing but Johanna and how she was getting on. How many wholesalers would she have to visit before she found one who liked Marie's baubles? Would she really get an order? Or would none of them want to buy from a woman? When the sun began to sink in the sky, a glowing red globe, they wondered when they could expect Johanna back. Was it a good or a bad sign that she was away for so long?

Peter joined them after his workday was over; he too was impatient. He suggested going to meet Johanna at the station, but Ruth and Marie were against the idea. What if one of the neighbors saw them all waiting for Johanna? It would only lead to prying questions. So Peter was reduced to pacing up and down in front of the door like a prison warden. Ruth and Marie left him to it.

It was almost eight o'clock when they finally heard him say, "She's coming!" They all rushed outside.

Johanna was as white as a sheet. She didn't wave her hand, or laugh, or call out *"We've got a contract!"* From the look on her face and her heavy gait, there could only be one explanation.

It had all gone terribly wrong.

They didn't dare look at each other. They were rooted to the spot as they watched Johanna approach. Neighbors passing by on the street watched the scene in surprise.

"Johanna, what's the matter? You look as though you've seen a ghost," Ruth cried out at last.

Johanna walked past them into the house, her shoulders drooping. Her dress was clinging to her back where the sweat had run down between her shoulder blades. She sat down at the table.

"I feel like I have." Her voice was as frail as an old woman's, and her eyes wandered aimlessly around the room.

Was it the heat? Or had Sonneberg reawakened painful memories of the rape? Had it all been too much for her?

Ruth and Peter exchanged worried glances while Marie put a glass of water in front of her sister.

Peter sat down on the bench next to her and put an arm protectively around her shoulders.

"It's all right now. You're back home with us." He held the water glass up for her.

Nobody knew what to say. It was so quiet that all they heard was the sound of Johanna drinking.

"I went to visit every wholesaler. I knocked on every door, every single one. They wouldn't even listen to what I had to say," she began at last.

Fat tears ran down her face.

"I felt like I had the plague and leprosy all at once. But in fact it was worse than that."

The others looked at each other.

Ruth felt the disappointment knotting painfully in the pit of her stomach.

"What are you talking about, for God's sake?" Peter asked, shaking her gently. "Did Woolworth come earlier than planned, or what happened? Why did nobody have time for you?"

Johanna shook her head. "At first I didn't understand what was going on," she said tearfully. "After the first shopkeeper was so rude to me I thought, he's just having a bad day, I'll try the next fellow. When the next one looked me up and down and said he had no time, I didn't think anything of that either. But then . . ." She put both hands to her face and sobbed at the top of her voice. "I've never felt so horrid in all my life. I mean . . . except when . . . but now . . ." Her words were lost in a fit of sobbing.

The others waited helplessly for her to calm down.

"When I asked the woman . . . in the perfumer's, she wouldn't tell me . . . I still had no idea what was going on," Johanna said at last in a tearful voice.

Ruth was growing angry on top of the disappointment. "So what is going on? Would you please be so good as to actually *explain* to us?"

Marie kicked her under the table.

"Strobel told the whole town that I stole from him and that's why he kicked me out." Johanna's face was devoid of expression. "Everybody thinks I'm a thief. *That's* what's going on!" The hysteria in her voice gathered strength. Her laugh cut through the silence as the others sat there in shock. "I'm done with Sonneberg. Once and for all. Even the dogs wouldn't give me the time of day there!"

13

Johanna was almost more distraught than she had been after the rape. She had been able to explain the attack by telling herself that Strobel was mad, that he was not in his right mind. Although he had raped her and robbed her of her innocence, deep inside, by some miracle, she had stayed whole. But his slander had wounded her innermost self; she, Johanna Steinmann, had lost her dignity. All the values that Joost had passed on to his daughters were shattered in a stroke. It was only a question of time before the rumors reached Lauscha as well. Perhaps it had already happened? Perhaps people were already making wicked remarks behind their backs?

She retreated to her room and spent days on end there, brooding in the summer heat. While the air outside shimmered in the heat wave that had descended on the village, she didn't want to see or speak to anyone.

Eventually an even worse suspicion dawned on her: perhaps she had been the reason Ruth left Thomas. Had he called her a thief and Ruth had come to her defense? Was that why Ruth was keeping quiet about why she had fled in the middle of the night?

Brooding and furious, she relived every humiliation of her visit to Sonneberg over and over again.

◆ ◆ ◆

"I won't put up with it any longer. She's hardly shown her face down here for days. When I look in on her, she turns her face to the wall. So I stand there feeling like a fool and have to leave again," Ruth fumed, pacing up and down the kitchen. "How long is this going to go on? This Woolworth is probably in town by now, and we still haven't got a wholesaler for your globes."

"How many times are you going to say that? Just put yourself in her shoes. Johanna's not doing all this just to annoy you." Marie was tired. She had spent the whole day working with enamel paint and still had a nasty smell in her nose. She also had a headache.

She went into the workshop and sat down at Joost's workbench. How long had it been since she had last had an evening's peace in here?

Ruth followed her.

"It doesn't fix anything to have her hiding in her room while we're down here worrying about her. But the worst of it is how she won't even talk to us."

"Look who's talking. You're silent as the grave yourself about what went wrong between you and Thomas."

"That's got nothing to do with anyone but me and him. But *this*—this is about all three of us! It's our future, our life, our . . ." Ruth fell silent.

"But Johanna's the one who's been libeled. And it's all Strobel's fault. I can hardly imagine what it's like. You stand there talking to people, and all the while they believe the most horrible things about you. And there's not a thing you can do about it. I wouldn't want to be going through what she's going through, that's all."

"And we're not, thank God," Ruth said bitterly.

"You can be very unkind, do you know that?" Marie said.

"And you only ever assume the worst of me. I don't mean that the way you think I do." She drew up her old chair from the workbench and sat down next to Marie.

"You heard what Johanna said: her name's mud in Sonneberg. But that doesn't mean that we're all tarred with the same brush now, does it?"

"I don't know. Really, it ought not to. But the wholesalers might lump us all together when they find out that we're Johanna's sisters," Marie answered. She had guessed what Ruth was driving at. It wasn't as though she too wasn't racking her brains about what to do next.

"Do you think so?" Ruth bit her lip. She looked as though she hadn't been expecting that answer.

"Actually I was going to suggest that I take your globes and show them to the wholesalers. But of course, if they show me the door just the way they did with Johanna . . ."

Marie looked askance at her. So she wasn't as brave as all that!

"I think we should ask Peter to show my baubles to his wholesaler."

Ruth looked up, relief showing on her face. "As you like. After all, they're your baubles."

And who had just been blathering on about *our* future and *our* life, Marie grumbled silently to herself.

Marie was already asleep when somebody shook her arm roughly.

"Wake up!" Ruth whispered in her ear. "I have to talk to you."

Marie stumbled downstairs after Ruth so as not to wake Johanna, and followed her into the kitchen.

"Are you mad? Why are you waking me up in the middle of the night? I can't spend my days lazing about like some people, I have to go to work in the morning," she said as Ruth put the gas lamp on.

The light shone unpleasantly harsh in Marie's eyes, so she turned the flame lower.

"I have an idea!" Ruth said, bursting with excitement. "I have a wonderful idea!" She bounced across the kitchen and knelt down in front of Marie. "Just imagine; there's a way I can help us all. If what I have in mind works, then we won't be dependent on anyone. We—"

"Ruth, please!" Marie chided her. "It's the middle of the night, and I'm not in the mood for riddles. Tell me what's buzzing about in that head of yours and then we can both go back to bed."

All at once Ruth looked like the fun-loving girl she had once been. Her cheeks were flushed, her eyes glowed with delight, and she laughed mischievously.

"Once you hear what I have in mind, you won't get a wink of sleep anyway!"

◆　◆　◆

The next morning Ruth got up earlier than usual. After looking in on Wanda, she went down to the washhouse. Marie happily ceded the mirror to her and even offered to go in and take care of breakfast. When Ruth nodded to her absentmindedly, their eyes met in the mirror.

"You really think you can do this?" Marie asked, her hand on the door handle.

"It's the only way," Ruth replied.

"It's not. As I said yesterday, we can always ask Peter . . ."

"You're right. But . . ." She nodded into the mirror to cheer Marie up, who was looking worried. "Just let me give it a try. The worst that can happen is that I get turned down. In which case we'd be right where we are now. But if my plan actually works . . . knock on wood . . ." Hurriedly, she rapped her knuckles against the wall. "But we shouldn't even talk about it. No need to tempt fate."

Once Marie had left, she washed herself from head to toe and carefully combed her hair. Then she took a thick strand between her fingers and held it up to the sunlight that shone through the narrow window. Was she imagining things, or had her hair lost some of its shine? It used to look better than this. She stepped back to the mirror. And wasn't her skin rather pale, despite all the time she'd been spending out in the fresh air? Had her eyes lost their sparkle? She put the brush down as a wave of sadness overcame her. She felt so old all of a sudden. Old and worn like a tool that had passed through many hands—this despite the fact that she had only fallen into *one* pair of hands. She gave a bitter laugh.

It took some effort to shake herself out of the joyless mood. She gave her hair another fifty strokes of the brush and made faces at herself in the mirror as she did so, trying out various expressions. She had to radiate confidence. She wasn't looking for Mr. Woolworth's sympathy—she wanted a contract.

No sooner had she finished putting up her hair than she was assailed by more doubts: Wasn't this hairstyle a bit too old-fashioned? The American must be used to women who were the height of style. She gently teased out a few strands, making sure not to ruin what she had just achieved and skeptically turned her head to the left and right. Yes, that was better, but now it looked rather too playful. She wound the strands around her finger until they curled gently. Much better. Glancing coquettishly at herself in the mirror, she decided she was still very pretty. And there was no point trying to compete with high-society ladies. She would just have to make the best of what she had.

With a practiced motion, she pulled her dress on over her head without putting even a hair out of place. She would have liked to wear her wedding dress, but that would have been impossible in the August heat. So she had settled for her second-best dress: the color was nothing impressive—a dull brown—but it was a well-cut garment with plenty of fabric and especially luxuriant skirts. The brown complemented her skin nicely. As she was putting on a necklace that Marie had recently made her from glass beads and silver wire, she suddenly had an idea. She ran out to the back of the house, picked a bunch of daisies, then hurried back into the wash-house and twined some of them into her hair. She pinned a final posy onto the shoulder of her dress. At last she was happy with how she looked.

When she went back into the house, Marie was about to leave for work.

"The basket with the baubles is out in the hallway. I put the biggest pieces on top, just make sure nothing gets cracked."

"And? Did she notice anything?"

"Johanna?" Marie shook her head. "Either she was pretending to be asleep when I went into the room to fetch the basket or she really was asleep. She didn't make a sound at any rate."

Ruth breathed a sigh of relief. "Thank God. I wouldn't want to explain all this to her." She turned to go into the kitchen and drink a quick cup of coffee.

Marie caught her sleeve. "Are you sure you'll manage? I mean, you haven't been to Sonneberg much."

"Why can't you trust me just a little?" Ruth asked, upset. "I'm no less intelligent than Johanna, am I? As long as I catch the slate-maker on his cart, I can be in town in no time. And if not . . ." She shrugged. "Then I'll just have to walk; I do know the way."

"But then the American will be out visiting the wholesalers by the time you get there," Marie protested. "And how will you find him then? Even if you cross paths somewhere in town, it's not as though you can just stop him on the street and introduce yourself."

Ruth gnawed at her lip. "That's the only thing that worries me," she admitted. "I've even wondered whether I should try to find out which hotel he's staying at."

"And then?"

"Don't play the fool," Ruth said, shaking her head disapprovingly. "Then I could wait for him there."

"That's certainly one way to do it," Marie conceded. "But what if he doesn't speak German?"

"Marie!" Ruth cried. "We talked about all that at length last night. He must know German. How else would he even get by? I can't imagine that every wholesaler in town speaks English." She turned abruptly and went into the kitchen. "And now I don't want to hear another word about it. The more I think of it, the more nervous I get."

14

When Marie left, Ruth went upstairs. She lifted Wanda from her cot, hastily changed her diaper, and then took her into the next room. Carefully she put Wanda down next to Johanna in bed, whereupon her daughter looked at her wide-eyed. Ruth hoped that she wouldn't start to cry.

"What's all this?" Johanna said ungraciously.

"You'll have to take care of Wanda today. I'm going out, and I'm not sure when I'll be back. I might even be gone for the night." As she spoke Ruth realized that she hadn't considered that possibility until now. But it wasn't all that unlikely, given that she might have to wait some time for Mr. Woolworth . . .

Johanna sat up in bed and took Wanda onto her lap.

"You're going out? Overnight, perhaps?" There was a note of curiosity in her voice. "Are you meeting Thomas?"

Ruth gave a noncommittal shrug. Johanna could believe whatever she liked. She tried to estimate what a night in a hotel might cost, and what she would have to take with her. She felt sick at the thought that she might have to take a room somewhere. Could a woman alone even do such a thing? And it must cost a fortune! Her palms were damp with trepidation as she took a fresh nightshirt from the wardrobe; she could pack her hairbrush and a few other things down in the washhouse. Then she went back to Johanna's bed.

"How do I look?" She did a little pirouette. When Johanna didn't answer straightaway, she felt her self-confidence wilt. Then she saw the admiration in Johanna's eyes.

"You look lovely. Any man who sees you will be enchanted, believe me," her sister said at last. She sounded absolutely convinced—and convincing.

Ruth, who had been discreetly holding her breath, heaved a sigh of relief. With any luck, what Johanna had just said would hold true for American businessmen.

"She hasn't had anything to eat yet," she said, nodding toward her daughter. "Can I ask you to take care of her? Marie can give you a hand this evening."

"Of course I'll look after her. What a question," Johanna said. She tickled Wanda's tummy, and the baby began to giggle.

Ruth had to bite back an unkind reply. There had been precious little "of course" from Johanna these past few days. She cleared her throat.

"I don't like to ask, but . . . could you lend me a little money?"

Johanna frowned. "Why do you need money if you're seeing Thomas?"

"I . . . umm, I have . . . an idea," Ruth stuttered. "So what do you say? Can you?"

"Help yourself. No need to get worked up." Johanna raised her hands in an appeasing gesture. "You know where my purse is. Just take what you need."

A smile played across Ruth's lips. If only it could all be as easy as this . . .

She suddenly felt bold and fearless. She stopped in the doorway and turned around.

"Wish me luck!" Grinning, she blew them both a kiss.

She could feel Johanna's surprised glance following her down the stairs.

She had just reached the outskirts of Steinach when the slate-maker who always used to pick up Johanna came around the corner with his old nag and rickety cart. Seeing Ruth, he drew up alongside her and let her climb on. Instead of putting the basket full of Marie's Christmas globes in the back of the cart with his crates of slates and pencils, she put it down between her legs. As they clip-clopped along the road, they passed several of the village women who were on their way to town to run errands. Ruth looked at their wicker carrying packs and was reminded of the ants she had seen on the forest floor when she had met Thomas there. Unlike the busy little ants, however, these women were clearly marked by hard work. They crept along the path, many of them with pain showing on their faces, their backs bent under their loads and their hands wiping away sweat or brushing away flies. Ruth knew how heavy a pack like that could be when it was filled with glass, and she wouldn't have traded places with them for anything in the world. Suddenly, she felt terribly important sitting up there in the slate cart.

Once they reached Sonneberg, she shouldered her pack and marched off. Nobody paid any attention to her; the town was full of women like her delivering wares. The narrow streets were heaving with activity: mail coaches, carriages, people on foot—all trying to get wherever they were going faster than anyone else. More than once Ruth was roughly shoved aside and had to struggle to recover her balance. She was so worried that her fragile wares might break that she ended up walking close to the houses. Her eyes darted around the streets all the while. The air was thick with the sound of voices speaking in Saxon and Thuringian dialects, as well as foreign languages. Ruth began to feel that her fears had been justified; it would be a small miracle if she actually met the American tycoon in this crowd. The only sensible thing to do was to track him down at his hotel.

Though she was parched with thirst and desperately wanted a glass of fresh lemonade or at least some cold water, she headed straight to the photographer's studio, where the pictures of Wanda were still waiting to be collected.

The photographer was much less polite than he had been during her first visit, and she wondered whether he too had heard the rumors that Johanna was a thief. He muttered angrily to himself as he slowly searched through a box for the envelope with her photographs. As Ruth stood there, her face expressionless, she felt her chances of getting any useful information from him dwindling. But as soon as she saw the pictures of Wanda, she couldn't help chuckling with delight. Her daughter looked like a little princess!

Her enthusiasm had an infectious quality, and the photographer smiled as well.

"I knew that these pictures would turn out to be something special! All *très, très chic!*" he remarked, with undisguised pride in his artistic achievement. "Look at the lighting! And how clear the lines are!"

Ruth beamed at him. "They are the most beautiful photographs I have seen in my life!" she said truthfully. He didn't need to know that they were also the only ones she had ever seen. She paid him the price they had agreed.

"It was my pleasure, Madame."

Ruth decided to try a little flattery. Perhaps that was the way to get him to open up. "You're a true artist. The people of Sonneberg should count themselves lucky to have a photographer like you in their midst. I should imagine you must be flooded with work, are you not?"

The man's face fell. "You would think so, wouldn't you?"

"But . . . ?" Ruth raised her eyebrows and toyed with a curl of hair.

He snorted. "Dolls, glass, toys—all they think about in this town is selling!"

Ruth rejoiced inwardly. "And the foreigners? After all, that American gentleman has been in town since yesterday, and everyone's expecting great things from his visit. I'm sure he would know the value of a fine photographer such as yourself."

The man snorted again. "Not at all," he said and waved a hand dismissively. "Not him. He seems to be a most parsimonious fellow."

"But . . . I thought . . . given all that we've heard about this Mr. Woolworth . . ."

"Oh no! When he's buying for business, money's no object!" The man was clearly happy to tell Ruth his woes. "Which is why the wholesalers all bow and scrape before him. Just this morning, the two Americans walked past my studio, and the wholesalers were all buzzing around them like moths around a flame!" He adopted a mocking tone. "'Step this way, sir! Do come in! No, this way first if you please!' But they don't give the rest of us the time of day. He's even staying at the cheapest hotel in town, and they say that he orders the simplest meals on the menu."

Ruth swallowed. That didn't sound like the man she'd been expecting to meet. She also noted that Woolworth had apparently not come alone.

"I've never seen an American," she confessed. "What does this Woolworth look like?"

"Oh, *chérie*," the photographer said, taking her hand across the counter and patting it. "He looks the way middle-aged men look. An ill-fitting suit, a bit of a belly, glasses, thinning hair."

Ruth couldn't conceal her disappointment.

"What were you expecting?" the man asked, amused. "You know, businessmen from all over the world come to Sonneberg— after all, I ended up here as well—but I learned one thing about them long ago: whether they come from Hamburg, Rome, or New York, in the end, they're only human like the rest of us."

By the time Ruth left the studio, she knew that Woolworth was staying at the Sun Hotel, and she had drunk a glass of water, which assuaged her thirst.

15

Ruth spent the whole day near the hotel, keeping an eye on the entrance. But there was no sign of Woolworth at lunchtime, or all through the afternoon. Ruth's feet ached, and the heat was making her unbearably thirsty again. She had leaned her basket up against a birch tree, but it offered little shade. As the hours passed, the shade disappeared altogether, and the heat became worse. Ruth found herself thinking of Wanda and felt like crying. The daisies in her hair had wilted and shriveled away. Ruth plucked them out, one by one, and threw them away. Her ringlets had lost their curl and hung limply, framing her face. Dark patches of sweat showed through her dress and Ruth grew more and more anxious: How would she ever make a good impression in this bedraggled state?

Passersby on the street cast curious or even suspicious glances at her, and in the end she felt so desperate that she plucked up her nerve and went into the hotel. It was so cool in the lobby that it was like plunging into cold water after the heat outside. Although she already knew that it was the cheapest hotel in town, she was struck by how sparsely furnished it was. There was only an unstaffed reception desk and a wooden bench. Ruth sat down on the bench and had hardly been there for five minutes when a door opened behind the desk and a man came toward her with a hostile look on his face.

"What do you want?"

Ruth shifted forward on the bench.

"I'm waiting for a guest," she replied with all the poise she could muster.

The man looked her up and down.

"And are you a guest of our establishment yourself, Madame?"

"No, I—"

"You can't wait here then," he said, grabbing her sleeve roughly and pulling her to her feet. "We don't want peddlers here," he hissed in her ear.

The next moment Ruth found herself back outside in the August heat. She glared over her shoulder at the man. What a pig! It wouldn't have inconvenienced anyone to allow her to sit on the bench a little longer.

She didn't dare loiter about in front of the hotel any longer. That man would probably go and fetch the police if she did. Half carrying and half dragging her basket, she walked around the corner. She felt a lump forming in her throat and tears gathering in her eyes. Her shoulders drooping—both from the weight of the basket and disappointment—Ruth came to a stop.

"You silly clod!" The man's voice rang out again and Ruth opened her eyes with a start. "How can anyone be so stupid? The bedspreads, I said! The bedspreads! Not the pillows!"

Ruth breathed out. She couldn't see who he was yelling at this time, but at least it wasn't her. Only then did she realize that she was standing at the back of the hotel. There were half a dozen washing lines stretched across its narrow backyard, all hung with shabby-looking pillows that had odd stains and not enough stuffing. Among them stood a chambermaid, almost hidden from view by the towering figure of the hotelier standing in front of her.

When the man left, the young woman began to take the pillows down from the lines. Ruth looked at her over the fence. She had small eyes and her mouth was set in a grim line that didn't suit her rosy cheeks. Ruth cleared her throat.

"Your boss seems to be a harsh taskmaster."

The maid turned her head. "So? What's that to do with you?" she spat.

"Nothing at all," Ruth said with disarming honesty. "It's just that I got on the wrong side of him myself a few minutes ago."

The girl looked at her mistrustfully but didn't ask any questions. She continued to tug at the pillows, pulling them off the line without bothering to unclip the pegs.

Ruth told her what had happened anyway. "I was sitting there on the bench as quiet as a mouse. I only wanted to wait for someone." Tears sprang to her eyes again at the thought of all her wasted effort. She fished a handkerchief from her purse and blew her nose.

"That's a fine necklace you've got," the chambermaid said, having obviously decided to talk to Ruth after all.

"Do you think so? My sister made it. She's very clever at that sort of thing." Ruth recognized the greed in the young woman's eyes. "Here! Why don't you try it on?" It only took her a moment to open the clasp and she held out the necklace over the fence.

"May I really?"

Ruth stretched her arm out farther. "Would I have offered otherwise? I know it will suit you nicely." She swung the necklace from side to side.

At last the girl reached out, taking it as reverently as if she held the emperor's crown.

"I've never had a piece of jewelry like this. Just a clasp for my hair. I could never buy myself anything as lovely as this with the money that old skinflint pays me!"

Ruth's heart beat faster. "If you like, you can have the necklace, I just need you to do me a little favor . . ."

A short while later, as the hotelier was on his way to the bank, Ruth went into the hotel through the service entrance. She followed her guide swiftly across the worn parquet floor and up a narrow staircase. Keys rattled and a door opened.

"This could cost me my job, so whatever you do, don't get caught!" the chambermaid whispered as she peered over her shoulder at the stairs.

Before Ruth could thank the girl, the door shut behind her. And Ruth was standing in Frank Winfield Woolworth's room.

The next few hours were at least as nerve-racking as the day spent in the baking sunshine. The longer Ruth waited there alone, the more scared she felt by the sheer effrontery of what she was doing.

It must have been about eight o'clock in the evening when she heard voices in the corridor. Ruth's heart began to beat wildly. What if they thought she had broken in? That she was a burglar? Where should she be standing when the man came in? At the window? Right by the door? By the table where she had set out Marie's baubles on a white cloth she had brought with her? As the voices drew nearer she hurried over to the table. *Dear God, please don't let him throw me out immediately,* she prayed silently.

"Actually, I agree with you," she heard a man's voice saying in measured tones. "But with all the expenses . . ." A key fumbled in the lock.

Please, God, make . . .

The door opened. A man came in and stopped, rooted to the spot, surprised and clearly angered as well.

"What the heck are you doing in my room?"

Ruth didn't need a translation.

"I've come from Lauscha," she replied in German. "I . . ."

Ruth hardly ever prayed but she began again now. *Dear God, let him understand German.* She gestured helplessly and swallowed. Her throat was dry. "I'd like to show you something." She pointed to the table and tried to smile. "Christmas globes."

Woolworth stared at her uncomprehendingly and with a distinctly unfriendly look on his face.

She clenched her hands around the back of a chair, just in case he planned to throw her out of the room.

Then another man walked in.

Ruth glanced at him out of the corner of her eye and instantly forgot what she had been trying to say. She had never seen such a handsome man in her life!

The two men talked to one another for a moment and then went to the table.

A moment later, the famous Mr. Woolworth was holding a glass globe, one painted with an ice-crystal pattern. Though the room was quite dark, the globe picked up what light there was and seemed to sparkle and glow. He turned again to his companion, and they exchanged a few words in English. He picked up a second globe, then a third. When he next spoke, his voice was oddly hoarse.

Though Ruth couldn't understand a word, she could tell that the man was interested. She unclenched her hands on the chair a little. Just when she had plucked up the courage to take another look at the handsome assistant, he turned to her. Their eyes met over the sparkle of Marie's globe.

"How on earth did you get into this room?" he asked in perfect German. "And what do you want?"

Ruth felt herself flush. "I would rather not answer your first question, since it would get someone into trouble." She lifted her hands apologetically and tried to smile. "But I will gladly tell you what I want. I've come from Lauscha to offer you these Christmas baubles for sale." Ruth blew a strand of hair from her face.

The man frowned but seemed satisfied with her answer. He and Woolworth exchanged a few more remarks.

Dear Lord, thank you!

Woolworth asked his assistant a question, pointing at Ruth as he did so. When she heard something that sounded like *Loosha*, she nodded.

He reached for more baubles, showing this one to his assistant, holding that one up in the last bit of light from the setting sun.

Ruth didn't dare look over at the second man again. Instead she took the opportunity to get a good look at Woolworth. No, she couldn't agree with what the photographer had said; it was only at first glance that Woolworth looked like any other middle-aged man. What set him apart from other men was not his clothing or his haircut but the way he moved, nimble and forceful all at once. And his eyes, which never stayed focused on one thing for more than a moment but took in the whole room. Ruth had the feeling that this man never missed even the smallest detail.

Standing there in her sweat-soaked dress, with her hair coming undone, she began to feel even more awkward. She tried to unstick the sweaty strands from her face without being too obvious about it. Her eyes had just wandered involuntarily back to Woolworth's companion when Woolworth himself turned to her, holding a silvered glass nut in his hand. He frowned and asked something in English.

"Mr. Woolworth would like to know why you are not represented through one of the wholesalers," the younger man translated. "After all, it's not standard practice for sellers to sneak into our hotel room." An amused smile played across his lips.

"Well, you see . . ." She bit her lip. The explanations she had so carefully prepared were gone in a puff of wind. There was nothing left for it but to tell the truth. "There are three of us. We're sisters.

Johanna, Marie, and myself. Oh, and my name's Ruth," she added. "Our parents are dead and we must fend for ourselves. Which is why Marie . . . she's the youngest"—Ruth swallowed nervously— "Marie blew these globes. She's very gifted. But it's not, umm, standard practice for women to sit down at the lamp. That's the workbench where the—"

"I know what the lamp is," Woolworth's assistant interrupted her, smiling.

Ruth felt herself blush again. Was he mocking her?

"No woman has ever dared blow glass before. It's strictly a man's job in Lauscha, but Marie does it," she said proudly. "None of the wholesalers want to take our wares because glass is men's work."

As the assistant translated everything she had said, Ruth held her breath. What would Woolworth say? He evidently liked the baubles. But would he have the same prejudices against a woman blowing glass?

A loud burst of laughter broke in on her doubts and fears.

Woolworth clapped a hand on Ruth's shoulder while speaking to her in English. She looked to the younger man for a translation.

"Mr. Woolworth says that he likes the idea that a woman made these baubles. He likes it a great deal!" the assistant said, smiling. "And he also likes the way you took the bull by the horns. He says that's something he would have done as a young man."

"Really?" Ruth's eyes widened. "You're not . . . pulling my leg?"

Both men laughed.

Ruth stood there and felt silly. While the men talked, she began to pack the baubles back into their basket. What came next?

As the assistant approached her, Ruth noticed that his dimples deepened when he smiled.

"Mr. Woolworth is very interested in these baubles. However, since he has other business appointments all evening, he suggests that the two of us sit down and work out the details of prices and delivery."

Ruth looked from one to the other and back again, then fixed her gaze on Woolworth. She took a deep breath and held out her hand toward him.

And Ruth heard her own voice say, "A pleasure doing business with you," as though she closed deals every day of the week.

Woolworth answered in English. "Here's to glass," he said. She understood that much, at least.

Ruth had to fight to stifle a smile. When the others back home heard about this . . .

"May I accompany you downstairs?" The assistant took her gently by the arm and gestured to the door with his other hand.

Ruth beamed at him. Johanna had never told her that business negotiations could be this thrilling.

16

When Woolworth's assistant handed Ruth's basket to the reception desk to look after, the hotelier's eyes almost popped out of his head. Then they went into the dining room.

Her head held high, Ruth sat down on the chair that he held out for her. She had never dreamed that she would get to go out to dinner with a man like him. By now, she hardly cared that she looked worn and disheveled; she simply enjoyed the curious glances that the other diners cast their way.

"I don't believe we've been properly introduced," Ruth's companion said as soon as they were seated. "My name is Steven Miles." He held his hand out over the table. He had a warm, firm handshake.

"My name's Ruth . . . Heimer. How do you happen to speak such good German, Mr. Miles?"

He laughed and brushed a short strand of black hair back from his forehead. "Well, you speak quite good German too. No, in all seriousness, my parents are from Germany. They emigrated to America just before I was born."

"So you're American."

He nodded. "Born and bred. And proud to be!"

A waiter appeared. He had a grubby dishcloth tucked into his waistband and black rims to his fingernails.

"Would the lady and gentleman care to dine?" he asked, handing Steven the menu and giving Ruth a disdainful glance.

"Bring us two glasses of sherry first. You do drink sherry?" he asked Ruth.

Not knowing what sherry was, she smiled apologetically and said, "I'd rather have a glass of lemonade."

Steven ordered her a lemonade without hesitating even a moment.

"That fellow was none too polite," he muttered as the waiter left the table. "What a day. Full of surprises!" he went on. His voice had been cool and distant as he spoke to the waiter, but now it was friendly again. He gave Ruth a boyish grin. "I never really thought I would enjoy a meal in this hotel."

Hoping that he meant that as a compliment, Ruth smiled at him. "We've a saying that you should always expect pleasant surprises. The unpleasant surprises will come anyway."

"Nicely put and sweetly said . . ." His gaze dropped to her lips for a moment, and then he looked up again. "And while we're speaking of surprises, the food here could be better, I'm afraid. A great deal better. If you don't mind, I'll choose for both of us."

Ruth nodded. Ever since they had entered the dining room, she had had the strangest feeling that everything she saw was magnified as if by a glass: the room with its tall, narrow windows that were badly in need of cleaning; the other guests—all five of them—at the tables along the wall.

And Steven Miles. More than anything else, Steven Miles.

He was of medium build, not especially big but not reedy like so many of the village boys, who never had enough to eat. He had thick hair that would probably stick out wildly in all directions if he didn't keep it down with pomade. Like Woolworth, he had a moustache, though his was not as bushy.

He had dark, intelligent eyes that were set ever so slightly too close together but that were lively and curious in a way that most men's were not.

"Your eyes remind me of a neighbor of ours," Ruth heard herself say. She felt mortified as soon as she spoke.

Steven Miles lowered the menu and looked at her attentively.

"Given that I don't know your neighbor, I can't tell whether that's a good or a bad thing."

Ruth had to laugh. "Don't worry! Peter Maienbaum is a very good man. He's a glassblower, and he's in love with my sister Johanna." As she spoke, she tried to work out just where the warm glow in her belly was coming from. Why did she feel so safe and happy with this man she had only just met?

When the waiter brought the drinks, Steven ordered two portions of goulash with potato dumplings.

Ruth hadn't had a bite to eat all day, but now she wasn't sure she'd be able to swallow a morsel.

Steven Miles suggested that they finish up with business matters before the food arrived.

"Since there's no middleman in this deal, we need to draw up a contract—in German of course. It will be based on the one we use for wholesalers, but it will take into account the fact that you yourselves are the suppliers." He put his briefcase on his lap and took out a notepad and pen.

Ruth nodded bravely. It would all work out, wouldn't it? What choice did she have but to trust this complete stranger?

"Who should I put in as supplier? Marie, or all three of you? That would make it Johanna, Marie, and Ruth Heimer," he said, his fountain pen poised above the page.

Ruth swallowed. What now?

"In fact my sisters' last name is Steinmann. I'm the only one who's a Heimer."

He frowned but was too polite to ask any questions.

"Steinmann is my maiden name. I'm married," Ruth whispered hoarsely. The palms of her hands were moist now. How could she ever have imagined she'd be able to close a deal?

"Married? And your husband? What does he have to say about your habit of sneaking into other men's hotel rooms?" It may have been meant as a joke, but to Ruth it sounded like an accusation.

"My husband doesn't know I'm here. We're separated, and I'm living with my sisters. And my daughter. Her name's Wanda. She's only eight months old. I . . . ."

Dear God, what now?

Before Ruth quite knew what was happening, tears had sprung to her eyes.

Startled, Steven ran his fingers through his hair, which immediately sprang out in all directions. The waiter was approaching their table with two plates, but Steven waved him away.

"Please don't cry. We'll . . . look after all that. Please don't worry. I'll take care of it all. Do please calm down." He held out a silk handkerchief to her.

Her hands trembled as she reached out and took it. It smelled of tobacco, and of him.

"There, there, that's better. I'll grant you that negotiating a contract can often be a fraught occasion, but emotions don't tend to start running high until we get to the terms and conditions—rather than the first line. I've seen grown men on the verge of tears, though, I'll tell you that!" He grinned, trying to defuse the situation.

Ruth wished the earth would swallow her up. There she was, sitting with Woolworth's assistant in a hotel restaurant, and all she could do was make a fool of herself. The thought was so painful that fresh tears sprang to her eyes. When she saw the helpless look that

Steven gave her, it was more than she could bear. Her voice was thick with tears as she choked out, "Please excuse me for a moment," then pushed her chair back and ran from the room, half-blind.

Since she wasn't sure where else to go, she simply stood outside the dining room. She sobbed quietly, relieved that neither the greasy waiter nor any guests were coming or going just then. She dabbed away her tears with the handkerchief and then finally went back into the room and sat down across from Steven Miles, careful to keep her face neutral.

"Please pardon my outburst," she said, laughing bitterly. "What a silly woman, you must be thinking. And you're quite right."

"Not answering back now, Ruth Steinmann, are you?" She ran her finger along the flatware that the waiter had brought while she was away.

"It's just that there's been so much going on lately that I hardly know what my own life looks like." She looked up at him, hoping he wouldn't see the touch of panic she felt sure was in her eyes. "Everything's topsy-turvy. Nothing's the way it used to be or the way it ought to be."

"Why don't you just tell me about it?" Steven asked quietly.

If anybody had told Ruth before that day that she would pour out her whole life story to a complete stranger, she wouldn't have believed it. But she did just that: she began with Joost's death, then told him about working for old Heimer and about Griseldis and Eva and all the others, and about the pittance they had been paid that first month.

Mostly, Steven Miles simply listened. Now and then—when Ruth stumbled in her story—he asked a question. Ruth heard herself confess her girlish dreams that she would one day meet a Polish prince. Glossing over the details of how Thomas had wooed her, she told him about the wedding itself and the celebrations. The table decorations! All those guests! The good cheer! It hurt to talk about it. As she told her tale, her lost innocence seemed to yawn beneath her feet like the mouth of a chasm that might swallow her whole at any moment. But when she looked into Steven's face and saw his concentrated, attentive expression, she knew she would not fall. It was such a relief to be able to be put down her burden. She told him how much Thomas had changed when the son he had longed for turned out to be a daughter he despised. She even heard herself telling how he had hit her. As she talked about the bruises his blows left, her voice was as neutral as it would have been describing curtain fabric. She told Steven how Thomas had torn out her hair and wrenched her arms up behind her back so that her elbows ached for days afterward. Then at last she described the night when Thomas had raised his hand to Wanda.

Steven reached his hand across the table to stroke her head, the way he might comfort a sorrowful child.

Ruth had to fight an urge to grab his hand and hold it tight. She looked at him.

"I . . . pardon me for telling you all this. I'm really not like this most of the time. Not even my sisters know that Thomas used to hit me."

"But why did you keep your misery to yourself?" he asked, leaning back in his chair and shaking his head, uncomprehending. "Did you want to protect your husband by keeping silent?"

Ruth shrugged.

"I was so horribly ashamed. You can hardly go around telling people that your own husband beats you. And anyway, it happens in a lot of families. Besides, it's not as though Johanna and Marie only had me to think of. They have enough to be getting on with in their own lives. Johanna more than either of us, even. She used to work for one of the wholesalers until recently, but he treated her very poorly." She blinked at him. "But that's another story. A very sad story, in fact, and rather horrible. But not even I am so much of a blabbermouth that I'd tell you that one as well."

He grinned. "That's the second time today you've refused to tell me someone else's secret."

"It's a matter of trust," Ruth replied flatly. "I think you would do exactly the same thing if you were in my position. You wouldn't abuse someone else's trust in you." As she spoke she realized that she could just as well have posed that as a question.

Steven nodded without saying a word. He scanned her face, gazing at her gently.

"What is it? Why are you looking at me like that?" Ruth asked, unsettled.

Before he could answer, the waiter appeared and lackadaisically served them their goulash. The brown gravy dribbled down the sides of both plates, staining the threadbare tablecloth. He put a dish in the middle of the table holding six potato dumplings and a puddle of the water they had been boiled in.

Ruth caught Steven's eye over the meal. They both laughed.

"I daresay that you have spent more pleasant evenings!" Ruth said, frowning apologetically.

"I have to agree with you there," Steven replied as he speared a dumpling with his fork. "Well, let's enjoy the meal! Did you know that Thuringian potato dumplings are world famous?"

In fact Ruth hadn't known, but she thought it was very kind of him to mention it.

17

Though the food had no taste, Ruth discovered after her first bite that she was terribly hungry. She ate the first dumpling almost without noticing and was already fishing for another one when she caught Steven's eye.

"Finally a woman who doesn't pick at her food like a sparrow!" he said appreciatively. "I'm afraid that back in New York eating has practically fallen out of fashion among the fair sex." He shook his head.

Instead of feeling flattered, Ruth stared at her plate in dismay. "I'm a real country bumpkin, aren't I?"

"Not in the least!" He leaned forward. "And you needn't feel ashamed of your tears, either. To be honest I even envy you a little that you can show your feelings that way. We businessmen are expected to have the emotional range of a cold fish," he said, grinning broadly. "I can't remember ever having enjoyed a mealtime so much!" His eyes were as dark and hot as coals.

Ruth felt her cheeks flush as he looked at her. He wasn't anything like a cold fish—quite the opposite.

"You're only saying that to make me feel better. How am I supposed to measure up against those fine ladies in New York?"

"Why on earth would you want to? There's really no need, you're a quite extraordinary woman in your own right."

She laughed. "You should try telling my husband that! 'Ruth and her crazy ideas!'" she scoffed. Though she had been tense and miserable just a few minutes before, she suddenly felt happy again. She didn't know why her mood was swinging so erratically. Had they not finished the contract yet because she was behaving so strangely? Or was it because of the way Steven Miles's eyes kept catching hers?

After they finished dinner, Steven produced the documents again. They decided that the suppliers should be named as "the Steinmann family," and then they worked through the contract point by point. When he quoted a quantity for delivery, Ruth felt dizzy for a moment.

"You really want three hundred of each of the baubles I brought?"

He nodded. "Can you deliver in those quantities? Or is it a problem if we order so much?"

"No!" she replied hastily. She couldn't actually say whether it was a problem; her brain was still racing to add up the numbers. "So . . . given that I brought twenty different styles today, that means our contract is for . . . six thousand globes?"

Steven nodded absentmindedly as he ran his pen down the page to the next line.

"We usually ask wholesalers to deliver to the harbor in Hamburg. However, in your case I suggest that Mr. Woolworth and I take responsibility for transport from Sonneberg to Hamburg. This will affect the price we pay you, of course."

Ruth bit her lip. "Of course. That goes without saying." In fact she didn't even know how she was going to get six thousand baubles as far as Sonneberg, but she would be hanged if she had to arrange transport all the way across Germany. Wouldn't Johanna be surprised when she saw that Ruth really had thought of all the details?

"Delivery would be no later than the thirtieth of September. That's the date by which all the globes have to be in Sonneberg, ready and waiting to be transported onward. If they're not, then the wares won't get to us in time for the Christmas sales." His gaze was level and businesslike now; it was as though they had never even mentioned personal matters. "You realize that would make the whole shipment worthless, of course?"

Ruth nodded uneasily. Six weeks? Could they manage that? How many nights were there in six weeks? And how many globes could Marie blow in a night? While Ruth's brain was spinning, Steven went on. "The last possible loading date for cargo from Hamburg to New York is the second of October. Then we have to add another six weeks for delivery and distribution in America, which means that Christmas tree decorations will reach the shops in mid-November."

Ruth sighed. "Christmas in New York. And Marie's baubles, right there in the middle of it all. I can hardly even imagine it." New York. The name itself sent a frisson through her. There were a thousand questions she wanted to ask him. About New York, about his employer and his family.

But Steven was not to be distracted. "You have to be able to imagine it. If there is one thing that Mr. Woolworth really can't abide, it's breach of contract. So please allow me to ask you one last question. An important question. Can you and your sisters really fulfill this order?"

There was a note of concern in his voice, but she couldn't tell whether it was personal or simply professional. Ruth had to pull herself together to concentrate on his question. Her gaze was steady as she answered him.

"We can meet it and more. Our globes will be in Sonneberg, ready and waiting for collection on September thirtieth. Even if I have to sit down at the lamp and blow them myself!"

He smiled. "Would it be too much if I said that I expected nothing less of you?"

Ruth had the feeling that she was blossoming before his very eyes, like a flower that finally had water.

"Nonetheless, if there are any difficulties, then you can always try reaching me in the Hamburg office."

"Hamburg? I thought you were from New York?" *How far is it to Hamburg?* Ruth wondered. Not as far as to New York, that much was certain.

"Mr. Woolworth wants to be quite sure that none of his Christmas wares get lost on the quayside in Hamburg and that they all end up on the right ship. Which means that I'm staying in Europe until everything's loaded and under way," Steven explained cheerfully.

They worked through all the other points fairly rapidly until they got to the issue that Ruth had racked her brains over even as she hatched her plan: the matter of payment.

"Before we start to talk figures, I want to make you the following offer," Steven began. "We'll pay you the same price we would pay a wholesaler for items of this kind. Less—let's say—ten percent for the delivery costs to Hamburg, which we shall be taking over." He looked at her questioningly.

Ruth's first impulse was to nod in agreement. What he said made sense. But then she realized something; the wholesaler Steven was talking about could only be Friedhelm Strobel. And he sold the globes that Karl Flein blew. Wasn't that what Johanna had said? Steven had already put pen to paper to fill in the blank when Ruth reached across the table and tapped him gently on the arm.

He looked up and clearly noticed her unhappy expression.

"I haven't even named a price that you could quibble with!"

Ruth managed to smile. "I don't wish to quibble. And I certainly don't wish to be brazen. Heaven only knows, maybe I'm talking my way into trouble here. It's just that . . ." Embarrassed, she tucked back a strand of hair, and a daisy she had missed earlier fell onto the table in front of her.

"What is it?" Steven asked, his eyebrows raised.

Ruth flicked the faded little flower across the tablecloth between finger and thumb. Well, no use dithering! She looked Steven in the eye. "Marie's baubles are a lot prettier than any of the others you buy. Marie's globes are painted, with whole winter landscapes. And many of them are silvered. That's a lot of extra work, let me tell you. Then there are the baubles that she blows into forms that she cast specially. The nuts for instance. And the pinecones. And—"

Steven raised his hands in surrender. "Stop! You've convinced me. Marie's baubles are a great deal more work to make, that's true."

At last they agreed on a price. Woolworth would pay one mark twenty pence for every dozen baubles, which came to six hundred marks for six thousand globes. Six hundred marks! She and Johanna and Marie all would have had to work for Heimer for more than a year to make that much, Ruth told herself jubilantly. Of course they would have to pay for materials and the gas they used, but even so there would be a tidy sum left over

The dining room was long empty by now, and the waiter was hovering so obtrusively over their table that Steven took a golden watch from his pocket.

"Good gracious me! After ten already. Time simply flew by in your company!" He looked at her with concern in his eyes. "How thoughtless of me to keep you here for so long. Is there even a train back to Lauscha at this hour?"

Ruth laughed. "Have you forgotten, Mr. . . . Miles, that we're countryfolk out here?" She would far rather have called him Steven. "The last train left a while ago. At this hour, the only way to get back is on foot."

"I cannot allow you to walk such a distance in the dark. We'll get you a room here in the hotel." He was already waving the waiter over. "If that's all right with you?"

Before Ruth could say anything, he was already giving orders. She thought of Wanda and hoped that she was all right, but even as the thought formed in her mind, she was already looking forward to sleeping in a hotel for the first time in her life.

A few minutes later, she held a wooden ball in her hand with two keys dangling from it. Steven explained that one of them was for her room and the other was for the front door of the hotel.

She giggled. "And when I think that at noon today I was sneaking in through the service entrance. I still can't quite believe that Mr. Woolworth didn't throw me out on my ear!"

"I have the feeling that they want to throw us out of here now though," Steven said, nodding toward the waiter, who was putting the gas lamps out one by one and looking over at them quite obviously as he did so.

"What a shame," Ruth heard herself say. "I would have liked to spend a little longer talking. Given that you know all about me by now, and I know hardly a thing about you . . ." She fell silent, embarrassed. What on earth had gotten into her?

Steven Miles seemed to hesitate. He looked from her to the waiter and then back again. "Let's leave this pit of vipers before that one starts to spit venom at us," he said and held out his hand.

It was the first time in her life that a man had helped her up from a chair. Feeling thoroughly pampered, she briskly stood up.

After she had collected her basket from the reception desk, they stood on the stairway that led up to the guest rooms, looking at one another. It was an awkward moment.

"I . . ." Ruth began hesitantly.

"I'd like . . ." Steven said at the very same time.

They both laughed and the moment passed.

"I don't quite know how to say this without . . . giving you the wrong impression." Steven smoothed his moustache with finger and thumb.

"Yes?" she croaked. Her knees felt suddenly weak, and she knew that it was not because of the long day she'd had.

"Oh, please forget that I spoke," she heard Steven say, to her disappointment. He waved the thought away.

"I wanted to ask you whether we might not continue our conversation in your room, or perhaps in mine. But goodness knows that's not a suggestion one can make to a lady—not even with the purest of intentions. Please forgive me for even having thought of it."

Before Ruth could answer, he had taken her basket over his shoulder.

"But I can at least take you as far as your room."

As they climbed the narrow stairs, Ruth didn't know whether to be disappointed or pleased.

They reached her room before she had a chance to think of some way to spend more time with Steven. She turned toward him one last time and gave him a wry grin. "Thank you—for everything. And do please thank Mr. Woolworth on my behalf, from the bottom of my heart. He has no idea what this order means for me and my sisters."

"I shall do that," Steven assured her. "Thank you for a lovely evening."

She could feel his breath in her hair.

Ruth swallowed hard. "I still don't know anything about you except your name, and who you work for."

For a tantalizing moment, she thought that he would kiss her.

But Steven simply stroked her hair gently.

"That will change. Sooner than you think, perhaps." His eyes locked onto hers. "You won't get rid of me so easily. I promise you that."

The room was surprisingly chilly, in all likelihood because hardly any sun came through the tiny window. Ruth sat down on the bed and found herself looking at the pillow, which had been hanging on the line in the garden at noon. The white linen began to shimmer in front of her eyes, and a thought buzzed round and round in her head.

I've met my Polish prince.
He's an American.

18

Steven. The globe order. Wanda. The strange smell of the room. Ruth slept fitfully, waking up again and again at the mercy of her confused thoughts—questions to which she had no answers, feelings that scared her.

She was happy when at last it started to get light. She opened the door a crack and listened for any noise out in the hall, but everything was quiet—she seemed to be the only one awake.

After she washed, she stood in front of the mirror that hung over the washbasin and began to unbraid her hair. It was a good thing she had remembered to bring her brush and comb. The old familiar routine of brushing her hair calmed her down, and her fingers were steady as she worked on one lock at a time until her hair hung down to her waist in a shimmering flood. After she had loosely plaited it and put it up in a figure-eight bun, she got dressed. Then she turned to and fro in front of the mirror, looking at herself appraisingly. She was pleased with what she saw. She had hung her dress up by the open window to air and now it looked smooth and fresh and smelled good too.

Just as she was preparing to leave, the church bells began to chime. Ruth counted one, two, three, four, five. Was it really only five o'clock? She strained to hear the next set of bells, and it, too, only chimed five times.

Ruth frowned. If she went downstairs now, she certainly wouldn't run into Steven.

She sat down on the bed and waited.

At seven o'clock sharp she picked up her basket and bag and left the room.

Please God, let me see him one more time!

A moment later, she saw him standing down below on the stairs. Ruth was shocked to feel her heart turn a somersault in her chest.

Woolworth was standing next to him, and they were peering at a stack of papers. Steven was so absorbed in the documents that he seemed not even to hear it when the hotelier greeted them with a cheerful "Good morning."

Ruth kneeled down slowly and undid the lacings on her shoe, then tied them up again as slowly as she could. Perhaps . . . if she waited a little longer, Woolworth might go in for breakfast and . . .

Just then, Steven looked up.

Ruth hurried to stand up straight and smiled at him uncertainly. What if he had no time for even a few words?

But then he was hurrying up the stairs toward her.

"Ruth! How fortunate that you're still here! It's a real stroke of luck. I was worried I might have missed you. The doorman didn't know for sure, and you weren't at breakfast . . ." He was babbling away like a brook.

"Have you already had breakfast?" Ruth asked.

"Of course. Mr. Woolworth is an early bird, as we Americans say. Well then . . ." Steven cleared his throat. "I'm not sure how to put this . . . perhaps it won't suit you at all . . ." He ran his hands through his hair and a little spike stuck up out of place.

Ruth had to stifle a giggle. "Yes?"

"It's like this: Mr. Woolworth has a couple of meetings this morning for which my presence is not strictly required. So he has been good enough to give me some time off today. And so I thought, if you would like, I might see you home? I mean, since it was my fault that you were stranded here last night."

Instead of heading off toward the railway station, Ruth decided to take the road that led to Steinach and then onward to Lauscha. Steven followed her as though he had never even heard of the railway between Sonneberg and Lauscha.

Four hours! Maybe even four and a half if they walked slowly, Ruth told herself happily as the last houses of Sonneberg disappeared behind them. She never would have even dared to dream that Steven would be coming along with her; she had to fight the urge to pinch herself. Ever since she had left Lauscha, Fortune seemed to be smiling upon her.

The sky shone that day as though newly scrubbed clean. There was not a cloud anywhere, not even the tiniest dab of white on the distant horizon. The pine forests on the slopes alongside the road were almost black against the brightness of the sky, and the birds were singing in the treetops. A cuckoo called from somewhere, *cuck-oo, cuck-oo*, tireless, yearning.

The scent of wild thyme hung in the air. Later, when the air had warmed a bit and the sun reached the edge of the forest, they would smell the heady and sensual perfume of the dog rose too.

Even the rushing Steinach brook was quiet, the water seeming to caress the stony bed rather than scour it clean. Instead of sending up the spray and droplets that usually cooled her on her walk, the stream merely babbled softly.

It would be a hot day; that much was certain.

Ruth tucked back a loose strand of hair from her forehead. She didn't care if she had to walk over burning coals this morning . . .

They didn't talk a great deal, at least not at first, though Ruth struggled to think of topics of conversation. Nothing came to mind. Why wasn't he saying anything? Was he bored by her company? Was the path too steep? Perhaps she shouldn't have let him insist on carrying her basket? She cast a sidewise glance in his direction and then burst out laughing.

"What's got into you, Steven? You look like the cat that got the cream!"

"That's how I feel!" he replied. "What could be better than walking through such a wonderful landscape with you on a day like this?" He grinned boyishly. "To tell the truth, I could just hug the whole world! Don't try to tell me you feel any different."

"If you hug the whole world, what's left over for me?" Ruth asked mischievously.

He stopped for a moment. "Perhaps . . . could I take your hand?" he said hesitantly. When she didn't answer at once, he continued. "The path is fairly rocky here. You might stumble."

"That would be very kind of you." Her hand trembled as she reached out and took his.

It was as though their hands were made for each other. Her hand lay snugly in his the way the glass Marie blew fit inside its form. From time to time he ran his thumb across the back of her hand, without knowing he did so. Tenderly, warmly.

For a while they talked about this and that and nothing at all. Steven asked how she had slept in the hotel, in a strange bed. Whether the little village they could see up ahead had a name. What the white stars blossoming in such profusion at the forest's edge were called.

"They're white aster, nothing special!" Ruth laughed. "When we were girls Marie and I plucked them by the armful. Then we'd sit on the bench behind the house and make chaplets for our hair." She looked at him. "We used to dance together too. We were so happy back then. Happy the way only children can be. In a few years' time I'll be making chaplets like that for Wanda."

Steven stopped. "Why do I hear such pain in your voice?"

Ruth stopped as well. "Do you?"

Their eyes locked on each other.

"I want you to be happy, Ruth." His voice was hoarse.

Can it be that I love this man? The question struck Ruth like a thunderbolt.

"Why?" she whispered. "You don't even know me."

"Why? Because we Americans are inveterate optimists!" Steven said, grinning shyly. He put out a hand and gently lifted her chin. "And because there's nothing that makes a woman more beautiful than to see her smile!"

The moment passed but the tenderness remained.

They walked on, hand in hand. When they saw the first houses of Steinach, Steven thought that they had reached Lauscha. Ruth laughed as she told him that they had just as far again to go. She didn't mention that it would also get steeper; he would see that for himself.

As he wiped the sweat from his brow, Steven wondered aloud at the black layer of grime that covered the village and its tiny houses. Ruth told him about the slate that the Steinach villagers dug out of the hillside, day and night, and the meager living that it gave them.

"The slate dust doesn't just get into every nook and cranny and all over people's clothes, it gets into their lungs as well," she explained. She went on to tell him about Eva's family, in which one of the younger children died every year. "I'm just happy I was born in Lauscha. Marie calls it a paradise of glass. Though if you ask me, it's not much of one."

"When I look around, I can see what your sister means," Steven answered, pointing up the mountain. "I've never seen such marvelous landscapes, not all the way from Hamburg to here. Look at the forests! Pine trees as thick as the hair on a bear's rump!"

"Yes, and when the sun's not shining it's as dark in here as if you were wrapped in a bearskin. But come winter you notice pretty quickly that you're not. It's cold enough to freeze your hands and the roads are so covered with snow that you can't even leave the village. It may look marvelous to you, but we'd all rather live somewhere a bit more ordinary."

Steven laughed.

"Do you know that you're quite extraordinary yourself?"

Ruth frowned at him.

"You're not just clever and beautiful, you're funny as well!" he said in a tone that suggested he couldn't quite believe it himself.

Ruth decided to change the subject and insisted that he tell her something about his family. His parents had emigrated years ago after his father and uncle had decided to open a branch of the family business in America as an import-export house. Steven and his three sisters had all been born in America. Ruth was astonished to learn that Sophie, Edna, and Jean, the youngest, all worked for Miles Enterprises. But if his family was as rich as all that . . .

He laughed at her confusion. "Just because a family has money, that doesn't rule out the daughters working! We're quite used to women in America earning their own money. Sophie has never let her husband stop her from working. She doesn't even need the money; her husband is a rich man himself." Sophie was the only sister who was married.

"But who looks after the housekeeping? And who takes care of the children?" she asked. Steven had already mentioned that he was the proud uncle of twins.

"The staff," he replied. "Sophie has no time for the housekeeping. She spends quite a few hours every week doing charity work, looking after the children of poor immigrants."

The things they got up to in America! Ruth shook her head in confusion.

"And why is it that the only son in your family is working for another firm?"

"I'll never learn as much anywhere else as I will under Woolworth's wing! My father expects me to join him in the family business eventually of course. But at the moment I have the good fortune to be able to watch two great business minds at work at once, and I cherish the hope that one day I may be a passable businessman myself."

Ruth sighed. "It all sounds so exciting! When I think of life in my little village . . ."

"What kind of businesswoman talks like that?" he asked, his eyes sparkling. "You and your sisters are trailblazers."

She looked at him skeptically.

"Look at what you just did," he insisted. "You got yourself a deal with one of the biggest chain stores in America. You're your own boss; you work in an industry that up till now had been exclusively the domain of men—my God, that's what I call entrepreneurial! Believe me, you're building yourselves a grand future here."

Ruth's thoughts turned to home, where Johanna was lying in bed humiliated and robbed of her honor. Where Marie was hoping to be able to sell even a single bauble. Where her own daughter would grow up without a father or any brothers and sisters and with only her mother to turn to. She took Steven's hand again and smiled painfully.

"If only I could see things your way. But what you call entrepreneurial, we call bitter necessity."

As they walked on she plucked a flower from one of the many wild rose bushes, a blossom that had just opened. She breathed deeply, drinking in all she could of the barely perceptible scent. Then she looked up.

"When I was a girl, I used to greet every new day that came. As soon as I opened my eyes I would wonder what lay ahead of me. Every morning I used to think that there were pleasant surprises in store. I never even wanted to consider that life had its dark side too. And Father used to encourage me in my beliefs. He only ever wanted the best for me. And for Johanna and Marie as well, of course." She shrugged in resignation. "How I wish I could still think the same way!"

19

"You did *what*?" Johanna's eyes threatened to pop out of their sockets. Flabbergasted, she stared at the sheet of paper that Ruth was holding out to her.

"I went to Sonneberg and showed Marie's baubles to Mr. Woolworth," Ruth repeated. Ruth laughed and Wanda gurgled happily in her arms.

Marie laughed even more loudly than Ruth and Wanda together, and she hopped up and down like a child.

"Don't you understand? The American wants to buy six thousand baubles from us. Six thousand! I can't quite believe it myself, not yet." She snatched the contract from Johanna's hand. "But here it is, in black and white!"

Johanna suddenly felt ashamed of herself. She had been upstairs in bed day in and day out, as though she were suffering from some dreadful disease. Wallowing in self-pity like a great crybaby. While outside, life had gone on like a giddily spinning top.

Ruth had been to see Woolworth? *That* Woolworth?

A contract for six thousand baubles?

"And there I was, silly goose, thinking you'd gone to meet Thomas!" She felt even more stupid just thinking about it. "So that's why you didn't go to work today!" she added, turning to Marie. "You wanted to wait for Ruth to come back with her news."

Ruth and Marie exchanged knowing glances. They both looked about fit to burst with self-importance.

Johanna looked at Ruth as though seeing her sister for the first time.

"The things you get up to!" she said, swinging both legs out of bed. She felt dizzy from the movement. "To tell you the truth, I don't know whether I would have dared."

"But the truth is that *you're* the businesswoman among us," Ruth said, looking at her with unmistakable pride.

Once she was on her feet Johanna didn't know whether to laugh or cry. Ruth and Marie were leaning in the doorway and looking at her as though they were expecting her to crawl right back into bed.

Her sisters! The Steinmann girls.

"Don't worry. I'm not going to lie down again," Johanna assured them as she reached for her clothes. "If we women are going to rule the roost again, then I can't just laze around on a feather bed!"

Ruth and Marie sighed with relief. Loudly.

Peter came by a little while later. Marie had already told him what was afoot the evening before, and when he saw Johanna sitting downstairs in the kitchen, he knew that Ruth had succeeded.

While Johanna bustled about getting supper ready, Ruth told the whole story, starting from the moment the photographer blurted out which hotel the American was staying in. They all listened, astonished and openmouthed, as Ruth explained how she had gotten the chambermaid to help her sneak into Woolworth's room. The bread and cheese sat on the table untouched. Who could even think of eating at a time like this? As Ruth recounted how Woolworth had picked up one bauble after another and looked at each in turn, Marie hung upon her every word.

"He was really impressed," Ruth told her sister.

Johanna reached for the contract. She read it through several times, then looked up, frowning. The others didn't fail to notice the question in her eyes.

"Look at that, it didn't take her long to find fault," Ruth remarked pointedly to Marie. Then she turned to Johanna and asked, "May we know just what displeases you here?"

"Nothing at all, nothing! It's all just as it should be," Johanna said, raising her hands appeasingly. "The delivery date will be tight, but there's nothing we can do about that. And the price is fine. And it was very clever of you to make sure that we only have to deliver as far as Sonneberg."

Ruth relaxed a little. "But?" she asked nevertheless, still apprehensive.

Johanna smiled helplessly. "I'm just wondering where we're going to get the money for so much glass stock and all the packing and gas if he isn't paying us an advance."

There were a thousand and one questions to consider that evening, some of which they could answer themselves, some of which they left to Peter. Anything that couldn't be settled straightaway was left for later.

It was already dark outside, with a strong wind rattling the windows by the time they finally had a plan.

The three sisters gratefully accepted Peter's offer to lend them the money they would need for materials. They were mighty surprised all the same that he had so much in savings.

Peter also offered to buy the glass stock for them from the foundry. When he suggested he could help blow the baubles as well, Marie turned him down in no uncertain terms. It was a matter of honor for her that she do it on her own. She was well used to sitting up at the lamp until late at night and had no doubts that she could manage the order. It would be a lot of hard work, but she didn't mind that. Ruth and Johanna would use Marie's samples as models to paint the globes and the other designs in the daylight hours before packing them up in the evenings. Marie didn't want to give up working for Wilhelm Heimer—best not to burn her bridges quite yet.

Although the sisters argued that they should keep their plans quiet for the time being, Peter said that it was probably impossible. The master glassmakers down at the foundry would wonder why he suddenly needed hundreds and hundreds of rods. And Fritz the crate-maker would ask the same question when Johanna went to order the packing materials.

Peter looked around the table at each of the women in turn. "Why keep it a secret? You should be proud of getting this order!"

Marie looked at him in an agony of embarrassment.

"Yes, of course. But what do you think the men will say when they find out . . ." She paused and made a wry face, but a moment later, she smiled. "Peter's right in fact; it's too late to get cold feet now!"

Johanna nodded. "Lauscha will just have to get used to the fact that we have our own roost to rule. There's always going to be someone who grumbles. And some who resent what we're doing. But we mustn't be discouraged," Johanna said, looking at Ruth. "Aren't you listening?"

Ruth sat up straight with a start. "I . . . sorry, what were you saying?"

Johanna smiled as she shook her head.

"I suppose you were still thinking of Sonneberg."

Ruth looked thoughtfully out the window, at the wind driving the rain against the pane.

"You have no idea how right you are."

20

Now that Johanna had snapped out of her trance, she took charge of everything much as before. Neither Marie nor Ruth had any objection when she went to Fritz the crate-maker and bargained with him on the price of the packing material. She also insisted on going into Sonneberg to buy the white enamel paint, tinsel wire, and other supplies they would need to realize Marie's designs. She even set out to organize the glassblowing itself.

"Why not start by blowing the globes that will take the most time to paint up?" she suggested to Marie. "Then while Ruth and I are painting those, you can get on with the rest of the order."

Most of the time, Ruth and Marie let Johanna give the orders; they liked having the old Johanna back again, rather than a sister who just lay in bed like an invalid. They only ever objected if they felt she was pushing them around too much. And when they did, Johanna actually managed to hold her tongue for a while and let the two of them work in peace.

It didn't take long for the rest of Lauscha to notice that something was going on at the Steinmann sisters' house. The lights were on until late at night and their neighbors wondered whether the women ever slept. And wasn't that the telltale flicker of a gas lamp through the windows, the kind that a glassblower used at his bench? The neighbors soon began stopping by and trying to get into the house under all sorts of pretexts: one woman came to borrow a cup of flour and another to ask for Ruth's help in sewing a winter jacket; one man came to ask whether he could take a look at Joost's old tools and perhaps buy one or two that he might need. When they saw what was really going on in Joost's workshop, some of them could hardly believe their eyes.

Marie, the youngest of the Steinmann girls, sitting at the lamp?

Reactions ranged from incredulity to downright disapproval. Many spoke of dark doings, and some even said it was the devil's work. Marie's conviction that she could do a man's job provided weeks of conversation, both in the village houses and down at the Black Eagle as well. When Peter came to tell them what was being said at the tavern, the sisters didn't know whether to laugh or cry. Thomas Heimer had the most to say. He told whoever would listen that he had known right from the start that there was something not quite right about the three of them. They were all stubborn, self-righteous little minxes, pampered and insolent and with their heads in the clouds. When somebody asked him why he had married one of them, and everyone else at the table burst out laughing, Thomas lunged.

"I'll not be made a fool of! Not by you, not by a woman, not by anyone!" he yelled, and shook the man until he almost fainted. After that nobody quite dared ask why Thomas's father saw fit to have one of these minxes still working for him—despite her devilry.

From then on, Thomas kept coming to their house at night. When the Black Eagle closed at ten o'clock, he stumbled through the streets, always drunk, and the whole neighborhood could hear him shouting for Ruth. Sometimes he grabbed hold of their gate and shook it, threatening all kinds of vengeance. The first few times, Ruth tried to calm him down, but no sooner had she leaned out the window than he became even more abusive. He called them witches, whores, and thieves. Deeply shaken, Ruth flushed and put her hands over her ears. On one occasion, when Thomas was being particularly nasty, the other two sat down at the kitchen table with her. Johanna reached over and prized Ruth's fingers apart as she wrung her hands.

"Let him shout! Nobody will think the worse of us because he's making a laughingstock of himself."

From then on, the sisters tried to ignore him when he turned up drunk at their door, and Peter usually managed to send Thomas away with threats.

As if it weren't enough to have the glassblowers heaping scorn upon them, Marie and her sisters also found that many of the local women spurned their company; conversation came to a stop or went on in hushed tones whenever Ruth or Johanna went into the village store. Some of the village women condemned the Steinmann sisters out of envy, others out of sheer incomprehension, but most of them did so out of fear. After all, if men saw them taking charge, they might get it into their heads that women could be the bread-winners of the family.

The only one who took Ruth aside when there were no eyes upon them was Mrs. Flein, the wife of Swiss Karl. She whispered in Ruth's ear.

"Back forty years ago, when my father had pneumonia, I sat down at his lamp, and I blew beads in secret." Mrs. Flein's cheeks flushed as though she were still proud of what she had done. "We didn't have the gasworks back then, and the flame wasn't as hot as it is today, but I made those beads all the same. If I hadn't, we'd all have starved. You tell your Marie that there's nothing wrong with what she's doing." She patted Ruth on the shoulder, then scurried away as though she didn't want to be seen with her.

But there were other reluctant admirers too, among them Wilhelm Heimer.

"Don't think for a moment that I approve of women getting up to that sort of mischief!" he boomed, so loudly that everyone in the workshop looked over at him and Marie. "But you've got the gift for it, and I've known that for a long time now!" Then he winked and dropped his voice so that only those standing nearby heard him say, "As long as your work here doesn't suffer, I'll turn a blind eye to whatever else you choose to do."

"Don't you think you've impressed Wilhelm any," Eva hissed at Marie, sounding for all the world like a jealous wife.

Griseldis and her son were regular visitors. Although Griseldis was skeptical at first, she warmed to the project when she saw how much thought the three sisters had put into the work. Sometimes she sat down at the table and helped them paint, while Magnus packed the baubles and stacked the cardboard boxes once they were full.

Week by week, the pile of boxes grew, climbing ever higher toward the ceiling. Soon there were boxes of baubles all over the house, and it was a nerve-racking business picking a path around them to make sure nothing toppled and fell.

Even with all the enmity they attracted and all the hard work, it was a good time for the Steinmann sisters. Though none of them knew how to put their feelings into words, they were proud to see Joost's old workshop come back to life and to be working together once more.

The bulk of the work fell to Marie, but she never once complained about putting in twenty hours a day. Instead she sat at Joost's bench and blew glass as though she'd been doing nothing else her whole life. She was quite carried away by the idea that her baubles soon would be hanging on Christmas trees all across

America. Johanna sometimes wondered whether there wasn't a touch of obsession in Marie's dedication. When she mentioned this to Peter, he replied dryly, "Is there even any such thing as dedication without obsession?"

For Johanna, too, the work was like stepping into freedom after doing nothing all summer long: she painted, finished, numbered the items, wrote the price tags, packed the baubles, tracked the inventory. Finally, it was her chance to show what she was made of. And she had to admit that there was a kernel of obsession inside her as well.

Ruth went around with a blissful smile on her lips all the time—almost entirely thanks to the letters the postman brought.

21

Dearest Ruth,

I hope that my letter finds you in good spirits and in good health? I am sure that there is much work to fill your days, so I almost feel guilty for taking up your valuable time with my letter.

Ruth, you cannot imagine how pleased Frank (Mr. Woolworth) is to be able to have your Christmas decorations in his catalog. Throughout the journey back to Hamburg he talked of little else but how he could hardly wait to see those baubles shining on his shop displays. You should know, most respected Ruth, that Woolworth stores are not like other shops; we do not have our wares stacked up out of reach on shelves behind a counter, but rather, everything is set out where the customers can help themselves. This means that everyone can pick them up, look as closely as they wish, and then choose whatever their heart desires. The customer is king, so Frank always says. My employer is quite sure, as am I, that your Christmas baubles will suit our customers' tastes exactly.

I am distressed to discover that even in the first paragraph I have already broken my resolution not to take up too much of your time. Ruth, you have made me into quite the chatterbox. There are a thousand things I wish to tell you. But where should I begin? Where should I stop? And yet I confess I find that a written letter is a poor substitute for being able to look into your eyes and listen while you talk in that lively and inimitable way you have. Please permit me to say that since we met, I have not stopped thinking of you. The evening we spent together, and then the walk we took through that incomparable landscape enchanted me. You, Ruth, enchanted me!

I am a man of numbers, a sober-headed chief clerk, and yet I find myself asking Fate what it could mean that we met. I hardly dare hope that you might consider our meeting anything more than a commercial transaction. Though this, too, has its charm—it seldom happens that I find myself negotiating with such a charming partner. Mr. Woolworth, by the way, says that he found the way you did business very "American." You may be assured that he means that as a compliment.

As I sit in my office and look out the window, I see steamers setting out for the New World every day. In only a few weeks I, too, will set foot aboard one of these oceangoing giants to accompany your Christmas baubles—and the many other glasswares from your home village—to America. But before that time comes, I wish you to know that I am considering a visit to Sonneberg on the 29th of September. Given the quantity of goods that are to be transported to Hamburg on the 30th, it might be a good idea for me to supervise the loading and packing of these wares myself. Most respected Ruth, if you chose to come from Lauscha to Sonneberg, we could be certain that the wares are treated with the due respect. After all, glass is very fragile, is it not?

I would be very pleased indeed to receive a few lines with your reply. I have already given you my address in Hamburg. You will *also find it on the back of the envelope to this letter. With hopes of a positive reply, I remain,*

 Yours sincerely,

 Steven Miles

◆   ◆   ◆

Lauscha, 9 September 1892

Dear Steven,

 Thank you for being so kind as to write. Your letter was delightful! (If one may say this sort of thing of a letter.) I would be very pleased if we could meet in Sonneberg on the 29th of September. Of course I plan to accompany our Christmas decorations—after all, I must make sure that they don't end up in a ditch by the side of the road somewhere between Lauscha and Sonneberg! Do you see now what you have done to me? No sooner do I have dealings with you than I begin to behave like a silly woman. Or at least write things that sound silly. Please ascribe this to the fact that I have as little experience in writing letters as I do in business affairs.

 I, too, find myself thinking of our meeting every day but I do not have the words to express my feelings as beautifully as you do.

 Perhaps I should tell you that the work is proceeding apace. Marie can hardly wait to sit down at her lamp every day. I believe that for her, it is more a pleasure than a chore. Johanna and I greatly enjoy the work of painting and finishing the pieces. It is quite another thing when we are producing the wares for ourselves, rather than working for someone else. It is a very fine feeling to be able to be proud of what one has done. Especially since my husband does whatever he can to humiliate and hurt me. He comes to our house almost every night, drunk, demanding that I come out. Once he lay in wait for me on the way to the village store and grabbed me roughly by the sleeve. I'll get what is due to me, *he said. Thank God that some of the villagers happened to pass by just then. I was honestly frightened. What if he does something to Wanda one day, simply to cause me pain? When I look into his eyes, all I see is rage. Impotent rage. He recently asked me, in all seriousness, why I left him. Can you imagine? Until he understands what he did wrong, he will not leave me in peace. Enough! Over and done with!*

Do not worry, dear Steven, I am not about to burst into tears again and tell you my sad story. Even today I feel quite ill at ease when I recall how I behaved that evening. I am still most grateful to you for your kind understanding. The only way I can explain my candor is to say that from the very outset I had the feeling that I could trust you wholly and purely. When you consider that in truth I have little experience with men—and that what little I have had could hardly be called joyful—this is in fact quite astonishing. But deep inside I know that you are different. And that is why I am already looking forward to seeing you again. By the way: when you look out of your window, please give the ocean liners my greetings. It must be a fine feeling to be so close to the "big, wide world"!

With warm wishes from the Paradise of Glass,
Ruth

◆　◆　◆

Hamburg, 15 September 1892

Dear Ruth,

Your letter made me the happiest man in Hamburg!

I must protest strongly against one thing that you said; you are a most gifted correspondent. The lines that you write are as lively and engaging as your conversation in person. When I read them, I feel almost as though I were sitting with you in the workshop while you and your sisters create your baubles with skillful hands. How I would love to be there with you in your Paradise of Glass—and what a beautiful name that is! Instead I threaten to drown under a mountain of paperwork. The greater the proportion of foreign goods offered for sale in Mr. Woolworth's shops, the greater, alas, the workload. Yet I do not wish to complain. It is always exciting, with every day that dawns, to watch how he is building a great business empire through his cunning maneuvers. Indeed, I feel honored to be allowed to work for such a great man as Frank Winfield Woolworth. And yet there are times, such as now, when I yearn to be able to pack my case and travel wherever I will. But, alas, life is not that simple. Yet when I hear, dear Ruth, how your husband mistreats and molests you, then I burn to depart with the next coach and tell this villain just what I think of him. What kind of life is that, if every day you must live in fear? You do not deserve this. Nobody deserves this.

By the time you read these lines it will be just a few days until we see one another again. Thus I know I cannot expect to receive another letter from you in the meantime. I can hardly wait to sit across the table from you once more, to look into your velvet brown eyes and then never look away. Dare I imagine that you, too, think of me from time to time? You, the Princess of the Paradise of Glass?

I remain, in joyful anticipation,

Yours sincerely,

Steven Miles

◆　◆　◆

Lauscha, 21 September 1892

Dear Steven,

I am counting the days until we see one another again the way a child counts the days to Christmas!

Your Ruth

22

It was Sunday evening in the fifth week of the six they had to complete the baubles. Marie had sensed for the first time that the glances thrown their way at church that morning had been a little less hostile. Perhaps Lauscha was gradually getting used to the idea that a woman could blow glass. As she raised her voice with all the others in a hymn, she felt that she could finally sing with an open heart once more. When they left church, Thomas was waiting as usual and tried to take Ruth aside. All she did was look him up and down and then leave him standing there. With Peter next to her and all the parishioners around, Thomas did not dare drag Ruth away by the arm or make a scene. The painful moment passed.

Once they got home, they no longer had a spare minute. As so often recently, the mood was tense: the long hours of work side by side had begun to eat away at their patience and good cheer. Hardly a day passed without some quarrel. Wanda had just begun teething, and her constant crying only heightened the tension. The situation had grown especially bad that Sunday. While Wanda shrieked and wept, Ruth gave her sage tea and smiled blissfully. She seemed to have not a care in the world.

Marie glanced up from the lamp several times, looking askance at the other two. She could feel a tension in her cheekbones. Quiet! All she wanted was a little quiet.

When Wanda could not be soothed either by tea or kind words, Ruth said, "She probably doesn't like the smell of the Epsom salts." She looked reproachfully at Marie as she spoke, as though her sister had invented the technique expressly to upset Wanda. Some of the Christmas baubles were dipped into a mixture of British gum and Epsom salts and then put out in a cool place to dry. The effect was marvelous; the salts formed crystals as the solution dried and looked like a fine layer of ice covering the glass. Mr. Woolworth had been especially taken by these globes.

"Then pick it up and put it somewhere else! Nobody's forcing you to sit down with Wanda right by the dipping pail," Marie grumbled in reply.

When Ruth took the baby upstairs for her lunchtime nap, Marie and Johanna breathed a sigh of relief.

"I couldn't have put up with that for much longer. How is anyone supposed to concentrate on work with all that crying?" Marie said, reaching for a rod of glass and warming it in the flame.

"That's what it's like with a baby in the house. Don't believe you cried any less. And Father still managed to get his work done."

"Father! I'm not Father!" As the glass began to glow orange-red, Marie took the rod from the flame, carefully set the cool end to her lips, and blew life into the glass. Although by now she had blown thousands of globes, it was always a special moment for her when the rod began to swell and take on a new shape. For a moment she forgot all about Wanda's crying and concentrated on her breath and on turning the globe around on its stem. Once it was exactly the same size as all the others, she took the rod from her lips. She used the tongs to expertly bring the globe's tail back in on itself to form a little loop for hanging on the tree. Then she gave the whole thing one last critical look and put it aside. She smiled.

"Watch the merry man dance, my dear, see him grin from ear to ear . . ." Ruth's voice reached them, bright and clear from upstairs.

Marie rolled her eyes.

"No sooner does the little one stop crying than Ruth starts making a racket. She's so cheerful it's quite disgusting. There must be something amazing in those letters she carries about and reads at every possible moment. How else can you explain the fact that she goes around smiling all the time?"

"You're being oversensitive," Johanna said, shaking her head in disapproval. "Just be glad she's feeling happy. After all she's been through."

"I'm fed up with it," Marie burst out. "I can't take any more of being told to spare someone this or consider her feelings about that. Everybody in this house gets special treatment but me. Neither of you care that I'm doing most of the work for this order. I've had no more than four hours' sleep a night for weeks on end. But nobody considers my feelings! After all, *I* haven't had anything *horrible* happen to me." Marie knew that she was being unfair but there was nothing she could do to stop the words tumbling out.

Ruth had come quietly into the room.

"What are you bleating away about down here? You sound like an old goat." She walked over to Marie and made to put her hand on her arm, but her sister brushed it away sharply.

"The best thing you could do is come and sit by me," Johanna said, beckoning Ruth over. "And keep quiet. Our little artist is disturbed by all this chatter."

Marie shot them a venomous glance. It was just like Johanna to take Ruth's side!

"I would be very grateful if I could work in peace for just a little while. It's quite enough that Eva spends all day every day chattering in my ear."

"I hope you're not seriously comparing me to that silly cow," Ruth snapped back.

"Old goat, silly cow—I don't know whether you've noticed, but we are in fact in a workshop here, not a farmyard!" Marie was trembling with rage. It wasn't like her to get so angry. She had always been the quiet one among the three sisters, the one who always gave way first whenever there was a disagreement. Perhaps it was lack of sleep that made her pick the fight this time.

Ruth seemed dumbstruck. And then Marie threw in one more jab.

"Or maybe it's these 'mysterious' letters you're getting that suggest this sort of comparison? Maybe some *silly ass* wrote them?" She smirked as she put her hands up to her head and waggled them about like donkey's ears.

Ruth was round the table so fast that it wobbled as she ran past. "You . . ."

The sound of glass chiming should have warned them both. But Marie was worked up, and Ruth was in a blind rage. She grabbed her sister's arm.

"You take that back. Right now!" she spat at Marie.

"I will not," Marie shouted, snatching her arm away. Habit made her careful not to knock into the gas pipe, but she never thought of the pail of gum-and-salts solution that Ruth had picked up and put behind her earlier.

"Careful!" shouted Johanna.

The pail tipped over.

Speechless with horror, the three women watched the liquid spill out over a pile of boxes.

Johanna was the first to collect her wits. She ran into the kitchen and came back with two dishcloths. She tried in vain to stem the tide of liquid, but it had already soaked through the thin cardboard of the boxes, leaving a layer of ice crystals behind as it dribbled over three hundred Christmas baubles packed and waiting for transport.

◆ ◆ ◆

"I'm cold." Ruth rubbed her hands together and then wrapped them in the folds of her skirt. Her eyes were red with weeping, and there was reproach written all across her face.

Johanna's eyes were also red. She slowly got to her feet.

"So am I. I'll shut that window now. There's no point in trying to air out the room. Nobody's ever died from a bad smell, but we may very well freeze to death!"

After the accident, they had flung open all the windows, but instead of the stinking cloud of fumes leaving the house, the cold autumn mist had crept in. Johanna rubbed her brow and groaned.

"I feel as though my skull might burst from the stink! And my bones hurt as well."

"What next?" Ruth's question was hardly more than a whisper.

"I don't know," Johanna confessed. "That's two hundred and fifty globes completely unusable, at least another hundred splashed, a whole pail of salts solution tipped over—and that costs money as well—and the floorboards are soaked. Then there's the smell . . ." She shook her head. "If it weren't all so terrible, I might even find it funny." She swallowed hard. She wanted to run upstairs the way Marie had done and hide away in a corner. But how would that have helped?

"More than three hundred globes, ruined! And so close to the end of the commission. I don't know whether to cry or grind my teeth. How on earth are we going to make up for the lost work? We were already falling behind," Johanna said.

There was desperation in Ruth's eyes as well. "If we can't fill the order . . . then we're sunk. We'll never get another."

"It hasn't come to that yet," Johanna said with more conviction than she felt. "In the worst case, we'll only be short by five hundred. Ruth!" she said, grabbing hold of her sister's arm. "Please don't cry!" But her own eyes were prickling as well.

"Steven Miles will think I'm nothing but an unreliable flibbertigibbet. And Mr. Woolworth will regret ever having signed a contract with us. I can still hear what Steven said: 'If there is one thing that Mr. Woolworth really can't abide, it's breach of contract.'" Ruth covered her face with her hands and let out a loud sob.

"Please calm down. All is not lost."

Ruth shot a hate-filled glance at the stairs.

"And it's all her fault! She's to blame for the whole miserable business. If she hadn't knocked over that pail . . ."

"Not so fast there. As I remember, you had something to do with it as well," Johanna said. "You made a dreadful scene when all she did was tease you a bit. You're not usually so sensitive. And the way you make such a song and dance about keeping your letters secret. If this Steven is only writing about the contract as you claim, then why can't we read them too? The way you're carrying on, anyone would think there was something else going on between you and Mr. Miles." It was not the first time the thought had crossed Johanna's mind, but until that moment, she had always thought it far too unlikely to bring up. But as soon as she saw Ruth glance sullenly away, it didn't seem so unlikely after all.

"Oh no," Johanna groaned. "You've fallen in love with that American. Ruth, please tell me it's not true!" Johanna had an overwhelming urge to get up and walk away as though the whole conversation had never taken place.

"I don't know whether I've fallen in love with him," Ruth said, suddenly embarrassed. "Sometimes I think I have," she added, just as naturally as if they talked about it every day. "But then I think I can't possibly have! I mean, I've only even met the man once."

For a moment Johanna felt a twinge of hope. Love at first sight—that was just for fairy tales. Even a child knew that.

"Back when I was in love with Thomas, I felt as though there were a thousand ants marching through my belly. All he had to do was look at me, and I flushed hot and cold. Ha! I can hardly believe there was a time when I couldn't wait for him to kiss me. That changed soon enough." Ruth laughed bitterly.

"But it's different with Steven." Her voice became soft. "I feel we have a real connection even though we've hardly touched. And he's so polite and responsive that I sometimes think he can read my mind. For instance he told the waiter to open the window before I could even mention that I wanted some fresh air. And then he ordered a coffee for me after the meal. He had no way of knowing what a coffee fiend I am." Ruth's eyes shone. "And his letters! He writes so wonderfully that I feel I already know him. I only hope I'm not making a fool of myself with all the nonsense I scribble down. You know quite well that I was never much for reading and writing."

With every sentence she spoke, Johanna's heart sank further. Her sister had it bad, worse than Ruth even realized herself. Although Johanna had the feeling that she should say something to put the whole matter in perspective, nothing came to mind. "*Even though we've hardly touched*"—well, at least the worst had not yet happened.

Quite without warning, Ruth reached across the table and took Johanna's hand.

"I'm so happy I can finally talk about it all. Perhaps I should have told you ages ago. But . . ." She shrugged. "It's all so personal, somehow." She smiled that blissful smile again. "Perhaps Steven wouldn't even want me talking about him like this. A matter of trust, do you understand?"

Johanna nodded, saying nothing, and Ruth seemed content with that.

"He's such a good listener. I would never have thought you could actually talk to a man the way we talked. He's a bit like Peter, in fact, just not so . . . matter-of-fact. He—" She broke off. "Oh, I really can't explain. At any rate, I've never felt so safe and happy with anyone." She sighed. "With Thomas I was never sure whether he really meant any of his compliments, because they were only ever about one thing. But I believe every word from Steven. Although . . ." Ruth laughed, embarrassed, and her cheeks flushed pink. "I do wonder what a businessman and man of the world like him sees in me."

Johanna couldn't sit and listen in silence any longer.

"You and your daydreams," she said, interrupting her sister. "It wasn't so long ago that you were in raptures over Thomas just the same way, and look what came of that. Just stop and think for a moment. You're married, and you have a child. You live here in the Thuringian Forest, while this man lives in New York. There are worlds between you. Even if he did have some feelings for you . . . what could possibly come of it?" Johanna felt a growing urge to grab Ruth by the shoulders and give her a good hard shake.

"I don't know," Ruth cried miserably. "And I don't even want to think about it. All I know is that I can hardly wait to see him again when he comes to collect our wares from Sonneberg. That's why nothing must go wrong with this order! I can't stand the thought."

"I'm glad we're agreed on that much at least," Johanna said dryly.

"If Steven weren't coming to Sonneberg, I would go to Hamburg to be with him!"

"You in Hamburg? Don't make me laugh! You have to pluck up your nerve just to go as far as Sonneberg." Johanna scoffed.

"You're horrid! You're just like Marie; she doesn't want me to be happy either." For a moment it looked as though Ruth might burst into tears again, but then she shook her head. "Perhaps that's the only way you know how to talk. Because neither of you knows what true love is like." She shut her eyes. "True love is much stronger than us mortals. It stops us from being scared of what tomorrow may bring."

Romantic twaddle! Ruth had obviously spent far too much time reading the *Arbor*. Johanna had no desire to continue the conversation, so she shoved her chair back and stood up. It was already late.

It was cold in the kitchen, and the house still stank of Epsom salts. She would have to go to Peter tomorrow and confess that they had no hope of filling the order without his help. Perhaps she would also have to have a good long talk with their resident artist to make her sit back down at the lamp. The last thing Johanna needed just then was to watch Ruth fluttering her eyelids and listen to her soppy talk.

Though Johanna was bone tired, she knew that she wouldn't get to sleep easily—not after Ruth's news.

23

At eight o'clock sharp on the morning of September 29, two draft horses pulling a wagon stopped outside the Steinmann house, snorting and shaking their manes. They belonged to a farmer from a nearby village who made a little extra money carrying cargo for the glassmakers of Lauscha. He looked around dubiously as he opened the tailboard for loading. He had never picked up anything from here before. But if he had any doubts as to whether it was the right place, they were answered the very next moment when the three sisters came out of the house, each balancing a stack of cardboard boxes in their arms. Peter and Magnus both insisted on being allowed to help load the wagon, so the farmer stood aside and watched, filling his pipe as they worked.

More and more boxes vanished into the belly of the wagon. By the time the last box had been loaded, the cargo was piled up almost six feet high. The young women watched hawkeyed as the farmer and Magnus lashed down the boxes with rope. At last everything was safely stowed.

"Done!" Johanna heaved a loud sigh. "We'll be able to move around the house again without glass chiming at every step."

"It looks like any old shipment of ordinary glassware, doesn't it?" Somehow Marie still couldn't believe that this huge mound of buff-colored boxes had actually been packed in their house.

"Very true. From the outside, there's nothing to suggest all the glitter and sparkle inside," Johanna replied.

Ruth, who had been staring into the dusty kitchen window, turned around.

"It's just as well. No one needs to know what we're transporting here. We'd just end up getting robbed on the road," she muttered, then turned again and looked at her dim reflection. She sighed fretfully as she tugged a lock of hair back into place, tucked another behind her ear and ran her finger along her eyebrows.

Johanna and Marie exchanged knowing glances. Ruth had spent more time in front of the mirror that morning than anywhere else. Even Wanda had been left to her own devices for once, lying in her pram and grumbling away.

"You take good care of the papers, now," Johanna told Ruth, not for the first time that day. "The lists give all the details they'll need on how many of each design are in the delivery. The authorities in Hamburg won't be able to draw up export papers if they don't have the right information. Once when I was working for Strobel, we—"

"Johanna, I know all that. You take good care of Wanda for me," Ruth said, her eyes shining like well-polished slate. "Don't worry. I know what I have to do."

Johanna snorted. "I'm not so sure about that," she said, then added softly, "Just don't go doing anything foolish when you and Steven . . ."

"Johanna, please don't start that again," Ruth murmured. She turned abruptly and blew a kiss at her daughter, who was watching the scene with a look of skepticism on her face. "Until tonight, little Wanda! If you're good, Mama will bring you back a present."

She was halfway up to the wagon seat when she suddenly climbed back down.

"What's the trouble now? Women!" the farmer grumbled. He had a whole day's work on the farm waiting for him when he got back from Sonneberg.

Ruth hugged Marie. "You see, we really did it. The Steinmann girls will show the world what we're made of."

Marie hugged her back. "Have a nice time in Sonneberg."

At last the wagon lurched into motion, its wheels creaking. Wanda began to cry. Johanna rocked the pram from side to side without taking her eyes off the wagon. Peter came to join her, and she did not protest when he put his arm around her shoulders.

Marie stood a little off to one side. The time had come. Thousands upon thousands of silvered pinecones, nuts, painted globes, and mirrored globes were setting off on their long journey to America. Everything that had been at the very center of her existence for the past few months was now gone forever, vanished from her life. She had wanted to go with the cargo as far as Sonneberg, but Ruth wouldn't hear of it and had insisted quite vehemently on going on her own. They had almost had another row over it. But then Johanna had taken Marie aside and told her in a few carefully chosen words what was on Ruth's mind.

"Let her meet this Steven one more time. Perhaps she'll realize then that she's just chasing rainbows. We can stay home with Peter and enjoy our day off," she added. But Marie waved the offer away. If she wasn't going to go to Sonneberg, then she just wanted some peace and quiet.

"It's an odd feeling—to know that the whole hustle and bustle is over, just like that," Johanna said, smiling.

Peter sighed. "That's just like you. Instead of celebrating, you stand out here feeling gloomy," he said, grinning reproachfully. "I think you should come over to my place. Or had you forgotten your promise that you would come and help me for a change?"

Before Johanna could say a word, he had taken hold of Wanda's pram and was pushing it toward his house. "What is it, are you planning to put down roots?" he called over his shoulder to Johanna, without turning round.

Johanna looked at Marie.

Marie nodded encouragingly to her sister. That left her and Magnus. He looked down and dug into the hard earth with the toe of his right shoe.

Marie shivered. She had forgotten to put on a jacket that morning in all the excitement, and the first frosts had begun a few days ago. It wouldn't be long now before the trees shed their colorful leaves. Unlike most people, Marie was looking forward to seeing the trees and branches bare. When their silhouettes showed sharp against the pale winter light, there was nothing to distract her from the fine filigree patterns the branches made.

She hugged herself tight. "What do you think—could there be a way to capture the seasons of the year on Christmas baubles?"

"All four seasons, on a ball?" Magnus was taken aback.

"A set of four globes, one for every season." Even as she spoke the globes began to take shape in Marie's mind. She would paint the globe for spring with yellow primroses. Summer—perhaps that could be a sun? No, because then there would be two globes painted yellow. So spring would have to be lily of the valley instead. Fall would be colorful leaves of course, in every shade of the forest. As for winter—well, that was obvious enough.

"Why didn't I think of it before?" She was so angry she stamped her foot.

"What's the problem?" Magnus asked. "Just paint that design for the next order."

"If there is one! We still don't know for sure whether anyone in America wants to buy them."

"You talk almost as much doom and gloom as my mother. I wouldn't have expected it of an artist like you."

Marie blushed. To change the subject, she asked, "How is Griseldis? I would have thought she'd move heaven and earth to be here with us this morning. I mean, since you both gave up all your evenings the last few weeks to help us out."

Magnus made a wry face. "Old Heimer has more work for her. He's insisted that she spend today cleaning the warehouse, because there are fresh supplies arriving early Monday morning."

"Today? On a Saturday?"

He nodded sourly. "I wish she at least got another mark in wages for all the extra work she puts in. But the old fellow just works her fingers to the bone."

"Do you mean to say she doesn't even get paid for the extra hours?" Marie frowned. Griseldis was always the last to leave the Heimer workshop in the evening. Ever since Edeltraud had died, hardly a day passed when Wilhelm Heimer didn't find some extra job for her. For some reason, he never asked that of Marie, or Sarah-the-snail.

Magnus laughed bitterly. "That's just what I mean to say. And even so, my mother feels she ought to get down on her knees and thank the old tyrant every day for letting her work for him."

Marie felt she had to say something in Griseldis's defense.

"Your mother is a good soul, and she's always ready to help. She helped us too. When I think of the way she came to our aid when Father died . . . Never mind these last few weeks!"

"But that was a matter of honor. Which is why my mother was so surprised when Johanna insisted on paying us for those few hours we put in. We can certainly use the money, but we would have helped you even without any pay."

Magnus was at least as kindhearted as his mother, Marie realized. It was a touching thought.

"Without those 'few hours' as you call them, we would never have gotten the whole shipment finished."

He waved her thanks away. "It's damned cold for the end of September. We'll have another hard winter ahead. What do you say—would you like a hot cup of tea? I could make us some, and Mother made an apple pie yesterday."

Marie hesitated for no more than a moment. "Why not? Perhaps I'd better get used to the idea that I don't have to work every waking moment from now on."

They were already halfway to Griseldis's house when Marie stopped in her tracks.

"What is it? Have you changed your mind?"

Marie bit her lip.

"Actually I'm still a bit upset that I didn't go to Sonneberg. It would have been a good opportunity to take a stroll round town."

"You mean stroll around town and spend some of your hard-earned money in the Sonneberg shops?" Magnus grinned.

Marie shook her head. "We haven't been paid a penny yet. Though for what I have in mind, I would happily spend all my savings. Well, perhaps another time . . ." Her voice gave away nothing of the longing she felt.

Magnus hopped from one foot to the other. Without looking at Marie he finally asked, "If you really would like to go to Sonneberg—well then, why don't we go? We could always walk if you don't want to spend the money for a train ticket. And who knows? If we're lucky, someone might stop and give us a ride some of the way." Magnus grew more enthusiastic with every word.

Marie, however, was torn. Was Magnus the right person to help her do what she was planning?

"I don't know. I would have to tell Johanna first. We had agreed that I would look after Wanda for half the day."

"I'll tell Johanna if you like. I'm sure she wouldn't mind you taking a little trip," Magnus said. "Should I go talk to her?"

Marie took hold of his sleeve. "Hold on! There's another thing: What if we happen to run into Ruth? She'll end up thinking I don't trust her to deliver the wares, and that would be very awkward."

"Sonneberg's not so small that you're always bumping into people around every corner," Magnus answered, sounding disappointed. "If you don't want to go with me, let's just forget it."

"That's not it," Marie said hurriedly. She laughed, embarrassed. "But there's one more thing . . . Just have a look at me . . . I can't go into town like this." She pointed at her legs.

One day she had started wearing Joost's old pants around the house; they didn't get in the way of the gas pipe the way her skirts always did. She soon realized that pants were fundamentally more practical than women's clothing and that she could slip them on in seconds and then have time for more important things. Ruth and Johanna had almost screamed the house down when they saw her wearing Joost's old rags, but Marie had nonetheless stuck to her new habit.

"Now that I think about it, I don't have anything fit to wear," she added.

Magnus crossed his arms. The corners of his mouth rose into a mocking grin.

"Marie Steinmann, can it be that you've lost your nerve?"

24

They had hardly been walking for half an hour when a wagon stopped and let them ride for a few pence. It was not even eleven o'clock when they arrived in Sonneberg. On the way there, Magnus had suggested all sorts of things they might do in town. When Marie finally mustered the courage to tell him what it was that she wanted to do, Magnus hadn't even batted an eye.

And so they marched out of the marketplace and headed straight for a little side alley. Marie could already read the shop sign from a long way off. "Books Old and New," it read, and underneath in smaller letters, "Books Bought and Sold, Alois Sawatzky." Her heart pounded.

"What if he doesn't have anything like what I'm looking for?" she whispered.

"We'll soon find out." Magnus put his hand on the handle and opened the door with a flourish. When the shop bell rang, Marie nearly jumped. Hesitantly, she followed Magnus inside.

It was not especially bright inside the shop, and Marie had to let her eyes adjust to the dim light. The smell—old, stale air with a sour note to it—took some getting used to as well. She had had no idea that books could smell so unpleasant.

"Is there anybody there? Mr. . . . Sawatzky? Hello!" Magnus called.

Marie was awestruck. Towering piles of books were stacked wherever she looked. The stacks in front of the windows were heaped so high that the daylight only came through the chinks in between.

"And there we were complaining about a few cardboard boxes in the house," she murmured.

"Good day, Sir, Miss, how can I help you?"

Marie spotted a man standing in the half dark between several piles of books.

"We're looking for a few books," Magnus replied. "My companion here can tell you more." He pointed to Marie.

Alois Sawatzky was much younger than she had imagined a bookseller would be. She would have felt rather less foolish telling her wishes to an old man.

"I'm looking for books on art."

"On art . . ." The man ran a finger through his beard. "What, in particular, do you have in mind?"

Marie breathed out slowly. "In particular? Well, what do you have in stock?"

"My dear young lady, my stock is so extensive that bibliophiles come from as far afield as Weimar to buy from me. I'll need you to give me one or two ideas as to what you want. Otherwise we could be here till tomorrow morning." He coughed.

"Well, you see . . ." Magnus began, about to come to her aid, but one look at Marie's face told him that she could cope with this arrogant young man quite well on her own. She took a deep breath and raised her chin.

"I would be most interested in a treatise on modern artistic styles. Everything that is *en mode*, so to speak." She fixed him with a gaze that Johanna would have been proud to see. *En mode*—if he could use fancy words, then so could she. "I would also be interested in any works you have on older traditions. The old masters and such." She waved her hand dismissively. "And if you happen to have anything on the history of glassblowing, that would be good as well. And then, I don't know whether any such book has ever been written, but something about drawing techniques—a drawing course, so to speak—for charcoal sketches in particular would be useful. And if there is any such thing for color drawing as well, then all the better. Apart from that, I would also be interested in . . . What is it?" She stopped, frowning.

The man's eyes had been growing wider and wider as she ran through her list.

"Could it be that your stock is not quite so extensive after all?" she asked in a gently mocking tone.

"Quite the opposite, my dear young lady." It wouldn't have taken much more, and he would be bowing and scraping in front of her. "I am certain that we can turn up a few treasures for you. If you would care to follow me? Allow me to lead the way." He pointed toward the back of the shop.

Marie smiled at him. Once he had turned his back, she winked at Magnus. They made their way together through the heaps of books until the man stopped.

"So, here we are! Perhaps the gracious lady would like to look at one or another book, with no obligation to buy of course?"

He pointed behind himself. Marie's worldly airs and graces fell away at once.

"Are these *all* books about art?"

The bookseller's smile grew wider.

"But of course! Or do you happen to know of any subject— with the exception of love—that has been written about more extensively than art?"

When she left the shop two hours later, Marie's cheeks were aglow. She was flushed all over as though she had a fever—and not just because she had spent all her savings. She hesitated when Magnus invited her for a beer—in part because she could hardly wait to get home and cut the string on the parcel of books and because she didn't know whether Magnus could afford to visit a tavern. She accepted all the same.

"But only on one condition: we don't run into Ruth!"

As they walked through Sonneberg, Magnus pointed out every shop they passed and had a tale to tell about each of them.

"Given that you've been running mail and messages between Lauscha and Sonneberg for only a few months, you certainly know your way around," Marie said admiringly. "I don't think I'd have even found my way back to the marketplace without you."

Magnus led them to a tavern that was tucked away off the main street. "Well, at least I'm good for something." Once they were settled at a table, he ordered two glasses of beer and two plates of bread and cheese.

Though Marie was about to protest, she realized that looking for art books had made her quite hungry. No sooner had the waitress put down the platter in front of her than Marie picked up a slice of bread and took a hearty bite.

"I keep my ears open when I'm running errands, that's all," Magnus said, picking up the thread of their conversation. "But God knows, it's hardly a job to be proud of. The way you work with your hands and your imagination, the way you mix craft and art—that's really something. Do you know that I almost envy that?"

Marie laughed. "Lots of people have ideas," she muttered, a touch embarrassed.

"But not as good as yours! Many glassblowers don't even do Christmas decorations. And the ones who make them . . . well, you should see the plain designs they use. No extra details, maybe a layer of mirror finish on the inside, and that's that. They're downright boring compared to your works of art."

"I don't know whether to even believe you," Marie said. Magnus's words were music to her ears but she felt self-conscious at his outspoken admiration.

"Believe away! After all, I'm the one who carries everybody's samples here and back again. But let's not talk about everyone else." He leaned across the table toward her. "Do you want to know what I really admire about you?" He didn't wait for an answer but kept straight on. "Your single-mindedness. You're so sure about everything you do. Whenever you . . ."

"Me, sure of myself?" Marie interrupted. "You've really gotten the wrong idea. I'm besieged by doubt the moment I sit down with my sketchpad or at the lamp. I'm always asking myself whether I'll be able to blow the shape. Or whether my designs can even work in glass." She shook her head. "I'm plagued by doubt most of the time in fact. Then I convince myself that I don't have the skills to create what I've pictured in my mind's eye. How could I? I mean, what little I do know I taught myself." She sighed.

"Have you never considered enrolling in the glassblowers' trade school in Lauscha?"

She gaped at him. "You mean where they teach technical drawing and modeling? But that's for the sons of glassblowers! Not for their daughters!"

"They might take you all the same. The way I hear it, they're not exactly oversubscribed . . ."

"That's the worst thing about it," Marie chimed in. "Either the boys don't want to learn anything or their fathers force them to sit down at the lamp just as soon as they're done with ordinary school!" She shrugged. "One way or another, that school's not for me. And as for the doubts I have . . . when it comes down to it, I don't think there ever can be any such thing as certainty in art. Oh, I don't know . . ." Even talking about it brought back all the helpless loneliness she had felt during the long nights at the lamp.

She had never talked about any of this, not even to Peter. In the end she was just a woman who was trying to persuade herself she could hold her own against the men in their trade. Who wanted not solely to understand the most difficult material any craftsman could work with but to master it.

"Which is why you bought all those books, isn't it?"

Marie laughed, embarrassed. "There won't be anything about Christmas tree decorations in any of them, but I'm bound to find something I can use. It's worth a try, isn't it?"

Magnus considered this for a moment.

"More than that," he answered, his voice ringing with conviction. "Perhaps you should spend a certain amount of time each day with your books from now on. Be your own tutor, so to speak."

Marie looked at him in astonishment. "That's just what I was going to do. Can you read my mind?"

Magnus grinned. "Perhaps I'm just good at knowing what an artist might be thinking. But joking aside"—he reached for her hand—"if you want my honest opinion, given how important your art is to you, you're not giving it nearly enough of your time."

"How can you say such a thing?" Marie protested, pulling her hand away. "Who spent night after night sitting at the lamp blowing glass these last six weeks? That was me, wasn't it?"

Magnus smiled. "That's exactly what I mean." When she frowned, he continued. "You were working to earn your living. Now you should take some time to develop your gifts as an artist. I can't imagine that the old masters like Rembrandt and Rubens would ever have become so famous if they had to paint night and day to make money."

"What you forget to mention is that many of the old masters reportedly starved to death," Marie said dryly. "You're also forgetting that neither Ruth nor Johanna has a job . . ."

Magnus nodded. "I know. You have a great deal resting on your shoulders. But all the same—whenever you have a moment free from working for Heimer, you should make some sketches, read your books, have a look at the illustrations. Oh, I envy you what's ahead."

Marie felt her excitement grow. Magnus was right! She could hardly wait to resume her studies, which she had neglected ever since Johanna and Ruth had moved in. All the same she cocked her head and looked at him critically.

"The way you talk, anyone might think you gave advice to self-proclaimed artists every day of the week. Why do you think you know so much about what's right for me?"

He beamed back at her. "Didn't you just say yourself that there are no certainties in art? But there's one thing I do know for sure: there's more to you than you even know yourself. You just have to bring it out."

Tears pricked at the inside of Marie's eyelids, and she had to swallow hard. "That's the first time anyone's had so much faith in me," she whispered. "You know what everyone else in the village says about a woman blowing glass."

"It makes sense that people need time to get used to something new," Magnus responded. "You and your sisters are a good way ahead of our time. But I'll tell you this: in a few years there'll be a great many more women blowing glass. And who knows—perhaps they'll even be allowed to enroll in the trade school."

Marie sighed. It did her good to hear Magnus's words. "That would be wonderful! Then at last I'd have somebody I could talk to about . . . all this."

"What do you mean? You've got me," he answered boldly.

She looked at Magnus as though seeing him for the first time: his even features; his dark brown eyes that seemed slightly lost; his dark eyebrows, just a shade too close together; his long, rather unkempt hair. Griseldis's son wasn't much to look at. His eyes didn't twinkle roguishly; his lips were rather narrow and didn't seem sensual or invite kisses.

And for all that Magnus was unusual. The way he had taken care of Johanna after her . . . misfortune had proved then and there that he was trustworthy. And he was a helpful soul with a gift for knowing what others were thinking . . .

Marie smiled at him. "I still think that most of your compliments are nothing but flattery, but they do me good all the same. Thank you," she added softly. "Do you know what? My first attempts at blowing glass were hard work, but now I'm ready to spread my wings. I'd like to make the most beautiful Christmas ornaments imaginable! I want children's eyes to light up with happiness when they see my Saint Nicholas on their trees. I want my baubles to bring a glow to even the poorest parlor. I want them to catch the light and cast it back a thousandfold; I want them to glitter like the stars on a clear night sky. Old and young, man and woman—I'd like everyone to find their own little paradise in my baubles!"

25

The farmer tried several times to start up a conversation with his pretty young passenger, but to no avail. Ruth simply stared straight ahead and smiled absentmindedly. Her mouth was dry, and she was so excited that she felt as if she kept forgetting to breathe. Her stomach was churning, and it took all her concentration to try to calm the collywobbles. All in vain—to her great embarrassment, she had to ask the driver to stop his wagon. Her panic grew when she saw that there was nowhere she could decently take shelter in the woods. At last she scurried behind a little copse of pines, but no sooner had she got there than the churning in her guts suddenly stopped.

When the first houses of Sonneberg came into view, Ruth was a bundle of nerves.

She was about to see Steven again at last!

When the farmer asked where he should direct his wagon, she had trouble concentrating. She swallowed several times and finally managed to tell him to go to the Sonneberg railway station. He shook his head and gave her an odd look.

On the way to the station, Ruth was already looking up and down the road for Steven, but she didn't see him anywhere. She would have known his head in any crowd, the way his hair sprang up.

Once they reached the station, the farmer turned his horses and brought the wagon up alongside the platform. Instead of dismounting, Ruth sat where she was on the bench.

How were they ever to find each other here?

She couldn't imagine a worse meeting place than this madhouse. Crates and cartons were piled high, people were coming and going, and men were conducting business, handing over sheaves of money or bills of lading. Tempers were short, and here on the crowded platform patience was not to be had at any price. Their cargo wobbled dangerously as wagons shoved and jockeyed for the best position to unload, and Ruth feared that the farmer's horses would shy at the loud shouts and crack of whips all around. Fortunately, they stood their ground without getting skittish.

Ruth, however, felt increasingly frazzled and disappointed. Her stomach was giving her trouble again. While the farmer began to untie the lines that held the cardboard boxes in place, Ruth spotted a sign that pointed to the public lavatory. After deliberating for a moment, she mumbled something about having an upset stomach, pointed vaguely toward the main entrance, and dashed off.

"I'll be back in five minutes," she called over her shoulder to the farmer.

This time Ruth managed to ease her bowels. When she was washing up and looked into the mirror, she was shocked at what she saw. Her face was dreadfully drawn and tense. She stuck her tongue out at her reflection.

"What a silly cow you are," she scolded herself. "No man would ever get so worked up." By the time she left the lavatory she had calmed down a little.

And then she saw him.

Steven!

He was standing there with a black notebook in his hand, counting the cardboard boxes as the farmer unloaded them and stacked them up. Ruth wondered how he had managed to find the right wagon amid all the confusion.

Her heart was in her throat. How should she greet him? She hoped she would be able to speak at all.

But before she could utter a word, Steven looked up. "Ruth!" he exclaimed. Beaming, he lowered the documents in his hands and came toward her.

"How are you? The driver told me that you have an upset stomach. I do hope it's nothing serious?"

Of course he had to spot her as she came out of the lavatory. Ruth felt her cheeks grow hot. "No, nothing, just a little chill," she murmured in embarrassment.

"You look a little pale still, if you don't mind my saying so."

His eyes. So full of concern for her, so . . . Ruth had to fight the impulse to fling her arms around his neck.

"I'm sure I do. I wasn't expecting all this excitement." She waved her hand in a gesture that took in the whole station.

"That's why I'm here," Steven said, seizing her hand and pressing it briefly. "I'll take care of everything. Marie's baubles will leave Sonneberg in one piece, and they'll arrive in New York unharmed."

His smile and the certainty he radiated could have calmed a herd of stampeding horses. Ruth had trouble keeping her happiness in check.

"Here are the inventories. Just as you asked, we've listed every design individually. And the codes on the cardboard boxes are all explained here." She pointed to the top of the first sheet.

How good he smelled. His face was just a few inches from hers as they bent over the papers together. There were blue shadows under his eyes.

"You look worn out," Ruth heard herself whisper. She had to resist the impulse to reach out and stroke his cheek until the fatigue vanished.

Steven looked up. "The thought of seeing you again robbed me of my sleep," he whispered back, not taking his eyes off her. Then he reached out and took the lists from her hand as though forcing himself to get back to business.

"Well then! Let's make sure we get this show on the road! The sooner the better. When we're done here, I'd like to invite you for a cup of hot cocoa. Are we agreed?"

Ruth nodded. She would have agreed to anything.

From that moment on, she didn't have to worry about a thing. Steven beckoned, and three laborers came over. Steven gave one of them a sheaf of papers, and the men began to load the cardboard boxes into several enormous wooden crates. Then the crates were taken away on a handcart. Steven pressed a few coins into the hand of the man who had taken the papers and suddenly it was over. The whole thing took less than a quarter of an hour.

Ruth was almost sorry it had all happened so fast. She would have been quite happy watching Steven for a while longer.

Steven insisted on taking care of business first. They had hardly taken their seats in the café before Steven started counting out the banknotes for Ruth, as discreetly as he could. Six hundred marks. When he was done, she put the fat wad of notes in her bag with trembling fingers. Six hundred marks—the reward for six weeks of hard work, missed sleep, arguments, and tears. She had never had so much money in her life.

With the smell of hot chocolate hanging over the table, her fears that they might not have anything to say to one another vanished into thin air.

The hours flew by as never before. One cup of cocoa became two, and then three. If anybody had asked Ruth afterward what they talked about she would hardly have been able to say. And yet it was almost as if not a day had passed since their last meeting, so easily did they pick up the threads of conversation. Though the talk itself was lively, they were also communicating at another level—for instance when Steven took a handkerchief from his breast pocket before Ruth had even wrinkled her nose to sneeze. The rage in his eyes when she told him about Thomas and the scenes he made in front of their house every night. The gleam in Ruth's eyes when Steven told her about the Christmas decorations that were about to go up in every Woolworth's store in America. Her delight when he told her every detail of Thanksgiving and its traditions.

"My mouth's already watering!" she said, laughing. "I can practically smell the turkey and the stuffing!"

"Have you ever thought what it would be like to leave Lauscha?" Steven's question took her breath away.

"Leave Lauscha?" She put a hand to her throat. She felt like she was choking.

All afternoon, she had somehow managed to forget the circumstances of their meeting, forget that the clock was ticking away as they laughed and gazed into one another's eyes. But his question brought it all back. As though she needed another reminder, the oak-cased grandfather clock at the end of the room struck six. The café would close at seven.

"How could I ever leave Lauscha?"

"It seems to me that the real question is how you could stay. What future do you have here?" Steven asked quietly. "After all you tell me about Thomas Heimer, I worry for your safety. That man isn't going to leave you alone. What if he's lying in wait for you or your daughter one day when there's nobody nearby?"

"He's not interested in Wanda," Ruth said, dismissing the idea.

Steven looked skeptical. "There's no shortage of tragedies that occurred because someone thought *if I can't have her, then nobody will . . .*"

Ruth raised her hands in despair. "Why are you frightening me like this? I'm married to him. I know that Thomas will never set me free—he's too proud for that—but that doesn't mean he's going to kill me." Tears sprang to her eyes. There was no future left for her anywhere; she had thrown it away long ago.

"Ruth, Ruth . . ." Steven whispered. He stroked her head gently. "Don't cry. I'm here. I'll take care of you."

How could that be? Steven had his life to lead, and she had hers. She sniffled as she told him so.

"Have you forgotten that I'm an American?" he answered with a roguish grin that didn't really suit her mood. "We Americans aren't so quick to knuckle under when things aren't going as we'd like. If we don't like the way things are, we change them. And I get the feeling that you can change things too." He lifted her chin.

Ruth wiped the last tears from her eyes.

"How many women would have spent their life alongside a husband who beat them rather than take the brave steps that you did and leave him?" Steven asked. When she didn't answer straightaway, he added, "Do you know any other woman who would have dared go to Mr. Woolworth's room looking for him? You began taking your fate into your own hands long ago."

"When you look at it like that, I suppose I did," she said, smiling a little. "Crying won't help matters, my father always used to say, you have to do something too."

She didn't quite know what they were talking about. What did he want her to say? Where was he going with this?

"Oh, Steven," she sighed. "Perhaps there might be some point in our talking like this if things were different. But as it is, even the kindest twist of fate wouldn't be enough to give me what I wish for most—which is to turn back the clock to before I was married."

"That's not what you really want," he said. "For one thing you wouldn't have your wonderful daughter"—he nodded at the photo of Wanda that Ruth had shown him—"and for another thing we would never have met."

"Well, that's true too," Ruth laughed. "You have a gift for finding the silver lining in any cloud."

He joined in her laughter.

"Wait, I have something for you." He bent down under the table for his briefcase then put a glass object in front of Ruth. It was shaped like a heart.

"A heart of glass?" She lifted it carefully and nestled it in the middle of her palm. It felt cool and soft. She held it up to the light.

"How beautiful." Her own heart suddenly felt even heavier. "Glass can break so easily . . ."

"I knew that you would see the hidden implication straightaway. Mr. Woolworth found this heart in a department store in England recently. He actually wanted to find a glassblower who could make us something like it last time we came. But unfortunately—or perhaps I should say thank heavens—we forgot the sample in our Hamburg office. What do you think? Could this be an order for you?"

So it was a sample, not a present. Ruth put the heart back down on the table. She shrugged.

"Marie can certainly manage it. What size order were you thinking?" If she had to die of a broken heart, she didn't want to starve to death as she did so, she thought with a touch of dark humor.

"One thousand items."

Ruth whistled softly. "That's quite a number! When would they have to be ready?" She held her breath. Would he come to Sonneberg to collect this order as well?

"By the end of November. The shipment will be traveling on one of the slower freighters, so the crossing will last four whole weeks. The hearts would arrive in New York at the beginning of January."

"That's hardly seven weeks away," Ruth said, biting her lip. Did that mean that Steven would be in Hamburg all that time?

"I'm afraid I can't extend the deadline. The hearts have to be in every Woolworth branch in America before the fourteenth of February. That's when Americans celebrate Saint Valentine's Day, the patron saint of lovers. Everybody who's in love buys a little present for their beloved, like this heart here, for instance. We put out special tables full of merchandise in all the stores for the occasion."

"What a lovely custom! Women who get a heart like this as a present could wear it on a velvet ribbon round their neck. Or hang it in the window on a thread, so that they think of their sweetheart whenever they look out the window." How Ruth would have loved to be one of those women. But before she could let herself feel saddened by that thought, she began to do the arithmetic.

"If we buy the glass stock straightaway and then make one hundred fifty pieces a week . . ." Why was she even bothering to calculate it, since she had no choice but to take on the order? She looked up and held out her hand to Steven. "It's a deal! Mr. Woolworth will have his hearts by the end of November."

Steven took her hand. But instead of shaking on the deal, he kissed it.

"Ruth."

He spoke her name as an endearment, dark and soft. Her fingers tingled. His lips were so warm on her flesh, his moustache tickled . . .

"If you will allow it, I will give you not just a heart of glass but a heart that beats wildly at the thought of you."

"Steven, please don't say these things," Ruth whispered, gently withdrawing her hand. She was in agony. "I thought of you every day, I dreamed of you every night," she confessed miserably. "You have no idea how much I wanted to hear you say such a thing, even though I know it's wrong. To know that you feel as I do, to know that it was more than just business for you when we met . . ." She stopped uncertainly. Was she making a fool of herself with this confession?

"But that's not all." She looked down at the floor. She could not look him in the eye and say what had to be said. "I wanted to hear those words so much, but they hurt me like red-hot needles. Because they promise me something that can never be." She stood up before Steven could help her to her feet. It hurt so much! "I have to go now. If I don't hurry, I'll miss the last train home."

26

Steven hastily paid for their drinks and hurried out after Ruth. He caught up with her in front of the café and insisted on going with her to the station.

Ruth wanted to sit down somewhere and burst into tears. The bag holding the money hung casually from her right arm, and she didn't even consider the possibility of purse snatchers. All she wanted to do was get away from the pain of meeting Steven. What had she really hoped would happen today? She was too exhausted to answer her own question.

"Stop, Ruth! I beg you!"

He was just as miserable as she was. All his confidence seemed to have deserted him, and the pain in her heart only deepened when she saw his shoulders drooping. Ruth walked on and Steven marched silently beside her. Their hands touched again and again. It was terrible and beautiful all at once.

The railway station was only two blocks away. Ruth took a deep breath, mustering her strength.

Only one more street and then two last turns. Ruth's heart was beating so loudly that it hammered in her ears.

Dear God, help me to do the right thing.

They walked together toward the great wrought-iron gate of the station. Ruth stopped.

"I can't."

She turned to him. "I can't just leave you like this."

The next moment she was clinging to his chest.

"Steven!"

"Ruth," he answered hoarsely and took her in his arms.

A few minutes later, they were running through the streets hand in hand as though the devil himself were at their heels, while the townspeople looked on in astonishment. Ruth suppressed the waves of shame and doubt and the pangs of guilt that threatened to overwhelm her. She even ignored the knowing look that the doorman at the Swan Hotel gave them. She had made her decision; she would be with Steven.

It was like putting down a heavy load. The clothes she wore were like chains that she could not remove fast enough. She undressed without shame, her movements sure. She did not have to look down at her bodice as she unhooked it. Nor could she have even if she had needed to. She only had eyes for Steven.

They were like flowers unfurling their blossoms in a perfumed garden. There was no need to touch; the invisible bond that united them was closer than any physical contact could ever be.

When at last they stood across from each other, entirely naked, Ruth took the pins from her hair. It fell down over her shoulders and settled there like a silken scarf. Then she shook her head proudly so that it hung behind her.

As they went to one another, Ruth drank in every detail of Steven's body. She stared at his manhood as though mesmerized, and a tremor of desire ran through her whole body. He was as beautiful as the Greek statues in the art book that Peter had given Marie. Back then, in another life.

"I've never seen a man naked," she whispered.

Steven laughed. "How can that be?" Slowly he reached his hand out toward her, and ran his fingertips down the valley between her breasts.

Ruth smiled in embarrassment. "It was always dark." *And it always happened very fast,* she thought. She waved a hand as though to drive off a troublesome insect. She didn't want to speak of that anymore. She didn't want to think of it.

Steven's eyes warmed her like two glowing fires as he led her to the bed.

When their naked flesh touched, desire flared in them both. His lips were strong, his kisses commanding, and Ruth thought she could taste a hint of cocoa on his tongue. She opened her mouth hungrily. More. More of this.

The feather pillow plumped up on each side of her head, getting in the way. She grabbed it and threw it off the bed. She wanted to cling closer to Steven, but he held her back.

He ran his fingers reverently over her breasts, then lowered his head. Ruth heard herself moan as his tongue playfully circled her right nipple. He raised his head and looked at her questioningly, but she just sank her fingers deeper into his arm.

While his lips caressed her left breast, his hands roamed up and down her body. Ruth felt her skin beginning to glow red hot under his touch. She thrust herself toward him once more.

But again Steven held her down, gently but forcefully.

"Easy does it," he whispered in English. "Easy and slowly."

He kissed her. Kisses light as feathers on her mouth, her eyes. In the middle of her forehead and on her hairline; his touch was so tender, his kisses were everywhere . . .

Suddenly his hand was on her mound of Venus. He did not stop stroking her, but his fingers moved down to the soft skin of her inner thigh. Ruth opened her legs gladly, impatiently. It felt wonderful to be stroked like that. His finger trailed across her labia as though quite by chance, and Ruth twitched like a kicking pony. She heard herself moan. It was a strange, full-throated sound.

Then Steven's hand began circling, circling. Hot waves seized hold of her, each stronger than the last. She screamed quietly. His fingers became bolder, burrowing into her flesh, and his lips insistently claimed her mouth.

Ruth clung to him. She didn't want to miss a moment of this bliss, the happiness that until that moment she had only ever dreamed of. What was happening here bore no resemblance to what Thomas had done to her, often against her will.

She was nevertheless unprepared for how readily her body responded when Steven finally entered her. He did not stop stroking her but instead kept time, his fingers like music on her skin, as he thrust deeply into her. Tears sprang to her eyes, hot tears of joy that she was glad to shed.

"I love you," Steven whispered hoarsely into her ear. Ruth didn't need to know any English to understand him.

"I love you too," she replied in German, her legs wrapped around his.

For the first time in her life, Ruth crossed the threshold to true love. Her body and her soul were as one with Steven.

Ruth stayed with him all night. She knew that Johanna and Marie would be worried. And that Wanda would be missing her. But she couldn't make herself care.

They had only this one night.

When they were not making love, they drifted off to sleep, her head on his chest, his arm around her protectively. It was only a light doze, however, for each was too aware of the other's presence to sleep soundly.

Clinging to one another, they watched the dawn light appear in the window. Ruth listened to Steven's heartbeat and wished she could stay forever in this hour between night and day.

"I love you." His voice was hoarse.

A hot wave of happiness washed over her.

"I love you too," she whispered.

"Could you see yourself coming to New York with me?"

His question was like a bolt from the blue. Her stomach twisted and cramped.

"I can't bear the thought of having to leave you in just a few hours. I've never had these feelings for anyone else! I was lost the moment I first saw you in Frank's room."

Steven sat up in bed and shifted around until he was kneeling. He took her hand.

"Ruth! You are the only woman for me. I want always to be here for you. I want to see your smile every morning. And at night, I want to fetch you the stars from the sky."

Ruth tried to concentrate on just one thing and to ignore everything else he was saying.

"And would you accept another man's child?"

"Did he ever show any interest in the child? Wanda is *your* daughter. Your angel. That's all that matters, as far as I'm concerned. I want to offer you both a home where you will have all the love you deserve, and everything else too."

"It's a beautiful dream." Ruth swallowed hard.

"No, it's not a dream." Steven's eyes were shining. "If you want it, it can all come true—and so much more as well! Love can move mountains, didn't you know that? Of course something like this needs careful thought and planning. Most importantly, I would have to get papers for you and Wanda."

"Papers?" she asked, as though everything else had long been settled.

"For the crossing, and for entry to America. I've already been asking around. The fact that you're married complicates matters somewhat. If my information on the laws here is right, you would actually need your husband's permission to emigrate."

Ruth sat up so fast that her head bumped the wooden headboard.

"He'll never do that! If he ever knew that I love another man . . ." Her eyes were wide with fear. "He must never find out. Never, do you understand?" she cried out. The thought that Thomas might do something to hurt Steven was too horrifying to contemplate.

"Calm down, my darling. Nobody need ever know anything if you don't want them to." Steven picked up his shirt from the floor and put it around Ruth's trembling shoulders. "There is another way," he said slowly and deliberately.

Ruth was becoming more and more confused with every sentence he spoke.

"What are you talking about?" she asked against her own will. These were just daydreams, she mustn't start to believe in them.

"I know somebody in New York who could create papers for you and Wanda under another name. Meaning that during the journey you would be somebody else, do you understand? Nobody would ask you about your husband—you'd be free! Free to be at my side. Free to live in New York, where we . . ."

"And my sisters?" Ruth interrupted softly.

The gleam in Steven's eyes died away.

"It will be difficult for you, I know, but you mustn't tell them anything. The danger that one of them might give you away is too great. Especially if Marie says something in the workshop."

"Marie wouldn't say anything. She can't stand Thomas."

"She might not intend to, but even a word out of place could put our plan in danger. Which is why it would be best to leave them behind and then let them discover the truth."

There were tears burning in Ruth's eyes as she freed herself from his embrace.

"*Leave them behind?* These are my sisters we're talking about! And Peter. My family, do you understand? Steven, I love you so much that it hurts. But what you're asking me to do . . . I'm not sure that I can." She put a hand to her brow. "You want me to vanish like a thief in the night. To leave my family forever—I can't bear the thought. But I also can't bear the prospect of having to live even one more day without you!" Her misery grew with every word she spoke. "Tell me, what should I do?"

Steven took her in his arms again and rocked her back and forth.

"I know that it's a lot to ask of you. You don't need to decide today. But it would mean a great deal to me if I knew that you were considering my suggestion while we're apart."

"When will we see one another again?" she choked out, her voice thick with tears as she clung to him. "Do you really have to go?" she asked, against her better judgment.

Steven gently prized open her fingers where they were clamped around his arm. He took her hand in his and kissed the palm.

"I'll be returning to Thuringia in mid-May. Until then, we can write to each other every week, every day! I promise you that as soon as I have the letter telling me your decision, I will do all that has to be done. When I come back to Europe in the spring, I could have all the papers for you and for Wanda with me. You'll see, the winter will just fly by. Before we know it, spring will be here. And we can begin our future together."

"I haven't said yes yet," Ruth told him, frowning.

"I know." He kissed her mouth and drew her close. "But I will pray every day that you do."

27

"Have you gone quite mad? How could you say yes to the American without asking me first?"

Marie took the contract for the Valentine gifts and shoved it back into Ruth's hand. Then she began leafing deliberately through one of her new books, as though Ruth's concerns had nothing to do with her.

"Now you're insulting me; that's just like you!" Ruth replied. "You're the one who's always going on about your skills as a glassblower. But instead of thanking me for getting you another order, you stab me in the back. This order is our big chance, don't you understand?" She waved the sheet of paper in Marie's face.

"Our chance for what? For us to end up looking like fools?" Marie retorted without looking up from her book.

Johanna stepped between her sisters.

"Now calm down, both of you. Whatever we have to say to one another, there's no need to shout, is there?"

"That's easy for you to say," Marie said mockingly. "You're not the one being asked to blow one thousand glass hearts in the next seven weeks."

She slammed her book shut and thumped it down on the tabletop.

"There's no way to make a heart by free-blowing. Which means I'll have to make a mold for it first. And not just one—I'll need at least a dozen to blow a thousand hearts because my plaster forms don't last as long as Strupp's." She looked accusingly from Johanna to Ruth. "Unless either of you has a special recipe?"

The only answer was an uncomfortable silence.

"If we had a mold from Strupp, then things would be different. But he can't make us one at such short notice," Marie threw in.

Not even Johanna knew what to do. She felt utterly overwhelmed by the new development. She and Marie had been awake half the night, worrying about Ruth and fearing the worst. When their sister finally came home, she offered not a word of explanation but simply handed them this sheet of paper. This was the last thing Johanna had expected.

She had been preparing for Ruth to return lovesick and distraught in floods of tears, so she had been racking her brains as to how best to comfort her sister. But by the look of it, Ruth didn't need a word of comfort. She looked calm and collected and seemed not to feel the slightest pang of guilt for having stayed away all night. She didn't say a word about Steven or what it had been like to see him again.

"I have to admit I never thought that the mold might be a problem. When I saw the heart, I thought it looked a lot simpler than your more elaborate baubles," Ruth said. "We could at least ask Emanuel Strupp whether he'd make us a form. The worst he can do is say no." Ruth turned to Johanna and gave her a nudge. "Are you even listening? You're not usually one to hold back from giving advice. This is about how we earn our living after all!"

Johanna looked up.

"It's strange. We never wanted anything more than to be able to stand on our own feet. To depend on nobody. Not on Wilhelm Heimer, and not on Thomas. And not on the wholesalers in Sonneberg either," she said, looking first at Ruth, then at Marie. "But now that it looks as though we could really do it, we're suddenly afraid. Instead of thinking how best to fill the order, we're squabbling. Maybe the others are right when they say that women can't rule their own roost?"

The other two looked stubbornly at the kitchen table and at the object that lay in the middle of it—the subject of the whole argument—the heart of glass.

Reluctantly, Marie reached out and picked it up. She turned it this way and that in her hands.

"*Who* says that women can't run a business?" she asked.

Johanna shrugged.

"I don't know. But supposedly there are people who say that sort of thing."

"They're wrong," Marie said, her face stern. "Even if I have to cast a dozen forms, we're filling the order. We Steinmann girls will show the world what we're made of!"

She put the heart down and reached her hands out to Johanna and Ruth.

But instead of joining hands with her sisters as they always had in the past to show their common purpose, Ruth jumped up and ran from the room.

Frowning, Marie watched her go.

"What's wrong with her? Why is she crying when everything's all right again?"

◆　◆　◆

The weeks that followed passed in the same rhythm as those that had gone before; Marie went to work for Heimer by day, then sat down at the lamp in the evening—often without even stopping to eat supper. Johanna and Ruth did the packing, eight glass hearts to a box. Although she was blowing into a mold, the same shape over and over again, the work made great demands on Marie, and when at last she would turn off the gas tap just before midnight, she was trembling with exhaustion.

Johanna watched with concern as Marie's features grew sharper and Joost's old pants flapped more loosely around her legs. From then on, she made sure always to bring Marie something to eat as she sat at the lamp, but most of the time Marie simply waved her away. "I'm fine," she would claim, rolling her eyes when Johanna gave her a worried look.

Ruth agreed that Johanna was fussing too much. "Marie was always thinner than either of us. I think it suits her," she said, shrugging. "Other women spend an age putting blush on their cheeks to try to look as radiant as Marie does naturally."

Johanna had to admit that Ruth was right; she hadn't quite noticed before, but over the past year Marie had grown to be a real beauty, which not even her curious costume of men's pants and a black workbench smock could disguise. Quite the opposite, it gave her a certain exotic charm.

◆ ◆ ◆

And then they had done it again: at the end of November Ruth and Johanna rode off to Sonneberg to deliver the merchandise to the railway station. Marie couldn't go because it was a weekday and she had to work for Heimer. Ruth was unusually quiet during the trip, her eyes downcast.

Johanna found the right train and took charge of the loading. After that, they went to find the bank where Steven had sent their payment. The counter clerk looked unimpressed by the sizeable sum he was counting out for them, and Johanna picked up the cash as though it were the most natural thing in the world. Their own money, earned by the work of their own hands.

◆　◆　◆

Christmas was suddenly upon them without any of the three sisters quite knowing where it had come from. On December 18, Ruth got another of the letters that had been arriving at the house ever more frequently, as well as a package from New York, which she opened three days before Christmas Eve—her excuse being that perhaps there was something inside that might spoil. Then she came out of the bedroom, proud as a queen, to show off a midnight-blue suit with a blouse of lilac silk. The ensemble was completed by a pair of dark mauve ankle boots. Neither Johanna nor Marie could believe that a man had chosen all this with such an eye for style and fine judgment of her size. And there was more to admire in Steven's package; he had sent two colorful silk shawls for Johanna and Marie, and a dress of rose-colored lace for Wanda. Ruth smiled quietly to herself as the others went into raptures over their gifts and praised Steven's generosity.

The only part of the Christmas holiday itself worthy of mention was Marie's lavishly decorated Christmas tree; when they saw the many new baubles that hung on it, Johanna and Ruth suddenly knew what Marie had been up to every evening behind closed doors in the workshop after they had filled the Valentine order. Their cries of delight were music to Marie's ears. For the first time in ages, she was pleased with herself and with what she had made: the glittering stars, the dewdrops that gleamed on the silvered pinecones, the wreaths of cream-colored Christmas roses. The new designs had come to her almost fully formed in her mind, without requiring long hours at her sketchpad first. They had taken shape in glass almost as easily. Perhaps studying her art books was already paying off? She rejoiced inwardly.

◆　◆　◆

When the postman approached their house on New Year's Day, Ruth was halfway out the door before he could even knock.

Marie looked out the window. "Ruth's giving the postman a whole stack of letters," she whispered to Johanna. "Is she worried that half of them might never arrive? She must be writing him several letters at once."

"You know Ruth. She's turned letter writing into a kind of religion," Johanna replied.

Marie scurried from the window before Ruth could spot her there.

"I would dearly love to know what she writes to him all the time. There's surely not that much to report?"

Johanna shrugged. "Apparently there is for Ruth. I could just as well ask why you bury yourself in those dusty old books all the time. They can hardly be that exciting."

"They are for me!"

"You see." Sighing, Johanna stood up. "I should imagine Ruth won't be in the mood to chat for the next few hours. So I'll make coffee just for the two of us."

She was just putting the water on to boil when Ruth came in, letting in a gust of ice-cold air.

"There's a letter to all three of us," she said, frowning as she held up a thick brown envelope. There was disappointment written all over her face. "I hope nothing went amiss with our delivery. What if half the baubles broke in their boxes?"

"Don't tempt fate," Johanna said. She was beside her in an instant and took the letter from her sister. She slit the envelope open with her fingernail, and two smaller envelopes slid into her hand. "This one's for you," she said, handing Ruth a cream envelope, which her sister put into her apron pocket as carefully as if it were an egg.

Johanna opened the other letter and unfolded a few sheets of thin notepaper, which all had the green Woolworth diamond as their letterhead. She read through the first lines in haste.

"That can't be true," she exclaimed, looking from one sister to the other. "A new order already? How can it be? There must be some mistake." She began to leaf wildly through the rest of the pages.

As she did so, Ruth pointed to the bottom of the first sheet. "That's Steven's handwriting. Johanna, I'm warning you, if you don't read us what he wrote straightaway then I won't be answerable for my actions!"

Johanna was busy deciphering the postmark.

"He wrote the letter on December thirteenth," she answered, frowning.

A moment later, Ruth snatched the letter from her hand and read out the lines that Steven had written.

Dear Ruth, Johanna, and Marie, You will surely be surprised to hear from me so soon. I am afraid I must tell you that we made a mistake in our calculations regarding your Christmas baubles.

"Does that mean that nobody wants to buy them?" Marie broke in, her eyes wide with distress. "Or are they too expensive for the Americans?"

Ruth rolled her eyes. "You're driving me mad, both of you!" she said, and resumed reading.

Here's what I have to tell you:

They sold out. Every single one of them. Down to the very last winter scene!

28

Ruth hastily threw another blanket over Wanda's pram before she pushed it outside, then shut the door behind her without saying good-bye to anyone. She felt for Steven's letter one last time. Certain that it was in her coat pocket, she pulled her mittens on and headed off, warmly bundled in her woolen jacket, overcoat, and shawl. If she had her way, she wouldn't be back for a while. She wanted nothing more than to read Steven's letter in peace.

The damp snow splashed up onto Ruth's skirt with every step, and she struggled to get the wheels of Wanda's pram to turn as she walked uphill. Even so, she basked in the warmth of the sun on her shoulders and neck where it shone down between the houses. The thaw was coming.

When Ruth neared the Heimer house, she quickened her pace. The last thing she wanted was to run into Thomas. It was enough to start the new year with *one* argument.

Only when she had left Lauscha behind did she stop to rest. She picked up a twig and gave it to Wanda to play with. While her daughter gurgled merrily away, Ruth walked onward into the forest. The snow was so thick on the branches that the pines were bent over like little old women. It gleamed almost silver in the sunlight, so bright that Ruth had to squint. She was in no mood to admire the beauty of the winter woods anyway.

"Thirty thousand Christmas baubles by mid-August—I won't do it!"

She could still hear Marie's words ringing in her ears.

She and Johanna had stopped their dance of joy as though thunderstruck.

"I won't go into mass production, do you hear me?" she had yelled at them. "I might just as well be working for Heimer. At least my workday there only lasts ten hours, and after that I'm free to think of new designs."

"But you could do all that and more if you gave up working for Heimer," Johanna had replied, pointing to Steven's letter. "It says here in black and white that you would have an absolutely free hand in designing the baubles! The only condition is that they mustn't be significantly more expensive than the last batch."

"You see, they're already imposing conditions," Marie had shot back. "And besides, when am I supposed to think up these new designs if I'm sitting at the lamp day and night? Magnus agrees with me," she had added, as though Griseldis's son had anything to do with it.

Ruth swallowed hard. She still didn't understand why Marie had dug in her heels. Instead of being pleased to have a guaranteed buyer for her new designs, instead of being overjoyed at being able to finally stop working for Heimer, all Marie had done was complain. Ruth was getting fed up with all this talk of art and artists. Marie didn't even realize how selfish she was being. She and Johanna couldn't blow glass after all, so when Marie got on her high horse about her "artistic development," she was jeopardizing her sisters' future. But Marie didn't seem to care. So much for "the Steinmann girls will show the world what they're made of"!

Ruth stopped abruptly. Perhaps it had been a mistake to leave right in the middle of the argument. But she simply couldn't bear all the squabbling, not with Steven's letter in her pocket. She wanted to hold on to that warm feeling of happiness and protect it. She felt through her overcoat for the letter. It was still there. Good.

The steeper the path became, the more Ruth's lungs ached. She was walking fast, which helped to clear her head. By the time she reached the bench on the hill with the view of the valley, she had calmed down somewhat. And that was as it should be. She wanted to read Steven's letter without that silly argument clouding her mood.

Wanda had fallen asleep. Ruth pulled the blanket all the way up to her nose and pushed the pram into a patch of sunlight. Then she sat down on the bench. The wood felt warm and dry. It was the first time she had been up here since she had left Thomas. Though she had been half expecting to be plagued by bad memories, she experienced nothing of the sort. Even the fact that she had lost her innocence here meant nothing to her now. It was almost as though it had happened in another life. She chased away the last thought of these things and made room in her mind for Steven.

Steven. Her great and distant love.

Ever since he had left, she had asked herself every morning whether she still loved him. And every time, the answer had been a resounding *Yes*.

Carefully she took Steven's letter from her coat pocket, and just as carefully she opened it.

My beloved Ruth!

How I wish I could be with you now, wherever you are. But the best I can manage is to send you my thoughts. And this letter.

Please do not be surprised that there are not more letters for you today. As always at this time of year, there has been a great deal of work, and I have hardly had time for anything else. Nevertheless I have done little else but think of you. Lovesick thoughts, foolish thoughts, happy and unhappy at once. Happy because of you. Unhappy because you are not with me—not yet at least.

Not a day has gone by when I do not yearn for you morning, noon, and night. Sometimes I even wake at night and see your angelic face before me. I hear your voice and the wonderful things you say. Sometimes I long for you so much that it hurts. Is it usual for a man to bare his feelings like this? I don't know. All I know is that I must.

Two days ago I was finally able to make contact with my adviser in these matters and explain my plan. He is prepared to obtain the necessary documents for you and Wanda. I await only your word. I do not wish to impose on you in any way but should tell you that my adviser would have to begin his preparations no later than the beginning of March *if he is to have everything ready by April 15, when my ship, the* Boston, *sails for Europe.*

"The beginning of March!" Ruth said aloud. That meant she would have to send Steven her decision within the next two weeks . . .

What do you say to the order—isn't it magnificent? The success of your Christmas ornaments truly exceeded all our expectations. Mr. Woolworth can hardly wait to receive the Valentine hearts as well. The Americans seem truly to love the glass artworks from the Thuringian Forest. In my estimation, you will never be short of work from us in the future. It goes without saying that these orders will always go to the Steinmann sisters, even if circumstances change. *There are things that can be better organized from here in America—if you understand my meaning. As I have said before, it is all a matter of planning and organization. But even more than that, it is a matter of the heart.*

Your heart.

And that is why I await your answer, with fear and anticipation, as soon as you are ready to send it.

Your own loving Steven.

Ruth put the letter down. Her heart ached so much that she had to press both hands to her breast. It was a miracle that a man she hardly knew could stir such deep feelings within her.

"I love you too," she whispered, and watched four little puffs of breath hang in the cold air for a moment like tiny clouds. Perhaps they would drift all the way across the Atlantic and reach him?

It was even harder going back downhill with the pram than it had been walking up. Ruth had to take care with every step not to slip. Her thin boots were soaked through and gave her no foothold in the snow. She held on tight to the push bar of the pram. Whatever happened—whether she stumbled, slipped, or fell—she would never let go of the pram with Wanda inside. Soon her arms were trembling and she began to sweat inside her heavy clothing.

Ruth breathed a sigh of relief when a cloud passed over the sun. But a moment later she felt oddly ill at ease; where before the world had been bright and warm, it was now gloomy and cold. And it grew darker with every step she took down into the valley. Suddenly she felt that the mountains were about to fall on her.

She only saw him when it was too late to change course—in among the first houses of the village. Her eyes darted all around, like a cornered animal looking about for a bolt hole. In vain. Thomas was standing in the middle of the street as though he had been waiting for her.

"Happy New Year!" he said, taking off his cap awkwardly.

"Happy New Year," Ruth muttered in reply. Without looking at him, she tried to walk past. As she went she hunched her shoulders unconsciously. Perhaps he would leave her alone.

But just as she was even with him, he grabbed her wrist.

"Ruth! Please stop, let's talk."

Thomas didn't look good. His chin was almost black with stubble and there were blue shadows under his eyes. The stench of beer on his breath was so strong that Ruth felt she could almost see it in the air.

Her husband.

All at once she felt unspeakably sad.

"What do we have to say to one another?" she said, taking her hand wearily from his grasp.

"Isn't it time to ring out the old and ring in the new?" He forced a smile. "Ruth, come back to me," he pleaded. "I . . . perhaps I wasn't always the best husband. But that will change, I promise you. I'll do better. I won't drink so much, if that's what you want. You and me, we were really something! Think of our wedding day . . ." He broke off as though unsure of what he was saying.

Ruth kept quiet. What could she even say? That it had all been a mistake, nothing but a mistake?

"If you like we can go to Sonneberg together and buy you something nice to wear. Or something for Wanda," he added, glancing briefly down at his daughter.

"These last six months without you, alone in the apartment . . ." He shook his head. "That's no life! And as for you, living with your sisters . . . that can't go on forever."

Ruth struggled for something appropriate to say—to no avail. She had nothing left to say to Thomas Heimer. It was as simple as that. The only thing she felt for him was a kind of pity. No matter how hard he tried, Thomas would never be able to quench her longing. And she could not quench his.

"Not a day has gone by when I do not yearn for you morning, noon, and night. . . . Sometimes I long for you so much that it hurts."

Encouraged by her silence, Thomas carried on trying. "We're still young, you and I. We've got our whole life before us. Who knows? Perhaps our next child will be a boy? And if not, that's all the same to me. We'll manage to make an heir at some point. All we need is patience. That's what my father says too. Look at us, three boys in a row."

Ruth could hardly believe her ears. Any pity she had felt was gone in a flash. "You're talking as though I were nothing but a brood cow! How can you blather on about having a son after all that's happened? The moment you raised your hand against Wanda you gave up every right as my husband." She would never forget that night. How he had staggered around the bedroom, drunk. *"Not answering back now, Ruth Steinmann, are you?"* How she had watched helplessly as he had leaned over the cradle and . . .

"We may still be married on paper, but as far as I'm concerned we divorced a long time ago! You let me past, Thomas Heimer."

"No, wait! Ruth, I'm begging you. For better or for worse, isn't that what they say?" He smiled awkwardly. "If we want it to be, the worst could be over now." He held tight to her sleeve.

"The worst is certainly over for me. Because I have nothing more to do with you," she replied icily. "Now let me past or I will scream the whole street down."

"Oh, is that so? Is there no end to your pride?" His voice had lost its wheedling tone as though a switch had been thrown. Now he was shouting at her. "Here I am, pleading like a good-hearted sap for you to come back to me, and you make a fool of me! If you think things can go on like this then you've reckoned wrong, Ruth *Heimer*! There are other means I can use. You can forget your talk of divorce! If you think . . ."

His shouting woke Wanda, whose tiny eyes looked reproachfully at Ruth as her little hands reached out for her.

Ruth felt a surge of cold rage.

"What I think has nothing to do with you," she interrupted him. "And I will not let you threaten me a moment longer!" She didn't even try to keep her voice down. She wanted everyone to hear what she had to say. She couldn't care less if all the neighbors up and down the street stuck their heads out their windows.

"Get out of my way," she repeated, more vigorously than before. She was nonetheless surprised when he did as she asked. She had been bracing herself for more insults. She took a step toward him.

"If I can give you some friendly advice, a bath wouldn't do you any harm. You stink as though you'd drunk a keg dry. But knowing what I do of you and your family, I wouldn't be at all surprised if that's precisely what you did for New Year's."

She gave him one last contemptuous glance, then walked on without turning back.

29

"I'm not sure I understand," Marie said, frowning. She turned to Peter, who sat beside her on the bench. "You're suggesting we knock through the wall between our house and yours to make a bigger workshop."

Johanna rolled her eyes. "We've already been over all this. Yes, that's the idea. Then we would have one big workshop where everybody could work together."

Ignoring Johanna, Marie went on. "And there would be two lamps in the workshop for three glassblowers: you, me, and Magnus."

She struggled silently to find some flaw in the plan, but nothing came to mind. Peter's idea could work! All the same, she didn't want to get ahead of herself. Had the others really understood that when she said she needed more time for herself, it was a matter of life and death for her, not just crazy talk as Ruth always said?

Peter nodded. "Of course we would have to talk to Magnus first to see if he's interested in learning to blow glass. And even if he is, we'll have to see whether he's got the knack for it. After all, glassblowing's not in his blood the way it is for us."

The way it is for us—Marie's breast swelled with pride.

"Magnus is a good friend of course, but I sometimes wonder just what *is* in his blood. What's he been doing ever since he came back? You can hardly call running errands a real job for a man, can you?" Johanna remarked, shaking her head. "Magnus a glassblower? I don't know. He's a nice lad, but can we rely on him? I fear we'll get him trained up and then he'll be off and away. To be honest, that's the part of the plan I like least."

"I don't like the way you talk about him," Marie said, her cheeks glowing. "Magnus can't help it that his father was a drunken sot rather than a glassblower. Why do you think he ran off the way he did? Because he couldn't stand it any longer! If Joost had been that sort of man then we would probably have done the same. I don't think he'll want to leave again. Quite the opposite, he's happy to be back. And he's keener on glassblowing than anyone I've ever met. But you . . ."

"Don't get so worked up! Surely I'm allowed to voice my doubts," Johanna broke in.

"Well, you don't have to be snippy about it. I would be glad to have Magnus working with us. A third glassblower would be a great help. Without him . . ."

"O-ho, so you're going to blackmail us now!" Johanna bridled. "If your *best friend* Magnus . . ."

"Enough!"

Peter's fist thundered down onto the tabletop. He stood up and went to the window. Then he turned and stared grimly at the two women.

"I've had it with all this bickering! One of you jumps up and runs out of the house as though the whole thing had nothing to do with her. Then you two come to me asking for my advice, but instead of putting your heads together you start squabbling like a pair of old women. Perhaps I was a little too quick to suggest we share a workshop. I can't imagine listening to this kind of quarreling every day. My work is too complicated to allow for that sort of distraction all the time."

Marie swallowed. It served them right.

"We really didn't mean it that way," Johanna said meekly. "We're just a little worked up. Because of the size of the order and the way Ruth ran off. And—oh, I don't know!"

"Johanna's right," Marie said through gritted teeth. "And you're right too. If we want to take on this job, then your plan is the only way to make it work."

Peter sat down at the table with a sigh. "Then let's get on with it." He turned to Johanna. "We will need three pairs of hands working at the lamp. Marie desperately needs time to work on new designs. Unless you think this Woolworth is the sort of man who would be happy to buy the same thing every year? If Marie can give him new designs all the time, you'll be guaranteed a repeat customer."

Marie's face brightened. She had enough ideas. For instance she wanted to cast a mold for the icicles that had gone wrong the first time she tried them and . . .

"I also think that we should take Griseldis on," Peter said. "We can find a few marks somewhere to match what Heimer pays her. Then we'll have the best silver-bath mixer anywhere in Lauscha."

Johanna looked at Peter in surprise, as though seeing him for the first time. Then she hugged him. "You have a real business head on your shoulders. What would we do without you? To be honest I was just like Marie at first; all I saw was a whole mountain of problems and questions. We were hardly expecting such a huge order, after all."

"Well, Johanna Steinmann, sometimes it does no harm to listen to what I have to say. Even if that doesn't come easily to you." Peter grinned. "Now let's get started." He scratched his head. "I love you all, of course, but I'm not going to leave my patients in the lurch. And I have to show up at the foundry for a few hours from time to time when they're firing the ovens. So I plan to spend half the day on the Christmas tree order, and the other half making my eyes. As for what becomes of my little glass critters, we'll just have to see. They bring in a pretty penny, but my heart's not really in them to the extent that I couldn't give them up."

Johanna frowned. "I do have one more question . . ." she said almost timidly.

Peter laughed. "Well go on, I don't bite! It's just that from time to time you Steinmann girls need to be told what's what. All three of you can be stubborn as mules, you know that. So, what is it?"

"If we have only one workshop, where will you consult with your patients about their eyes? They surely don't want to sit for a fitting in among all our baubles."

"We'll wall off a corner of the workshop," Marie said before Peter could answer. Now that they had a plan in place, she didn't want to hear of any further obstacles. She wanted to draw, to think up new designs for her globes. "While we're at it, let's wall off a little cubbyhole for me as well. Sometimes, I just need to have a little time to myself." Marie was expecting Johanna to raise some further objection, but none came.

"Here's one possible answer." Peter pulled out a pencil and paper from the table drawer and sketched out a plan of the new workshop in a few lines. "The two gas connections will have to stay in front where they are now. That means the other workbenches will have to go here in the middle, which works well because that gives us the most room for painting, silvering, and packing."

"And for other decoration work," Marie put in. "I'm thinking that some globes will be wrapped with tinsel wire and others glued with little glass beads and . . ."

"That doesn't matter now. We're just talking about how to use the space," Johanna interrupted impatiently.

Peter gave both of them a warning glance.

"Then we could put in a table for Marie and another one for me, here." He sketched in two rectangles as he spoke. "You could study and work here, and have all the peace and quiet you need."

Study in peace and quiet . . . Marie's eyes gleamed.

"I would need a bookshelf as well, and somewhere to keep my papers," she said.

"That should be easy," Johanna said. "If we take the wardrobe from upstairs in Father's room and use that to help wall off your corner from the workshop, you can keep everything you need in there. That would also give us more storage space upstairs."

"Storage space!" Marie exclaimed, putting a hand to her mouth. "We haven't given that a thought. Where in the world are we supposed to store ten thousand baubles?" They discussed ideas for hours, and the air in Peter's workshop was thick with excitement, happiness, and a touch of fear about what the future might bring. They all forgot about lunch until Peter put bread and cheese on the table sometime in the afternoon. When Marie ran next door to fetch some wurst, there was still no sign of Ruth. How could anybody be so childish?

Nobody paid much attention to the food. One or the other of them was constantly reaching with greasy fingers for the pencil and paper to jot down an idea. As the list of tasks grew and grew, the business began to take shape.

Johanna was slicing herself a second piece of bread when she put down the knife and wiped her hands on her apron.

"Actually there's one more thing we haven't thought of . . ."

"What would that be?" Peter asked.

He cast her a glance so full of yearning that Marie felt a pang of sympathy for him. She knew so well that feeling of being so close to her goal and yet so far away!

"A name. Our business needs a new name! May I?" She pointed to the pencil in Peter's hand.

He handed it over. "You always do what you want anyway." He shrugged, trying to seem indifferent, but Marie sensed that this was about much more than a name.

"So here you all are!"

Three heads turned as Ruth appeared in the doorway.

"I was calling for you next door. I could have called till I was blue in the face!"

She picked Wanda up in a practiced grip and put her on one hip while she closed the door behind her with the other.

"I'm so hungry I could eat half a pig! I went right up into the forest, can you imagine?" Before she sat down, she picked up a slice of bread from the basket and took a hearty bite. "What are you doing there?" she asked, pointing to the list in Johanna's hand.

Marie looked at her sister, speechless. Just that morning, they had been quarreling and now she was acting as though they had never argued at all.

"If you think we're going to start again from the beginning for your sake, you're wrong," Johanna replied icily. She turned the notepad over so that Ruth couldn't even see what was written there.

"Well pardon me! I daresay I'll find out soon enough."

Ruth cut a few thin slices of cheese and popped them into Wanda's mouth bit by bit. Her movements were flustered.

"I ran into Thomas."

The others looked at each other. So that was why Ruth was so jittery.

"And? Did he make trouble again?" Peter asked, frowning.

Ruth shook her head.

While they all listened to Ruth describe her encounter, Peter reached for Johanna's notepad and pulled it toward him unobtrusively. He hesitated for a moment, then turned it over as though it were the card upon which his whole game depended.

Marie peered over his shoulder as he read, and she wanted to whoop with joy.

Peter put down the notepad and grinned.

"Not quite what I'd imagined, but it's a start," he whispered to Johanna.

Ruth looked from one to the other, exasperated.

"Is anybody even listening to me? What do you have there anyway?" Before Peter could stop her, she had snatched the pad from his hand.

"Steinmann and Maienbaum, glassblowers." She looked up, baffled. "What's that supposed to mean?"

Life was never the same again in the Steinmann house, and the three sisters were once more the talk of the whole village.

Marie and Griseldis gave notice the same day. Wilhelm Heimer stood there openmouthed and had to watch his best painter and his best silver-mixer walk out of the workshop without looking back.

Hammers swung, and the wall between the Steinmanns' house and Peter's was broken down and replaced by new support timbers. Though the space was still not as big as the Heimer workshop, it was much larger than the two little rooms it replaced. Furniture was moved around, and the men from the gasworks came to extend the gas pipes by another couple of yards.

Peter and Magnus hung a sign that read "Steinmann-Maienbaum, Glassblowers" between the two houses, and everyone who walked past stopped to wonder at it; Marie had painted the letters as pine-tree branches and created a frame of red and dark-blue Christmas baubles all around them. The effect was astonishing and eye-catching. As well as the artistry involved, the sign's message also stirred great interest; Peter and the Steinmann sisters were joining forces when he wasn't even married to one of them. Surely that was just another sign of how things could go wrong when women ruled the roost.

While Johanna and Marie went down to the foundry to order new stock, Ruth went to Sonneberg with Wanda to send confirmation to Woolworth that they were accepting his order. She sent another letter that same day, with trembling fingers and pounding heart.

◆　◆　◆

It was not yet mid-January when production began in the new workshop. Although they had never worked together like this before, their daily routine soon became that of a close-knit team. In the mornings Peter and Marie sat at the lamp and blew glass. The finished baubles went on to Ruth and Griseldis at the next table, who silvered them. Thanks to Griseldis's special recipe, the baubles had exactly the right silvery gleam, with no gray streaks or dull spots. Johanna congratulated herself more than once on her decision to take on Griseldis, and she cheerfully forgot that it was actually Peter who first made the suggestion.

Johanna spent most of her mornings doing paperwork; she worked out a system for numbering all the items and then wrote them out on labels and cardboard boxes in the afternoons. When she was done with that, she wanted to prepare a catalog; she had to think of the future after all.

Around midday, Magnus sat down at Marie's lamp and practiced blowing the globes. Either Peter or Marie watched over his shoulder as he worked, giving advice or correcting his posture. Although he didn't become a talented glassblower overnight, he managed to blow simple globes—even if they all varied somewhat in size.

While the silvered globes were drying on a bed of nails, they all sat down around the table and ate the lunch that Griseldis made early each morning. She had insisted from the start on taking on the task.

"If you're going to employ an old woman like me, then I want to make myself useful. Otherwise you might just as well have taken on one of the young village girls!" she had told Johanna as she kneaded the potato dough with wet hands to make dumplings. Neither Johanna nor Ruth was sorry to be rid of the hard work of cooking, and they enjoyed the luxury of sitting down to lunch at a table that was properly set. They set great store by the fact that there were enough plates for everyone.

After lunch the silvered globes would be dry and the women sat down, under Marie's guidance, to decorate them. While the first winter landscapes had been painted with white enamel, they now had a broad palette in shades of red, blue, and green. And they had a full range of decorations as well, including glass beads and tinsel wire as fine as human hair. Whenever Marie looked at the sparkling, shining treasures all around her, her heart leaped. With all the glowing colors, the silver bath, and other shimmering materials, the workshop looked like a fairy's grotto or a storehouse where comets waited before shooting across the sky. Sometimes Marie felt that she was an enchantress. With the time to finally try out new shapes and designs, her imagination knew no limits. Where she had once had a dozen different designs, she now had three dozen or more. The others grumbled that even if Johanna did ever get started on her catalog, she would never be able to finish it because of Marie's boundless imagination.

Other glassblowers soon started to say that Marie's baubles were more beautiful than anyone else's. Again and again, they stopped by and tried to get into the workshop under some pretext or another in an attempt to catch a glimpse of Marie's designs. But Johanna was unbending here; apart from Peter's patients, nobody else was allowed in the workshop. She didn't want Marie to suffer the same fate that Karl Flein had met with his glass roses.

While Marie spent the afternoons working on new designs just as they had agreed, Peter made glass eyes to written specifications that arrived by post. He had as many orders as ever, and he had patients who came directly to him.

His fears that the patients would be distressed by the chatter, song, and laughter in the workshop were soon banished. Rather they felt quite at ease in the bustling, happy atmosphere. Fate had been unkind to them once when they lost an eye, but after their consultations with Peter many didn't want to leave, so they sat down at the workbenches with the women and watched as they painted and finished the pieces.

Although next Christmas was still nearly a year away, it wasn't long before a visitor asked whether perhaps he could buy some of the splendid globes. At first Johanna wanted to refuse—after all, they were working to fill an order for America—but she soon reconsidered. The first to ask was a man who had come from Nuremberg with his daughter. Johanna let him choose twelve globes, which she packed for him in a cardboard box. Then she asked double the price that Woolworth was paying. The gentleman handed over the money without a murmur of protest and thanked Johanna over and over for accommodating him. As Peter and Johanna shook his hand to say good-bye, neither of them could have guessed that they had just won a major new client.

Nor did they immediately make the connection when a letter arrived a few weeks later from a Nuremberg department store, asking about terms and prices. Peter only realized as he was reading it through for the second time that one of the "Hoffmann Brothers & Sons" must have been the father of little Siegrun, who had lost an eye in a riding accident. He hadn't known until that moment that the man was also part owner of one of the largest stores in Nuremberg. After a flurried exchange of letters—and a box of samples sent to Nuremberg—Steinmann and Maienbaum, glassblowers, had another order to fill.

◆ ◆ ◆

When in late February the postman arrived at their door with a telegram from America, everybody was too busy to be surprised.

A telegram from America? Why not?

All the same everyone was eager to hear what news could be so important that it would be sent at such expense. It wasn't the way their client usually communicated with them.

As always, Ruth took delivery of the mail. She unfolded the sheet as she came in from the street.

"I hope the shipment of Valentine hearts arrived all right," Johanna murmured. Though everything in the workshop was running as smoothly as could be, she was still prone to fits of worry. The humiliation she had suffered at the hands of the Sonneberg wholesalers was like a thorn in her flesh. It always began to itch anew whenever she dared believe that success was here to stay.

All eyes were on Ruth as she stood rooted in the doorway, staring at the sheet.

"How long are you going to keep us in suspense?" Johanna snapped nervously. "Peter, don't you even care that there's news from America?"

Peter was consulting with a war veteran about a new eye. He sighed and put the color card aside. He didn't like being interrupted at such a critical moment.

With one hand at her throat, as though gasping for air, Ruth croaked, "The telegram is from Steven. He says, 'Valentine hearts arrived. Well done.'" She looked up.

"Thank God!" Johanna said. "For a moment I feared the worst."

"Does he write anything about how the hearts are selling?" Marie asked.

Ruth shook her head. "He's coming to Sonneberg in May. He wants to look at your new baubles when he comes. Which must mean . . ."

"Ruth! Why don't you just read what he wrote?" Johanna spat. "The telegram's addressed to all three of us after all!"

Peter's patient followed what was going on with lively curiosity; he had not expected the consultation to be so interesting.

Ruth finally read it aloud.

Valentine hearts arrived. Well done. Arriving Sonneberg 14 May. Meet Swan Hotel. Request one sample each design from new collection. To Ruth Heimer, All preparations in place. Schedule tight. Stop.

She looked up. "That's all. Happy now?" She made a face at Johanna.

"All preparations in place. What does he mean by that?" Marie asked, frowning.

"Mr. Woolworth probably just doesn't want to miss Ruth for anything," Peter said, then turned to Ruth and went on. "You must have made quite an impression on the man."

"The telegram's not from Woolworth though, it's from his assistant Steven Miles!" Johanna said, casting a meaningful glance at Peter.

Marie shook her head. "It sounds very odd to me all the same," she insisted. "What do we care if his schedule's tight? My word, he should see ours!"

The others laughed.

Ruth gazed into space as though none of this had anything to do with her.

Marie wasn't ready to change the subject though.

"They want to see new baubles, isn't that wonderful? It's a lucky thing I already have some put aside. I'll be sure to spend more time on my new designs from now on." She looked triumphantly around the room, but there was no reaction except from Magnus, who nodded his approval.

They soon all went back to work and nobody paid any more attention to Ruth. She walked through the room like a sleepwalker and knelt down where Wanda was sitting on a blanket, playing listlessly with some wooden blocks. Glad of the distraction, she stretched out her little arms to Ruth.

"My angel. My sweet little girl!"

"Mama . . ."

Ruth brushed Wanda's blonde locks away from her forehead, then held her tight, cheek to cheek.

"It'll happen soon. Soon."

Nobody but Wanda heard her whisper.

31

The next few weeks were not easy for Ruth.

She felt so distraught that on some days, her secret threatened to choke her. She longed to be able to tell Johanna and Marie everything, to prepare them for what was to come. She wanted to talk to them about the long journey she was about to undertake, and she wanted their advice on what to bring along and what to leave behind. Instead she had to think it through on her own, figuring out whether Wanda would need her winter coat for the trip on the ocean steamer or whether a jacket would be enough—after all, she could hardly pack everything from the baby wardrobe in her bag.

How she would have loved to share her coming happiness with her sisters. And to weep with them too. But she could do none of that. Ruth knew that emigrating on forged papers, as she planned to do, was some sort of crime. The lonelier she felt, the more deeply she regretted having promised Steven to keep silent, but she would rather have bitten off her tongue than break her promise. When it all became too much for her, she left the room before she could spill the beans.

With every day that she secretly crossed off the calendar, everything felt more final. Suddenly even the most ordinary activity was charged with meaning, and she found herself thinking, *This is the last sack of flour I'll ever bring home from the store in the wheelbarrow* or *That was the last time I'll ever buy new shoes for Wanda from Mrs. Huber.* When Easter came, she put a bouquet of daffodils in the window, and wondered whether they even had daffodils in New York. The very idea of New York was often too much for her. Ruth instinctively shied away from thinking about the distant city of which she knew so little and what life would be like there. If she had done that, her fear of the future would have overwhelmed her.

When the swallows began to build their nest under the window in the washhouse, Ruth knew that she would already be gone by the time their chicks began to chirrup.

The worst part was when somebody tried to include her in any plans. When Johanna asked her whether she'd like to take the train out to Coburg when summer finally came, Ruth had trouble holding back the tears. At last she managed to summon up a scrap of enthusiasm and muttered, "What a good idea!" At lunch one day she said how much she liked Griseldis's sour pickles, and the good old soul promised to make a few more jars for the Steinmann sisters that July when gherkins were in season. Ruth felt like a heel. She was going to leave all these dear people, leave them in secret and forever!

The only time the melancholy could not touch her was when she was sitting with the others in the workshop. Instead of thinking *This is the last set of ice crystals I will ever paint with my sisters*, she took comfort in the thought that these Christmas decorations would be going with her on the long voyage across the ocean. She would probably not be there to watch Marie work on her new idea of a series of baubles in the shape of bells, but she would hold the finished items in her hands when she got to New York. Perhaps she would be able to hang them on her own tree next Christmas! And so every time she picked up a globe, opened the bottle of silver solution, or took a brush into her hand, it soothed the pain of her imminent departure. Whatever else might happen, the glass would always be there to connect her to her sisters—and to Lauscha.

And so day followed day, and week followed week.

◆ ◆ ◆

"Well then, I'm going over to see Magnus." Marie was already half-way out the door, with a light jacket over her shoulders and her sketchpad under her arm, when Johanna called her back.

"Do you have to spend every evening with him? I really don't know what you see in him," Johanna said irritably. "Magnus is a nice lad of course, but . . ."

"But what? He's a nice lad, and that's enough for me," Marie shot back. "Perhaps that's just what I like about him—the fact that he's not always asking something from me, that he's not always prodding at me the way you do. He takes me as I am, and I do the same with him."

Ruth pretended not to see Johanna look to her for support, and carried on brushing Wanda's shock of blonde hair with a soft brush. She didn't know what Marie saw in Magnus either—she thought he was rather a dull dog—but she certainly wasn't going to stick her nose in like Johanna.

"I don't know why you're always picking on Magnus. He was the one who picked you up off the street and brought you back home. But you seem to have forgotten about that," Marie said to Johanna. "And you have no cause to complain about his work. He's blowing almost as many globes as Peter or I. He turns up on time and he's reliable to boot," she added defiantly.

"You're right," Johanna conceded. "All I meant is that . . . he's so quiet. And he hardly ever laughs."

"I'm sure that he saw some terrible things when he was out in the world," Marie said, and there was suddenly a note of pity in her voice. "But I don't spend my time poking and prodding at him like Griseldis does, trying to discover his secrets. I can let him be sad if he must. In fact he's something of an inspiration to me." And with that, she left, slamming the door behind her.

Johanna shook her head as she watched her go.

"Will you just listen to that? His sorrow's an inspiration to her."

"Let her be," Ruth replied with a grin. Johanna was puffing herself up like a broody hen again.

Ruth put Wanda gently down on the bench—she had fallen asleep while her mother was brushing her hair—and frowned.

"Do you think that the two of them . . . are more than just friends? Marie and a man—to be honest I never even considered that," Ruth said.

Johanna sighed. "Well, she is still our little sister. But I suppose we need to get used to the idea that she's grown up by now."

Well hark who's talking! Ruth thought. Who was it after all who always wanted to make Marie's decisions for her?

But she kept this thought to herself and instead said, "That's not what I meant. Rather . . . well you have to admit that when she goes around wearing pants like that with her hair combed straight back she doesn't really look very feminine. And she's never shown any sign of being interested in men."

Johanna nodded but said nothing.

Ruth stood up to take Wanda upstairs to bed. When she came back, Johanna was still sitting there.

"When I think about it, we haven't had much luck with men, have we?" Johanna raised her eyebrows ironically.

I have! Ruth thought, but she shrugged noncommittally. "That depends. Isn't the saying that you make your own luck?"

Johanna looked up. "I wouldn't have expected you to agree."

"Why not?" Ruth answered. "Nobody forced me to marry Thomas. And he and I are the only ones to blame for the failure of our marriage. We were never right for one another, from the very start, but I saw that too late. Or rather I was too blind to see it."

"You say that so calmly," Johanna said in surprise. "It's as though you were talking about the weather, but it changed your whole life."

"Thomas is over and done with as far as I'm concerned, whatever it might say in the parish registry. There's nothing for me to get worked up about. Sometimes it's helpful just to see things plain . . . Perhaps you should try that." To her horror, the conversation was venturing into deep waters. It wouldn't be long before she started talking about Steven.

"Just to see things plain . . . that's the sort of thing that Peter might say . . ." Her sister heaved a deep sigh.

Ruth frowned and looked over at her. "So what about you two? Is anything ever going to come of that or not?"

Johanna looked up as though she had been expecting just this question.

"I don't know. I don't think so. Oh, it's all so crazy." She ran her hand through her hair. "He's spent years telling me that we were meant for one another and that he was just waiting for me to see it."

"And now?" Ruth hadn't noticed any change in Peter's behavior toward Johanna. But she hadn't been paying much attention either. "Does this mean you've realized now that you love Peter and he's lost interest?"

The only answer was another deep sigh. "I don't know that I would put it that way. But more and more often these days, I find myself wishing he would take me in his arms," Johanna admitted. "Sometimes I want to do that to him . . ." she added, blushing.

She clearly had trouble admitting this, so Ruth bit back a mocking remark. All the same she couldn't quite keep the sarcasm from her voice.

"Why have you suddenly changed your tune after all these years?"

"It's not so sudden as all that. In the last six months I've begun to notice that Peter is more than just a big brother. It might sound strange, but the real reason is what happened with Strobel. After that I began to watch Peter more closely. To be honest for a while I was just waiting to catch him out in some sort of wickedness—after all, he's a man too. But I never did, thank God." There was admiration in her voice. "Peter stands above the world in so many ways. He's so self-assured, and his whole demeanor is so . . . engaging! Whenever I look over at him at work these days, I keep thinking: there's a man who can really make a woman feel safe. I can even imagine him putting his arms around me and kissing me, because I know that it would be nothing like what Strobel . . ." She turned her eyes away.

"Why don't you try telling *him* everything you've just told me?" Ruth asked.

Her sister waved a hand. "I'd just feel silly. After all these years . . . And who knows what he thinks of me these days. He hasn't tried anything for ages." She looked up sadly. "If he still loves me, why doesn't he do something, say something?"

Ruth couldn't suppress her smile any longer. "He's a fairly clever man, if you hadn't noticed." If Peter had kept up his overtures toward her sister, Johanna certainly wouldn't be talking this way now. Ruth sighed. It was so simple! All she had to do was help Johanna see what was right in front of her . . .

"Do you still have the atlas that Peter gave you two Christmases ago?"

Johanna nodded glumly. "It's upstairs. Why?"

"If you want my opinion, Peter was giving you much more than just a book there." Ruth laughed. "That Christmas I only had eyes for my new brush set, but I can still hear what he said as though it were yesterday: You have to find out for yourself where you really belong!"

A little smile flitted across Johanna's face. "I'm surprised you remember."

"Sometimes people say things you can only understand in hindsight," Ruth remarked thoughtfully. "You think you know what you want from life, and then in the end it turns out to be quite the opposite. Just look at me: I thought that I would find fulfillment by marrying a Heimer, and that turned out to be a great disappointment. And you thought you would find fulfillment in the world of commerce. You never even dreamed that commerce could come to Lauscha, did you now? We don't always find happiness where we expect it. Sometimes we have to approach it the long way around . . ." She broke off. "And sometimes happiness is somewhere else entirely."

Johanna was looking at her skeptically. "You're not usually one for such wise words. I just wonder what all this has to do with Peter?"

If I carry on like this, I'll talk myself into trouble, Ruth thought. She had turned into such a chatterbox that if she had known the name of the ocean liner that she would be boarding next week, she would probably have blurted that out to Johanna too.

"When Peter gave you that gift, he was telling you that he was willing to wait for you," she said hastily. "And I see no reason why that should have changed. But if you think he's going to tell you he loves you another dozen times, then you're probably wrong. He has his pride, after all. Whether you like it or not, it's your turn now."

"Do you really think so?" Johanna asked despondently.

Ruth nodded emphatically. "He can't peer into your head, so you'll have to tell him—or show him—how you feel."

Johanna was still gazing into empty space, her expression downcast.

"I don't know whether I can. I'm . . . not good at that sort of thing. You know that quite well."

Ruth smiled. Johanna was right there, no doubt about it. All the same, she nodded encouragingly.

"It's not all that hard, believe me. All you have to do is wait for the right moment and then grab your happiness with both hands and never let go."

32

It was almost nine o'clock on Saturday morning.

Peter should have been sitting at his lamp already. Wanda had picked up the card of sample eye colors from his table the week before and thrown it on the floor. He really had to make a new set since he could hardly offer his patients a pile of glass shards from which to choose their colors. But another five minutes of rest wouldn't do him any harm, he decided, and he lay back down. He had all day, after all, and he hoped he might have some peace and quiet too.

He could hear the clattering of pots and running water from next door—Marie was probably putting the water on for coffee. Ever since they had taken down the wall between the two workshops, he could hear most of what went on over there: Wanda crying or the sisters arguing, visitors at the door, or Marie cursing like a sailor as she worked on her sketches. If he didn't make a conscious effort not to listen, he could hear everything. He had also heard Ruth leave early that morning—indeed, it had been more like the middle of the night. At any rate, the birds had not yet begun to sing. Instead of leaving the house quietly with Wanda, she had trotted up and down the stairs countless times, opening and closing every door in the house so that anyone might think there was an army marching through. Unless he was much mistaken, she had even opened his door and looked in. He had wondered what in the world she thought she was looking for, but just pulled the covers up over his head as far as they would go.

He plumped up his pillow and settled his head again. Women! But Ruth's noisy departure had been pretty typical of the entire week. He wouldn't have been able to bear so much commotion in the house every day of the year. Even Marie had called by every half hour or so. "Should I give Ruth this bauble to take with her, or that one?" And "Do you think I should put in some of my sketches on paper as well?" Not that she had ever been happy with his answers. Every single time, she had run off to Magnus right afterward to ask his opinion too.

And all because Woolworth's agent was coming today. And this despite the fact that they already had the order, signed and sealed, and there were only a few details left to sort out. If even that . . . Perhaps it was just that Ruth and her American prince wanted another chance to meet. Peter had been more than somewhat surprised when Johanna had told him about all that. Ruth writing letters? On the other hand, what else did she have to do with her time?

The door slammed loudly shut once more, and Peter remembered that Marie had planned to go up to the forest with Magnus this morning. They were going to gather snail shells to use in casting new molds. He made a face. That was another task awaiting him. In an unguarded moment, he had promised Marie that he would sound out old Strupp over a glass of beer or two and try to find out what went into his special mixture for the molds. He knew already that this was doomed to failure—Emanuel Strupp would never get so drunk that he would reveal his secret recipe. So they would just have to go on using their own lesser molds, even though they always eventually shattered.

Snail shells! On a Christmas tree. Peter had to grin. Was that the kind of thing that Americans would like? He would have liked to know where her ideas came from.

Then he heard the patter of feet down the stairs. Johanna, barefoot. Ever since business had taken off in the workshop, she had almost boundless energy. Although sometimes she could have done them all a favor by giving herself and everyone else a little rest. Now for example. Once she started on her chores, it would be the end of his quiet lie-in.

The next moment he heard the smashing of broken glass and a loud cry from Johanna.

He sighed and swung his legs out of the bed. Since it seemed like he would have no peace this morning, he decided to go and look in on Johanna. Now that the Steinmann sisters had robbed him of a quiet start to the weekend, the least they owed him was a cup of coffee.

Peter could see from the stairs that the shards of a glass bowl lay scattered on the kitchen floor. What was odd was that Johanna wasn't already busy sweeping them up.

She was at the table with her back to the door, sitting bolt upright.

He called "Good morning!" from the doorway just to be sure he didn't startle her.

She didn't turn around to face him, didn't return his greeting, didn't explain how the accident had happened.

Peter raised his eyebrows. Was this Johanna's famous morning moodiness?

"Have you looked out the window up toward the meadows yet? The last of the trees have burst into flower, and there are white blossoms wherever you look. It almost looks as though it's been snowing."

He sat down across from Johanna, resolved to ignore whatever was bothering her. But one look at her face was enough to shatter that resolve. It was white as chalk. Before he could even ask her what was wrong, she held a sheet of paper out to him. Her hands were trembling.

A letter. He recognized Ruth's handwriting.

"I just can't believe it," Johanna said in a hollow voice. "It can't be true, can it?"

He read it through three times, then put it aside. He was speechless.

"She can't really mean it. She wants to give us a shock, that's all," Johanna said, blinking as though there were something in her eye. "It's a stupid joke. She'll be back this evening. Of course she will!"

Who was she trying to convince? Herself? Ruth wasn't the kind of woman to play stupid tricks like that. Which was precisely what made the letter so unsettling.

He took Johanna's hand. "I think we'll have to get used to the idea that Ruth's not coming back."

"Why do you say that?" Johanna asked, withdrawing her hand reproachfully.

"Because that's how it is," he said gruffly.

"But she hardly knows this Steven!" she cried out in despair. "How can she follow a total stranger to the other side of the world? To an uncertain future? What if he tires of her tomorrow? And she has a child. And she's married. It's madness!"

"Well, I don't know . . . is it? What does she really have to lose? Try to put yourself in her shoes."

Johanna's features hardened. "I can't possibly know what goes on in her mind."

Peter ignored her remark. "What kind of future would she have in Lauscha? She didn't want to go back to Thomas, not for all the world; she made that clear enough. Was she going to live in this house forever?"

"Would that have been so bad? We're here too, after all. We could have taken care of her and Wanda."

"Think about it. Ruth would never have settled for that. She needs something else. More . . . how can I even put this? More *sparkle* in her life. And a man who tells her how beautiful she is, a man whose love she can bask in." Peter didn't feel entirely comfortable talking about such sensitive topics. Johanna's mood seemed to brighten a bit, however.

"And you think this Steven's the man? Don't you think that he was . . . after something else?" There was still a trace of skepticism in her voice.

"He wouldn't have to go to such lengths for *that*," Peter said decisively, pointing to the letter.

"She never said a word, not the whole time. Did she think she couldn't trust us?" Johanna's upper lip was trembling now. "If only she had just told us what she and Steven were planning! After all, we won't stand in her way."

"Don't cry now. That's not what Ruth would want." Peter shook her arm gently.

There were hot tears running down Johanna's face. "I'll miss her so much . . ." she sobbed.

"Come here," he said, and opened his arms. She clung to him like a fledgling seeking the warmth of the nest.

For a while they just sat there, her head on his chest, his arms wrapped tightly around her. He could feel her heartbeat and every breath she took. The hair at the nape of her neck was a little damp and clung to her skin. He blew softly onto it, and the strands lifted in the puff of air.

Peter felt a lump in his throat. He swallowed hard.

Damn it all, even if she stayed as stubborn as a mule to the end of her days, he would always love her.

Johanna broke free of his grasp a moment later. She rooted around in the pocket of her apron for a handkerchief, then blew her nose loudly. When she had put it back in her pocket, she looked at Peter, her eyes bright.

"Ruth's beginning a new life in America. Marie has her art . . ." She reached for his hand.

Her fingers were still wet with tears when he took hold of them.

"Now we just have each other," she whispered, and her eyelids fluttered like a butterfly's wings. "Or are you fed up with me by now?"

Peter couldn't even shake his head. His heart was full to bursting with love. How long he had waited to hear her say something like this! Why did joy and sorrow always come hand in hand?

Johanna was looking at him. Expectantly, uncertainly.

"You won't get rid of me so easily; you know that," he said at last, and managed to smile.

As he spoke, he saw something blaze up in her eyes that he had looked for in vain all these years—a woman's love.

She curled up in his embrace.

33

Steven had told her that with only five hundred cabin-class passengers and eighteen hundred in steerage, the *Valkyrie* was one of the smaller ocean liners. But when their carriage had stopped in front of the ship during a sightseeing tour of the Hamburg docks the day before, it had looked anything but small to Ruth. No, it was a giant—a giant of gleaming gray metal.

This impression was only reinforced as she followed Steven up the gangway with Wanda on her arm. The people down on the quayside looked so tiny. She couldn't even see the stern of the ship from where they were standing now, and its gleaming silver flanks seemed to stretch away forever. Ruth had read an article about the ocean liners in one of the magazines that Johanna used to bring home from Sonneberg; in the article, the ships were referred to as "floating cities." The writer had described the elegant restaurants and ballrooms on board, and noted that a person could lose his way among the endless mirror-lined halls and staircases. When she had read it, Ruth had thought that whoever wrote the article must be vastly exaggerating.

They shuffled forward at a snail's pace, stopping to wait with almost every step, because the passengers ahead were held up.

Steven had told her that it would be evening by the time the last passenger had been assigned a cabin. However, since the line for first class was significantly shorter than those for second and third class, he expected that they would have their cabins that morning.

Though Wanda was rather heavy in her arms, Ruth didn't mind the wait. On the contrary—she looked all around with boundless curiosity. Ruth drank up every detail like a sponge: the hectic activity on the quayside, the families saying farewell, the elegantly dressed gentlemen and even more elegantly dressed ladies all around them. Hats seemed to be the latest fashion, and there was hardly a woman in line who didn't have some fantastic creation perched on her head. Ruth put her hand to her head self-consciously and adjusted her own hat, a startling item made of velvet with a thick plume of purple feathers on the side. She pulled it a little farther down over her brow. When Steven had insisted on buying matching hats for all of her outfits, his generosity had been almost too much for her. But now she was glad she looked like the other ladies who were boarding the ship.

Steven turned to her.

"Are you quite sure you don't want me to take Wanda?"

Ruth shook her head. "We're all right, thank you. You have to hold the papers anyway." She pointed to the sheaf of documents that he had fanned out in his right hand.

"It'll all be fine, you'll see," he whispered, then turned to face forward again.

The more Steven assured her of this, the more nervous Ruth became.

She had had no time to worry about the papers on the journey to Hamburg or during the last two days here. There had been so much to see, to buy, to try on or try out. And everywhere, Steven was at her side, smiling with delight, ready to encourage her to any excess. Coffee and cakes in an English tea shop? Why not? A rocking horse for Wanda, with real horsehide? Of course they had room for that in their luggage. When Ruth complained that her feet ached after going around to so many shops, Steven snapped his fingers and called for a hansom cab. When Ruth climbed in, relieved that she didn't have to walk all the way back to the hotel on the Alster waterfront, she was quite startled to find that the cab took them not to the hotel but to a stylish beauty salon where Steven booked a pedicure with a dainty, almost doll-like woman. While the woman's soft hands pampered Ruth's feet and rubbed in soothing, scented oils, Steven and Wanda went for a walk in a nearby park. When she went to join them later, her heart almost burst with happiness at the sight of the two of them busily feeding the pigeons.

She loved this man so much that it hurt.

A smile flitted across Ruth's face, smoothing away the worry. Those days in Hamburg had been like a glimpse into a kaleidoscope, which revealed new marvels and adventures at every turn. Her fears had simply vanished in the flood of new impressions. And if she did feel a pang of worry or a twinge of regret, Steven made it vanish in the night.

But now, here on the gangway, there was nothing to distract from the question of what would happen if her papers were found to be forged.

There was only one passenger left in front of them, an older gentleman who was having his papers checked and cabin assigned.

Ship's officers in navy-blue uniforms stood to the left and right of the head of the gangway and greeted every passenger with a friendly "welcome aboard." Ruth could see a whole army of uniforms behind them. She longed to be aboard—not only because they would wait on her hand and foot but also because that would mean she had made it past the two border policemen, who stood in front of the serried ranks of uniformed ship's staff. They had stern faces and watchful eyes.

"Your papers please!"

With a charming smile, Steven handed the papers to the policeman on the left.

The man glanced at the two passports and then began to leaf through his thick sheaf of papers to find their names on his list.

Ruth was about to breathe a sigh of relief when he handed Steven's passport back to him, stamped several times over. But when he opened her passport, he seemed to find much more to interest him there. He raised his eyebrows and glanced at her curiously.

Ruth made an effort to gaze straight ahead, her eyes fixed on the wrought-iron decoration of the grand double doors, which had been thrown open wide for the passengers to enter through. How much longer was this man going to spend staring at her documents?

She felt his eyes on her face again. Should she try to stare him down with a haughty look?

Just then, Wanda showed the particular talent children have for knowing when their mother's attention has drifted. Seizing her chance, she took hold of the feathers that were nodding so intriguingly right in front of her nose. With her little hand, Wanda grabbed Ruth's hat by the brim, and the next moment it flew from the gangway in a high, curving arc.

"My hat!"

"The hat!" cried Steven and the border policeman.

Wanda beamed at the faces turned toward her.

"Welcome aboard, Baroness von Lausche."

The man bowed slightly and handed her the passport. His face had cleared, the frown was gone, his lips were no longer pursed, and he even seemed to smile slightly.

"And do take care that the little lady doesn't throw anything else overboard!"

The passport felt so good in her hand! Ruth gave the man one of her most dazzling smiles.

"I shall be sure to!"

Steven had taken two adjoining first-class cabins, and now a young steward who could hardly have been older than Ruth led them there. He unlocked both cabins and promised to have their luggage for the voyage brought up in the next half hour. Steven handed him a banknote and the man bowed as he took it. Then he hurried away, his footsteps swallowed up by the dark blue carpet with the yellow fleur-de-lis motif.

Wanda was kicking and squirming, and as soon as they were in the cabin, Ruth put her down on the floor.

"Steven!" She put a hand to her mouth. "This cabin is even bigger than our room at the Hotel Savarin! And it's beautiful. Look at that: the windows really are round!" She ran across to one of the three portholes and ran her fingers across the curved glass. Her eyes fell on the wall next to it.

"They've even hung an oil painting. Aren't they afraid we'll steal it?" She giggled.

Her eyes gleamed as she gazed around the room, taking it all in. Across from the bed, a small sofa and two dainty armchairs were arranged around a small table—she had read about such suites in the ladies' magazines Johanna used to bring her—and the whole of the wall behind them was taken up by a built-in wardrobe. Even though Steven had been more than generous when buying her clothes, everything she had with her would fit comfortably into just one section.

"I would never have dreamed of such luxury. I don't know what to say." Ruth sat down on the bed, taken aback. The pale beige silk bedcover was so generously draped that it fell in folds to the floor.

Wanda was doing her best to climb up onto the sofa, babbling merrily all the while.

Steven sat down next to Ruth and took her hand.

"I'm glad you like it. When I'm traveling with Mr. Woolworth, I seldom get the chance to enjoy first class." He laughed. "Frank doesn't set much store by a well-kept room; he'd rather sleep wherever is cheapest."

If not even Woolworth traveled in such style . . . All of a sudden Ruth felt scared by the splendor. Could Steven even afford this?

She shook herself. "Steven, I don't want you running up bills just on my account. Maybe there are some less expensive cabins elsewhere on the ship. Shouldn't we at least ask? As long as the ship doesn't sink and you're by my side, I really don't care where we sleep." She could see out of the corner of her eye that Wanda had managed to clamber up onto the sofa.

Steven took her chin gently in his right hand. When her eyes were gazing straight into his, he smiled and said firmly, "My love, I don't want you to worry about anything anymore. Not about money or anything else. You should just be happy and enjoy what life has to offer. Do you remember what I promised you our first night together? I want to make your life a paradise on earth. Please let me do that."

She was about to answer him when a movement distracted her. Her mouth curled up in an involuntary smile.

Sensitive to her every shift in mood, Steven followed her glance and then laughed.

Wanda had put Ruth's shawl on. Holding her mother's handbag on her lap, she sat in the middle of the sofa like a princess.

"It looks like Wanda's taken to her new lifestyle like a duck to water!" He waved at Wanda. "But is that surprising? Given her lineage?"

Ruth groaned. "Don't remind me! Why on earth did your forger friend do that to us?" Baroness Ruthwicka von Lausche—it was bad enough that the fellow had decided to make her an aristocrat, but the name itself was ridiculous.

Steven just laughed. "I think Ruthwicka was a wonderful idea. What if he'd made you an Amanda? Or an Ottilie? Either you'd have jumped every time I called you by the new name, or you wouldn't have reacted at all. And I think that being a baroness suits you wonderfully."

"Do you think so?" she asked, half reconciled to the idea. She had to admit that it had a certain mystique.

"I certainly do. You'll be the talk of the whole ship. Now then!" He stood up and offered Ruth his hand. "I suggest that we go and take our first look around."

No sooner had they stepped into the first salon than other passengers drew them into conversation. Wherever they went, there was always someone who wanted to introduce himself and talk for a while. The fact that they would be spending the next two weeks in one another's company seemed to make people inclined to talk.

Casting off from the quayside at Hamburg was a tearful occasion, but once it was over, the bell rang for the first dinner seating. When one of the stewards led them to their table, Ruth was momentarily alarmed; she had been expecting a table just for Steven, Wanda, and herself, not this great round table seating eight diners. But a moment later, she felt Steven's hand on her back, lending her courage and confidence.

At the beginning of the meal Ruth still felt rather awkward and chose to smile at their fellow passengers rather than take part in conversation. But once Steven had introduced her, their reactions left her no chance to feel insecure. And Wanda's lovable nature made the whole situation easier. Ruth's daughter conquered the whole of the *Valkyrie* with her cherubic smile. Before the evening was over, one waiter brought her extra little treats, an old gentleman at the table knotted his napkin into animal shapes to entertain her, and one of the ladies had picked her up and walked her around for a while. Ruth swelled with pride as she watched complete strangers succumb to her daughter's charms.

When dinner was over, they finally had a moment alone. Steven suggested a stroll around the deck before they went to sleep. Ruth agreed—she would have agreed to anything!

They stopped on the sundeck amidships, a lonely spot lit by two gas lamps. Ruth put Wanda down on one of the deck chairs, which were arranged in neat rows awaiting the passengers who would lie there the next day to drink in the sun. Steven covered her with his jacket.

Arm in arm they stood at the railing and savored the breeze on their faces.

"I've never seen the sunset so red," Ruth said, her eyes gleaming as she pointed west.

"It's because there's nothing here to block the sun's rays. It has room to show its full splendor. And over there, where the sun glows warmest, that's your new home," Steven whispered in her hair as the red ball sank slowly but inexorably down into the boundless sea before them.

"I'm so happy I could cry," Ruth whispered. And in fact, a few tears spilled down her cheeks.

Steven pulled her closer.

"You mustn't cry; you should be happy. Learn from your daughter's example!"

"What about her?" Ruth asked quietly, fighting the tears.

"She seems to be enjoying her new life with all her heart. It's an unusual gift that a child has, and it's one that's well worth emulating." Steven laughed quietly. "Anybody watching Wanda today might believe that she had been born with a silver spoon in her mouth!"

Ruth's gaze wandered lovingly over Wanda's small body and blonde curls, bright against the dark cloth of Steven's jacket. No, there had been no silver spoons where she came from. Ruth looked back at Steven, her eyes gleaming with pride.

"If anything, it was a *glass* spoon!"

AFTERWORD

All the names and characters are my own invention, as is the story I have told.

It is true, however, that glass Christmas tree decorations were invented in Lauscha, though there is no way to know which family first began to make them. Indeed, it seems clear today that there was no single "inventor" but rather that several different glassblowers simultaneously developed the idea. Researchers believe that the first glass Christmas ornaments were produced by the mid-nineteenth century, rather earlier than in my book. We can also be sure that for many, daily life was much harder than I have described.

It is true that Frank Winfield Woolworth exported Lauscha baubles to America and that these sold remarkably well in his stores.

Lauscha remains the glassblowing capital of Germany today.

ACKNOWLEDGMENTS

I would like to thank everyone whose help shaped this story, but above all Michael Haberland and his family, who create Christmas ornaments in their glassblowing workshop using the old techniques.

I would also like to thank Dr. Helena Horn of the Museum of Glass Arts in Lauscha, who gave me valuable advice on books to read, both in person and through her catalog *400 Jahre Glas aus Thüringen* (*400 Years of Thuringian Glass*).

Readers who want to know how the story of the Steinmann sisters progresses can follow their lives in the sequel, *The American Lady*.

ABOUT THE AUTHOR

© Privat

Petra Durst-Benning lives near Stuttgart, Germany, with her husband, Bertram, and their dog, Eric. Before writing her first novel she worked as an import/export translator and edited a magazine for dog owners. All this changed with the publication of *The Silver Thistle*, which was set against the background of the peasant uprising in Germany in 1514. Her next dozen books take place in times ranging from the sixteenth century to the nineteenth century, and are set in Germany, France, Russia, and America. They bring tales of historical times, love and family, happiness and hardship to an ever-growing readership. *The Glassblower* is the first part of a trilogy.

ABOUT THE TRANSLATOR

Samuel Willcocks is originally from Brighton on the south coast of England but now lives with his family in the historic city of Cluj, Transylvania, where he spends as much time in the cafés as he does in the libraries. A keen reader in many genres including science fiction and historical novels, he studied languages and literature in Britain, Berlin, and Philadelphia before winning the German Embassy Award (London) for translation in 2010. He has been a full-time translator from Czech, German, Romanian, and Slovene ever since. When not overindulging in cakes or dictionaries, he can be found at book festivals and other literary events, sharing his enthusiasm for Central European books and writers.